Ghost Stories
and
Weird Tales

Ghost Stories
and
Weird Tales

H. Russell Wakefield

COACHWHIP PUBLICATIONS
GREENVILLE, OHIO

Ghost Stories and Weird Tales, by H. Russell Wakefield
© 2025 Coachwhip Publications edition
Cover image: © FokasuArt

H. Russell Wakefield, 1888-1964
CoachwhipBooks.com

ISBN 1-61646-599-9
ISBN-13 978-1-61646-599-5

Contents

Stories from 'Weird Tales'

They Return at Evening

(1928)

That Dieth Not

Part I

Well, that's over! I expected an ordeal and found almost a farce. There is something to be said for being a Local Notable. For example, deferential condolences and preferential treatment (and no awkward questions) from the Coroner when one's wife is found dead at the bottom of the steps into the garden. With what censorious disdain old Weldon brushed aside the curiosity of Mr. Trench Senior! Now I have prosecuted Trench Junior for poaching three times; consequently Trench Senior does not love me. So I was none too pleased to see him on the Jury. I knew he would be nasty if he saw a chance, and he asked a very nasty and intelligent question. For if she had tripped on the top steps I doubt if she would have fallen so far, and if she had slipped lower down, why such shattering injury? Why indeed! You didn't deserve such a pulverising rebuke, Mr. Trench, but I'm very glad you got it!

And now that it is all over I can reflect without anxiety. Reflect that I am a murderer and, as such, if I got my deserts, a doomed and execrated pariah. No more loose generalisation was ever made than that whoever commits adultery—and, of course, any other sin or crime—in his heart, is guilty of that offence. Every man of imagination who is tempted commits sins in his heart as often as he is tempted, but not one in ten thousand commits them with his hand. Myriads of men must

9

have played with the idea of killing their wives, but *I killed mine.* Is there no difference? Consult the Shade of Ethel! No, I realise perfectly that I possess a kink which should have resulted in a six-foot drop. That I might never kill again, and that it was only by an acute combination of circumstances that I did so once, is beside the point.

A murderer should die—if he is sane and sober and selfish.

And am I so sure I could never commit another? I am not so sure. I have no remorse. There might be something to be said for a murderer who bitterly repents (though I'd hang him), but as for me—why shouldn't I murder again if someone again drove me to such an extremity of exasperation?

I rehearse all this—why and to whom? Why, because, murderer though I am, I feel compelled to tell the story of this repulsive episode impartially, and so rid my mind of it and, perhaps, forget it, for, murderer though I am, otherwise I believe myself to be reasonably decent and civilised, and I want to see what sort of defence I can muster. And to whom do I address myself? Well, it has long been a theory of mine—more than that, a profound conviction—that the minds of men are far more complex, bifurcated and stratified than is generally accepted or perceived. There is more than one "I" pervading my consciousness. There is the "I," the murderer, who is sitting here recalling, sifting and writing down. "I" number one, let us call him; but there is also "I" number two, who is compelled to observe "I" number one. It has been suggested that there is also a "number three" watching "number two," and so on *ad infinitum.* It may be so, but for me there is a limit set to the terms in the series, and it is fixed at "number two." I often feel compelled to explain to him the actions of "number one," though I do not feel he is or wants to be a judge, but just an aloofly interested spectator; in no sense a "conscience," but poised in another layer of consciousness. It is with such vague precision that this duality works in me And I want to explain to this watcher just how I came to kill Ethel. He may or may not be particularly interested, but he is in the unfortunate position of being compelled to listen!

I was thirty-one, wanting an heir, an ingenuous lover of beauty, and Ethel was certainly beautiful, and, I thought, a destined mother of robust children. That is why I proposed to her. I am wealthy, "a prominent local figure"; Ethel had an allowance of £40 a year—that is why she accepted me. She was highly intelligent in a debased feminine way, and she never used her brains to better purpose than in her behaviour to me during our engagement. A lovely piece of acting! Quite flawless. Such a lover of the country, adoring children, so docile, unselfish and interested in everything which interested me! What a treasure I believed I was about to acquire! Before the end of our honeymoon I began desperately to doubt it. She let me know quite uncompromisingly that she intended to "social push" with vigour and success. Now I am by nature a recluse, a detester of crowds, a loather of London: I make friends slowly and doubtingly, though most firmly now and again. But I flinch from "acquaintances" and the claims upon one's time and nerves they entail. It was, therefore, with incredulous dismay that I discovered Ethel was determined that we should spend six months in London and three months in fashionable resorts, and that I was to spend those six months playing the sedulous host and involving myself in an incessant spate of fatuous entertainment. When I had somewhat absorbed this shock I told her that it was the tradition in my family personally to look after the estate during most of the year, that I must work very hard if my book on "The Future of the Novel as an Art Form" was to be ready in time, that I wanted children, and that her programme was impossible. And then I had my first taste of that most wicked temper. Had I faced up to it and fought her, I believe I could have gained a precarious victory, but it was so horrible, so disgusting and intolerable that I gave way. It was a fatal blunder, for she then knew she possessed a most potent weapon against me. I did not capitulate unconditionally, but I felt exasperatedly certain that I should have to renew the battle before I should be able to enforce my side of the bargain.

Well, I agreed to do what she wanted for one year; to take a house in London for the Season and a Villa on the Riviera for the winter. I should have considered this quite reasonable if she had not been granted every opportunity before our marriage to understand what sort of person I am; and if she had not so cunningly and wickedly concealed from me what manner of woman she was. And though it is very plausible to say that my love for her should have made me delighted to please her, that is really vast rubbish, for the deep, dominating characteristics of a man's temperament can never be changed, while one can love and cease to love and love again.

Though it caused my vitality to droop and drain, I fulfilled my part of the contract. I took a monstrosity in Bruton Street, gave four huge parties, attended dozens of other huge parties, was forced to carry on disjointed chat through *Tristan* in a box, sit through *Rigoletto* in a stall, and poison my system in Night Clubs; so learning to despise humanity—or rather that brand of it—as no man should be taught. Had I possessed a constitution which would have allowed me to drink my critical sense to drowsing point, I might have tolerated such a *régime*, but, unfortunately, my grandfather had mortgaged the family liver.

As I withered Ethel bloomed. Her polluted sense of values and her intense social vanity made her revel in this frenetic round of snobbery, this eternal return of jostling, aimless futility.

I was not a success. My temperament nipped me below the arm-pits and dragged me round, the skeleton at the feast, though I never caused any awed hush to fall upon the assembly.

"Arthur, I do wish you'd make an effort to seem to enjoy things," Ethel once said. "The other night I overheard

George Willard say that you were the World's Worst Flat-tyre at a party. It makes me feel so ashamed and embarrassed."

"Do you think I care what that chinless, brainless, Bateman-drawing thinks about me?" I replied, knowing I was a fool to argue.

"Well, he's the son of a Duke," said Ethel; "and what do you mean by a 'Bateman-drawing'?"

"Oh, he was a pupil of Rembrandt," I replied inanely.

"You pretend to know all about Art, but the other day, when Lady Frowse was trying to discuss the Academy with you, you looked absolutely 'gaga.'"

"Lady Frowse," I replied, "was quoting verbatim from the notice in the *Times,* which, unfortunately, I had already read."

Then Ascot, jostle, clothes, and equine interludes—then Cowes, jostle, different clothes and the occasional belching of a decrepit cannon. And then Ethel went off to twitter in butts, and I, thank God, to Paradown and peace.

I made good progress with my book; my intense feeling of release fortunately stimulating my creative energy. I had also plenty of time to think, though nothing very pleasant to think about. I had the most bitter and smarting self-contempt. To think that I could have been such an utter flaming fool as to have ruined my life by a fatuous idealisation of a certain fortuitous combination of pigment, cuticle—and the way the blood shone through it, hair—and the way the light caught it, bones—and the way their envelope draped round them. A perilous privilege, "a sense of beauty." But had I ruined it? I considered the chances. Ethel was perfectly happy, rapidly stabilising her position amongst the Right People, with my cheque book as her entrenching tool and her temper to animate my fountain pen, with her beauty and her sexlessness and her unscrupulousness to get what she wanted from men and to keep her from ever repaying the debt. What a way to think about one's wife! Humbug! There was no other way to think about her. No, there would be no co-respondent to encourage and supplicate! And I could do nothing, unless I refused to fill my fountain pen, and I could not do that, for I had only myself to blame, and I was ready to blame myself. At present I could see no hope.

I lived a life of extreme asceticism, feeling feebly that by so doing I was defying and rejecting Ethel. Once I had been fool enough to regard women as mentally almost indistinguishable, and it had been merely by the physical criterion I had separated one from another in my mind. Now that I had been taught to despise the dangerous deceptiveness of eyes and breasts, colouring and curves and all those superficial stimulants which excite the featherless biped man to idealise the featherless biped woman, I realised what I should have known a year before—that I could only love someone with a mind I could respect. "What care I how fair she be, if she's naught but fair to me?"

Ethel came down at the end of October, her waist heavy with social scalps. A title had the same effect on her as the sound of a hunting horn on a pack of hounds. It gave her a delicious sense of excitement and well-being. When on one occasion she was addressed by a Minor Royalty for one thrilling moment, I believed she was about to die of joy. And, bitterly as she learned to loathe me, I am certain the fact she was loathing the current number of one of the oldest baronetcies in England gave her a soothing sense of social pride.

I had been working very hard on a delicate and highly contentious section of my book, and was inclined to be irritable and "on edge." Luckily at first Ethel was fairly amenable. For one thing, she had the Riviera to which to look forward, for another she was learning to ride, an art which she had been instructed was a necessary accomplishment for an English Gentlewoman. She learned quickly, and looked as nearly palatable as any Gentlewoman can when topped by a silk hat. The servants hated her, for her attitude towards them veered from touchy insolence to obviously insincere blandishments, and that they disliked both variants they showed most definitely though courteously.

As a Local Notable it was my duty to introduce Ethel to those of my neighbours and friends she had not already met in London, and for this purpose I gave a series of week-end parties. The fact that I do not puncture or pursue the fauna of Wiltshire by any of the traditional methods has not prevented me from being on most excellent terms with my neighbours. I think I can say I have worked pretty hard at those often tiresome jobs which the occupation of a prominent local position entail. I am regarded as a bit of a freak— as was my father before me, but my idiosyncrasies give them something to talk about, and there is a "Dear Oldness" about their references to me which mark the absence or passing of criticism. I was curious to observe how my good friends would regard my good lady. Well, the Elderly Ladies Who Knew, knew she was not quite a lady. The young women envied her clothes and looks, but I do not think they envied me. The men behaved in a robustly gallant manner towards her, partly out of consideration to me and partly because her beauty was within limits overwhelming. But I think they reserved judgment. A few fledglings fell in love with her and they *did* envy me. How I should have rejoiced to have settled some money on her and danced at her wedding to one of them!

She played her part rather well, but that which has fundamental flaws betrays itself inevitably by superficial cracks. Her breaks were not shattering, but they were palpable, and not one of them went by the Elderly Ladies Who Knew. She was quite unconscious of them. I usually said nothing, but I had to protest against one. She had repeated with the eager placid certainty of the natural scandalmonger a scabrous little rumour about the morals of Lady Pount's niece in the presence of her Aunt. While undressing, I suggested that the study of Debrett should not be pursued too academically, and that the art of knowing Who is Who should be an applied art, in so much as it might prevent awkward pauses in the hour of anecdote. And I gave as an instance the choice little canard she had repeated that evening. At which she lost her temper uneasily.

"I can't remember all those people! How was I to know they were related? It's true, anyway, and I think she ought to be shown up, it's disgusting."

"Nothing," I said, "is worth an awkward pause, not even the exposure of notorious evil-livers. Some people have a sixth sense for knowing how to avoid them. Of such is the Kingdom of Heaven."

A short but violent scene ensued.

So we scrambled along the broad, well mile-stoned path to mutual hostility. I made occasional halfhearted attempts to persuade myself that Ethel was other than she was. She felt, when she inspected her wardrobe and my broad acres and stable, and all those joys which I had brought into her life, that there were sufficiently compensating "Betters" for the "Worse."

And then it was time for the Riviera, its boomed beauty, its bloody brood. What a region! I have cruised the Mediterranean fairly extensively, and it is no Sea for me. What merits the Southern Latins may once have possessed is a matter of opinion; that they retain any to-day seems to me untenable. A breed of pimps, parasites and horse-torturers, the choicest surviving examples of that cretin civilisation which is Catholicism's legacy to the world. And it has always seemed to me that members of races vastly their intellectual and moral superiors become debased and degraded when brought in contact with them, though I know the region attracts the worst.

Ethel was so happy. She changed her clothes at intervals during the day, and made the acquaintance of a Grand-Duke, who was accompanied by a selection from his harem. Her delight in this encounter was so unconcealed that the nobleman for some time believed that she was anxious to be enrolled in his service! She "adored" the Casino. I took one look at those tables. A vice is known by the company it collects. There must be something to be said for opium. It makes glad the heart of Chinks, it induced *The Ancient Mariner,* and made De Quincey immortal. Booze has many excellent songs, Boris Goudonov, and missed partridges to its credit. Even murder can point to detective stories—the favourite literature of our Great Ones, and the support of hangmen's families. But gambling has nothing to justify its existence unless it be Revolver Smith's dividends and A New Use for Old Piano Cases. My absence from this Rouge et Noir midden didn't matter, for Ethel had many friends who considered it a Green Baize Paradise.

I mooned about aimlessly, did a little work, pretended at dropsical meals that I was having a good time, and then one day decided I could stick no more of it. So I informed Ethel and quelled the inevitable typhoon by reminding her she was there at my expense and that she could stay there alone at my expense if she chose, otherwise we'd both return to England at my expense. This syllogistic presentation of the case impressed her, and I returned alone.

On the journey home I had an opportunity for coolly regarding things in themselves, with particular reference to my marriage. By then I knew for certain that Ethel would never leave me of her own accord. She had everything she wanted, a title, money to burn, a circle of sycophants, a husband she could dominate. Could she? I supposed so, for the dread of scenes is the beginning and end of feminine domination in the case of men of my type, weak, introspective, with sensitive ears and a tantalising tolerance. I say *tantalising* because, were I asked to prescribe for the matrimonial troubles of others, I should be cool, hard, a rationalist, a regarder of facts in the face. I should prescribe for those in my state a drastic, cauteristic remedy, and feel confident of its efficacy. "No sentimentalist need apply" I should inscribe on my brass plate.

"Physician, heal thyself,'" the hardest of all hard sayings! But this is how I should prescribe in a case such as mine. "Force a divorce, you will never be happy. You know her chief concern is money, settle some on her. Living with her seems the Devil, well, take him by the horns."

Perfectly sound, common sense itself, but I couldn't do it.

A week after getting back I received a cable, "Returning immediately. Ethel."

This unexpected announcement filled me with a vague excitement. What had she been up to? Something which might lead to a solution—a dissolution? I enjoyed twenty-four hours of such straw-clutching, and then she arrived, and, as was her wont, went straight and viciously to the point. "I'm going to have a baby, and I won't have a baby. You've got to help me. It'll spoil everything. I don't care how much you want it. Tell me someone to go to."

"I shall do nothing of the kind," I replied. "Certainly I want you to have a child, and you'll be much happier. Now, Ethel, be unselfish about this!"

"Happier! Unselfish! I like that. You don't have to spend nine foul months, be cut out of everything, and probably have your figure ruined. I refuse to argue about it. Will you help me?"

"No, I won't," I said.

She said no more, but in ten minutes she was on her way to London. I heard nothing more from her for a fortnight, and then one evening she came back. She went straight to her room, refused to see me, and dined in bed.

However, I went up to her after dinner.

She was shaking with anger, and her eyes were those of a trapped lynx.

"I told you I didn't want to see you, but now you're here let me tell you this, I will never bear your child."

I think it was then, when I saw her hatred for me, that I first knew I hated her, and I suppose the murderer in me first woke to life.

She was as good as her word. She had a miscarriage two weeks later, and became quite lighthearted again. One day she came into my dressing room when I was shaving to tell me that, as she was not quite fit enough to hunt, she was going up to London, and had taken a suite at Claridge's. And then I received the worst shock of my life. She bent down for a moment to smell a bowl of roses on the dressing table. I had my razor in my hand, and for a moment I believed I could not restrain myself from cutting that lovely throat. With an agonising effort of self-control, I flung the razor on the floor. Ethel glanced up quickly, and, I suppose, partially understood the look in my face, for she put her hands to her eyes and ran from the room. She went up to London after breakfast, leaving me to my thoughts.

For the rest of the day I could not control my nerves nor stay still for a moment, for my brain continually forced that hideous picture before my eyes. I could see her writhing on the carpet, the blood gushing from her throat. And that night, each time I fell into an uneasy doze, it came as a fleeting dream vision more vivid and more vile. I knew I was receiving a most urgent warning, that my subconsciousness was telling me that inevitably, if I continued to see her, one day I should kill her.

The next morning I met Margaret Pascal. It was the only time I have figured in one of those coy sexual situations beloved by the authors of scenarios, for I found her embraced by barbed wire in Far Wood. After I had disentangled her and noticed the lovely junction of her legs and feet, we began a vague little talk. I told her my name. "This is all yours then," she said. "Was I trespassing?"

"Technically, yes," I replied. "But please commit the offence as often as you like."

"I am staying with the Franks," she said, "and was just wandering about. As a matter of fact, I adore birds, and there's a shrike's larder in that thorn just there, and I wanted to examine the grisly little feast."

She had a curiously deep and individual voice, and one can fall in love with a voice at first hearing, as I did. While we inspected the sorry and dismembered collation, each drawn, quartered and impaled remnant fluttering in the breeze, I appraised her. I had learned bitterly to distrust women's looks, so I paid little attention to her physical attributes. It was a certain combination of sweetness and intelligence, of gentleness and determination, and her all-pervading rightness, which lulled and soothed and stirred and excited me. She told me afterwards that I had the same immediate effect on her. A certain tension established itself, a happy unease.

When we parted I asked her if she would like me to show her over a part of the estate which was specially famous for its birds and beasts, for I had forbidden my keepers to shoot or trap there. She said she would love it, and I arranged to fetch her in the car early next day.

I found my mood had completely changed. I could even examine Ethel's photograph with a whistling ease, for everything else I had a bounding pulse and a flattering eye. And I knew why—it was because I was falling in love with Miss Pascal, and that it would make me exquisitely happy so to do. I could hardly realise Ethel existed, and felt quite carefree whether she did or not. I knew the reaction must come, but for the moment I was anaesthetised and thinking only of the morrow.

I called for Margaret early. The Franks are pleasant hunting, shooting and horticultural nonentities, and I think they were a little astonished at my precipitance; for my reputation is not exactly that of one who chooses to spend a whole day alone with a strange female. But it was the happiest day I had ever spent. I found in Margaret just that congruent complement of myself—association with which makes life worth living—and nothing else does. She was twenty-nine, very straight and strong. Her features I never have bothered about, though I gathered that a good many other men had. She has an admirable instinct for pictures, music and the written word, and her critical sense is quick and certain. I gathered she had practised at all three for a time, but had gallantly renounced each in turn, realising she could never transcend mediocrity. "I prefer," she said, "to criticise the successes of others happily, than to face my own failures with angry tears in my eyes. In many a second-rate painter and writer is buried a first-rate critic. A little talent is a cruel thing."

In the afternoon I took her for a fifty-mile run. Driving a car is one of my few accomplishments, and a lust for speed one of the very few unexpected traits in my character (a capacity for flinging my wife down a row of steps is the only other one I can recall).

My Ponitz has done 110 miles an hour at Brooklands and is the fastest car on the road I have ever known. Motor shop is the most boring of all, for fooling about with a car is for most people merely a substitute for thought. It is not so with me. Timid by nature, I resolved to conquer this timidity Driving was an agony to me at first; I imagined a crash at every corner, and a corpse in every adjacent pedestrian, but slowly I gained confidence, and then my curious, restless mania for speed asserted itself.

I asked Margaret if she minded fast driving. "Go ahead," she replied, "and I'll tell you afterwards." There was a perfect three-mile straight on the way home, and we touched eighty. She was in her element. "Take me again," she cried. "It was simply glorious, and I've never seen such perfect control. I don't mean to be personal, but it seemed to me you became a different person as soon as we reached sixty, somehow defiant and austere."

"How far would you like to go next time?" I asked. "Past the Plunge of Plummet?" and felt a fool for asking. She looked at me sharply and flushed slightly.

"Your wife might have something to say to that. By the way, when is she coming back?"

"Not yet awhile," I answered irritably. "Would you like to come to-morrow?"

"I'd love it," said Margaret, "but till I know you better you mustn't take me too far." She said that lightly, but with a certain emphasis.

My recent social experiences had taught me that the average young woman of her class was at best a *demi-vierge,* and such a remark from such an one would merely have implied encouragement for a casual intrigue, but I knew Margaret hadn't a trace of the promiscuous rip in her make-up, and I knew she knew I loved her, and that she mistrusted her powers of resistance. This went to my heart.

So it began, and it moved swiftly. A few days later we decided that it was impossible for her to stay on with the Franks and continue to see me each day. So I took a flat in Paris, and there we lived together. "In sin," you suggest, number two. If you like to, call it so. When one has lost and found oneself in a woman, what the respectable sensualist focuses his smutty spectacles upon and the Law deliciously terms "misconduct" becomes of the most petty importance. It is not quite negligible, for in that hopeless, tantalising longing for complete fusion, when four eyes almost become two, and two minds just not one, when in fleeting seconds of ecstasy the illusion of this complete unison is attained, that mechanical conjunction is inevitable. But to those who love imaginatively and therefore hunger and thirst and lust and strive to isolate themselves from the rest of mankind, this physically compelled commonplace loses its significance. It was only Margaret who could make me dread to die.

I told Ethel I should be abroad for a while, but she showed no interest in the information. By the time a month was up Margaret and I were just not one person, and I the unhappiest man in the world, for even if the view Prometheus enjoyed from his eyrie was the loveliest in the world, he must for ever have turned his eyes away from it to search for that speck in the sky. And often when I was alone with Margaret and for the moment utterly happy and at peace, it seemed that Ethel's face crept in between us, and once again

I felt that foul longing to get my hands to her throat. She would never divorce me. I knew it, and I could not force permanently on Margaret the uneasy, furtive alternative. She would have accepted it gladly and made the best of it, but I could not do it. "You preferred to murder your wife," I hear you murmur with some irony, number two. Yes, number two, I preferred to murder my wife.

We travelled back together, and I drove Margaret back to her flat in Gloucester Place. On the way we were held up by a traffic block at the Marble Arch. A car halted beside us, and as I glanced casually at it it seemed familiar. And then I saw Ethel, smoking a cigarette and talking to an elderly man with jackal's eyes. She saw me a second later. The cigarette dropped from her hand, and she craned forward to see who was with me, and then the dam broke and we went on down Great Cumberland Place.

"That was my wife in that car," I said to Margaret.

I saw her hand tremble. "Did she see us? Does it matter?"

"She certainly saw me," I replied, "and it matters not at all. But if I know her, she's the most frightened woman in London."

We parted miserably and uncertainly, comforting each other with vague hopes of some solution.

When I got back to Paradown, Ethel was waiting for me. She was shaking with the rage of terror as she rushed at me.

"Who was that woman you were with? Someone you picked up in Paris, I suppose. That's what you call working at your rotten book! Who is she?"

"A Miss Pascal," I said.

"Have you been living in Paris together?"

"Yes."

"Are you in love with her?"

"Yes," I said wearily.

"Oh, you are, are you? and planning to get rid of me. Well, I'm afraid you won't find it so easy. Remember this; I'll never divorce you or give you a chance to divorce me.

You beast and hypocrite! Pretending to be so cold and pious, and then sneaking off to Paris with the first low woman you can find!"

I said nothing. The only chance to bring her scenes to a close was to keep silence. Replying merely fed them.

"Can't you speak, you beastly fool? Are you trying to get rid of me?"

"No," I replied, "but I think we'd do better to separate."

"Oh, you do! Well, you've had my answer. I'll never leave you. I've seen you look like a fiend at me, as if you wished I were dead, but if I were, I'd still come between you and that strumpet."

The application of that disgusting epithet to Margaret began to rouse the killer in me, but I rallied all my self-control to subdue it.

"Well, then," I said, "there's no need for such a scene as this. If you insist, you shall remain my wife in name, but in nothing more. I cannot inhabit the same house with you, but I will make you as generous an allowance as I can afford."

"I imagine," sneered Ethel, "that when that little drab has been through your pockets it won't be so generous!"

I got up to leave the room, and this completely destroyed the remnant of her self-control. Her lips pouring out a stream of foul abuse, she came for me, struck me with all her force in the mouth, spat in my face, and then rushed over to my writing table, opened the drawer which contained all the notes I had been working on for the last six months, and flung them by handfuls in the fire. Something snapped in my brain. When she had finished she ran from the room, and I followed her stealthily. She went through the door into the garden to get air, I suppose. Just as she reached the top step I seized her by the shoulders and hurled her down. Her head struck the bottom step, and she writhed over on to her back and lay still. Trembling with horror and yet elation, I crept back to my study, and the butler found her an hour later.

Well, number two, there is my story. I suppose rather a commonplace sex-crime narrative. I'll read it again in ten years' time. I wonder if I shall believe it ever happened!

PART II

Which consists of a letter written by Sir Arthur Paradown to his friend, Mr. Weldon, the Coroner.

My dear Weldon,
Seven months ago you held an inquest on my first wife. It will now be your dubious pleasure to perform that office on me, and I am sending you with this letter an account of the events leading up to that first inquest; this will reveal the incidents leading up to the second. And I am doing so because I have a favour to ask of you. Can you forget for a few hours the fact that I was a murderer, and remember that I was a fairly conscientious landowner and did my best for the County and helped a few people to be a little happier? If you can, do you think you can be a little unprofessional and tell the Jury that I have written you a private letter which explains my suicide, and that it has persuaded you that I was not insane, and then treat these documents as secret? What harm can it do! And it can do good, for my present wife is expecting to have a child in six months' time, and I do not want the stigma of my insanity to rest on Margaret's baby. Will you do this for me? Read what follows, and then decide—

Murderer's sob-stuff is a peculiarly repellent brand, so I will merely state that when, six months later, I married Margaret, I knew for the first time utter cloudless happiness—for just six weeks, and then one evening after dinner, when we were sitting in my study, the telephone bell rang. Margaret took off the receiver and listened for a moment.

"It's making such a weird noise," she said.

"Give it to me," I replied, and put it to my ear.

"You thought you were rid of me, didn't you, you murderer! But as you killed me, I shall kill you!"

I knew the voice.

I made a casual remark, lest Margaret should suspect something was wrong, and went out into the garden to recover from what had been a terrific shock, and to regain my balance.

"Subjective or objective?" That is the old, old question on these occasions. In the first case I was mad, subject to hallucinations, in the second—well, then, a mystery of a different sort. There was little to choose between the alternatives. I certainly felt as sane as ever, but perhaps murder itself is a symptom of deep-rooted mental disease which could break out in other ways. My whole being rejected this hypothesis. But I had a dreadful certainty that in either case my doom had been spoken. This certainly must have branded itself upon my face, for Margaret was only half persuaded there was nothing wrong when I went in again.

I had three days' respite.

Margaret tolerated broadcasting, and our set was in use on most evenings. I used to stop work and come in to hear the news. On this occasion, after the usual ponderous catalogue of minutiae, listeners, as usual, were promised a "Little Piano Music" as a reward for their patience. Instead—as far as I was concerned, a voice suddenly cried out, "Sir Arthur Paradown murdered me, his wife, on March 9th."

I gripped my chair and glanced at Margaret, but she was placidly reading. "It's very clear to-night," she said.

It was ridiculous and yet dreadful. I felt a deep horror of myself, an awful sense of isolation and distress. The question was—could I face this persecution? But then, I might be mad! I'd see a specialist the next day. In any case I was involved in something foul. My loathing for Ethel was such that, had she been with me, I would have strangled her in cold blood.

The specialist found nothing the matter, and was obviously puzzled at my visit. I told him I fancied I heard sounds which were imperceptible to others. It sounded vague and lame. He made a few obvious remarks about possible overwork, which were so nauseatingly inadequate to my trouble that I hurried away. Of course I'd only gone to him in panic, it was a witch-doctor I needed.

Margaret, as arranged, rang me up at the club at lunchtime. Just as she had finished reciting a list of things she wanted me to do for her, her voice went blurred, and through it came another: "Are you beginning to be sorry you murdered me? You can tell me when I come to you at Paradown."

In the agonised daze which from then on always ensued on these occasions, I drove back home. "When I come to you." What had she meant by that?

When Margaret came out to greet me, I took her in my arms and kissed her, and let the small, clean fraction of my soul sink into her.

"What's the matter, my darling?" she asked, looking anxiously into my eyes.

"Sweetest," I replied, "if I should die, think only this of me. I adored you. There might have been a time for such a word." I felt unstrung, diseased, clinging to her, yet forced from her by that deadly secret she never could nor should share.

"What is it, Arthur, my dearest? You've suddenly changed. Something has happened. Tell me! Tell me! Whatever it is you can tell *me*."

A surging, clanging fury of despair and self-pity raced through me and then suddenly left me, left me limp and lying with a certain despair and subtlety about over-work and liver and moodiness, rounded off with a desperate sort of "Soon be all right again" coda.

Margaret forced some sort of reassurance on herself and went to bed. I stayed up with my thoughts.

The bitterest knowledge which flays the brain of those who are at once vile and highly sensitive is that of the misery they inflict on those who love them. I know some who with a hardy egoism declare that the simple must suffer and the complex must cause them to suffer, that that is an inexorable law of life, and that the sufferings of the simple are simple, tolerable little pangs, those of the complex insufferable agonies, and that the only judge of a complex temperament should be another equally complex. Alas, when murder is the symptom of complexity that flattering unction fails of its purpose. Ethel had timed her re-entry well. She just gave me time to realise the full extent of the happiness of which she would deprive me, and she doubled my misery by reflecting it back again from Margaret. How I longed to get my hands on her!

Just before going up to bed I went out into the garden. As I came through the door I saw her standing there on the top step with her back to me, just as at that other time. And then it seemed as though I was rent and torn apart, and that a shadow leapt from me, a furtive poised thing, which took her by the shoulders and hurled her—hurled her—

Margaret found me lying there, and, poor darling, sent for dear old Fritaker, who tried to pretend his feet were scientifically pacing the bottom when he was hopelessly out of his depth.

"Nervous strain," he diagnosed. "Bed, and feeding up," he prescribed. I felt like quoting *Macbeth* to him.

Yet bed and feeding up and an aching determination to spare Margaret contrived to patch me up, and for fleeting moments I felt some little reassurance. The "symptoms" of my disorder were not renewed, still I felt that Ethel knew her business, and would torture me with finesse. In that case could I train myself to nerve myself against her? Could I face the worst she could do, leading otherwise a normal,

sufficiently tolerable existence? Could I deceive and so pro-
tect Margaret? I must fight for her. My rotting brain might
merely be breeding these phantoms in its corruption, though
relatively there seemed to me little difference between being
haunted by Ethel objectively and haunting myself with her
subjectively. In any case I would fight. I sent for my lawyer
and had my affairs put finally in order, and a week later got
up and resumed my normal life. And for some days nothing
happened, and I began to wonder if, perhaps, I had had some
obscure nervous disorder—a lesion which had healed itself.

And then one evening, just before dusk, when Margaret
was in the garden, I had occasion to go up to my dressing-
room for some papers. I opened the door. There was a coffin
almost at my feet, housing a shrouded figure. There was a
dark patch where the head of this figure should have been,
and from it came something which slithered writhing down
the shroud, and then the figure began slowly to rise.

I shut the door and cowered shuddering in the passage.
When I felt I had strength to move I went down, drank a
glass of brandy, and kept out of Margaret's way till dinner.
But by that time she was seriously frightened about me and
watching me closely, so she knew at once I had had a "relapse." I assured her that such ups and downs were to be expected, but agreed to go up to London with her for a change.
Anything to make her happy, and one place was as good as
another to one in my case. We went up the next day.

I was out alone seeing my publisher the next morning,
and when I got back to the hotel I asked the lift-attendant if
my wife was in. He said she was, as he'd seen a lady entering
our suite. She was not there, however, so I asked him if he
was quite certain, and he said that he was. Just then his bell
rang, and a moment later he came up again with Margaret.
His face was a study in astonishment. I tipped him and told
him it was all right. I imagine he suspected that Salt Lake
City was my spiritual home.

I only mention this little incident, Weldon, as evidence that these appearances were, up to a point at least, perceived by others, and therefore some evidence of my sanity.

What undermined and pierced me was that as my life grew more shadowed Margaret and I were being prised apart. She was still my darling, and the fact that she loved me the sole justification for my living, but I felt I was living in an extra dimension, as it were, that the shadow of what I had done and what I was suffering was erecting a barrier between us, and soon I should be alone with my secret, isolated and yet in some deadly way still Ethel's husband. I could see that Margaret felt this vaguely, too, and that she knew something was sweeping us apart. I used to wonder miserably how I seemed to her, and what torturing, confused, despairing realisation must have come to her. If only I could have told her! But her belief in me was all I had to cling to, and I could not tell her that I had flung Ethel down those steps! And yet, if I could have got my hands on Ethel's throat, I'd have been a murderer again. That obscene, meagre, despicable, mercenary, murdered fool! The best thing I ever did was to crack that evil little skull. She may have had her revenge, but if there are steps in Hell—melodrama! and likely to make a bad impression on you, my dear Weldon.

My poor darling Margaret thought a little amusement would be good for me, so we went to see some picture by Charlie Chaplin that evening. It would have done me more good if Ethel hadn't come in and sat down next to me and begun to produce the picture, for something went snap in my head and there were the steps at Paradown, and Ethel came out, and I behind her, and down she went, and then her crushed and bleeding face grew and grew and thrust itself into mine. And I found myself back at Paradown in bed in my room and Margaret, white and wretched, and with a certain dread and despair on her face, bending over me. And then I remembered, and could not face her eyes. That was yesterday morning.

In the evening old Fritaker doped me, and Margaret went to bed in another room. Eventually I dozed off, and woke again, and then, as I turned sleepily, someone slipped into my arms. For a moment I had the ecstasy of feeling Margaret's heart beating against mine. And then I doubted, shook, and turned on the reading lamp beside the bed, and there was Ethel. For a moment she was warm and whole, and then she glazed, swelled and burst asunder, and became a seething bladder of corruption.

That, my dear Weldon, was five hours ago. It is now 6.30. This dirty little tale is ready for its envelope addressed to you. One bullet stands between me and release—for I can't fight *that*—and, I hope, between my hands and Ethel's throat. I'm not mad, I'm not mad, I swear it!

Or Persons Unknown

Mr. James Ponders rubbed his nose, and then read again his brother's letter:—

Dear Jim,

I've just got back from Madeira, and am so sorry to hear about poor old Reynolds. How you must miss him! Have you got anyone else yet? If not, I have someone I can recommend with perfect confidence. He is a man of the name of Millin, who was my valet for a time many years ago; I don't suppose you remember him. He left me to take up 'butling,' and was with Harry Roper till his death. He then went to Sir Roger Wallington, a very curious cove. You may remember that there was a mighty mystery about his passing. Well, Millin was suspected of having murdered him, not that there was any motive brought forward, but simply because he was sleeping in a room near by, and there was no other man in the house. Superficially it looked fishy. However, there was no real evidence against him, and he was never arrested. Now when I read the case I *knew* quite positively that Millin was innocent. He is one of the best fellows in the world, kind, thoughtful, a gentleman if ever there was one, besides being as efficient and hardworking as they're made. So I asked him to come to see me. When he came, looking weary and worn, he suddenly blurted out the very curious story which I hope you'll permit him to tell to you.

Now you know what an arrant old sceptic I am, neverthe-less I believed every word of this very curious story, though it tends to drive a hole clean through all my scandalous and antediluvian materialism.

Now there are many more things in *your* heaven and earth than in mine, so if I can believe it, you should have no diffi-culty in doing likewise. If you can, that act of faith will give you the finest servant in Europe, and a charming companion. His past has made it impossible for him to get a decent job, so I have been looking after him for the last two years. This seems a heaven-sent opportunity to do you and him a very good turn. At any rate see him. He is 46 and a bachelor. I hope you're flourishing; I should like to pay you a visit in June some time, if you'd like to have me.

Leonard.

P.S.—His address is 38, Mustard Row, Clapham.

Certainly Mr. Ponders missed Reynolds, his devoted com-panion for 25 years. To middle-aged bachelors with large Tudor houses, dwarfed social senses and a great appreciation of personal comfort, to perhaps a little bit selfish gentry of this sort, their butlers are, next to themselves, the most important people in the world. Mrs. Dupine did her best, Mr. Ponders conceded, but he had noted several little un-pleasant omissions during the last three weeks. He had inter-viewed several highly recommended and rotund individuals since Reynolds' death, but none of them had really appealed to him.

But was there anything less appealing than to have al-ways near one somebody who had been seriously suspected of having cut his master's throat! for that was how Sir Roger had come to his end, as he remembered. Might not such an one, encouraged by the success of his first—if it were his first—butchery, proceed with careful and cunning planning to commit another!

Had these questions been raised by anyone but his brother Leonard, Mr. Ponders would have scorned to put himself
to the trouble of answering them. But his brother Leonard
was without exception the finest judge of character he knew.
He was *inspired,* his instinct flawless. He *could* not disregard
his opinion in this case. Mr. Ponders was rather a timid, and
perhaps a little old-fashioned and prejudiced person, but he
prided himself on his courage and open-mindedness. Would
he have a claim to either if he refused to see this Mr. Millin?
He would not. Besides, it sounded as though his story might
be of interest to an earnest student of psychic phenomena.
And he *did* want a butler. So he straightway sat down at his
bureau in that glorious study, the pride of that famous show-
place, Ponders Manor, in the County of Bucks, the ancestral
seat of the Ponders line, and wrote a note to Mr. Millin in
his flowing yet staccato script, asking him, were it convenient to him, to come down the following Thursday. He suggested the 11.30 train from Marylebone. A car would meet
him at Great Missenden. All this would be, of course, at his,
Mr. Ponders' expense.

He also wrote to his brother Leonard. Then he looked at
his watch and found it was 4.30. Chess time for a man of
habit, so out came the ivory pieces, the chequered board, and
the book of the New York Tourney, and he began studiously
analysing that mighty tilt, "Capablanca *v.* Alechin, Round I."

On the next evening he received a note from Mr. Millin
respectfully announcing his intention of catching the 11.30
next Thursday.

Mr. Ponders looked forward to this interview with controlled trepidation. Fancy meeting someone—all alone in
his study—who but for the lack of a little evidence might
have been hanged—might have been "jerked," they called it,
didn't they?

Certainly, but for Leonard, he would not have put himself in such a position.

However, when 12.40 saw Mr. Millin entering the study his trepidation wavered and died. He saw an erect and rather lean figure appropriately garbed in black with a gold watch-chain. But it was Mr. Millin's face that almost persuaded Mr. Ponders forthwith to engage him without further ado. His features were nondescript, but there was something in his expression, so candid, benign, if a little dejected, the expression of one who had known terror and danger, which encountering, he had conquered—at a cost, that went straight to Mr. Ponders' really kind little heart.

He opened the conversation with a conventional gambit, describing the circumstances—already well-known to Mr. Millin—by which the latter found himself there.

Mr. Millin paid murmured thanks to the kindness of all concerned.

"And now, Mr. Millin," said Mr. Ponders, "I will be frank with you. My brother has told me about your connection with Sir Roger Wallington, the difficult position in which you were placed, and your explanation. The latter, I understand, takes the form of a rather remarkable story which my brother believed implicitly. In some way, I take it, it explains the mystery of Sir Roger's death?"

"In some way, I suppose it does, sir," replied Mr. Millin, "but it is so unlikely a tale that I wouldn't have had the courage to tell it to anyone but Sir Leonard. But he's always been so good to me that I dared to tell it to him. You can imagine my relief, sir, when he believed it. I quite understand that you, sir, wouldn't dream of taking me into your service unless you believed it too, and thought it freed me from all suspicion concerning Sir Roger's death."

"That is so," said Mr. Ponders. "Let me hear it."

"Well, sir, after Mr. Roper's death I was out of a position, and seeing Sir Roger's advertisement in the *Morning Post* I answered it, and received a request from Sir Roger to go down to see him.

"Sir Roger was a remarkable-looking gentleman, sir—very tall and strong, with very hard blue eyes, and a contemptuous, nervous, fighting look about him; yet somehow I took a fancy to him.

"'Well, Millin,' he said, 'so you think you'd like to be my butler. Five strong men have thought that in the last eighteen months, and then—they have decided otherwise. The fellow who's here now, for example, Mr. Peters, well—*he's* decided otherwise. He spent some time in America, Millin. The United States have much to be said for them, but they're not good for British butlers. Have you been abroad?'

"'Only for one day, sir,' I said, 'from Brighton to Boulogne and back.'

"'I shan't hold that up against you. I rather like the look of you—you look *soothing*. I want someone soothing. Would you like to try it?'

"I said I would, sir (for one thing, the wages Sir Roger offered were much above the average).

"'Very well,' he said, 'come next Wednesday and stay as long as you can stick it.'

"I had some dinner with the servants before leaving, and what I heard made me realise I was taking something on. Apparently Sir Roger had always been famous for his tempers; during the War he had been wounded in the head, and still had a good deal of pain, and his rages had become very hot indeed, sir.

"'Well, old man, I wish you luck,' said Peters, 'take out some All-Risk insurance, and when you see his chin go kind of down and back and his mouth open, and his left hand begin to twitch, and his eyes begin to spit blood, you'll know you were the wise guy, isn't that so, Mary?' (Mary was one of the housemaids, sir, with whom, I found, this Peters had been too free.)

"'How often does he get that way?' I asked.

"'Ordinary times about once a month. Depends how things are. But when this poacher bird Black Jack gets busy—

well, I won't pump the breeze up you, one of these sunny days you'll know what I haven't said! Anyway, I'm through, thank Theodore! Last Monday he threw a four-pound vase at my head, and I only side-stepped it by a millimetre. I'm not as young as I was. I'm off to Philadelphia next Thursday morning, so I should worry! Anyway, just remember when Black Jack is working his nets you watch his Lordship's eyes when you take in his early morning brandy and soda, and *keep on your toes!'*

"Well, sir, I didn't like this chap's way of carrying on, though his obvious relief at leaving his job made me think twice, but I am easy to get on with as a rule, I wanted work badly, and the pay was very tempting. Also I thought this Peters was the wrong sort of person for Sir Roger, with all his American slang and loud ways. There was another thing which helped to persuade me to accept. Elm Court is a very beautiful place, and I'm very partial to good surroundings."

"It is!" said Mr. Ponders. "The finest medium-sized Tudor House in Great Britain, and the grounds are perfection."

"Yes, sir. After I had been in Sir Roger's service for a week or so, I found out, sir, that he was subject to fits of heavy drinking. He was fairly moderate most of the time, sir, but about once a week he'd drink nearly a bottle of whisky besides other things. The housekeeper, Mrs. Miles, who had been with him many years, told me the habit was growing upon him. I was glad to find, sir, he seemed to take a liking to me; in fact, he quite made a friend of me. He saw very few people; it seemed he had got the wrong side of many of the gentry in the neighbourhood through rubbing them up the wrong way; it was as if he enjoyed doing it.

"Now and again he'd have some friends down from London, but he only entertained the local people, sir, when the Judge came down for the Assizes at Lewes. Otherwise he kept to himself, spending his time riding, looking after the farms on the estate, and, in the season, shooting. Peters had been right about the poachers. Sir Roger had the finest shoot in that part of the world, and the poachers were always at it. It was partly because he was so badly liked, for I found out that a lot of the local chaps were on the poachers' side and helped them. This Black Jack was the worst. The local people seemed to be very much afraid of him, and didn't like to talk about him. They were superstitious about him and very careful to keep on his right side. They told some funny tales. The first time I saw him was in the village about three weeks after I arrived. He was tall and slim and very dark, a good bit of the gipsy in him, I should say, sir. His face was like a hawk's, and he had a very piercing look, a nasty customer to get up against, he seemed to me. He had his dog, Scottie, with him, a big mongrel, a mixture of collie and lurcher he looked, who'd got the name of being the cleverest at his job in the county, a savage, cunning looking brute. Well, Black Jack came up to me with a cheeky contemptuous look on his face. 'You're the new bottle-washer at the Hall, aren't you,' he said. He had almost a gentleman's voice, sir. 'Well, I don't suppose you'll stay any longer than the other bottle-washers. You haven't met Scottie, have you?' The dog bared its teeth and snarled and growled. 'Doesn't seem to like you, never does seem to like Hall folk, somehow; can't think where he learnt to hate 'em. Well, tell that old — of yours I shall be working the East Side for the next week or so,' and he sauntered off.

"I gave Wilkins, the head-keeper, the tip. 'That's like his blasted sauce,' he said. 'I'll get that fine gentleman one of these days! I've had enough of him. It'll mean a new job for me if I miss him this time. I sometimes think he's got the Devil on his side. Say nothing to the master if you like a quiet life.'

"Well, Black Jack started his business as he said he would. He and his gang cleaned up the coverts on the East Side, but none of them was caught. Directly the poaching began the master began to drink. He was out every night, and his temper was something I'd never seen before, but he never actually went for me—Wilkins got it, though, sir. He and three other keepers got the sack, and a new lot came in. Wilkins didn't seem sorry to go. He told me he'd had enough of it, and that the master's cursing was too bad to put up with.

"It was a difficult time for me, sir. Sir Roger was drinking hard and up most of the night, chasing after Black Jack, and he'd come in at four and five in the morning, and I had to wait up for him. The servants were a great trouble. Sir Roger hated to see any of the maids about the house, and when he sacked one of the girls he found dusting his study at seven one morning all of them gave notice. However, I calmed them down and got Sir Roger to raise their wages. After a time Black Jack took his gang elsewhere, and things were a bit more peaceful for a few days.

"One day, early in February, Sir Roger drove up to town, taking Godson, the chauffeur, with him. He had said he'd be back about five, but it was a quarter past eight when they arrived—on foot. When I opened the door I knew that something had happened and that he'd had one of his rages. His face was always white and heavily lined after them, and his eyes looked swollen and red. He pushed past me without saying a word and began drinking whisky in his study. Presently he rang and said he would not dine, but that I was to bring him some sandwiches. When I got down to the servants' hall I found Godson, sitting at the table, his head in his hands. He looked up at me, and his face was haggard.

"'I'm through!' he said. 'The —'s mad, bloody mad'—he was never one to swear as a rule, sir.

"'What's up?' I asked, 'where's the car?'

"'What's up!' he cried; 'that —'s up the pole! I tell you I'm through. I'll tell you what sort of a blasted, bloody lunatic he is! When I met him at the Club I could see he'd been drinking, but he would drive coming home. I've never seen him wilder, we ought to have been killed ten times. I was just beginning to think we'd get through when we reached that switchback in the woods near Ollen. I should think we touched 90 on the way down. As we reached the bottom I saw there was someone standing at the side of the road half way up the hill. Suddenly he began braking hard and peering ahead. It was then I could see the chap in the road was Black Jack. Just as we were drawing up to him that dog of his bounded out into the road behind him. Then I felt the car swing. He drove her straight at Black Jack, missed him by a foot, and then swung back and caught the dog fair and square. The next thing I knew was that I was lying on my ear in a field. Both front tyres had gone, and we'd bust clean through a gate, bounced on the plough, and then turned half over in a dew-pond.

"'Well, His Highness was out in a flash, and I followed him back to the road. When we got there Black Jack was bending over the dog. When he saw us he picked it up and walked towards us. Sir Ruddy Roger went to meet him. Black Jack lifted his cap, and then held up the dog by the back of his neck. Its face was all bloody and dusty and smashed up.

"'"Good evening, Sir Roger," said Black Jack. "Scottie's dead all right, you got him at last, you got him!"

"'"Get to hell from here, you poaching blackguard!" cried the Guv'nor. "Certainly I've got one of you, and if ever you come on my land again I'll get you, too!"

"'"I was rather fond of Scottie," said Black Jack, "and knew all his tricks. He'd got some funny tricks, too; don't be too sure you've done with him!" Then suddenly his face went hard and fierce, and there were tears in his eyes. He shoved the dog's muzzle right into the Guv'nor's face and gave a funny little sharp whistle which seemed to scream in one's head, and he muttered something in some foreign language, gipsy, I guess, and I got the idea that the dog was listening as if it was alive again, and in a twinkling Jack and the dog had disappeared—into the woods I suppose, but it was quick work.

"'The Guv'nor never said a word, but started off to walk home, and here we are, and the ruddy car can drown for all

I care! I leave to-morrow. He can get some other stiff to be killed with him. I'm through. Christ, I've got a head!'

"'You go to bed,' I said, 'I'll get the car brought in in the morning.'

"He was as good as his word, sir; he left before lunch and I never saw him again.

"The next afternoon I had to go down to the village, and at once I noticed a change. Nobody from the Hall was ever much welcomed there, but I had always been treated with civility, and some of them were quite friendly. That day they looked at me out of the corners of their eyes, and were short and abrupt in their manner. It made me feel very uncomfortable, sir."

"What had Sir Roger done to make himself so unpopular with the local people?" asked Mr. Ponders.

"Well, sir, he was a harsh landlord, and never put himself out to please. In this way he was very unlike his father. I think that's what they hated most about him."

"I remember Fred Wallington," said Mr. Ponders. "A genial, easy-going old fox-hunter. Well, go on."

"Of course I couldn't get anything out of them, but they were behaving so queerly that I sent one of the maids, who had a sweetheart working in the local public-house, the Bee and Clover, to see if she could pick up anything. When she got back she said that Joe had 'been funny,' and that she'd had to make a bit of a scene before she could get anything out of him, and that he'd only mutter that Black Jack had said something the night before. He'd come in for a drink and left almost at once. When she asked what he'd said, he wouldn't answer, but had left her and gone home. She'd never seen him like that, she'd said. So putting two and two together, sir, I made out that Black Jack had made some sort of threat against the master which the local people believed he would carry out, and so they wanted to have as little to do with the Hall as possible. I thought the master seemed a bit uneasy at dinner that night. Sometimes he'd seem to be listening to something, and several times I noticed him giving sudden quick looks into a dark corner there was between the door and the serving table. After dinner he went out on to the lawn and walked in a stealthy sort of way over towards the clump of big cedars.

"Well, my pantry window looked out that way, and I saw the master suddenly come running back, and then I heard him slam the window of the morning-room. When I took in the whisky and soda he was looking a little queer, I thought. His face was flushed and his eyes were sort of screwed up, sir, as if he wasn't sure if he could see something or not.

"The next morning when I went to call him I found him wide awake—which I never remembered him being before.

"'Whose dog is that?' he asked, as soon as I came in.

"'What dog, sir?' I asked.

"'I don't know,' he answered shortly. 'I was restless during the night, and got up, and I saw it on the lawn. Find out whose it is and keep it away. Tell whoever owns it I shall have it shot if I see it again.'

"'Very good, sir,' I said.

"I made some enquiries, but no one knew anything about it, and the new keeper told me both his dogs had been sleeping in his kitchen from eight o'clock on.

"The master was all right through the day, but as soon as dusk came on he seemed worried and not himself. We were all a bit on edge, sir, for it was then the Noise began.

"It was quite faint at first. Now, sir, I know I shall never be able to explain what it was like, because the strange thing was that we couldn't really say we heard it, not through one's ears, that is to say. It was as if it was going on inside one's head. Also it was as much a shake as a noise; when it got worse it made everything in the house—how would you call it, sir?"

"Vibrate?" suggested Mr. Ponders.

"Yes, sir, as for what sort of sound it was, it reminded one of what Godson had said about Black Jack's whistle, it seemed to scream in one's head. You know that high noise bats make, piercing, but so high one can only just hear it. Well, sir, it was like that a thousand times louder, and it never stopped from dusk till dawn for a second. It seemed to cut us at the Hall from the rest of the world, close us in, as it were. I can't tell you, sir, how horrible it was at its worst, but at first it was quite soft, though all the servants noticed it, and kept going to the windows to look out, and wondering what it was.

"At dinner that night Sir Roger was very queer. He had just started on the soup when I saw his eyes go to the dark corner I mentioned before, sir. He never touched another mouthful of anything, but all the time his eyes travelled round the room as if he was following something about. Once or twice when he seemed to follow it right up to his side, he half started from his chair, but he always had great self-control of a sort, that is to say, he hated to make any kind of exhibition of himself before other people, sir, and he held himself in, though I could see his knuckles go white as he hung on to the chair. He got up half way through dinner and went back to the morning-room. When I took in his coffee he was peeping through the blind on to the lawn.

"When I came in he turned round rather slowly and said, 'You know that dog I spoke to you about. It's here again. Take the rook-rifle and see if you can find it. I thought I heard it barking just now in Grey Fallow.' (Grey Fallow, sir, is a big copse in the Park, up the hill a bit, about three hundred yards from the wild-rose hedge which cuts the Park off from the lawn.)

"'There,' he said, 'can't you hear it?'

"'I'll see if I can find it, sir,' I said, and got the rifle out, for I thought it would upset the master if I said I couldn't hear anything. By the time I'd reached the rose-hedge I felt I wanted to turn back, but I went through the gate up towards Grey Fallow. There was just a little moon coming through the clouds. Suddenly I felt I couldn't go any further. It was cowardice, I expect, sir, but there were two shadows which seemed to be coming from something standing, and another one crouching just inside the wood, which were more than I could face up to, sir. And then I found myself walking through the open window into the morning-room.

"'Well?' asked the master.

"'I couldn't see anything, sir.'

"'Damn you,' he said, 'I can hear it now; give me the rifle and pour me out a whisky and soda!'

"Some time later I was working in the pantry when I heard a shot. I looked out, but at first I couldn't see anything. Then the moon came through, and I picked out the master crouching down beside the big cedar. 'What's he up to?' I wondered, and it was then for the first time I felt a sinking, creepy feeling, sir, as if I'd give anything to be up in London with people and lights. But I was fond of the master, sir, and I felt it was up to me to look after him, and I made up my mind to stick it out.

"When I went back to the morning-room to ask about orders for the next day he was on his knees peering through the blind. I went out and knocked loudly, and he was sitting in his chair when I came in again, but his left hand was twitching quickly. I was going to take the rifle out to be cleaned, but he told me to leave it there till the morning.

"It was from then, sir, that the bad time really began. It was all right till dusk came, and the master was quite boisterous and good-humoured during the day, but as soon as the sun was down, and that sound began, and the master started to be funny, and all the maids got agitated and hysterical, it was as much as I could stand.

"When I say the master started to be funny, I mean that he got silent and watchful and absorbed in something. From then on he ate nothing at dinner, though he usually went

in and sat down for a time. On the third night, after he
had been staring at the dark corner and round the room
for a time, he suddenly jumped to his feet and seemed to
fling something from him. His face was working, sir, and he
pointed his hand to the door. 'Turn that dog out! Turn that
dog out!' he shouted.

"I was badly taken aback, but I pretended to drive something out of the door. This finished the footman, who ran
away the next morning. I wasn't sorry, as I thought I'd better have the master to myself. It was from then on I had to
pretend all the time when I was with him at night, for there
was no doubt by now, sir, that he was seeing some dog most
of the time, and he was scared of it. I had to sit with him in
the evening with a whip in my hand and let fly in the direction he pointed to. Then he made me come and sleep in the
room next to his. The sound got steadily worse and became
something shocking, sir, and the maids went one by one. It
seemed to drive them crazy, and they'd sit with their hands
to their ears crying. I replaced them at first and offered every
kind of high wages, but it was no good, they wouldn't stay,
and very soon Mrs. Miles and I were left alone. She was a brave
woman, sir, she said she'd stick till she died, if necessary."

"Did Sir Roger hear this sound?" asked Mr. Ponders.

"Not as we did, sir, but he was always hearing barking
and snarling and something scratching at the door. He hated
that worst of all. Time after time he'd tell me through the
tube from his room to mine that there was a dog at his door.
I always got up, but, of course, there was nothing there.

"I expect you wonder, sir, why I didn't take it for granted
it was D.T.s—delirium tremens I should have said, sir, and
fetched a doctor, and I often thought of it, but the master
was not drinking so heavily now as before the trouble began.
Then again the doctor would have probably come during the
day, and found the master almost himself. Besides, I don't
believe he would have seen a doctor, he always hated and
despised them."

"You didn't think it was drink, then?" he asked.

"I didn't know what to think. You see, sir, there was that Sound."

"I wonder you could stick it."

"Well, sir, I did long to go, but if Mrs. Miles could put up with it I could, and I felt I had to stand by the master in the bad time. I was quite attached to him, sir, and I shouldn't have felt right about leaving him in the lurch. I tried to get him to go up to London and stay at the club, but he wouldn't hear of it.

"There began to be a lot of talk in the neighbourhood, for the maids said things before they left, and all the villagers and local people round were certain it had something to do with Black Jack. He had never been seen since that night his dog was killed, but he was believed to be somewhere about. It was a funny thing the local people had a curious knowledge when he was about, and they were always right.

"The master got worse and worse. He couldn't seem to stay in the house after dark unless I was with him. He'd be out all night in the grounds, and I'd sometimes catch a sight of him crouching and hiding, and sometimes he'd come running back as if something was after him. He took to sleeping heavily during the day, but he had bad dreams then, and he said some funny things in his sleep.

"I felt he must be getting near the end of his tether.

"When the Judge came down I never for a moment believed he would attempt to entertain him, but, to my dismay, sir, he insisted, and asked thirty people to meet him. Of course, I had to get a lot of help down from London. The only good thing about it was, I felt, that some of the gentlemen might see what a state he was in and help me to do something for it.

"It was a terrible evening. The Sound was wicked that night. The hired chaps got the wind up, sir, as soon as it began, and kept asking what the hell it was, and several of them tried to slip away. It made all the guests nervous and uneasy.

"The master made an effort for a time; it was a very brave effort, sir, but after a time his eyes went to the corner by the door, and suddenly he gave a sharp movement and then his eyes flitted about as if he was following something. Twice he half rose from his chair as if something was getting at him. Of course, the guests noticed it and, although they made a pretence of talking, I could see them watching the master. The hired men lost their heads and were dropping plates and waiting shockingly. The Noise got so bad that everything was quivering and shaking, and I could see the guests were beginning to get horrified and very uneasy. I felt something was going to happen. Suddenly the master jumped to his feet and began flinging all his glasses and anything he could pick up from the table into the dark corner, shouting, 'Go! go! go! Drive it out, I tell you! Drive it out!' and then he fell in a heap on the floor. Some of the gentlemen helped me to carry him up to his room, and then they left, and glad to go they were. One of them, Sir Marcus O'Reilly, took me aside, and asked if this sort of thing had been going on long. I said for just three weeks. 'Well,' he said, 'it's delirium tremens, and a bad case. I'll do something about it in the morning. He can't go on like this.'

"Would you believe it, sir, the master pulled round about midnight and spent the rest of the night out in the Park!"

"Did you ever see anything unnatural, except those shadows, I mean?" asked Mr. Ponders.

Mr. Millin paused. "There was just something I did see—marks very like those made by the muddy paws of some animals outside the master's bedroom door several times, and one time, when Sir Roger woke me up and told me the dog was on his bed, there were some marks on the blanket.

"There was one funny little thing. The master was fond of cats, and kept six of them. Well, as soon as the Sound began, they all disappeared and were never seen again, and the keeper told me his dog wouldn't go near the hall after dusk. But I don't think I ever saw anything, though the master made it all seem so real that it was enough to make anyone see things.

"Well, sir, the next night it happened—I had managed to get to sleep about two o'clock—the master was out as usual. Suddenly I was awakened by hearing him rushing down the passage. I heard his door slam and then he began shouting, 'Get down! Down, you brute! Down! Down! Down!' and then I heard everything in the room begin crashing about. Just as I reached my door there was a terrible screaming and choking kind of cry—the most awful sound I ever heard, sir.

"I rushed to his room and turned on the light. He was lying across the bed, his throat torn open and the blood pouring out. He was dead already. As I lifted him and tried to staunch the blood I noticed something about his eyes. There was something sort of photographed in them."

"What?" asked Mr. Ponders sharply.

"Well, sir, it might have been the head of a dog smashed up and bleeding.

"When I went to pull down the blinds, my eye was caught by a shadow coming out from the big cedar. It was like the one I had seen in Grey Fallow. And it almost seemed as if I saw another shadow, which was leaping and bounding towards it—and then they both disappeared. And then I noticed the Sound had stopped.

"I got the doctor and the police as soon as I could. The doctor was very puzzled. He said he'd never seen a wound like it, and couldn't imagine how it had been caused.

"Next day the London police came down, and, of course, it began to be a bit unpleasant for me, being so near in the next room like that, and no one else about. They cross-examined me for a long time. All I could say was that the master had been queer for a long time and taken to roaming in the grounds at night, that I had been woken up by hearing him scream and had rushed in to find what I have described, sir. But it sounded weak and fishy. The Inspector heard something in the village about Black Jack, and tried his best to

find him, but he was never seen again. The inquest was ad-
journed several times, and I think everyone expected me to
be arrested, but when the doctor had given his evidence it
seemed to me that everyone in the Court felt there was something that couldn't be explained about the business, and the
verdict was 'Murder by a person or persons unknown.' After
that the police left me alone, but I suppose most people still
believe I did it. And then I came up to London and saw Sir
Leonard. I've never been able to get another place. As soon
as they hear I was with Sir Roger they turn me down.

"Well, that's my story, sir, and it's the whole truth and
nothing but the truth, though I know how it must sound."

"Did you ever think of telling the whole truth and nothing but the truth to the police?" asked Mr. Ponders.

"They wouldn't have stood for it, sir. I'm sure they
wouldn't."

"Well, Mr. Millin," said Mr. Ponders smiling, "my brother has praised you more than I have known him praise many
people, but even he never suggested you had the imagination
to invent that story. Do you know why—amongst other reasons—I believe every word of it? It's because I've heard it
before."

"Heard it before, sir!"

"Well, almost. Do you see that black and red book on the
shelf just behind you?"

"Yes, sir."

"Well, that contains an account of a very, very similar
happening in the year 1795 in this county, not ten miles
away. It is called 'A True Account of the Curious Events connected with the death of Mr. Arthur Pitts.' You shall read it
when you are installed here. By the way, how soon can you
come?"

Mr. Millin's eyes were very bright as he answered, "Any
time which will suit you, sir."

"He Cometh and He Passeth By!"

Edward Bellamy sat down at his desk, untied the ribbon round a formidable bundle of papers, yawned and looked out of the window.

On that glistening evening the prospect from Stone Buildings, Lincoln's Inn, was restful and soothing. Just below the motor mowing-machine placidly "chug-chugged" as it clipped the finest turf in London. The muted murmurs from Kingsway and Holborn roamed in placidly. One sleepy pigeon was scratching its poll and ruffling its feathers in a tree opposite, two others—one coyly fleeing, the other doggedly in pursuit—strutted the greensward. "A curious rite of courtship," thought Bellamy, "but they seem to enjoy it; more than I enjoy the job of reading this brief!"

Had these infatuated fowls gazed back at Mr. Bellamy they would have seen a pair of resolute and trustworthy eyes dominating a resolute, nondescript face, one that gave an indisputable impression of kindliness, candour and mental alacrity. No woman had etched lines upon it, nor were those deepening furrows ploughed by the higher exercise of the imagination marked thereon.

By his thirty-ninth birthday he had raised himself to the unchallenged position of the most brilliant junior at the Criminal Bar, though that is, perhaps, too flashy an epithet to describe that combination of inflexible integrity, impeccable common sense, perfect health and tireless industry which was Edward Bellamy. A modest person, he attributed his success entirely to that "perfect health," a view not lightly to be challenged by those who spend many of their days in those Black Holes of controversy, the Law Courts of London. And he had spent nine out of the last fourteen days therein. But the result had been a signal triumph, for the Court of Criminal Appeal had taken *his* view of Mr. James Stock's motives, and had substituted ten years' penal servitude for a six-foot drop. And he was very weary—and yet here was this monstrous bundle of papers! He had just succeeded in screwing his determination to the sticking point when his telephone bell rang.

He picked up the receiver languidly, and then his face lightened.

"I know that voice. How are you, my dear Philip? Why, what's the matter? Yes, I'm doing nothing. Delighted! Brooks's at eight o'clock. Right you are!"

So Philip had not forgotten his existence. He had begun to wonder. His mind wandered back over his curious friendship with Franton. It had begun on the first morning of their first term at Univ., when they had both been strolling nervously about the quad. That it ever had begun was the most surprising thing about it, for superficially they had nothing in common. Philip, the best bat at Eton, almost too decorative, with a personal charm most people found irresistible, the heir to great possessions. He, the crude product of an obscure Grammar School, destined to live precariously on his scholarships, gauche, shy, taciturn. In the ordinary way they would have graduated to different worlds, for the economic factor alone would have kept their paths all through their lives at Oxford inexorably apart. They would have had little more in common with each other than they had with their scouts. And yet they had spent a good part of almost every day together during term time, and during every vacation he had spent some time at Franton Hall, where he had

had first revealed to him those many and delicate refinements of life which only great wealth, allied with traditional taste, can secure. Why had it been so? He had eventually asked Philip.

"Because," he replied, "you have a first-class brain, I have a second or third. I have always had things made too easy for me. You have had most things made too hard. *Ergo,* you have a first-class character. I haven't. I feel a sense of respectful shame towards you, my dear Teddie, which alone would keep me trotting at your heels. I feel I can rely on you as on no one else. You are at once my superior and my complement. Anyway, it has happened, why worry? Analysing such things often spoils them, it's like over-rehearsing."

And then the War—and even the Defence of Civilisation entailed subtle social distinctions.

Philip was given a commission in a regiment of cavalry (with the best will in the world Bellamy never quite understood the privileged role of the horse in the higher ranks of English society); he himself enlisted in a line regiment, and rose through his innate common sense and his unflagging capacity for finishing a job to the rank of Major, D.S.O. and bar, and a brace of wound-stripes. Philip went to Mesopotamia and was eventually invalided out through the medium of a gas-shell. His right lung seriously affected, he spent from 1917-1924 on a farm in Arizona.

They had written to each other occasionally—the hurried, flippant, shadow-of-death letters of the time, but somehow their friendship had dimmed and faded and become more than a little pre-War by the end of it, so that Bellamy was not more than mildly disappointed when he heard casually that Philip was back in England, yet had had but the most casual, damp letter from him.

But there had been all the old cordiality and affection in his voice over the telephone—and something more—not so pleasant to hear.

At the appointed hour he arrived in St. James's Street, and a moment later Philip came up to him.

"Now, Teddie," he said, "I know what you're thinking, I know I've been a fool and the rottenest sort of type to have acted as I have, but there is a kind of explanation."

Bellamy surrendered at once to that absurd sense of delight at being in Philip's company, and his small resentment was rent and scattered. None the less he regarded him with a veiled intentness. He was looking tired and old—forcing himself—there was something seriously the matter.

"My very dear Philip," he said, "you don't need to explain things to me. To think it is eight years since we met!"

"First of all let's order something," said Philip. "You have what you like, I don't want much, except a drink." Whereupon he selected a reasonable collation for Bellamy and a dressed crab and asparagus for himself. But he drank two Martinis in ten seconds, and these were not the first—Bellamy knew—that he had ordered since 5.30 (there *was* something wrong).

For a little while the conversation was uneasily, stalely reminiscent. Suddenly Philip blurted out, "I can't keep it in any longer. You're the only really reliable, unswerving friend I've ever had. You will help me, won't you?"

"My dear Philip," said Bellamy, touched, "I always have and always will be ready to do anything you want me to do and at any time—you know that."

"Well, then, I'll tell you my story. First of all, have you ever heard of a man called Oscar Clinton?"

"I seem to remember the name. It is somehow connected in my mind with the nineties, raptures and roses, absinthe and poses; and the *other* Oscar. I believe his name cropped up in a case I was in. I have an impression he's a wrong 'un."

"That's the man," said Philip. "He stayed with me for three months at Franton."

"Oh," said Bellamy sharply, "how was that?"

"Well, Teddie, anything the matter with one's lungs affects one's mind—not always for the worse, however. I know that's true, and it affected mine. Arizona is a moon-dim region, very lovely in its way and stark and old, but I had to leave it. You know I was always a sceptic, rather a wooden one, as I remember; well, that ancient, lonely land set my lung-polluted mind working. I used to stare and stare into the sky. One is brought right up against the vast enigmas of time and space and eternity when one lung is doing the work of two, and none too well at that."

Edward realised under what extreme tension Philip had been living, but felt that he could establish a certain control over him. He felt more in command of the situation and resolved to keep that command.

"Well," continued Philip, filling up his glass, "when I got back to England I was so frantically nervous that I could hardly speak or think. I felt insane, unclean—mentally. I felt I was going mad, and could not bear to be seen by anyone who had known me—that is why I was such a fool as not to come to you. You have your revenge! I can't tell you, Teddie, how depression roared through me! I made up my mind to die, but I had a wild desire to know to what sort of place I should go. And then I met Clinton. I had rushed up to London one day just to get the inane anodyne of noise and people, and I suppose I was more or less tight, for I walked into a club of sorts called the 'Chorazin' in Soho. The door-keeper tried to turn me out, but I pushed him aside, and then someone came up and led me to a table. It was Clinton.

"Now there is no doubt he has great hypnotic power. He began to talk, and I at once felt calmer and started to tell him all about myself. I talked wildly for an hour, and he was so deft and delicate in his handling of me that I felt I could not leave him. He has a marvellous insight into abnormal mental—psychic—whatever you like to call them—states.

Some time I'll describe what he looks like—he's certainly like no one else in the world.

"Well, the upshot was that he came down to Franton next day and stayed on. Now, I know that his motives were entirely mercenary, but none the less he saved me from suicide, and to a great extent gave back peace to my mind.

"Never could I have imagined such an irresistible and brilliant talker. Whatever he may be, he's also a poet, a profound philosopher and amazingly versatile and erudite. Also, when he likes, his charm of manner carries one away. At least, in my case it did—for a time—though he borrowed £20 or more a week from me.

"And then one day my butler came to me, and with the hushed gusto appropriate to such revelations murmured that two of the maids were in the family way and that another had told him an hysterical little tale—floating in floods of tears—about how Clinton had made several attempts to force his way into her bedroom.

"Well, Teddie, that sort of thing is that sort of thing, but I felt such a performance couldn't possibly be justified, that taking advantage of a trio of rustics in his host's house was a dastardly and unforgivable outrage.

"Other people's morals are chiefly their own affair, but I had a personal responsibility towards these buxom victims—well, you can realise just how I felt.

"I had to speak about it to Clinton, and did so that night. No one ever saw him abashed. He smiled at me in a superior and patronising way, and said he quite understood that I was almost bound to hold such feudal and socially primitive views, suggesting, of course, that my chief concern in the matter was that he had infringed my *droit de seigneur* in these cases. As for him, he considered it was his duty to disseminate his unique genius as widely as possible, and that it should be considered the highest privilege for anyone to bear his child. He had to his knowledge seventy-four offspring alive, and probably many more—the more the better for the future of humanity. But, of course, he understood and promised for the future—bowing to my rights and my prejudices—to allow me to plough my own pink and white pastures—and much more to the same effect.

"Though still under his domination, I felt there was more lust than logic in these specious professions, so I made an excuse and went up to London the next day. As I left the house I picked up my letters, which I read in the car on the way up. One was a three-page catalogue raisonné from my tailor. Not being as dressy as all that, it seemed unexpectedly grandiose, so I paid him a visit. Well, Clinton had forged a letter from me authorising him to order clothes at my expense, and a lavish outfit had been provided.

"It then occurred to me to go to my bank to discover precisely how much I had lent Clinton during the last three months. It was £420. All these discoveries—telescoping—caused me to review my relationship with Clinton. Suddenly I felt it had better end. I might be mediaeval, intellectually costive, and the possessor of much scandalously unearned increment, but I could not believe that the pursuit and contemplation of esoteric mysteries necessarily implied the lowest possible standards of private decency. In other words, I was recovering.

"I still felt that Clinton was the most remarkable person I had ever met. I do to this day—but I felt I was unequal to squaring such magic circles.

"I told him so when I got back. He was quite charming, gentle, understanding, commiserating, and he left the next morning, after pronouncing some incantation whilst touching my forehead. I missed him very much. I believe he's the devil, but he's that sort of person.

"Once I had assured the prospective mothers of his children that they would not be sacked and that their destined contributions to the population would be a charge upon me—there is a codicil to my will to this effect—they brightened up considerably, and rather too frequently snatches of

the Froth-Blowers' Anthem cruised down to me as they went
about their duties. In fact, I had a discreditable impression
that the Immaculate Third would have shown less lachrymose
integrity had the consequences of surrender been revealed
ante factum. Eventually a brace of male infants came to contribute their falsettos to the dirge—for whose appearance
the locals have respectfully given me the credit. These brats
have searching, calign eyes, and when they reach the age of
puberty I should not be surprised if the birth statistics for
East Surrey began to show a remarkable—even a magical—
rise.

"Oh, how good it is to talk to you, Teddie, and get it all
off my chest! I feel almost light-hearted, as though my poor
old brain had been curetted. I feel I can face and fight it
now.

"Well, for the next month I drowsed and read and drowsed
and read until I felt two-lunged again. And several times I
almost wrote to you, but I felt such lethargy and yet such
a certainty of getting quite well again that I put everything
off. I was content to lie back and let that blessed healing
process work its quiet kindly way with me.

"And then one day I got a letter from a friend of mine,
Melrose, who was at the House when we were up. He is the
Secretary of 'Ye Ancient Mysteries,' a dining club I joined
before the War. It meets once a month and discusses famous
mysteries of the past—the *Mary Celeste,* the 'McLachlan
Case,' and so on—with a flippant yet scholarly zeal; but that
doesn't matter. Well, Melrose said that Clinton wanted to
become a member, and had stressed the fact that he was a
friend of mine. Melrose was a little upset, as he had heard
vague rumours about Clinton. Did I think he was likely to
be an acceptable member of the club?

"Well, what was I to say? On the one side of the medal
were the facts that he had used my house as his stud-farm,
that he had forged my name and sponged on me shamelessly.
On the reverse was the fact that he was a genius and knew

more about Ancient Mysteries than the rest of the world put together. But my mind was soon made up; I could not recommend him. A week later I got a letter—a charming letter, a most understanding letter, from Clinton. He realised, so he said, that I had been bound to give the secretary of the Ancient Mysteries the advice I had—no doubt I considered he was not a decent person to meet my friends. He was naturally disappointed, and so on.

"How the devil, I wondered, did he know—not only that I had put my thumbs down against him, but also the very reason for which I had put them down!

"So I asked Melrose, who told me he hadn't mentioned the matter to a soul, but had discreetly removed Clinton's name from the list of candidates for election. And no one should have been any the wiser; but how much wiser Clinton was!

"A week later I got another letter from him, saying that he was leaving England for a month. He enclosed a funny little paper pattern thing, an outline cut out with scissors with a figure painted on it, a beastly-looking thing. Like this!"

And he drew a quick sketch on the table cloth.

Certainly it was unpleasant, thought Bellamy. It appeared to be a crouching figure in the posture of pursuit. The robes it wore seemed to rise and billow above its head. Its arms were long—too long—scraping the ground with curved and spiked nails. Its head was not quite human, its expression devilish and venomous. A horrid, hunting thing, its eyes encarnadined and infinitely evil, glowing animal eyes in the foul dark face. And those long vile arms—not pleasant to be in their grip. He hadn't realised Philip could draw as well as that. He straightened himself, lit a cigarette, and rallied his fighting powers. For the first time he realised, why, that Philip was in serious trouble! Just a rather beastly little sketch on a table-cloth. And now it was up to him!

"Clinton told me," continued Philip, "that this was a most powerful symbol which I should find of the greatest help in my mystical studies. I must place it against my forehead, and pronounce at the same time a certain sentence. And, Teddie, suddenly, I found myself doing so. I remember I had a sharp feeling of surprise and irritation when I found I had placarded this thing on my head and repeated this sentence."

"What was the sentence?" asked Bellamy.

"Well, that's a funny thing," said Philip. "I can't remember it, and both the slip of paper on which it was written and the paper pattern had disappeared the next morning. I remember putting them in my pocket book, but they completely vanished. And, Teddie, things haven't been the same since." He filled his glass and emptied it, lit a cigarette, and at once pressed the life from it in an ash tray and then lit another.

"Bluntly, I've been bothered, haunted perhaps is too strong a word—too pompous. It's like this. That same night I had read myself tired in the study, and about twelve o'clock I was glancing sleepily around the room when I noticed that one of the bookcases was throwing out a curious and unaccountable shadow. It seemed as if something was hiding behind the bookcase, and that this was that something's shadow. I got up and walked over to it, and it became just a bookcase shadow, rectangular and reassuring. I went to bed.

"As I turned on the light on the landing I noticed the same sort of shadow coming from the grandfather clock. I went to sleep all right, but suddenly found myself peering out of the window, and there was that shadow stretching out from the trees and in the drive. At first there was about that much of it showing," and he drew a line down the sketch on the table cloth, "about a sixth. Well, it's been a simple story since then. Every night that shadow has grown a little. It is now almost all visible. And it comes out suddenly from different places. Last night it was on the wall beside the door into the Dutch garden. I never know where I'm going to see it next."

"And how long has this been going on?" asked Bellamy.

"A month to-morrow. You sound as if you thought I was mad. I probably am."

"No, you're as sane as I am. But why don't you leave Franton and come to London?"

"And see it on the wall of the club bedroom! I've tried that, Teddie, but one's as bad as the other. Doesn't it sound ludicrous? But it isn't to me."

"Do you usually eat as little as this?" asked Bellamy.

"'And drink as much?' you were too polite to add. Well, there's more to it than indigestion, and it isn't incipient D.T. It's just I don't feel very hungry nowadays."

Bellamy got that rush of tip-toe pugnacity which had won him so many desperate cases. He had had a Highland grandmother from whom he had inherited a powerful visualising imagination, by which he got a fleeting yet authentic insight into the workings of men's minds. So now he knew in a flash how he would feel if Philip's ordeal had been his.

"Whatever it is, Philip," he said, "there are two of us now."

"Then you do believe in it," said Philip. "Sometimes I can't. On a sunny morning with starlings chattering and buses swinging up Waterloo Place—then how can such things be? But at night I know they are."

"Well," said Bellamy, after a pause, "let us look at it coldly and precisely. Ever since Clinton sent you a certain painted paper pattern you've seen a shadowed reproduction of it. Now I take it he has—as you suggested—unusual hypnotic power. He has studied mesmerism?"

"I think he's studied every bloody thing," said Philip.

"Then that's a possibility."

"Yes," agreed Philip, "it's a possibility. And I'll fight it, Teddie, now that I have you, but can you minister to a mind diseased?"

"Throw quotation to the dogs," replied Bellamy. "What one man has done another can undo—there's one for you."

"Teddie," said Philip, "will you come down to Franton to-night?"

"Yes," said Bellamy. "But why?"

"Because I want you to be with me at twelve o'clock to-night when I look out from the study window and think I see a shadow flung on the flagstones outside the drawing-room window."

"Why not stay up here for to-night?"

"Because I want to get it settled. Either I'm mad or— Will you come?"

"If you really mean to go down to-night I'll come with you."

"Well, I've ordered the car to be here by 9.15," said Philip. "We'll go to your rooms, and you can pack a suitcase and we'll be there by half past ten."

Suddenly he looked up sharply, his shoulders drew together and his eyes narrowed and became intent. It happened that at that moment no voice was busy in the dining-room of the Brooks's Club. No doubt they were changing over at the Power Station, for the lights dimmed for a moment. It seemed to Bellamy that someone was developing wavy, wicked little films far back in his brain, and a voice suddenly whispered in his ear with a vile sort of shyness, "He cometh and he passeth by!"

As they drove down through the night they talked little. Philip drowsed and Bellamy's mind was busy. His preliminary conclusion was that Philip was neither mad nor going mad, but that he was not normal. He had always been very sensitive and highly strung, reacting too quickly and deeply to emotional stresses—and this living alone and eating nothing—the worst thing for him.

And this Clinton. He had the reputation of being an evil man of power, and such persons' hypnotic influence was absurdly underrated. He'd get on his track.

"When does Clinton get back to England?" he asked.

"If he kept to his plans he'll be back about now," said Philip sleepily.

"What are his haunts?"

"He lives near the British Museum in rooms, but he's usually to be found at the Chorazin Club after six o'clock. It's in Larn Street, just off Shaftesbury Avenue. A funny place with some funny members."

Bellamy made a note of this.

"Does he know you know me?"

"No, I think not, there's no reason why he should."

"So much the better," said Bellamy.

"Why?" asked Philip.

"Because I'm going to cultivate his acquaintance."

"Well, do look out, Teddie, he has a marvellous power of hiding the fact, but he's dangerous, and I don't want you to get into any trouble like mine."

"I'll be careful," said Bellamy.

Ten minutes later they passed the gates of the drive of Franton Manor, and Philip began glancing uneasily about him and peering sharply where the elms flung shadows. It was a perfectly still and cloudless night, with a quarter moon. It was just a quarter to eleven as they entered the house. They went up to the library on the first floor which looked out over the Dutch Garden to the Park. Franton is a typical Georgian house, with charming gardens and Park, but too big and lonely for one nervous person to inhabit, thought Bellamy.

The butler brought up sandwiches and drinks, and Bellamy thought he seemed relieved at their arrival. Philip began to eat ravenously, and gulped down two stiff whiskies. He kept looking at his watch, and his eyes were always searching the walls.

"It comes, Teddie, even when it ought to be too light for shadows."

"Now then," replied the latter, "I'm with you, and we're going to keep quite steady. It may come, but I shall not leave you until it goes and for ever." And he managed to lure

Philip on to another subject, and for a time he seemed quieter, but suddenly he stiffened, and his eyes became rigid and staring. "It's there," he cried, "I know it!"

"Steady, Philip!" said Bellamy sharply. "Where?"

"Down below," he whispered, and began creeping towards the window.

Bellamy reached it first and looked down. He saw it at once, knew what it was, and set his teeth.

He heard Philip shaking and breathing heavily at his side.

"It's there," he said, "and it's complete at last!"

"Now, Philip," said Bellamy, "we're going down, and I'm going out first, and we'll settle the thing once and for all."

They went down the stairs and into the drawing-room. Bellamy turned the light on and walked quickly to the French window and began to try to open the catch. He fumbled with it for a moment.

"Let me do it," said Philip, and put his hand to the catch, and then the window opened and he stepped out.

"Come back, Philip!" cried Bellamy. As he said it the lights went dim, a fierce blast of burning air filled the room, the window came crashing back. Then through the glass Bellamy saw Philip suddenly throw up his hands, and something huge and dark lean from the wall and envelop him. He seemed to writhe for a moment in its folds. Bellamy strove madly to thrust the window open, while his soul strove to withstand the mighty and evil power he felt was crushing him, and then he saw Philip flung down with awful force, and he could hear the foul, crushing thud as his head struck the stone.

And then the window opened and Bellamy dashed out into a quiet and scented night.

At the inquest the doctor stated he was satisfied that Mr. Franton's death was due to a severe heart attack—he had never recovered from the gas, he said, and such a seizure was always possible.

"Then there are no peculiar circumstances about the case?" asked the Coroner.

The doctor hesitated. "Well, there is one thing," he said slowly. "The pupils of Mr. Franton's eyes were—well, to put it simply to the jury—instead of being round, they were drawn up so that they resembled half-moons—in a sense they were like the pupils in the eyes of a cat."

"Can you explain that?" asked the Coroner.

"No, I have never seen a similar case," replied the doctor. "But I am satisfied the cause of death was as I have stated."

Bellamy was, of course, called as a witness, but he had little to say.

About eleven o'clock on the morning after these events Bellamy rang up the Chorazin Club from his chambers and learned from the manager that Mr. Clinton had returned from abroad. A little later he got a Sloane number and arranged to lunch with Mr. Solan at the United Universities Club. And then he made a conscientious effort to estimate the chances in Rex v. Tipwinkle.

But soon he was restless and pacing the room. He could not exorcise the jeering demon which told him sniggeringly that he had failed Philip. It wasn't true, but it pricked and penetrated. But the game was not yet played out. If he had failed to save he might still avenge. He would see what Mr. Solan had to say.

That personage was awaiting him in the smoking room. Mr. Solan was an original and looked it. Just five feet and two inches—a tiny body, a mighty head with a dominating forehead studded with a pair of thrusting frontal lobes. All this covered with a thick, greying thatch. Veiled, restless little eyes, a perky, tilted, little nose and a very thin-lipped, fighting mouth from which issued the most curious, resonant, high and piercing voice. This is a rough and ready sketch of one who is universally accepted to be the greatest living

Oriental Scholar—a mystic—once upon a time a Senior Wrangler, a philosopher of European repute, a great and fascinating personality, who lived alone, save for a brace of tortoiseshell cats and a housekeeper, in Chester Terrace, Sloane Square. About every six years he published a masterly treatise on one of his special subjects; otherwise he kept himself to himself with the remorseless determination he brought to bear upon any subject which he considered worth serious consideration, such as the Chess Game, the works of Bach, the paintings of Van Gogh, the poems of Housman, and the short stories of P. G. Wodehouse and Austin Freeman.

He entirely approved of Bellamy, who had once secured him substantial damages in a copyright case. The damages had gone to the Society for the Prevention of Cruelty to Animals.

"And what can I do for you, my dear Bellamy?" he piped, when they were seated.

"First of all, have you ever heard of a person called Oscar Clinton? Secondly, do you know anything of the practice of sending an enemy a painted paper pattern?"

Mr. Solan smiled slightly at the first question, and ceased to smile when he heard the second.

"Yes," he said, "I have heard of both, and I advise you to have nothing whatsoever to do with either."

"Unfortunately," replied Bellamy, "I have already had to do with both. Two nights ago my best friend died—rather suddenly. Presently I will tell you how he died. But first of all, tell me something about Clinton."

"It is characteristic of him that you know so little about him," replied Mr. Solan, "for although he is one of the most dangerous and intellectually powerful men in the world he gets very little publicity nowadays. Most of the much-advertised Naughty Boys of the Nineties harmed no one but themselves—they merely canonised their own and each other's dirty linen, but Clinton was in a class by himself.

He was—and no doubt still is—an accomplished corrupter, and he took, and no doubt still takes, a jocund delight in his hobby. Eventually he left England—by request—and went out East. He spent some years in a Tibetan Monastery, and then some other years in less reputable places—his career is detailed very fully in a file in my study—and then he applied his truly mighty mind to what I may loosely call magic—for what I loosely call magic, my dear Bellamy, most certainly exists. Clinton is highly psychic, with great natural hypnotic power. He then joined an esoteric and little-known sect—Satanists—of which he eventually became High Priest. And then he returned to what we call civilisation, and has since been 'moved on' by the Civil Powers of many countries, for his forte is the extraction of money from credulous and timid individuals—usually female—by methods highly ingenious and peculiarly his own. It is a boast of his that he has never yet missed his revenge. He ought to be stamped out with the brusque ruthlessness meted out to a spreading fire in a Californian forest.

"Well, there is a short inadequate sketch of Oscar Clinton, and now about these paper patterns."

Two hours later Bellamy got up to leave. "I can lend you a good many of his books," said Mr. Solan, "and you can get the rest at Lilley's. Come to me from four till six on Wednesdays and Fridays, and I'll teach you all I think essential. Meanwhile, I will have a watch kept upon him, but I want you, my dear Bellamy, to do nothing decisive till you are qualified. It would be a pity if the Bar were to be deprived of your great gifts prematurely."

"Many thanks," said Bellamy. "I have now placed myself in your hands, and I'm in this thing till the end—some end or other."

Mr. Plank, Bellamy's clerk, had no superior in his profession, one which is the most searching test of character and adaptability. Not one of the devious and manifold tricks

of his trade was unpractised by him, and his income was
£1,250 per annum, a fact which the Inland Revenue Authorities strongly suspected but were quite unable to establish. He
liked Mr. Bellamy, personally well enough, financially very
much indeed. It was not surprising, therefore, that many
seismic recording instruments registered sharp shocks at
four p.m. on June 12th, 192-, a disturbance caused by the
precipitous descent of Mr. Plank's jaw when Mr. Bellamy
instructed him to accept no more briefs for him for the next
three months. "But," continued that gentleman, "here is a
cheque which will, I trust, reconcile you to the fact."

Mr. Plank scrutinised the numerals and was reconciled.

"Taking a holiday, sir?" he asked.

"I rather doubt it," replied Bellamy. "But you might suggest to any inquisitive enquirers that that is the explanation."

"I understand, sir."

From then till midnight, with one short pause, Bellamy
was occupied with a pile of exotically bound volumes. Occasionally he made a note on his writing pad. When his clock
struck twelve he went to bed and read *The Wallet of Kai-Lung*
till he felt sleepy enough to turn out the light.

At eight o'clock the next morning he was busy once more
with an exotically bound book, and making an occasional
note on his writing pad.

Three weeks later he was bidding a temporary farewell to
Mr. Solan, who remarked, "I think you'll do now. You are an
apt pupil; pleading has given you a command of convincing
bluff, and you have sufficient psychic insight to make it possible for you to succeed. Go forth and prosper! At all times I
shall be fighting for you. He will be there at nine to-night."

At a quarter past that hour Bellamy was asking the
door-keeper of the Chorazin Club to tell Mr. Clinton that a
Mr. Bellamy wished to see him.

Two minutes later the official reappeared and led him
downstairs into an ornate and gaudy cellar decorated with

violence and indiscretion—the work, he discovered later, of a neglected genius who had died of neglected cirrhosis of the liver. He was led up to a table in the corner, where someone was sitting alone.

Bellamy's first impression of Oscar Clinton remained vividly with him till his death. As he got up to greet him he could see that he was physically gigantic—six foot five at least, with a massive torso—the build of a champion wrestler. Topping it was a huge, square, domed head. He had a white yet mottled face, thick, tense lips, the lower one protruding fantastically. His hair was clipped close, save for one twisted and oiled lock which curved down to meet his eyebrows. But what impressed Bellamy most was a pair of the hardest, most penetrating and merciless eyes—one of which seemed soaking wet and dripping slowly.

Bellamy "braced his belt about him"—he was in the presence of a power.

"Well, sir," said Clinton in a beautifully musical voice with a slight drawl, "I presume you are connected with Scotland Yard. What can I do for you?"

"No," replied Bellamy, forcing a smile, "I'm in no way connected with that valuable institution."

"Forgive the suggestion," said Clinton, "but during a somewhat adventurous career I have received so many unheralded visits from more or less polite police officials. What, then, is your business?"

"I haven't any, really," said Bellamy. "It's simply that I have long been a devoted admirer of your work, the greatest imaginative work of our time in my opinion. A friend of mine mentioned casually that he had seen you going into this Club, and I could not resist taking the liberty of forcing, just for a moment, my company upon you."

Clinton stared at him, and seemed not quite at his ease.

"You interest me," he said at length. "I'll tell you why. Usually I know decisively by certain methods of my own whether a person I meet comes as an enemy or a friend. These tests have failed in your case, and this, as I say, interests me. It suggests things to me. Have you been in the East?"

"No," said Bellamy.

"And made no study of its mysteries?"

"None whatever, but I can assure you I come merely as a most humble admirer. Of course, I realise you have enemies—all great men have; it is the privilege and penalty of their pre-eminence, and I know you to be a great man."

"I fancy," said Clinton, "that you are perplexed by the obstinate humidity of my left eye. It is caused by the rather heavy injection of heroin I took this afternoon. I may as well tell you I use all drugs, but am the slave of none. I take heroin when I desire to contemplate. But tell me—since you profess such an admiration for my books—which of them most meets with your approval?"

"That's a hard question," replied Bellamy, "but *A Damsel with a Dulcimer* seems to me exquisite."

Clinton smiled patronisingly.

"It has merits," he said, "but is immature. I wrote it when I was living with a Bedouin woman aged fourteen in Tunis. Bedouin women have certain natural gifts"—and here he became remarkably obscene, before returning to the subject of his works; "my own opinion is that I reached my zenith in *The Songs of Hamdonna*. Hamdonna was a delightful companion, the fruit of the raptures of an Italian gentleman and a Persian lady. She had the most naturally—the most brilliantly vicious mind of any woman I ever met. She required hardly any training. But she was unfaithful to me, and died soon after."

"The Songs are marvellous," said Bellamy, and he began quoting from them fluently.

Clinton listened intently. "You have a considerable gift for reciting poetry," he said. "May I offer you a drink? I was about to order one for myself."

"I'll join you on one condition—that I may be allowed to pay for both of them—to celebrate the occasion."

"Just as you like," said Clinton, tapping the table with his thumb, which was adorned with a massive jade ring curiously carved. "I always drink brandy after heroin, but you order what you please."

It may have been the whisky, it may have been the pressing nervous strain or a combination of both, which caused Bellamy now to regard the mural decorations with a much modified sang-froid. Those distorted and tortured patches of flat colour, how subtly suggestive they were of something sniggeringly evil!

"I gave Valin the subject for those panels," said Clinton. "They are meant to represent an impression of the stages in the Black Mass, but he drank away his original inspiration, and they fail to do that majestic ceremony justice."

Bellamy flinched at having his thoughts so easily read.

"I was thinking the same thing," he replied; "that unfortunate cat they're slaughtering deserved a less ludicrous memorial to its fate."

Clinton looked at him sharply and sponged his oozing eye.

"I have made these rather flamboyant references to my habits purposely. Not to impress you, but to see *how* they impressed you. Had you appeared disgusted, I should have known it was useless to pursue our acquaintanceship. All my life I have been a law unto myself, and that is probably why the Law has always shown so much interest in me. I know myself to be a being apart, one to whom the codes and conventions of the herd can never be applied. I have sampled every so-called 'vice,' including every known drug. Always, however, with an object in view. Mere purposeless debauchery is not in my character. My Art, to which you have so kindly referred, must always come first. Sometimes it demands that I sleep with a negress, that I take opium or hashish; sometimes it dictates rigid asceticism, and I tell you, my friend, that if such an instruction came again to-morrow, as it has often come in the past, I could, without the slightest effort, lead a life of complete abstinence from drink, drugs and women for an indefinite period. In other words, I have gained absolute control over my senses after the most exhaustive experiments with them. How many can say the same? Yet one does not know what life can teach till that control is established. The man of superior power—there are no such women—should not flinch from such experiments, he should seek to learn every lesson evil as well as good has to teach. So will he be able to extend and multiply his personality, but always he must remain absolute master of himself. And then he will have many strange rewards, and many secrets will be revealed to him. Some day, perhaps, I will show you some which have been revealed to me."

"Have you absolutely no regard for what is called 'morality'?" asked Bellamy.

"None whatever. If I wanted money I should pick your pocket. If I desired your wife—if you have one—I should seduce her. If someone obstructs me—something happens to him. You must understand this clearly—for I am not bragging—I do nothing purposelessly nor from what I consider a bad motive. To me 'bad' is synonymous with 'unnecessary.' I do nothing unnecessary."

"Why is revenge necessary?" asked Bellamy.

"A plausible question. Well, for one thing I like cruelty—one of my unpublished works is a defence of Super-Sadism. Then it is a warning to others, and lastly it is a vindication of my personality. All excellent reasons. Do you like my *Thus spake Eblis?*"

"Masterly," replied Bellamy. "The perfection of prose, but, of course, its magical significance is far beyond my meagre understanding."

"My dear friend, there is only one man in Europe about whom that would not be equally true."

"Who is that?" asked Bellamy.

Clinton's eyes narrowed venomously.

"His name is Solan," he said. "One of these days, per-haps—" and he paused. "Well, now, if you like I will tell you of some of my experiences."

An hour later a monologue drew to its close. "And now, Mr. Bellamy, what is your role in life?"

"I'm a barrister."

"Oh, so you *are* connected with the Law?"

"I hope," said Bellamy smiling, "you'll find it possible to forget it."

"It would help me to do so," replied Clinton, "if you would lend me ten pounds. I have forgotten my note-case—a frequent piece of negligence on my part—and a lady awaits me. Thanks very much. We shall meet again, I trust."

"I was just about to suggest that you dined with me one day this week?"

"This is Tuesday," said Clinton. "What about Thursday?"

"Excellent, will you meet me at the Gridiron about eight?"

"I will be there," said Clinton, mopping his eye. "Good-night."

"I can understand now what happened to Franton," said Bel-lamy to Mr. Solan the next evening. "He is the most fascinat-ing and catholic talker I have met. He has a wicked charm. If half to which he lays claim is true, he has packed ten lives into sixty years."

"In a sense," said Mr. Solan, "he has the best brain of any man living. He has also a marvellous histrionic sense and he is *deadly*. But he is vulnerable. On Thursday encourage him to talk of other things. He will consider you an easy victim. You must make the most of the evening—it may rather revolt you—he is sure to be suspicious at first."

"It amuses and reassures me," said Clinton at ten fifteen on Thursday evening in Bellamy's room, "to find you have a lively appreciation of obscenity."

He brought out a snuff box, an exquisite little masterpiece with an inexpressibly vile design enamelled on the lid, from which he took a pinch of white powder which he sniffed up from the palm of his hand.

"I suppose," said Bellamy," that all your magical lore would be quite beyond me."

"Oh yes, quite," replied Clinton, "but I can show you what sort of power a study of that lore has given me, by a little experiment. Turn round, look out of the window, and keep quite quiet till I speak to you."

It was a brooding night. In the south-west the clouds made restless, quickly shifting patterns—the heralds of coming storm. The scattered sound of the traffic in Kingsway rose and fell with the gusts of the rising wind. Bellamy found a curious picture forming in his brain. A wide lonely waste of snow and a hill with a copse of fir trees, out from which someone came running. Presently this person halted and looked back, and then out from the wood appeared another figure (of a shape he had seen before). And then the one it seemed to be pursuing began to run on, staggering through the snow, over which the Shape seemed to skim lightly and rapidly, and to gain on its quarry. Then it appeared as if the one in front could go no further. He fell and rose again, and faced his pursuer. The Shape came swiftly on and flung itself hideously on the one in front, who fell to his knees. The two seemed intermingled for a moment . . .

"Well," said Clinton, "and what did you think of that?"

Bellamy poured out a whisky and soda and drained it.

"Extremely impressive," he replied. "It gave me a feeling of great horror."

"The individual whose rather painful end you have just witnessed once did me a dis-service. He was found in a remote part of Norway. Why he chose to hide himself there is rather difficult to understand."

"Cause and effect?" asked Bellamy, forcing a smile.

Clinton took another pinch of the white powder.

"Possibly a mere coincidence," he replied. "And now I must go, for I have a 'date,' as they say in America, with a rather charming and profligate young woman. Could you possibly lend me a little money?"

When he had gone Bellamy washed his person very thoroughly in a hot bath, brushed his teeth with zeal, and felt a little cleaner. He tried to read in bed, but between him and Mr. Jacobs's 'Night-Watchman' a bestial and persistent phantasmagoria forced its way. He dressed again, went out, and walked the streets till dawn.

Some time later Mr. Solan happened to overhear a conversation in the club smoking-room.

"I can't think what's happened to Bellamy," said one. "He does no work and is always about with that incredible swine Clinton."

"A kink somewhere, I suppose," said another, yawning. "Dirty streak probably."

"Were you referring to Mr. Edward Bellamy, a friend of mine?" asked Mr. Solan.

"We were," said one.

"Have you ever known him do a discreditable thing?"

"Not till now," said another.

"Or a stupid thing?"

"I'll give you that," said one.

"Well," said Mr. Solan, "you have my word for it that he has not changed," and he passed on.

"Funny old devil that," said one.

"Rather shoves the breeze up me," said another. "He seems to know something. I like Bellamy, and I'll apologise to him for taking his name in vain when I see him next. But that bastard Clinton!—"

"It will have to be soon," said Mr. Solan. "I heard to-day that he will be given notice to quit any day now. Are you prepared to go through with it?"

"He's the Devil incarnate," said Bellamy. "If you knew what I'd been through in the last month!"

"I have a shrewd idea of it," replied Mr. Solan. "You think he trusts you completely?"

"I don't think he has any opinion of me at all, except that I lend him money whenever he wants it. Of course, I'll go through with it. Let it be Friday night. What must I do? Tell me exactly. I know that but for you I should have chucked my hand in long ago."

"My dear Bellamy, you have done marvellously well, and you will finish the business as resolutely as you have carried it through so far. Well, this is what you must do. Memorise it flawlessly."

"I will arrange it that we arrive at his rooms just about eleven o'clock. I will ring up five minutes before we leave."

"I shall be doing my part," said Mr. Solan.

Clinton was in high spirits at the Café Royal on Friday evening.

"I like you, my dear Bellamy," he observed, "not merely because you have a refined taste in pornography and have lent me a good deal of money, but for a more subtle reason. You remember when we first met I was puzzled by you. Well, I still am. There is some psychic power surrounding you. I don't mean that you are conscious of it, but there is some very powerful influence working for you. Great friends though we are, I sometimes feel that this power is hostile to myself. Anyhow, we have had many pleasant times together."

"And," replied Bellamy, "I hope we shall have many more. It has certainly been a tremendous privilege to have been permitted to enjoy so much of your company. As for that mysterious power you refer to, I am entirely unconscious of it, and as for hostility—well, I hope I've convinced you during the last month that I'm not exactly your enemy."

"You have, my dear fellow," replied Clinton. "You have been a charming and generous companion. All the same, there is an enigmatic side to you. What shall we do to-night?"

"Whatever you please," said Bellamy.

"I suggest we go round to my rooms," said Clinton, "bearing a bottle of whisky, and that I show you another little experiment. You are now sufficiently trained to make it a success."

"Just what I should have hoped for," replied Bellamy enthusiastically. "I will order the whisky now." He went out of the grill-room for a moment and had a few words with Mr. Solan over the telephone. And then he returned, paid the bill, and they drove off together.

Clinton's rooms were in a dingy street about a hundred yards from the British Museum. They were drab and melancholy, and contained nothing but the barest necessities and some books.

It was exactly eleven o'clock as Clinton took out his latchkey, and it was just exactly then that Mr. Solan unlocked the door of a curious little room leading off from his study.

Then he opened a bureau and took from it a large book bound in plain white vellum. He sat down at a table and began a bizarre procedure. He took from a folder at the end of the book a piece of what looked like crumpled tracing paper, and, every now and again consulting the quarto, drew certain symbols upon the paper, while repeating a series of short sentences in a strange tongue. The ink into which he dipped his pen for this exercise was a smoky sullen scarlet.

Presently the atmosphere of the room became intense, and charged with suspense and crisis. The symbols completed, Mr. Solan became rigid and taut, and his eyes were those of one passing into trance.

"First of all a drink, my dear Bellamy," said Clinton.

Bellamy pulled the cork and poured out two stiff pegs. Clinton drank his off. He gave the impression of being not quite at his ease.

"Some enemy of mine is working against me to-night," he said. "I feel an influence strongly. However, let us try the little experiment. Draw up your chair to the window, and do not look round till I speak."

Bellamy did as he was ordered, and peered at a dark façade across the street. Suddenly it was as if wall after wall rolled up before his eyes and passed into the sky, and he found himself gazing into a long faintly-lit room. As his eyes grew more used to the dimness he could pick out a number of recumbent figures, apparently resting on couches. And then from the middle of the room a flame seemed to leap and then another and another until there was a fiery circle playing round one of these figures, which slowly rose to its feet and turned and stared at Bellamy; and its haughty, evil face grew vast, till it was thrust, dazzling and fiery right into his own. He put up his hands to thrust back its scorching menace— and there was the wall of the house opposite, and Clinton was saying, "Well?"

"Your power terrifies me!" said Bellamy. "Who was that One I saw?"

"The one you saw was myself," said Clinton smiling, "during my third reincarnation, about 1750 B.C. I am the only man in the world who can perform that quite considerable feat. Give me another drink."

Bellamy got up (it was time!). Suddenly he felt invaded by a mighty reassurance. His ghostly terror left him. Something irresistible was sinking into his soul, and he knew that at the destined hour the promised succour had come to sustain him. He felt thrilled, resolute, exalted.

He had his back to Clinton as he filled the glasses, and with a lightning motion he dropped a pellet into Clinton's which fizzled like a tiny comet down through the bubbles and was gone.

"Here's to many more pleasant evenings," said Clinton. "You're a brave man, Bellamy," he exclaimed, putting the glass to his lips. "For what you have seen might well appall the devil!"

"I'm not afraid because I trust you," replied Bellamy.

"By Eblis, this is a strong one," said Clinton, peering into his glass.

"Same as usual," said Bellamy, laughing. "Tell me something. A man I knew who'd been many years in the East told me about some race out there who cut out paper patterns and paint them and send them to their enemies. Have you ever heard of anything of the sort?"

Clinton dropped his glass on the table sharply. He did not answer for a moment, but shifted uneasily in his chair.

"Who was this friend of yours?" he asked, in a voice already slightly thick.

"A chap called Bond," said Bellamy.

"Yes, I've heard of that charming practice. In fact, I can cut them myself."

"Really, how's it done? I should be fascinated to see it."

Clinton's eyes blinked and his head nodded.

"I'll show you one," he said, "but it's dangerous and you must be very careful. Go to the bottom drawer of that bureau and bring me the piece of straw paper you'll find there. And there are some scissors on the writing table and two crayons in the tray." Bellamy brought them to him.

"Now," said Clinton, "this thing, as I say, is dangerous. If I wasn't drunk I wouldn't do it. And why am I drunk?" He leaned back in his chair and put his hand over his eyes. And then he sat up and, taking the scissors, began running them with extreme dexterity round the paper. And then he made some marks with the coloured pencils.

The final result of these actions was not unfamiliar in appearance to Bellamy.

"There you are," said Clinton "That, my dear Bellamy, is potentially the most deadly little piece of paper in the world. Would you please take it to the fireplace and burn it to ashes?"

Bellamy burnt a piece of paper to ashes.

Clinton's head had dropped into his hands.

"Another drink?" asked Bellamy.

"My God, no," said Clinton, yawning and reeling in his chair. And then his head went down again. Bellamy went up to him and shook him. His right hand hovered a second over Clinton's coat pocket.

"Wake up," he said, "I want to know what would make that piece of paper actually deadly?"

Clinton looked up blearily at him and then rallied slightly.

"You'd like to know, wouldn't you?"

"Yes," said Bellamy. "Tell me."

"Just repeating six words," said Clinton, "but I shall not repeat them." Suddenly his eyes became intent and fixed on a corner of the room.

"What's that?" he asked sharply. "There! there! there! in the corner." Bellamy felt again the presence of a power. The air of the room seemed rent and sparking.

"That, Clinton," he said, "is the spirit of Philip Franton, whom you murdered." And then he sprang at Clinton, who was staggering from his chair. He seized him and pressed a little piece of paper fiercely to his forehead.

"Now, Clinton," he cried, "say those words!"

And then Clinton rose to his feet, and his face was working hideously. His eyes seemed bursting from his head, their pupils stretched and curved, foam streamed from his lips. He flung his hands above his head and cried in a voice of agony:

"He cometh and he passeth by!"

And then he crashed to the floor.

As Bellamy moved towards the door the lights went dim, in from the window poured a burning wind, and then from the wall in the corner a shadow began to grow. When he saw it, swift icy ripples poured through him. It grew and grew, and began to lean down towards the figure on the floor. As Bellamy took a last look back it was just touching it. He shuddered, opened the door, closed it quickly, and ran down the stairs and out into the night.

Professor Pownall's Oversight

A NOTE BY J. C. CARY, M.D.:
About sixteen years ago I received one morning by post a parcel, which, when I opened, I found to contain a letter and a packet. The latter was inscribed, "To be opened and published fifteen years from this date." The letter read as follows:

"Dear Sir,

"Forgive me for troubling you, but I have decided to entrust the enclosed narrative to your keeping. As I state, I wish it to be opened by you, and that you should arrange for it to be published. I enclose five ten-pound notes, which sum is to be used, partly to remunerate you, and partly to cover the cost of publication, if such expenditure should be found necessary. About the time you receive this, I shall disappear. The contents of the enclosed packet, though to some extent revealing the cause of my disappearance, give no index as to its method.—E.P."

The receipt of this eccentric document occasioned me considerable surprise. I attended Professor Pownall (I have altered all names, for obvious reasons) in my professional capacity four or five times for minor ailments. He struck me as a man of extreme intellectual brilliance, but his personality was repulsive to me. He had a virulent and brutal wit

83

which he made no scruple of exercising at my and everyone else's expense. He apparently possessed not one single friend in the world, and I can only conclude that I came nearer to fulfilling this role than anyone else.

I kept this packet by me for safe keeping for the fifteen years, and then I opened it, about a year ago. The contents ran as follows:

The date of my birth is of complete unimportance, for my life began when I first met Hubert Morisson at the age of twelve and a half at Flamborough College. It will end to-morrow at 6.45 p.m.

I doubt if ever in the history of the human intellect there has been so continuous, so close, so exhausting a rivalry as that between Morisson and myself. I will chronicle its bare outline. We joined the same form at Flamborough—two forms higher, I may say, than that in which even the most promising new boys are usually placed. We were promoted every term till we reached the Upper Sixth at the age of 16. Morisson was always top, I was always second, a few hundred marks behind him. We both got scholarships at Oxford, Morisson just beating me for Balliol. Before I left Flamborough, the Head Master sent for me and told me that he considered I had the best brain of any boy who had passed through his hands. I thought of asking him, if that were so, why I had been so consistently second to Morisson all through my school career; but even then I thought I knew the answer to that question.

He beat me, by a few marks, for all the great University prizes for which we entered. I remember one of the examiners, impressed by my papers, asking me to lunch with him. "Pownall," he said, "Morisson and you are the most brilliant undergraduates who have been at Oxford in my time. I am not quite sure why, but I am convinced of two things; firstly, that he will always finish above you, and secondly, that you have the better brain."

By the time we left Oxford, both with the highest degrees, I had had remorselessly impressed upon me the fact that my superiority of intelligence had been and always would be neutralised by some constituent in Morisson's mind which defied and dominated that superiority—save in one respect: we both took avidly to chess, and very soon there was no one in the University in our class, but I became, and remained, his master.

Chess has been the one great love of my life. Mankind I detest and despise. Far from growing wiser, men seem to me, decade by decade, to grow more inane as the means for revealing their ineptitude become more numerous, more varied and more complex. Women do not exist for me—they are merely variants from a bad model: but for chess, that superb, cold, infinitely satisfying anodyne to life, I feel the ardour of a lover, the humility of a disciple. Chess, that greatest of all games, greater than any game! It is, in my opinion, one of the few supreme products of the human intellect, if, as I often doubt, it is of human origin.

Morisson's success, I realise, was partly due to his social gifts; he possessed that shameless flair for making people do what he wanted, which is summed up in the word "charm," a gift from the gods, no doubt, but one of which I have never had the least wish to be the recipient.

Did I like Morisson? More to the point, perhaps, did I hate him? Neither, I believe. I simply grew profoundly and terribly used to him. His success fascinated me. I had sometimes short and violent paroxysms of jealousy, but these I fought, and on the whole conquered.

He became a Moral Philosophy Don at Oxford: I obtained a similar but inevitably inferior appointment in a Midland University. We used to meet during vacations and play chess at the City of London Club. We both improved rapidly, but still I kept ahead of him. After ten years of drudgery, I inherited a considerable sum, more than enough to satisfy all my wants. If one avoids all contact with women one can live marvellously cheaply: I am continuously astounded at men's inability to grasp this great and simple truth.

I have had few moments of elation in my life, but when I got into the train for London on leaving that cesspool in Warwickshire, I had a fierce feeling of release. No more should I have to ram useless and rudimentary speculation into the heads of oafs, who hated me as much as I despised them.

Directly I arrived in London I experienced one of those irresistible impulses which I could never control, and I went down to Oxford. Morisson was married by then, so I refused to stay in his house, but I spent hours every day with him. The louts into whom he attempted to force elementary ethics seemed rather less dingy but even more mentally costive than my Midland half-wits, and, so far as that went, I envied him not at all. I had meant to stay one week; I was in Oxford for six, for I rapidly came to the conclusion that I ranked first and Morisson second among the chess players of Great Britain. I can say that because I have no vanity: vanity cannot breathe and live in rarified intellectual altitudes. In chess the master surveys his skill impersonally, he criticises it impartially. He is great; he knows it; he can prove it; that is all.

I persuaded Morisson to enter for the British Championship six months later, and I returned to my rooms in Bloomsbury to perfect my game. Day after day I spent in the most intensive study, and succeeded in curing my one weakness. I just mention this point briefly for the benefit of chess players. I had a certain lethargy when forced to analyse intricate end-game positions. This, as I say, I overcame. A few games at the City Club convinced me that I was, at last, worthy to be called Master. Except for these occasional visits I spent those six months entirely alone: it was the happiest period of my life. I had complete freedom from human contacts, excellent health and unlimited time to move thirty-two pieces of the finest ivory over a charming checkered board.

I took a house at Bournemouth for the fortnight of the Championship, and I asked Morisson to stay with me. I felt I had to have him near me. He arrived the night before play began. When he came into my study I had one of those agonising paroxysms of jealousy to which I have alluded. I conquered it, but the reaction, as ever, took the form of a loathsome feeling of inferiority, almost servility.

Morisson was six foot two in height; I am five foot one. He had, as I impartially recognise, a face of great dignity and beauty, a mind at once of the greatest profundity and the most exquisite flippancy. My face is a perfect index to my character; it is angular, sallow, and its expression is one of seething distaste. As I say, I know my mind to be the greater of the two, but I express myself with an inevitable and blasting brutality, which disgusts and repels all who sample it. Nevertheless, it is that brutality which attracted Morisson, at times it fascinated him. I believe he realised, as I do, how implacably our destinies were interwoven.

Arriving next morning at the hall in which the Championship was to be held, I learned two things which affected me profoundly. The first, that by the accident of the pairing I should not meet Morisson until the last round, secondly, that the winner of the Championship would be selected to play in the forthcoming Masters' Tournament at Budapesth.

I will pass quickly over the story of this Championship. It fully justified my conviction. When I sat down opposite Morisson in the last round we were precisely level, both of us having defeated all our opponents, though I had shown the greater mastery and certainty. I began this game with the greatest confidence. I outplayed him from the start, and by the fifteenth move I felt convinced I had a won game. I was just about to make my sixteenth move when Morisson looked across at me with that curious smile on his face, half superior, half admiring, which he had given me so often before, when after a terrific struggle he had proved his

superiority in every other test but chess. The smile that I
was to see again. At once I hesitated. I felt again that sense
of almost cringing subservience. No doubt I was tired, the
strain of that fortnight had told, but it was, as it always
had been, something deeper, something more virulent, than
anything fatigue could produce. My brain simply refused to
concentrate. The long and subtle combination which I had
analysed so certainly seemed suddenly full of flaws. My time
was passing dangerously quickly. I made one last effort to
force my brain to work, and then desperately moved a piece.
How clearly I remember the look of amazement on Morisson's face. For a moment he scented a trap, and then, seeing
none, for there was none, he moved and I was myself again. I
saw I must lose a piece and the game. After losing a Knight,
I fought with a concentrated brilliance I had never attained
before, with the result that I kept the game alive till the ad-
journment and indeed recovered some ground, but I knew
when I left the hall with Morisson that on the next morning
only a miracle could save me, and that once again, in the test
of all tests in which I longed to beat him, he would, as ever
at great crises, be revealed as my master. As I trotted back to
my house beside him the words "only a miracle" throbbed in
my brain insinuatingly. Was there no other possibility? Of
a sudden I came to the definite, unalterable decision that I
would kill Morisson that night, and my brain began, like the
perfectly trained machine it is, to plan the means by which
I could kill him certainly and safely. The speed of this decision may sound incredible, but here I must be allowed a
short digression. It has long been a theory of mine that there
are two distinct if remotely connected processes operating in
the human mind. I term these the "surface" and the "subsur-
face" processes. I am not entirely satisfied with these terms,
and I have thought of substituting for them the terms "conscious" and "subconscious." However, that is a somewhat aca-
demic distinction. I believe that my sub-surface mind had

considered this destruction of Morisson many times before, and that these paroxysms of jealousy, the outcome as they were of consistent and unjust frustration, were the minatory symptoms that the content of my sub-surface would one day become the impulse of my surface mind, forcing me to plan and execute the death of Morisson.

When we arrived at the house I went first to my bedroom to fetch a most potent, swift-working, and tasteless narcotic which a German doctor had once prescribed for me in Munich when I was suffering from insomnia. I then went to the dining-room, mixed two whiskies and soda, put a heavy dose of the drug into Morisson's tumbler, and went back to the study. I had hoped that he would drink it quickly: instead, he put it by his side and began a long monologue on luck. Possibly my fatal move had suggested it. He said that he had always regarded himself as an extremely lucky man, in his work, his friends, his wife. He supposed that his rigidly rational mind demanded for its relief some such inconsistency, some such sop. "About four months ago," he said, "I had an equally irrational experience, a sharp premonition of death, which lingered with me. I told my wife—you will never agree, Pownall, but there is something to be said for matrimony: if I were dying I should like Marie to be with me, gross sentimentality, of course—I told my wife, who is of a distinctly psychic, superstitious if you like, turn of mind, and she persuaded me to go to a clairvoyant of whom she had a high opinion. I went sceptically, partly to please her, partly for the amusement of sampling one of this tribe. She was a curious, dingy female, slightly disconcerting. She stared at me remotely and then remarked, 'It was always destined that he should do it.' I plied her with questions, but she would say nothing more. I think you will agree, Pownall, that this was a typically nebulous two-guineas' worth." And then he drained his glass.

Shortly afterwards he began to yawn repeatedly, and went to bed. He staggered slightly on entering his room. "Good-night, Pownall," he said, as he closed the door, "let's hope somehow or other we may both be at Budapesth."

Half an hour later I went into his room. He had just managed to undress before the drug had overwhelmed him. I shut the window, turned on the gas, and went out. I spent the next hour playing over that fatal game. I quickly discovered the right line I had missed, then with a wet towel over my face, I re-entered his room. He was dead. I turned off the gas, opened all the windows, waited till the gas had cleared, and then went to bed, to sleep as soundly as ever in my life, though I had a curiously vivid dream. I may say I dream but seldom, and I never before realised how sharp and convincing these silly images could be, for I saw Morisson running through the dark and deserted streets of Oxford till he reached his house, and then he hammered with his fists on the door, and as he did so he gave a great cry, "Marie! Marie!" and then he fell rolling down the steps, and I awoke. This dream recurred for some time after, and always left a somewhat unpleasant impression on my mind.

The events of the next day were not pleasant. They composed a testing ordeal which remains very vividly in my mind. I had to act, and act very carefully, to deceive my maid, who came screaming into my room in the morning, to fool the half-witted local constable, the self-important local doctor, and carry through the farce generally in a convincing mode. I successfully suggested that as Morisson had suffered from heart weakness for some years, his own Oxford doctor should be sent for. Of course I had to wire to his wife. She arrived in the afternoon—and altogether I did not spend an uneventful day. However, all went well. The verdict at the inquest was "natural causes," and a day or two afterwards I was notified that I was British Chess Champion and had been selected for Budapesth. I received some medal or other, which I threw into the sea.

Four months intervened before the tournament at Budapesth; I spent them entirely alone, perfecting my game. At the end of that period I can say with absolute certainty that I was the greatest player in the world; my swift unimpeded growth of power is, I believe, unprecedented in the history of chess. There was, I remember, during this time, a curious little incident. One evening after a long, profound analysis of a position, I felt stale and tired, and went out for a walk. When I got back I noticed a piece had been moved, and that the move constituted the one perfect answer to the combination I had been working out. I asked my landlady if anybody had been to my room: she said not, and I let the subject drop.

The Masters' Tournament at Budapesth was perhaps the greatest ever held. All the most famous players in the world were gathered there, yet I, a practically unknown person, faced the terrific task of engaging them, one by one, day after day, with supreme confidence. I felt they could have no surprises for me, but that I should have many for them. Were I writing for chess players only, I would explain technically the grounds for this confidence. As it is, I will merely state that I had worked out the most subtle and daring variants from existing practice. I was a century ahead of my time.

In my first round I was paired with the great Russian Master, Osvensky. When I met him he looked at me as if he wondered what I was doing there. He repeated my name as though it came as a complete surprise to him. I gave him a look which I have employed before when I have suspected insolence, and he altered his manner. We sat down. Having the white pieces, I employed that most subtle of all openings, the Queen's bishop's pawn gambit. He chose an orthodox defence, and for ten moves the game took a normal course. Then at my eleventh move I offered the sacrifice of a knight, the first of the tremendous surprises I sprang upon my opponents in this tournament. I can see him now, the quick searching glance he gave me, and his great and growing agitation. Every chess player reveals great strain by much the same symptoms, by nervous movements, hurried glances

at the clock, uneasy shufflings of the body, and so forth: my
opponent in this way completely betrayed his astonishment
and dismay. Time ran on, sweat burst out on his forehead.
Elated as I was, the spectacle became repulsive, so I looked
round the room. And then, as my eyes reached the door, they
met those of Morisson sauntering in. He gave me the slightest look of recognition, then strolled along to our table and
took his stand behind my opponent's chair. At first I had no
doubt that it was an hallucination due to the great strain to
which I had subjected myself during the preceding months:
I was therefore surprised when I noticed the Russian glance
uneasily behind him. Morisson put his hand over my opponent's shoulder, guided his hand to a piece, and placed it
down with that slight screwing movement so characteristic of
him. It was the one move which I had dreaded, though I had
felt it could never be discovered in play over the board, and
then Morisson gave me that curious searching smile to which
I have alluded. I braced myself, rallied all my will power, and
for the next four hours played what I believe to be the finest
game in the record of Masters' play. Osvensky's agitation was
terrible, he was white to the lips, on the point of collapse,
but the Thing at his back—but Morisson—guided his hand
move after move, hour after hour, to the one perfect square.
I resigned on move 64, and Osvensky immediately fainted.
Somewhat ironically he was awarded the first Brilliancy Prize
for the finest game played in the tournament. As soon as
it was over Morisson turned away, walked slowly down the
room and out of the door.

That night after dinner I went to my room and faced
the situation. I eventually persuaded myself, firstly, that
Morisson's appearance had certainly been an hallucination,
secondly, that my opponent's performance had been due to
telepathy. Most people, I suppose, would regard this as pure
superstition, but to me it seemed a tenable theory that my
mind, in its extreme concentration, had communicated its
content to the mind of Osvensky. I determined that for the

future I would break this contact, whenever possible, by getting up and walking around the room.

Consequently on the next day I faced my second opponent, Seitz, the champion of Germany, with comparative equanimity. This time I defended a Ruy Lopez with the black pieces. I made the second of my stupendous surprises on the seventh move, and once again had the satisfaction of seeing consternation and intense astonishment leap to the German's face. I got up and walked round the room watching the other games. After a time I looked round and saw the back of my opponent's head buried in his hands, which were passing feverishly through his hair, but I also saw Morisson come in and take his stand behind him.

I need not dwell on the next twelve days. It was always the same story. I lost every game, yet each time giving what I know to be absolute proof that I was the greatest player in the world. My opponents did not enjoy themselves. Their play was acclaimed as the perfection of perfection, but more than one told me that he had no recollection after the early stages of making a single move, and that he suffered from a sensation of great depression and malaise. I could see they regarded me with some awe and suspicion, and shunned my company. It was also remarkable that, though the room was crowded with spectators, they never lingered long at my table, but moved quickly and uneasily away.

When I got back to London I was in a state of extreme nervous exhaustion, but there was something I had to know for certain, so I went to the City Chess Club and started a game with a member. Morisson came in after a short time—so I excused myself and went home. I had learnt what I had sought to learn. I should never play chess again.

The idea of suicide then became urgent. This happened three months ago. I have spent that period partly in writing this narrative, chiefly in annotating my games at Budapesth. I found that every one of my opponents played an absolutely flawless game, that their combinations had been of a profundity and complexity unique in the history of chess. Their play had been literally superhuman. I found I had myself given the greatest human performance ever known. I think I can claim a certain reputation for will-power when I say the shortest game lasted fifty-four moves, even with Morisson there, and that I was only guilty of most minute errors due to the frightful and protracted strain. I leave these games to posterity, having no doubt of its verdict. To the last I had fought Morisson to a finish.

I feel no remorse. My destruction of Morisson was an act of common sense and justice. All his life he had had the rewards which were rightly mine; as he said at a somewhat ironical moment, he had always been a lucky man. If I had known him to be my intellectual superior I would have accepted him as such, and become reconciled, but to be the greater and always to be branded as the inferior eventually becomes intolerable, and justice demands retribution. Budapesth proved that I had made an "oversight," as we say in chess, but I could not have foreseen that, and, as it is, I shall leave behind me these games as a memorial of me. Had I not killed Morisson I should never have played them, for he inspired me while he overthrew me.

I have planned my disappearance with great care. I think I saw Morisson in my bedroom again last night, and, as I am terribly tired of him, it will be to-morrow. I have no wish to be ogled by asinine jurymen nor drooled over by fatuous coroners and parsons, so my body will never be found. I have just destroyed my chessmen and my board, for no one else shall ever touch them. Tears came into my eyes as I did so. I never remember this happening before. Morisson has just come in—

A FURTHER NOTE BY J. C. CARY, M.D.:
Here the narrative breaks off abruptly. While I felt a certain moral obligation to arrange for the publication, if possible, of this document, it all sounded excessively improbable. I am

no chess player myself, but I had had as a patient a famous Polish Master who became a good friend of mine before he returned to Warsaw. I decided to send him the narrative and the games so that he might give me his opinion of the first, and his criticism of the latter. About three months later I had my first letter from him, which ran as follows:

"My Friend,
"I have a curious tale to tell you. When I had read through that document which you sent me I made some enquiries. Let me tell you the result of them. Let me tell you no one of the name of your Professor ever competed in a British Chess Championship, there was no tournament held at Pesth that year which he states, and no one of that name has ever played in a tournament in that city. When I learnt these facts, my friend, I regarded your Professor as a practical joker or a lunatic, and was just about to send back to you all these papers, when, quite to satisfy my mind, I thought I would just discover what manner of chess player this joker or madman had been. I soberly declare to you that those few pages revealed to me, as a Chess Master, one of the few supreme triumphs of the human mind. It is incredible to me that such games were ever played over the board. You are no player, I know, and therefore, you must take my word for it that, if your Professor ever played them, he was one of the world's greatest geniuses, the Master of Masters, and that, if he lost them his opponents, perhaps I might say his Opponent, was not of this world. As he says, he lost every game, but his struggles against this Thing were superb, incredible. I salute his shade. His notes upon these games say all that is to be said. They are supreme, they are final. It is a terrifying speculation, my friend, this drama, this murder, this agony, this suicide, did they ever happen? As one reads his pages and studies this quiet, this—how shall we say?—this so deadly tale, its truth seems to flash from it. Or is it some dream of genius? It terrifies me, as I say, this uncertainty,

for what other flaming and dreadful visions have come to
the minds of men and have been buried with them! I am,
as you know, besides a Chess Master, a mathematician and
philosopher; my mind lives an abstract life, and it is therefore a haunted mind, it is subject to possession, it is sometimes not master in its house. Enough of this, such thinking
leads too far, unless it leads back again quickly on its own
tracks, back to everyday things—I express myself not too
well, I know—otherwise, it leads to that dim borderland in
which the minds of men like myself had better never tres-
pass. We see the dim yet beckoning peaks of that far country,
far yet near—we had better turn back!

"I have studied these games, until I have absorbed their
mighty teaching. I feel a sense of supremacy, an insolence,
I feel as your Professor did, that I am the greatest player in
the world. I am due to play in the great Masters' Tournament
at Lodz. We shall see. I will write you again when it is over.

"Serge."

Three months later I received another letter from him.

"J. C. Cary, M.D.
"My Friend,
"I am writing under the impulse of a strong excitement, I
am unhappy, I am—but let me tell you. I went to Lodz with
a song in my brain, for I felt I should achieve the aim of my
life. I should be the Master of Masters. Why then am I in
this distress? I will tell you. I was matched in the first round
with the great Cuban, Primavera. I had the white pieces. I
opened as your Professor had opened in that phantom tourney. All went well. I played my tenth move. Primavera settled himself to analyse. I looked around the room. I saw, at
first with little interest, a stranger, tall, debonair, enter the
big swing door, and come towards my table. And then I remembered your Professor's tale, and I trembled. The stranger
came up behind my opponent's chair and gave me *just that*

look. A moment later Primavera made his move, and I put out my hand and offered that sacrifice, but, my friend, the hand that made that move *was not my own.* Trembling and infinitely distressed, I saw the stranger put his arm over Primavera's shoulder, take his hand, guide it to a piece, and thereby make that one complete answer to my move. I saw my opponent go white, turn and glance behind him, and then he said, 'I feel unwell. I resign.' 'Monsieur,' said I, 'I do not like this game either. Let us consider it a draw.' And as I put out my hand to shake his, it was my own hand again, and the stranger was not there.

"My friend, I rushed from the room back to my hotel, and I hurled those games of supreme genius into the fire. For a time the paper seemed as if it would not burn, and as if the lights went dim: two shadows that were watching from the wall near the door grew vast and filled the room. Then suddenly great flames shot up and roared the chimney high, they blazed it seemed for hours, then as suddenly died, and the fire, I saw, was out. And then I discovered that I had forgotten every move in every one of those games, the recollection of them had passed from me utterly. I felt a sense of infinite relief, I was free again. Pray God, I never play them in my dreams!

"Serge."

The Third Coach

The only objection I have to the Royal Porwick Golf Club is that the sixth green is only separated by a narrow lane from the Royal Porwick Lunatic Asylum—or rather from its exercise enclosure—the saddest playground I have ever seen. So-called mad people fill me with dread, and yet a certain shamefaced fascination. "There, but for the grace of God, goes Martin Trout"; though why that grace stopped short of these poor lost souls is a curious mystery understood only by reverend gentlemen.

So whenever I was approaching the sixth green—a hole I played by some muscular aberration consistently well—I felt a flickering unease, hoping to Heaven the inmates were locked in their cells; yet if they were out at their pathetic exercises I could not keep my eyes off them.

There was one considerable compensation, however, in this proximity, for it was through it that I made the acquaintance of Lanton, one of the Asylum doctors. I not only took a strong personal liking for him, but he interested me deeply. He is a distinguished alienist, and passionately absorbed in the study of insanity, and yet at the same time he detests his job.

Many a time he has had to cancel a round with me, and nearly always for the same reason, that he has been assaulted by a patient. "Didn't get the hyoscine hydro—bromide (or whatever it was) in quite quick enough," he will say, as he surveys me quizzingly yet wearily through a pair of rainbow eyes, "and the Asylum chairs are infernally hard. It took four of our strongest warders to keep him from creating a vacancy on the staff." As time went on the strain began to tell, and he has lost his resiliency, but he has always remained a charming, and I felt heroic, person. He has promised to chuck it if he gets a definite danger signal, for he has the wrong temperament to resist the withering experiences of his day's work much longer.

Those patients who are allowed out take their daily walk along a deserted bye-road which runs parallel to the third hole, and one day when I was playing with Lanton, that shuffling, damned parade was passing by just as I hit a quick, short hook into the hedge bordering the road. As I walked towards it my eye was caught by an individual walking alone and writing busily in a note-book. He was dressed in a round clerical hat, a "dog-collar," a clerical frock-coat, a pair of riding breeches, and brown boots. As I approached he looked up at me with an extremely penetrating, cunning, and yet preoccupied expression on his face—and then he went on with his writing.

When we had finished the round I described him to Lanton, and asked who he was.

"The Reverend Wellington Scot," he replied. "And a very curious case. If you would like to know more, come down to my study this evening. That's all about him now."

When I arrived at the Asylum, Lanton was just about to set out on his evening round.

He went to a drawer and got out a note-book.

"Read this while I'm away. I'll be back in about an hour. There are the drinks and Goldflakes."

When he had gone I picked up the note-book, and saw that it was filled with a very delicate script. I began to read.

I remember that the reason for my being in the Pantham district that day was that I was paying a visit to a widowed lady of means whom I wished to interest in a Benefit Scheme. (A Benefit Scheme is a scheme which benefits me.) I was "Mr. Robert Porter" on this occasion. Ten pounds richer than when I left it, I was approaching Pantham Station along a small road which topped the railway embankment. I noticed casually a train approaching—it was too early to be mine—when suddenly I saw sparks flashing up from it. It rocked violently, left the rails, and crashed into a bridge. I saw that the third coach was smashed to matchwood and bodies were hurled from it on to the side of the embankment. I started to run—not for assistance, as you might naturally but erroneously imagine, but to get the story through to the *Evening News*—which might well result in my returning £20 to the good.

Suddenly I stopped in my tracks, for I subconsciously realised there had been something very peculiar about that accident. What was it? And then I knew. *I had not heard a sound.* I ran back to the top of the embankment, and there was merely a placid row of metals shining in the sun.

Whereupon I sat down on the grass and thought things over. Like most superior men I am somewhat superstitious. I was, therefore, convinced that there was some reason why I, alone of all mankind, should have been vouchsafed this vision. The only supernatural personage for whom I have any respect is the Devil, for I believe he looks after his own, which is more than can be said for any of the more reputable deities. I regarded this singular apparition as a hint from him, and carefully recalled the hour of its occurrence in my note-book. I enquired casually at the station, and found there was no train passing Pantham at that time. The vision then probably referred to the future—to some new train not yet in Bradshaw. There were many conceivable ways by which I might benefit by a railway accident. The Editor of *Truth*, for example, might be in that third coach, or various other personages whose demise would not be regretted by me. Pursuing this train of thought I journeyed back to London.

Now I have described myself as a superior man. I had better explain that. A superior man is one who rises superior to his environment. All great moralists from Mr. Pecksniff to the Bishop of London would agree with me there.

Again, a superior man is one who, by grasping some simple principle concerning humanity and acting ingeniously upon that knowledge, makes a satisfactory livelihood. "Ninety five per cent. of human beings are mugs," for example, which is the one I have acted upon. The Bishop and Mr. Pecksniff might shake their heads over this, but I am convinced it is true.

My father followed a peculiar profession. He conveyed second-rate racehorses from one part of the globe to another. Sometimes he'd be conducting a brace of duds to Jamaica or over to Ireland or France. He received frequent bites and hacks from his charges, but he expected them and, I believe, was invariably kind to these glorified "screws." Consequently he was away a great deal, but, as this traffic was sporadic, had much spare time, most of which he spent in conveying pints of stout from a pot to his belly.

My mother was a good-tempered slut, and the only quarrels she ever had with the Pater concerned their respective shares of that filthy fluid. Apart from her good temper and her thirst, there is nothing to record concerning her.

My father, a squat, bow-legged little gnome, had that complete, unquestioning belief in the mingled credulity and rascality of his fellow-men which those who are connected professionally with the Sport of Kings invariably share. "Racing," he was wont to declare, "consists of mugs, bloody mugs, crooks, bloody crooks and 'orses."

"And which are you?" asked my mother.

"I ain't neither. I just helps the crooks to skin the mugs by movin' about the 'orses. I've seen too much of it. I've seen blokes who was pretty artful at the doings in the ornery way become just too bloody silly whenever they 'ear the bookie's chorus."

He was so convinced of the peculiar opportunities afforded to bookmakers for plumbing the depths of human simplicity that he suggested having me apprenticed to their profession, but my mother threw a pot at his head for suggesting it. "I didn't bear my boy to be a bookie," was her inflexible decision. All the same, these repeated references to mugs and crooks had the effect of convincing my childish mind that the world was entirely peopled by these two classes. As an example of the lasting effect of those lessons learnt in infancy, I remain of that opinion to this day.

Most of the money for my education went to quenching my parents' thirst, but I was taught to read and write, and acquired the rest myself. In my errand boy days the only literature I could afford was a newspaper, but this was sufficient to enable me to test the truth of my father's generalisation. For the most part it seemed to me triumphantly to support it.

Let me give a few examples. The head of the firm for which I worked was one of the greatest commercial figures in England, and the papers frequently contained articles from his (secretary's) pen dilating on the blessings of thrift, hard work and early marriage to "Miss Right"—yes, he actually used that expression. Yet everyone from the Managing Director to myself knew that he gambled wildly, ill-treated his wife, and kept a succession of decorative harpies labelled "dancing girls."

Then one of our assistants helped herself to the till and was given three months. She was anaemic, scrawny, middle-aged, yet the papers described her as a "pretty girl." I marked that down; obviously for some obscure reason the populace preferred their minor female criminals to be "pretty," and the papers fostered this harmless inanity. I found eventually that this rule applies to all women under fifty who earn mentions in the Press.

Again. We resided in a semi-slum near the Marylebone Road, and one of our neighbours brought to a close an argument with another of our neighbours with a chopper. The papers described this as a "West-End Chopper Attack," yet anything less "West-End," as I understood the expression, than Milk Row was hard to imagine. I marked that, too. Obviously the populace found something more stimulating in a West-End Chopper Attack than in a Chopper Attack in other areas. This extraordinary psychological mystery took me some time to solve, but I learnt to understand it perfectly. And so as I matured and read and read and read, I realised that there is an absolute and comprehensive difference between life as it appears in the Press and life as it really is. I shall not enlarge upon that, for anyone who compares what he reads in the papers about Sex, Religion, Sport, Business, the Theatre, the many-coloured globe of human activity, with what he experiences himself, knows this to be beyond dispute. When I had proved to my satisfaction that my father was right I thought very hard. Ninety-five per cent. of human beings must *like* to be mugs and mugged, I decided, must prefer soft tales to hard truths, they must find a solace and a stimulant in being incessantly bamboozled by the other five percent., newspaper proprietors, bookies, bishops, financiers and politicians. Certainly there must be a percentage of mugs amongst these professional men, but roughly they represent my father's "crooks," in other words, exploiters of the mass credulity of the ninety-five per cent. This is not a thesis on human behaviour, so suffice it to say that I eventually definitely decided the inhabitants of Great Britain were ninety-five per cent. mugs and five per cent. crooks, and I used to find great amusement and instruction in following the workings of this truth down the most obscure and unexpected bye-ways of our comic civilisation. I was then eighteen, a very junior clerk. Not to act upon a profound conviction is laziness and cowardice, so I had to make up my mind which I was to be, mug or crook, exploiter or exploited.

With the necessity for this decision harshly exercising my mind, I went to the White City one evening to observe the reactions of humanity to the spectacle of a succession of thin, rather graceful hounds in pursuit of a metal mechanism, which I discovered about as much resembled a hare as poor Miss Flint resembled a "pretty girl."

As a spectacle it had its points. That deep, dark pool circumscribed by a green and tan track, the focus for the eyes of ninety-five thousand half-wits and five thousand live-by-wits, the curious surging, harsh hum of the Worst Hundred Thousand, the sudden appearance in the distance of half-a-dozen tiny white two-legged figures with still tinier four-legged figures pacing beside them, wandering round the vast arena till they reached a sort of chicken house into which the two-legged hoisted the dangling four-legged, who, stirred by the sound of a bell and the sight of an individual ascending a peculiarly lousy tower, whimpered and grumbled and thrust eager paws through the bars. All this was admirably calculated to put the mugs into the right mood for the crooks' purposes. I wandered about amongst the excited, liquor-sprung horde, fighting their way to rows of leather-lunged sharps who, wedged like unsavoury sardines, bellowed out their inane jargon, and exchanged pieces of cardboard with their lamentable faces gummed upon them for the silver and paper of the Triumphs of Evolution—and I made up my mind.

Some exploiter, a politician as far as I remember, once, in a gust of vote-snatching sentimentality, declared he was on the side of the angels; he would have been hard put to find an ally at the White City, and he would certainly not have found one in me.

It would be humiliating and debasing to be a Private in the ranks of muggery, far better to be an Officer and a crook. Only so could I keep my self-respect. I consider that this was the decision of a philosopher and a superior man, and I have never changed my opinion.

How to begin? I carefully studied the pages of *Truth,* an organ I have always found most useful; it is an encyclopaedia of muggery. Its editor has kept on my track, but he is at a hopeless disadvantage, for there is a sucker born every minute and a reader of *Truth* perhaps once a day, odds too great even for a Labouchere. The present editor is a charming personality, and I have to thank his ably conducted periodical for many of my most remunerative conceptions, but I'd have liked him in that third coach all the same.

I decided to make a beginning with a Begging Letter. It hardly sounded like that, for it was manly, suggesting rows of medals, a patient little wife, and many hostages to fortune. It ended with a pathetic suggestion of suicide, and a defiant repudiation of the dole. I sent this to a carefully selected list, and netted £84 13*s.* 2*d.*, and then I knew that bounding sense of exhilaration which a man gains from finding that he is destined for success in his life's work.

Shortly after, I noticed one who was clearly a policeman in mufti hanging about, so I changed my address. A week later *Truth* had a paragraph about me, and was good enough to congratulate me on my epistolary skill, which, it suggested, would eventually bring me to a place where I should have few opportunities of exercising it.

My next conception concerned that shocking instance of human callousness, the Holiday Cat, or rather the cat that doesn't get a holiday, or a square saucer of milk, when its thoughtless owner is at Southend. In a carefully composed epistle I reminded a large number of maiden ladies of this sickening victimisation, and stated that I should devote any funds provided to the cause of feline felicity. I enclosed with it a portrait of a tortoiseshell animal in an advanced state of emaciation. £122 10*s.* 3¾*d.* (and another change of address).

This time *Truth* sat up and took notice. By a flash of genius it suggested that the honest victim of circumstances, "Wilfred Town," and the humane Cat Lover, "John Reddy," were one and the same person, and expressed the opinion that this combined individual was well worthy of mention in its Cautionary List.

From these crude beginnings I advanced to far greater subtlety and versatility, till I was making a steady £2,000 a year—sometimes more. But for one thing I could have retired long ago, and that is the scandalous and narrow-minded and anachronistic bar which prevents women from entering the Church of England Ministry. Clergymen are no good for charitable schemes, but they are invariably attracted by possibilities of getting a new suit of clothes by means of a little investment proposition. Maiden ladies, while they like a flutter at times, are splendidly charitable. The combination of these two—a maiden lady parson! Well, it's time our legislators were up and doing.

I was convicted once, but knowing more than a little law got off on appeal, and *Truth's* exuberation was short-lived. I have had seventy-four aliases and seventy-four changes of address.

Except in their charitable aspect, I had practically no dealings with women for many years, but then it occurred to me that the right type might be useful to me for business purposes. There are many little jobs for which a woman is better than a man—one of them is getting money out of men. I didn't mean to embark upon blackmail—it earns too long a sentence nowadays—and is extremely hazardous, but it is possible for women to get money from men without going to extreme lengths. I resolved to keep my eyes open. It was about this time that I had that curious experience at Pantham.

I was having tea at an A.B.C. shop one afternoon when the waitress banged down my cup and splashed some of its contents over my spats. I began to remonstrate angrily, and found myself looking into a pair of black indomitable eyes—battle, murder, and sudden-death eyes. So I laughed it off and began watching her as she went from table to table. She was tall and powerfully built, and her face I was convinced,

was that sort which compels men—for some queer reason which has always been a mystery to me—to behave in
fatuous, unexpected, and erratic ways. I could see by the
expression on it that she was furiously discontented and in
the mood to do something drastic and dangerous to improve
her lot—in the mood to exploit male mugs, I diagnosed.

I returned to this shop the next day and had a few words
with her. But those few words on my part were very carefully
chosen, and she agreed to dine with me that night. She was
in the mood I had guessed—prepared to slip a double dose
of strychnine into every cup of tea, coffee, or bovril in the
establishment. She passionately desired pretty clothes, ease,
and power. She expressed utter contempt for every member
of my sex. I believed her when she said she was a virgin.
Very gently and delicately I began to explain my means of
livelihood, and suggested she should come into partnership.
This delicacy I found was quite unnecessary, for she agreed
with enthusiasm, and like a true enthusiast expressed herself
ready to begin work at once.

We started to live together the next day—quite platon-
ically, I may say. I spent £200 on a trousseau for her and
carefully instructed her in the technique of her business. She
was a wonderfully apt pupil and "quick study."

Within a week she had a wealthy married member of the
Stock Exchange neatly on the hook. We had agreed that she
should retain 75% of any small sums and the value of any
presents she received, and when I say that my 25% represented £84 in five months, the generosity of this expert in
American Rails cannot be questioned. But then he began to
get a little frightened and rather bored, and he gave Charity
to understand that she was about to have a more amenable
successor. The critical moment! Now blackmail was barred, so
Charity merely rang him up at his home and his office about
ten times a day, and he found her waiting for him weeping
bitterly every time he entered and left the Exchange, much

to his chagrin and the amusement of the man at the door and his fellow-members. There is no law against ringing up business men at home or at the office, or exhibiting all the symptoms of a broken heart in Threadneedle Street, however much susceptible stockbrokers may regret the fact. Charity acted beautifully, and, I believe, aroused genuine sympathy in the breast of this speculator's solicitor as he handed her a cheque for £2,000, which she and I divided equally as per contract. And she was brilliantly still a virgin!

I grew to admire her greatly, and though we had no sexual relationship whatsoever, sometimes when I heard her turning over in bed, or saw her coming back naked from her bath I knew vague stirrings and excitement. But I repressed them vigorously and, indeed, they were never much more than the ripples on a pond as compared with the combers off the Horn of the average Mug.

Our combined income for the next three years averaged £5,000, not one penny of which went into the coffers of the Chancellor of the Exchequer. By now I was a badly wanted and notorious person, but I have a sixth sense for evading the constable, and I could see retirement and ease before me very soon, when the one thing I had considered inconceivable happened. Charity fell in love with a poor man in the middle stage of consumption, who most improvidently and prematurely caused her to be with child. After she had told me this she cut short my remonstrances and protests, by informing me she must have money to marry on, and that I must supply it to the tune of £2,000 a year for six years.

I replied I would make it £200 a year for three years, and not a penny more.

"In that case," she said, "I go round to the Editor of *Truth* to-morrow and tell him everything."

"And ruin yourself!" I replied. "What's come over you? Be sensible. Have the baby quietly, leave this young dying fool for ever, and concentrate on business. A child might be useful to us. I'll think that point over."

"I shouldn't waste your valuable time if I were you," she answered, "and don't be too sure I shall ruin myself. You're the big game they are after. If I give you away they won't bother about me, and I doubt if they could convict me, anyway. And I don't mind betting the papers will pay me anything I like to ask for my story after you've been jugged."

"Give me time to think," I said.

Was she bluffing? I didn't believe so. She was probably right. The police would merely use her as evidence against me, and she would be able to get thousands of pounds for her version of the last three years. Yet pay her £2,000 a year for six years! It would *just not* ruin me, and she knew it. The gross ingratitude!

I tried to get her to lower her terms, but she was adamant.

"I don't feel well, and am going down to Folkestone to-morrow for a week. I shall expect your answer directly I return," was her ultimatum.

I spent the most wretched night of my life. I saw all that I had planned for going by the board. Sooner or later I should be forced into extreme recklessness by this dreadful drain on my resources, and then, "Ten years' hard labour" at least. This little vixen I had reared! Making her teeth meet in the hand which had fed her, for the sake of some broken-lunged piece of worm-fodder. I'd like to have flung her into a cell full of drunken stokers! And then I dozed off, and woke in the most confident, buoyant mood. That is why I am superstitious, for I have had this experience several times—just when I have felt that I was trapped at last, I have had these sudden flashes of confidence and ease, and always something has happened to save me. It would come this time! I went to see Charity off, pretending to be in despair, and imploring her to make some concession.

"Oh, shut up!" she said. "I'm not doing this for myself, I'm doing it for Jim. He's sweet and he's straight and I love him. Words you don't know the meaning of, you mixture of dirty crook and frozen fish, so you can work for him or go to clink and work for His Majesty, and you've got a week to choose."

She had just got into a coach about half-way up the train, and I was about to leave when my eye was caught by an individual in clerical attire who was sauntering down the platform and glancing sharply at the people upon it. As he drew near he seemed vaguely familiar to me. Suddenly he saw me, and gave me a quick, meaning look. He passed close to me, and as he went past he said slowly and distinctly, "There's more room in the third coach."

The third coach! The third coach! And in a flash I saw a third coach turn to matchwood.

"There's more room in front, Charity," I said. "Come along!" The compartment was packed, and she came readily. Just as we reached the third coach the whistle went, and I bundled her into a compartment already filled to the brim. She gave me a venomous glance as the train pulled out.

And then I looked round for that slightly familiar individual. He was far down the platform by now, but he turned round, saw me, waved his hand, and disappeared. As the train was passing out I happened to catch my reflection in a window glass, and then I knew why he had seemed familiar, for his face was mine!

I left the station and took a taxi to Pantham Station. During the hour's run I was in a state of high excitement.

About a mile from the station we were stopped by a policeman. "You can't go down this road," he said, "there's been a smash on the line."

"What train?" I asked anxiously.

"The down Folkestone express."

"My God!" I cried. "I had a friend in it!"

"Well," he said, "they've got the killed and injured on the side of the embankment, you'd better go down there; anyway, they want help."

It wasn't a pleasant sight. I identified Charity by the remnant of her watch-garter which was still hanging to what had been her leg. Then, saying nothing to anyone, I went away. Otherwise she was never identified.

And then, for some reason or other, I became a clergyman. I don't really know why. In fact I think I've become that individual who told me about that third coach.

Here the delicate little script came to an end, and a moment later Lanton came back.

"Finished?" he asked. "Well, what do you think of it?"

"A very rascally and curious tale," I replied.

"But the most curious part of it is," said Lanton, "that there's not a word of truth in it."

"What!"

"The Reverend Wellington Scot was a mild, timid, East End curate. Going down for a holiday to Folkestone he was in the Pantham disaster, and hurled from the third coach on to his head. He was unconscious for ten days, and when he came to he had to come here. He spends every moment writing that story in notebooks. He completes it twice a week. We read it carefully to see if his narrative ever changes, but it is always almost word for word the same. He is very docile and easy to manage so long as he is allowed to write. For an experiment we took his writing materials away, whereupon he delivered himself of the most appalling filth and blasphemy I have ever heard. He never speaks unless he is spoken to. When he first came in his face was round, chubby, and ingenuous in expression; it has slowly lengthened, hardened, and its expression has become cunning, watchful and malevolent. That is the story of the Reverend Wellington Scot."

"And the explanation?" I asked.

Lanton shrugged his shoulders.

"How can there be one? I have known somewhat similar cases, though never so perfect, where some injury to the head has changed the disposition and to some extent the memory, but, as I say, never to this extent. As a matter of fact one can find traces of the curate in that narrative. A quotation from Shelley, a familiarity with strange types, a distaste for sex and so on, and, of course, the closing sentences; otherwise he is, as he appears in his story, the precise opposite of what he actually was. Perhaps you may have missed almost the most remarkable thing. His description of the accident, as seen in his vision, is precisely identical with that of the two eyewitnesses of it, yet, of course, he never could have seen it, and he hasn't read a word since he recovered consciousness. I said just now there wasn't a word of truth in that narrative, but that in a sense is presumptuous and unscientific. The fashionable theory to-day is that we each one of us create our own particular god and our own particular universe—it is subjectivity's innings. We certainly create our own truths. Fortunately in the case of most of us our truth roughly corresponds with the truth of others. The Reverend Wellington Scot's violently diverges, so we have to lock him up. He has been here a year, and I found he went to a Greyhound Racing Meeting at the White City the night before the accident. Would you like to see him again?"

"Yes and no. On the whole, yes."

Lanton took me along a corridor and unlocked a door. The Reverend Wellington Scot was seated at a table, his face partly shaded by a reading lamp. He was writing busily, but looked up after a moment and shot that penetrating glance at me.

"I hope you have everything you want, Mr. Scot," said Lanton.

"Yes, thank you, sir," he replied, in the mild, slightly clipped, slightly sing-song voice of a stage-curate, "but I have one little question to ask of you, should the words watch-garter be hyphenated, in your opinion, or not?"

"Hyphenated, I think," replied Lanton.

"I am much obliged to you, and glad to find that we are in agreement. I suppose, sir, I shall be here for some little time yet?"

"Oh yes, just for a little while longer," said Lanton. "Good-night."

"Good-night, sir," he replied, his pencil already busy again.

"Poor devil," I said, as we walked back to Lanton's study. "Is he happy?"

"Perfectly," replied Lanton. "There ought to be a deep truth hidden somewhere in that fact; and now for a drink."

The Red Lodge

I am writing this from an imperative sense of duty, for I consider the Red Lodge is a foul death-trap and utterly unfit to be a human habitation—it has its own proper denizens—and because I know its owner to be an unspeakable blackguard to allow it so to be used for his financial advantage. He knows the perils of the place perfectly well; I wrote him of our experiences, and he didn't even acknowledge the letter, and two days ago I saw the ghastly pest-house advertised in *Country Life*. So anyone who rents the Red Lodge in future will receive a copy of this document as well as some uncomfortable words from Sir William, and that scoundrel Wilkes can take what action he pleases.

I certainly didn't carry any prejudice against the place down to it with me: I had been too busy to look over it myself, but my wife reported extremely favourably—I take her word for most things—and I could tell by the photographs that it was a magnificent specimen of the medium-sized Queen Anne house, just the ideal thing for me. Mary said the garden was perfect, and there was the river for Tim at the bottom of it. I had been longing for a holiday, and was in the highest spirits as I travelled down. I have not been in the highest spirits since.

My first vague, faint uncertainty came to me so soon as I had crossed the threshold. I am a painter by profession, and therefore sharply responsive to colour tone. Well, it was a

brilliantly fine day, the hall of the Red Lodge was fully lighted, yet it seemed a shade off the key, as it were, as though I
were regarding it through a pair of slightly darkened glasses.
Only a painter would have noticed it, I fancy.

When Mary came out to greet me, she was not looking
as well as I had hoped, or as well as a week in the country
should have made her look.

"Everything all right?" I asked.

"Oh, yes," she replied, but I thought she found it difficult to say so, and then my eve detected a curious little
spot of green on the maroon rug in front of the fire-place. I
picked it up—it seemed like a patch of river slime.

"I suppose Tim brings those in," said Mary. "I've found
several; of course, he promises he doesn't." And then for a
moment we were silent, and a very unusual sense of con-
straint seemed to set a barrier between us. I went out into
the garden to smoke a cigarette before lunch, and sat myself
down under a very fine mulberry tree.

I wondered if, after all, I had been wise to have left it all
to Mary. There was nothing wrong with the house, of course,
but I am a bit psychic, and I always know the mood or character of a house. One welcomes you with the tail-writhing
enthusiasm of a really nice dog, makes you at home, and at
your ease at once. Others are sullen, watchful, hostile, with
things to hide. They make you feel that you have obtru-
ded yourself into some curious affairs which are none of
your business. I had never encountered so hostile, aloof, and
secretive a living place as the Red Lodge seemed when I first
entered it. Well, it couldn't be helped, though it was dis-
appointing; and there was Tim coming back from his walk,
and the luncheon gong. My son seemed a little subdued and
thoughtful, though he looked pretty well, and soon we were
all chattering away with those quick changes of key which
occur when the respective ages of the conversationalists are
40, 33 and 6½, and after half a bottle of Meursault and a
glass of port I began to think I had been a morbid ass. I was

still so thinking when I began my holiday in the best possible way by going to sleep in an exquisitely comfortable chair under the mulberry tree. But I have slept better. I dozed off, but I had a silly impression of being watched, so that I kept waking up in case there might be someone with his eye on me. I was lying back, and could just see a window on the second floor framed by a gap in the leaves, and on one occasion, when I woke rather sharply from one of these dozes, I thought I saw for a moment a face peering down at me, and this face seemed curiously flattened against the pane—just a "carry over" from a dream, I concluded. However, I didn't feel like sleeping any more, and began to explore the garden. It was completely walled in, I found, except at the far end, where there was a door leading through to a path which, running parallel to the right-hand wall, led to the river a few yards away. I noticed on this door several of those patches of green slime for which Tim was supposedly responsible. It was a dark little corner cut off from the rest of the garden by two rowan trees, a cool, silent little place I thought it. And then it was time for Tim's cricket lesson, which was interrupted by the arrival of some infernal callers. But they were pleasant people, as a matter of fact, the Local Knuts, I gathered, who owned the Manor House; Sir William Prowse and his lady and his daughter. I went for a walk with him after tea.

"Who had this house before us?" I asked.

"People called Hawker," he replied. "That was two years ago."

"I wonder the owner doesn't live in it," I said. "It isn't an expensive place to keep up."

Sir William paused as if considering his reply.

"I think he dislikes being so near the river. I'm not sorry, for I detest the fellow. By the way, how long have you taken it for?"

"Three months," I replied, "till the end of October."

"Well, if I can do anything for you I shall be delighted. If you are in any trouble, come straight to me." He slightly emphasised the last sentence.

I rather wondered what sort of trouble Sir William envisaged for me. Probably he shared the general opinion that artists were quite mad at times, and that when I had one of my lapses I should destroy the peace in some manner. However, I was duly grateful.

I was sorry to find Tim didn't seem to like the river; he appeared nervous of it, and I determined to help him to overcome this, for the fewer terrors one carries through life with one the better, and they can often be laid by delicate treatment in childhood. Curiously enough the year before at Frinton he seemed to have no fear of the sea.

The rest of the day passed uneventfully—at least I think I can say so. After dinner I strolled down to the end of the garden, meaning to go through the door and have a look at the river. Just as I got my hand on the latch there came a very sharp, furtive whistle. I turned round quickly, but seeing no one, concluded it had come from someone in the lane outside. However, I didn't investigate further, but went back to the house.

I woke up the next morning feeling a shade depressed. My dressing-room smelled stale and bitter, and I flung its windows open. As I did so I felt my right foot slip on something. It was one of those small, slimy, green patches. Now Tim would never come into my dressing-room. An annoying little puzzle. How on earth had that patch—? Which question kept forcing its way into my mind as I dressed. How could a patch of green slime . . .? How could a patch of green slime . . .? Dropped from something? From what? I am very fond of my wife—she slaved for me when I was poor, and always has kept me happy, comfortable and faithful, and she gave me my small son Timothy. I must stand between her and patches of green slime! What in hell's name was I talking about? And it was a flamingly fine day. Yet all during breakfast my mind was trying to find some sufficient reason for these funny little patches of green slime, and not finding it.

After breakfast I told Tim I would take him out in a boat on the river.

"Must I, Daddy?" he asked, looking anxiously at me.

"No, of course not," I replied, a trifle irritably, "but I believe you'll enjoy it."

"Should I be a funk if I didn't come?"

"No, Tim, but I think you should try it once, anyway."

"All right," he said.

He's a plucky little chap, and did his very best to pretend to be enjoying himself, but I saw it was a failure from the start.

Perplexed and upset, I asked his nurse if she knew of any reason for this sudden fear of water.

"No, sir," she said. "The first day he ran down to the river just as he used to run down to the sea, but all of a sudden he started crying and ran back to the house. It seemed to me he'd seen something in the water which frightened him."

We spent the afternoon motoring round the neighbourhood, and already I found a faint distaste at the idea of returning to the house, and again I had the impression that we were intruding, and that something had been going on during our absence which our return had interrupted.

Mary, pleading a headache, went to bed soon after dinner, and I went to the study to read.

Directly I had shut the door I had again that very unpleasant sensation of being watched. It made the reading of Sidgwick's *The Use of Words in Reasoning*—an old favourite of mine, which requires concentration—a difficult business. Time after time I found myself peeping into dark corners and shifting my position. And there were little sharp sounds; just the oak-panelling cracking, I supposed. After a time I became more absorbed in the book, and less fidgety, and then I heard a very soft cough just behind me. I felt little icy rays pour down and through me, but I would *not* look round, and I *would* go on reading. I had just reached the following passage: "However many things may be said about Socrates, or about any fact observed, there remains still more that might be said if the need arose; the need is the determining factor. Hence the distinction between complete and incomplete description, though perfectly sharp and clear in the abstract, can only have a meaning—can only be applied to actual cases—if it be taken as equivalent to *sufficient* description, the sufficiency being relative to some purpose. Evidently the description of Socrates as a man, scanty though it is, may be fully sufficient for the purpose of the modest enquiry whether he is *mortal* or not"—when my eye was caught by a green patch which suddenly appeared on the floor beside me, and then another and another, following a straight line towards the door. I picked up the nearest one, and it was a bit of soaking slime. I called on all my willpower, for I feared something worse to come, and it should *not* materialise—and then no more patches appeared. I got up and walked deliberately, slowly, to the door, turned on the light in the middle of the room, and then came back and turned out the reading lamp and went to my dressing room. I sat down and thought things over. There was something very wrong with this house. I had passed the stage of pretending otherwise, and my inclination was to take my family away from it the next day. But that meant sacrificing £168, and we had nowhere else to go. It was conceivable that these phenomena were perceptible only to me, being half a Highlander. I might be able to stick it out if I were careful and kept my tail up, for apparitions of this sort are partially subjective—one brings something of oneself to their materialisation. That is a hard saying, but I believe it to be true. If Mary and Tim and the servants were immune it was up to me to face and fight this nastiness. As I undressed, I came to the decision that I would decide nothing then and there, and that I would see what happened. I made this decision against my better judgment, I think.

In bed I tried to thrust all this away from me by a conscious effort to "change the subject," as it were. The easiest subject for me to switch over to is the myriad-sided, useless, consistently abused business of creating things, stories out of pens and ink and paper, representations of things and moods out of paint, brushes and canvas, and our own miseries, perhaps, out of wine, women and song. With a considerable effort, therefore, and with the edges of my brain anxious to be busy with bits of green slime, I recalled an article I had read that day on a glorious word "Jugendbewegung," the "Youth Movement," that pregnant or merely wind-swollen Teutonism! How ponderously it attempted to canonise with its polysyllabic sonority that inverted Boy-Scoutishness of the said youths and maidens. "One bad, mad deed—sonnet—scribble of some kind—lousy daub—a day." Bunk without spunk, sauce without force, Futurism without a past, merely a *Transition* from one yelping pose to another. And then I suddenly found myself at the end of the garden, attempting desperately to hide myself behind a rowan tree, while my eyes were held relentlessly to face the door. And then it began slowly to open, and something which was horridly unlike anything I had seen before began passing through it, and *I* knew It knew I was there, and then my head seemed burst and flamed asunder, splintered and destroyed, and I awoke trembling to feel that something in the darkness was poised an inch or two above me, and then drip, drip, drip, something began falling on my face. Mary was in the bed next to mine, and I *would not* scream, but flung the clothes over my head, my eyes streaming with the tears of terror. And so I remained cowering till I heard the clock strike five, and dawn, the ally I longed for, came, and the birds began to sing, and then I slept.

I awoke a wreck, and after breakfast, feeling the need to be alone, I pretended I wanted to sketch, and went out into the garden. Suddenly I recalled Sir William's remark

about coming to see him if there was any trouble. Not much
difficulty in guessing what he had meant. I'd go and see
him about it at once. I wished I knew whether Mary was
troubled too. I hesitated to ask her, for, if she were not, she
was certain to become suspicious and uneasy if I questioned
her. And then I discovered that, while my brain had been
busy with its thoughts my hand had also not been idle, but
had been occupied in drawing a very singular design on the
sketching block. I watched it as it went automatically on.
Was it a design or a figure of some sort? When had I seen
something like it before? My God, in my dream last night! I
tore it to pieces, and got up in agitation and made my way
to the Manor House along a path through tall, bowing, stip-
pled grasses hissing lightly in the breeze. My inclination was
to run to the station and take the next train to anywhere;
pure undiluted panic—an insufficiently analysed word—that
which causes men to trample on women and children when
Death is making his choice. Of course, I had Mary and Tim
and the servants to keep me from it, but supposing they had
no claim on me, should I desert them? No, I should not.
Why? Such things aren't done by respectable inhabitants of
Great Britain—a people despised and respected by all other
tribes. Despised as Philistines, but it took the jaw-bone of an
ass to subdue that hardy race! Respected for what? Birken-
head stuff. No, not the noble Lord, for there were no glit-
tering prizes for those who went down to the bottom of the
sea in ships. My mind deliberately restricting itself to such
highly debatable jingoism, I reached the Manor House, to
be told that Sir William was up in London for the day, but
would return that evening. Would he ring me up on his return? "Yes, sir." And then, with lagging steps, back to the
Red Lodge.

I took Mary for a drive in the car after lunch. Anything
to get out of the beastly place. Tim didn't come, as he preferred to play in the garden. In the light of what happened I

suppose I shall be criticised for leaving him alone with a nurse, but at that time I held the theory that these appearances were in no way malignant, and that it was more than possible that even if Tim did see anything he wouldn't be frightened, not realising it was out of the ordinary in any way. After all, nothing that I had seen or heard, at any rate during the daytime, would strike him as unusual.

Mary was very silent, and I was beginning to feel sure, from a certain depression and oppression in her manner and appearance, that my trouble was hers. It was on the tip of my tongue to say something, but I resolved to wait until I had heard what Sir William had to say. It was a dark, sombre, and brooding afternoon, and my spirits fell as we turned for home. What a home!

We got back at six, and I had just stopped the engine and helped Mary out when I heard a scream from the garden. I rushed round, to see Tim, his hands to his eyes, staggering across the lawn, the nurse running behind him. And then he screamed again and fell. I carried him into the house and laid him down on a sofa in the drawing-room, and Mary went to him. I took the nurse by the arm and out of the room; she was panting and crying down a face of chalk.

"What happened? What happened?" I asked.

"I don't know what it was, sir, but we had been walking in the lane, and had left the door open. Master Tim was a bit ahead of me, and went through the door first, and then he screamed like that."

"Did you see anything that could have frightened him?"

"No, sir, nothing."

I went back to them. It was no good questioning Tim, and there was nothing coherent to be learnt from his hysterical sobbing. He grew calmer presently, and was taken up to bed. Suddenly he turned to Mary, and looked at her with eyes of terror.

"The green monkey won't get me, will it, Mummy?"

"No, no, it's all right now," said Mary, and soon after he went to sleep, and then she and I went down to the drawing-room. She was on the border of hysteria herself.

"Oh, Tom, what is the matter with this awful house? I'm *terrified*. Ever since I've been here I've been terrified. Do you see things?"

"Yes," I replied.

"Oh, I wish I'd known. I didn't want to worry you if you hadn't. Let me tell you what it's been like. On the day we arrived I saw a man pass ahead of me into my bedroom. Of course, I only *thought* I had. And then I've heard beastly whisperings, and every time I pass that turn in the corridor I *know* there's someone just round the corner. And then the day before you arrived I woke suddenly, and something seemed to force me to go to the window, and I crawled there on hands and knees and peeped through the blind. It was just light enough to see. And suddenly I saw someone running down the lawn, his or her hands outstretched, and there was something ghastly just beside him, and they disappeared behind the trees at the end. I'm terrified every minute."

"What about the servants?"

"Nurse hasn't seen anything, but the others have, I'm certain. And then there are those slimy patches, I think they're the vilest of all. I don't think Tim has been troubled till now, but I'm sure he's been puzzled and uncertain several times."

"Well," I said, "it's pretty obvious we must clear out. I'm seeing Sir William about it to-morrow, I hope, and I'm certain enough of what he'll advise. Meanwhile we must think over where to go. It is a nasty jar, though; I don't mean merely the money, though that's bad enough, but the fuss— just when I hoped we were going to be so happy and settled. However, it's got to be done. We should be mad after a week of this filth-drenched hole."

Just then the telephone bell rang. It was a message to say Sir William would be pleased to see me at half past ten to-morrow.

With the dusk came that sense of being watched, waited for, followed about, plotted against, an atmosphere of quiet, hunting malignancy. A thick mist came up from the river, and as I was changing for dinner I noticed the lights from the windows seemed to project a series of swiftly changing pictures on its grey, crawling screen. The one opposite my window, for example, was unpleasantly suggestive of three figures staring in and seeming to grow nearer and larger. The effect must have been slightly hypnotic, for suddenly I started back, for it was as if they were about to close on me. I pulled down the blind and hurried downstairs. During dinner we decided that unless Sir William had something very reassuring to say we would go back to London two days later and stay at a hotel till we could find somewhere to spend the next six weeks. Just before going to bed we went up to the night nursery to see if Tim was all right. This room was at the top of a short flight of stairs. As these stairs were covered with green slime, and there was a pool of the muck just outside the door, we took him down to sleep with us.

The Permanent Occupants of the Red Lodge waited till the light was out, but then I felt them come thronging, slipping in one by one, their weapon fear. It seemed to me they were massed for the attack. A yard away my wife was lying with my son in her arms, so I must fight. I lay back, gripped the sides of the bed and strove with all my might to hold my assailants back. As the hours went by I felt myself beginning to get the upper hand, and a sense of exaltation came to me. But an hour before dawn they made their greatest effort. I knew that they were willing me to creep on my hands and knees to the window and peep through the blind, and that if I did so we were doomed. As I set my teeth and tightened my grip till I felt racked with agony, the sweat poured from me. I felt them come crowding round the bed and thrusting their faces into mine, and a voice in my head kept saying insistently, "You must crawl to the window and look through the blind." In my mind's eye I could see myself crawling stealthily across the floor and pulling the blind aside, but who would be staring back at me? Just when I felt my resistance breaking I heard a sweet, sleepy twitter from a tree outside, and saw the blind touched by a faint suggestion of light, and at once those with whom I had been struggling left me and went their way, and, utterly exhausted, I slept.

In the morning I found, somewhat ironically, that Mary had slept better than on any night since she came down.

Half past ten found me entering the Manor House, a delightful nondescript old place, which started wagging its tail as soon as I entered it. Sir William was awaiting me in the library. "I expected this would happen," he said gravely, "and now tell me."

I gave him a short outline of our experiences.

"Yes," he said, "it's always much the same story. Every time that horrible place has been let I have felt a sense of personal responsibility, and yet I cannot give a proper warning, for the letting of haunted houses is not yet a criminal offence—though it ought to be—and I couldn't afford a libel action, and, as a matter of fact, one old couple had the house for fifteen years and were perfectly delighted with it, being troubled in no way. But now let me tell you what I know of the Red Lodge. I have studied it for forty years, and I regard it as my personal enemy.

"The local tradition is that the second owner, early in the eighteenth century, wished to get rid of his wife, and bribed his servants to frighten her to death—just the sort of ancestor I can imagine that blackguard Wilkes being descended from.

"What devilries they perpetrated I don't know, but she is supposed to have rushed from the house just before dawn one day and drowned herself. Whereupon her husband installed a small harem in the house; but it was a failure, for each of these charmers one by one rushed down to the river just before dawn, and finally the husband himself did the same. Of the period between then and forty years ago I have no record, but the local tradition has it that it was the scene of tragedy after tragedy, and then was shut up for a long time. When I first began to study it, it was occupied by two bachelor brothers. One shot himself in the room which I imagine you use as your bedroom, and the other drowned himself in the usual way. I may tell you that the worst room in the house, the one the unfortunate lady is supposed to have occupied, is locked up, you know, the one on the second floor. I imagine Wilkes mentioned it to you."

"Yes, he did," I replied. "Said he kept important papers there."

"Yes; well, he was forced in self-defence to do so ten years ago, and since then the death rate has been lower, but in those forty years twenty people have taken their lives in the house or in the river, and six children have been drowned accidentally. The last case was Lord Passover's butler in 1924. He was seen to run down to the river and leap in. He was pulled out, but had died of shock.

"The people who took the house two years ago left in a week, and threatened to bring an action against Wilkes, but they were warned they had no legal case. And I strongly advise you, more than that, *implore* you, to follow their example, though I can imagine the financial loss and great inconvenience, for that house is a death-trap."

"I will," I replied. "I forgot to mention one thing; when my little boy was so badly frightened he said something about 'a green monkey.'"

"He did!" said Sir William sharply. "Well then, it is absolutely imperative that you should leave at once. You remember I mentioned the death of certain children. Well, in each case they have been found drowned in the reeds just at the end of that lane, and the people about here have a firm belief that 'The Green Thing,' or 'The Green Death'—it is sometimes referred to as the first and sometimes as the other—is connected with danger to children."

"Have you ever seen anything yourself?" I asked.

"I go to the infernal place as little as possible," replied Sir William, "but when I called on your predecessors I most distinctly saw someone leave the drawing-room as we entered it, otherwise all I have noted is a certain dream which recurs with curious regularity. I find myself standing at the end of the lane and watching the river—always in a sort of brassy half-light. And presently something comes floating down the stream. I can see it jerking up and down, and I always feel passionately anxious to see what it may be. At first I think that it is a log, but when it gets exactly opposite me it changes its course and comes towards me, and then I see that it is a dead body, very decomposed. And when it reaches the bank it begins to climb up towards me, and then I am thankful to say I always awake. Sometimes I have thought that one day I shall not wake just then, and that on this occasion something will happen to me, but that is probably merely the silly fancy of an old gentleman who has concerned himself with these singular events rather more than is good for his nerves."

"That is obviously the explanation," I said, "and I am extremely grateful to you. We will leave tomorrow. But don't you think we should attempt to devise some means by which other people may be spared this sort of thing, and this brute Wilkes be prevented from letting the house again?"

"I certainly do so, and we will discuss it further on some other occasion. And now go and pack!"

A very great and charming gentleman, Sir William, I reflected, as I walked back to the Red Lodge.

Tim seemed to have recovered excellently well, but I thought it wise to keep him out of the house as much as possible, so while Mary and the maids packed after lunch I went with him for a walk through the fields. We took our time, and it was only when the sky grew black and there was a distant rumble of thunder and a menacing little breeze came from the west that we turned to come back. We had to hurry, and as we reached the meadow next to the house there came a ripping flash and the storm broke. We started to run for the door into the garden when I tripped over my bootlace, which had come undone, and fell. Tim ran on. I had just tied the lace and was on my feet again when I saw something slip through the door. It was green, thin, tall. It seemed to glance back at me, and what should have been its face was a patch of soused slime. At that moment Tim saw it, screamed, and ran for the river. The figure turned and followed him, and before I could reach him hovered over him. Tim screamed again and flung himself in. A moment later I passed through a green and stenching film and dived after him. I found him writhing in the reeds and brought him to the bank. I ran with him in my arms to the house, and I shall not forget Mary's face as she saw us from the bedroom window.

By nine o'clock we were all in a hotel in London, and the Red Lodge an evil, fading memory. I shut the front door when I had packed them all into the car. As I took hold of the knob I felt a quick and powerful pressure from the other side, and it shut with a crash. The Permanent Occupants of the Red Lodge were in sole possession once more

"And He Shall Sing . . ."

Mr. Cheltenham, a rather dusty and musty, yet amiable-looking person, a veteran of some sixty publishing seasons, was seated at his desk in his charming if a little rickety office in Willoughby Court, one placid September afternoon, reflecting drowsily on an aphorism which an American publisher friend had yapped at him during luncheon. "It's a sort of joke amongst authors in America to say, 'Now Barabbas was a publisher.'" "Well," thought Mr. Cheltenham, "if that were so, every scribe in the Province should have come to howl for his release. Three-quarters of all the books I have published would never have been born but for me. By my instinct and initiative they are conceived; I midwife them and wet-nurse them. I ensure that they are beautiful. In most cases only too soon I am compelled to recognise they are dead, and remainder their remains. And my remuneration for carrying out these versatile functions, genital, obstetric, and cenotaphic, is microscopic. And the lazy ingrates who pretend to their parentage compare such philanthropists to a brigand!" Indignation brushed the poppies from his eyes, and he went back to his proof-reading. A little later his telephone bell rang. "A gentleman to see you. Yes, sir, a Mr. Kato, sir, about a manuscript." "Oh, show him up," answered Mr. Cheltenham resignedly. A moment later the door opened and an exotic and singular personage entered. His tiny feet were embraced by patent leather boots and white spats. A pair of plus-four

knickerbockers peeped out through a loose dark garment like
a priest's robe. Above protruded a short, tubby body, above
that a sallow expressionless face with fluttering almond eyes.
His right hand was clutching a bowler hat, his left a package
of some kind. This apparition sat down on the chair pointed
out to him by Mr. Cheltenham, and remained silent. "Well,
Mr. Kato," said the publisher, "and what can I do for you?"
Mr. Kato thereupon raised his left hand and placed on the
table a beautifully bound manuscript on which were painted
in a panel some sentences Mr. Cheltenham supposed were
Japanese. "I have this book, which I wish to bring to notice
of poetic public persons," he said in a clipped, toneless voice.

Mr. Cheltenham picked up the manuscript. "I take it you
wish to have it published," he said. He saw it consisted of
a number of short poems. "The usual tripe," he thought to
himself, for he had met these Orientals before who spend
many ingenious days translating into deliberately naive English the lesser-known works of their compatriots and palm-
ing them off as their own.

"Well, Mr. Kato," said he, "it is easier to sell a boot-legger
a case of ginger-pop than for a publisher to support a wife
and family on the publication of verse. If poets are determined to inflict on a patient public the dreams they dream
and the visions they see, it is only fair that they should foot
the bill—that the piper should pay for the paper and the
printing and remunerate the publisher—in this case shall we
say myself—for the time and trouble he gives to the prepara-
tion of the book. Are you willing to contribute towards the
cost of production?"

"If it must be so," replied Mr. Kato. "It is the poetic fame
which I desire."

"Very well, then," said the publisher, "but first of all I
must satisfy myself that the work is worthy to bear my im-
print. My standard is high—if I find it reaches that standard
I will have an estimate prepared, and then put my proposals

before you. You shall have my decision within a week. Good afternoon."

Mr. Kato rose, shook hands, put on his bowler and walked towards the door. Now Mr. Cheltenham had been very uncharacteristically brusque and tart during this short interview, for he had not been quite at his ease. It was no doubt owing to his drowsiness, but it had seemed to him that Mr. Kato's outline had been curiously smudgy and wavering, and as he walked away he had the impression that the little Jap's shadow was walking out behind him, as if two little Orientals were passing across the room to the door. But the sun had long ceased to throw shadows into Willoughby Court. He took the MS. home with him that night, and after dinner began to look through it. It was entitled, *And He Shall Sing As Best He Can.* That pleased Mr. Cheltenham at once, for he recognised it as a quotation from *The Gates of Damascus,* that masterpiece of Flecker, a poem he considered of extreme delicacy, subtlety, and rhythmic and verbal beauty. That Mr. Kato should have chosen such a title gained the publisher's sympathy at once.

For the next hour he knew one of those rare moments in a publisher's life when he realises that something of genius has been placed in his care, and that for evermore it will be identified with his name. For the poems in that lovely MS. were perfection. By some miracle of good taste the delicate, urbane, autumnal imagery, in which the Oriental poet clothes his thought as he delicately shrugs his shoulders at life, had been transmitted into an English idiom at once the poets' own, and yet perfectly adapted to it. Its mastery and flawless precision sent tingles of pleasure through every nerve in Mr. Cheltenham's body. Golden visions surged through his brain; "good simile that about poetry and ginger-pop, but was it always true? Brooke, Housman, Masefield—no, there *had* been best sellers in rhyme and metre"; and through Mr. Cheltenham's head hummed the princely beat of printing machines, 2,000, 5,000, 30,000, 100,000! He re-read the first ten pieces and his mind was made up. He had a winner, a philistine-proof, reviewer-proof, bookseller-proof, inevitable certainty! There on his table was a masterpiece. He went glowing to bed. Perhaps on that account he slept fitfully. Four or five times it seemed to him that a tiny Mongolian face came and stared imploringly into his eyes, and grew and grew till crack! something snapped in his brain and he awoke. Though all Japs looked much alike to him, this officious visitor did not remind him of Mr. Kato.

The next morning he rushed down to his office and dictated the following comparatively ingenuous document:—

"Dear Sir,

"I have read your verses. They seem to me to be sufficiently competent and original to have a chance of success. So much so that I have decided to take a risk with them, and shall not ask you to bear the whole cost of production.

"I am prepared to suggest a joint venture with you. I propose that we share the costs, which will amount to £200 for 1,500 copies, and that we likewise divide between us any profits which may accrue. We will share advertising expenses, starting with an outlay of £50. If this scheme appeals to you I will have an agreement drawn up for you to sign. I shall be glad to hear from you.

"Faithfully yours,

"Charles Cheltenham."

For the rest of the day he worked steadily, though every now and again he picked up the poems to reassure himself that he had not been too generous, and each time his confidence increased. The next morning Mr. Kato rang up to say that he accepted the proposal, and would call on the publisher at five o'clock the next day.

Mr. Cheltenham spent the morning preparing a rather subtle agreement, and it was ready for Mr. Kato when he arrived at 5.15. The publisher had worked hard and was feeling quite drowsy when the little man entered the room, so much so that once again he experienced the silly illusion that Mr. Kato's shadow had come in with him.

"Well," he said, rousing himself, "I spent a delightful evening reading your poems, and I think them admirable, and I am looking forward to being your partner in their production and publication. I have the agreement here"—he glanced down at his desk—"which I shall ask you to—I must overcome this drowsiness," he thought to himself, for it had seemed to him that a shape like a small thin hand had fallen across the page, and he had started to brush it away when he had paused—"which I shall ask you to examine. But first I will read you the main clauses."

"Quite pleased," said Mr. Kato.

Mr. Cheltenham began to mumble rapidly through the first paragraph—"An agreement between Charles Cheltenham, hereinafter referred to as the Publisher, and F. Gonesara, hereinafter—Gonesara?" he repeated puzzled, and then looked up with a smile. "Why I should have made such a mistake with the name I cannot"—and then he paused, for Mr. Kato was not looking his best. His eyes were staring and his hands were working, and he was muttering to himself in a foreign tongue. "Please excuse," he murmured, "and read remainder of contractual document." Mr. Cheltenham did so perfunctorily and hurriedly, for he had the impression Mr. Kato was not listening, and was anxious to be gone. When he had finished the latter took it up and almost ran from the room. As he got up the publisher saw, or seemed to see, that shadow rise with him and dart away behind him.

The agreement came back the next day, laconically labelled "O.K. J. Kato."

Then did Mr. Cheltenham get exceedingly busy. He decided it should be a beautiful little book bound in batik, price 7*s*. 6*d*.

He had some of the poems typed out and sent to certain influential literary critics of his acquaintance for their opinion, and there were many other details to attend to. He had a highly-trained mind, and by that evening everything concerning the production of the book was settled.

He worked late, till long after his small staff had gone home.

Shortly before leaving he had occasion to go down to the ground floor for the estimate book which his manager guarded. On returning to his room it seemed to him that a small figure was leaning over his desk, but a second later it was gone.

Hallucinations had not been included in the content of Mr. Cheltenham's experience up till then, and he walked home to his flat in Westminster in rather a thoughtful mood. "Possibly," he said to himself, "I have been overworking."

Several days passed in an eminently satisfactory manner. Mr. Kato signed his agreement without demur. The influential literary critics were one and all most enthusiastic, and eager to know all there was to be known about the author. That suggested a problem to Mr. Cheltenham. Should he treat Mr. Kato as a mysterious and enigmatic figure, and rouse interest in him in that way, or should he do the usual thing and supply full details.

He decided first of all to see what facts concerning his career Mr. Kato could supply. He wrote him the usual letter strongly urging him to overcome that loathing for publicity which he probably cherished.

He received a reply by return of post:

"Dear Charles Cheltenham,
"Please excuse. I am, as you would say, middle classes Jap Gentleman, formally in Rice Affair. Therefore complete void of interesting publicity dope.
"J. Kato."

There were some Japanese characters under the signature. When he had read this missive and decided to treat Mr. Kato as a mystery, Mr. Cheltenham ruminated, and not for the first time, on the incredible workings of the creative imagination. How was it possible for a person who could write "Please excuse"—"Formally in Rice Affair"—to be the author of the many masterpieces in *And he shall sing as best he can?* He gave it up.

He wondered what might be the meaning of the delightfully decorative postscript.

When he went to lunch at his Club, he took the letter with him—Sanders of the Far Eastern section of the British Museum was usually to be found there. He was in on this occasion and talking very loudly, wittily, and provocatively in the smoking-room.

He glanced casually at the letter which the publisher held out to him. Then it seemed to hold his attention. "A morbid prophet, your friend," he said, "but I have always understood that even the shortest experience of publishers sharply stimulates a suicidal neurosis."

"Publishers, like saxophones and beards," replied Mr. Cheltenham, "should be exempted by a truce of God from being made subjects of the cheap jokes of inferior humorists for Eternity. And now tell me what those Jap words mean."

"Well," said Sanders, "they follow on the signature, so the whole thing reads 'J. Kato who will die on Feb. 13th!'"

Mr. Cheltenham was taken sharply aback.

"Is that what it says?" he replied sharply. "What's the fool mean?"

As he walked back to his office he felt for the first time a slight diminution of his enthusiasm for the book, a vague premonition of coming fear, such as a swimmer far out in a calm and golden sea might know when he felt the first pull of a strong and hostile current.

His experiences during the next fortnight were not calculated to reassure him. During that period he found it

necessary to stay late at the office several times, and he
felt a growing dislike to doing so. He was tempted to keep
his manager back on some excuse, but he was a considerate
employer who realised what staying late means for the inhabitants of the outer suburbs. The reason for this lively distaste
was something which after dark kept visiting the corners of
his eyes. He could never see it clearly; it was always on the
margin of vision, but it was uncomfortably suggestive of a
small, dark man.

He found himself looking up quickly to try to catch it
when he should have been concentrating on agreements and
estimates, but it was always just too quick for him. He stood
it as long as he could, and then went to see a famous nerve
specialist who had written a treatise on Abnormal Psychology which Mr. Cheltenham had published.

The latter described his solitary symptom and was subjected to a rigorous examination. "Well," said the specialist,
when he had finished, "all I can say for a confirmed celibate
and 'sedentary brain worker' you are disgustingly fit physically, and, I should judge, mentally. If you see a small dark
man out of the corner of your eye you can take it from me
he's there. But it is a curious story. Tell me frankly, do you
know any possible explanation?"

The publisher received the verdict with mixed feelings,
and he paused before replying. To say that the appearance of
this phenomenon coincided with his acceptance of a book of
poems seemed merely to darken counsel, so he answered—
not quite frankly—that he had no such explanation to offer.

"Then," said the doctor, "let me know how things turn
out, for honestly I'm interested and curious—and don't stay
late at the office." Still a victim of mixed feelings, Mr. Cheltenham found his zeal for Mr. Kato and his work steadily
diminishing. A genuine lover of good books and a sincere
and single-minded person, he hated to feel this irrational repulsion for what was after all indisputably a work of genius,
and, from a publisher's point of view, the book of a lifetime.

The best thing to do was to hurry the book out. It was occupying too much of his time and his thoughts. That reminded him the proofs were late. He rang up the printer, whose representative came round to see him. "Proofs to-morrow, for certain, sir. You'd have had them before, but—well, there's been a sort of a little trouble," and he gave Mr. Cheltenham a funny, deprecating, dubious glance.

"What sort of trouble—machine trouble?" asked the publisher.

"It sounds a bit of a yarn," replied the printer, "and it's only what I've been told, but the men in the setting room, who've been working overtime, say they keep seeing a little dark chap—well, they don't exactly see him, but they know he's there—it fusses them."

"Do you mean an actual person?" asked Mr. Cheltenham perfunctorily.

"Well," replied the printer, "the men don't seem to think so, it sounds ridiculous and is probably 'all my eye'—I only mention it to account for the delay. They get gassing and fussing, and won't get on with the job. However, as I say, to-morrow for certain."

After his departure Mr. Cheltenham sat staring at the wall and drumming on his table for a while. Then he rang for his typist and dictated a letter to Mr. Kato, informing him that the proofs of his book would be ready for him if he would call in the next day. He, Mr. Cheltenham, would then explain to him, Mr. Kato, what it was necessary for him to do regarding them. Then, in accordance with doctor's orders, he went home early.

Mr. Kato arrived punctually at 3.30, and the publisher was immediately impressed by his appearance. He looked shrunken and wasted. His face was drawn and hollowed, and his eyes were those of one from whom sleep has gone, and to whom fear has come.

Mr. Cheltenham began apologising for the leisurely behaviour of the proofs, but Mr. Kato obviously took little interest on what he was saying. "The publication date will be February 13th"—as he said this, Mr. Cheltenham paused. Till he made the remark he had not considered the date of publication definitely. Why then had he mentioned February 13th so decisively? The date seemed vaguely familiar, as if he had heard it recently in some other connection.

"Yes," said Mr. Kato listlessly.

"You don't look very fit, if I may say so," said Mr. Cheltenham. "I hope you're not worrying about the book. I can assure you there's not the slightest need to. Everything is progressing quite satisfactorily, and I feel certain that you will have an amazingly favourable Press."

"I do not worry about it," said Mr. Kato—and then paused, his haggard eyes fixed on Mr. Cheltenham's face. ("As if," thought the latter, "he wants sympathy pretty badly, and I'm the first person who has shown him any.")

Suddenly Mr. Kato's expression changed, he looked sharply behind him, and a hunted look overspread his face. "Please excuse," he muttered, "my nerves are not so good, I think," and he got heavily up and went out.

"Unless he does something about it," thought the publisher, "this will be the last as well as the first book he has his name to. Funny thing! If I'd written it, I should be thrilling with excitement to see it published, but he seems bored to death with it. He is the easiest author I've ever had to deal with. Poets are usually the devil—fussing about perfectly fatuous little details and trying to teach me my business. But he's a model."

The printer was as good as his word, and the proofs arrived the next morning and were immediately sent off to the author for correction, and they arrived back the following afternoon. "Pretty quick work, that," thought Mr. Cheltenham in astonishment. Having finished his other work, he took up the proofs and began to look through them. And then he got one of the greatest surprises of his life. The printers had warned him that, being a rush job, the proofs would probably be full of mistakes. There was one Mr. Cheltenham noticed in the title of the very first poem, "Cherry" being spelt with one "r," but Mr. Kato had not altered it. The publisher turned over the galley slips. There was not one single correction from beginning to end, yet a quick scrutiny showed him there were many and some ludicrous errors. He put down the proofs and sat back in his chair. He knew he was in the presence of a mystery, and many thoughts passed through his mind. Gradually the several, single, isolated puzzles began to knit themselves into coherency. "Curse the fellow, whoever he is," he said to himself, "this means another late night." As he took up his pen and began to make the first correction that strange drowsiness he knew so well seized him once more . . .

When he awoke the clock was just striking eight. "Good Lord," he thought, "I've been to sleep for two hours and a half and not one stroke of work have I done at these cursed—" and he leapt to his feet, for there on the first page was an added "r" in the margin opposite the title of the first poem, and in the poem itself an epithet had been struck out and another substituted in a delicate, exotic handwriting, which was certainly not his own. He turned the pages rapidly, and on nearly every one was some alteration or revision, which Mr. Cheltenham saw at a glance was invariably completely right. He turned back to the title page, and there was Mr. Kato's name neatly crossed out and "F. Gonesara" substituted. Mr. Cheltenham was frightened, and he knew it. He reached for his hat and coat and ran from the room and down the stairs; just as he reached the ground floor he saw out of the corner of his eye a small, dark figure on the landing above.

Mr. Cheltenham had a will of his own when he chose to utilise it, and for the next few weeks he resolutely refused to allow his mind to wander along forbidden and dangerous paths, even when there was that curious incident at the binder's. He never stayed late and kept himself busy. Contrary to his custom he took several manuscripts home and read them in bed till his eyes closed. Eventually his plans and preparations for the publication of *And he shall sing* were completed, advertising space was booked, review copies sent out, the trade supplied, and there was nothing to do but wait for February 13th, the date of publication. On February 12th he spent a very quiet day. Business was good. The latest masterpiece of his best-seller, Miss Vera de Vere, *Passionate Desire*, was selling passionately. He had no worries, he dined lightly and drank sparingly. It was, therefore, all the more unexplicable that he should have been afflicted with the most dreadful nightmare of his life.

At first he seemed to be standing against the wall of a room, a very silent and dark room, incapable of moving hand and foot, gripped and held by a malicious power which was quite determined he should do its bidding. But Mr. Cheltenham wanted to leave that room very, very badly. He longed with a desperate longing not to have to witness the horror which he knew was coming. Gradually his eye grew accustomed to the darkness, and then he could pick out the dim outline of the room, and then a shaft of moonlight came pouring in its thin radiance. He saw he was in a bedroom, looking down on a bed in which someone was lying motionless. He knew something vile was about to happen before his eyes: he strained at his invisible bonds, but inexorably they held him. By the light of the moonbeam he could see the room was carpetless, the worn polish of the floor reflected the moonlight hazily. And then Mr. Cheltenham saw that a plank was rising slowly. Once again he strained at his bonds. The plank rose steadily and stealthily, and suddenly something had moved up from under it, and had climbed out and was crouching on the floor.

Mr. Cheltenham trembled violently. That something, he knew, was or had been human. For a moment it stayed motionless, and then it began crawling stealthily towards the bed. A foul and deadly stench filled the room, and the publisher swayed reeling to his knees. He saw that that

Something was naked, livid, and that blood was streaming jerkily from its rotting lips. Mr. Cheltenham flung himself on the floor, and with a terrible effort turned his head away—and he found himself clawing at the carpet beside his own little iron bed, sweating and whimpering. Distressed and nauseated, he made no attempt to go to sleep again, but read Pickwick for the rest of the night.

He had not been at his office long the next morning when his bell rang.

"Chief Inspector Walsh to see you, sir."

"Show him up," replied Mr. Cheltenham, who spent the next few moments puzzling over the possible causes of this visitation. Had the author of *Passionate Desire* overstepped the liberal bounds allowed her? He never read her books himself, but his manager had assured him that her latest was no more stimulating than usual. A knock on the door, and in stepped a large, dominating personality, hairy and red-faced. "Good morning, sir," said he, "I've come about a Mr. Kato. I want to know if you can give me any information about him."

"I've just published his book this morning," replied Mr. Cheltenham, "but I'm afraid I know absolutely nothing personal about him. Why, has he got into some trouble?"

"Well," said the Inspector, "I think you can put it that way. He was found murdered in his bed this morning."

The publisher started to his feet.

"Murdered! By whom?"

"Well, sir, it's a funny case, a very funny case, you might say. The instrument used was a book—his own book, I take it, and whoever did it was a strong man, for he'd brought it down on his face so that he's—not a pretty sight, but that's not the end of it. One of my men noticed a board in the floor was loose. It was pulled up, and underneath was a body, much decomposed, with its throat cut. He was a Jap, too. Looks like a feud of some kind. Kato killed this chap and another chap got him. I came to see you, sir, because nothing is known of this Kato, and except some letters from you we found nothing suggesting he had any friends or acquaintances in this country. The Embassy people know nothing about him."

"As I say," replied Mr. Cheltenham, "I knew him purely in a business way, but I do think there was some mystery about him, for I had come to the conclusion that he was not the author of the book which he pretended to have written."

"How's that?" asked the Inspector.

"It is a collection of extremely subtle and beautiful poems," replied the publisher, "and from my experience of Kato I am convinced he could not have written them. He was always very nervous and uneasy, by the way."

"Don't you be too sure he didn't write 'em, sir," said Mr. Walsh. "Besides your letters, the only papers we found in his rooms were poems, stacks of them. I've brought some of them along, and in view of what you say I'd like you to look through them and see if they shed any light on the business, and then I'm afraid I must ask you to come along and identify the body.

"Must I really do that?" said Mr. Cheltenham.

"I'm afraid so, sir; you're the only person who seems to know anything about him, and you'll be wanted at the inquest."

"Very well," replied the publisher, "I'll ring you up when I have looked through these papers."

"Much obliged, sir," said the Inspector, and left the room.

The first thing Mr. Cheltenham did was to send for his manager.

"Dixon, I have decided to withdraw *And he shall sing.*"

"But, sir—"

"I'm afraid there are no 'but's' about it. I'll explain to the Trade and the reviewers, you hustle up and get the books back; there aren't many out yet, and reviewers don't hurry over poetry."

Some people may remember a curious little mystery about a book of poems—it had another title—which was reviewed enthusiastically in one or two papers, but apparently never published. A few copies are in existence, and sell for good sums when a collector consents to part.

Mr. Cheltenham destroyed every copy he could get hold of. Perhaps an impulsive and unnecessary performance, but he felt he could do no other. Having completed his plans for the withdrawal of the book he turned to the inspector's bag and its contents. They were "poems," as he had said, the feeblest, most bathetic, utterly commonplace rubbish on which Mr. Cheltenham in a long and bitter experience had ever cast his eyes. "It is the poetic fame which I desire," these words came back to his mind as he thrust the heap back into the bag. Perhaps he understood; and "F. Gonesara"? He shrugged his shoulders and took a taxi to Mr. Kato's flat in a typical Bloomsbury street.

The Inspector was waiting for him.

"Well?" he said.

"Mr. Walsh," replied Mr. Cheltenham, "when you have time I have a story to tell you, one you may not believe, but I think if you *could* believe it you would be saved a lot of useless work on this case. And now let's get the beastly ordeal over."

"Any time you like, sir. Come with me." He led the publisher along a passage and opened a door, and they entered a room. Mr. Cheltenham recognised it, as he had expected, and when he saw the bed and a red-stained sheet upon it, he trembled again—and then the Inspector went forward and drew back the sheet.

The Seventeenth Hole at Duncaster

Mr. Baxter sauntered out of his office in the Dormy House at Duncaster Golf Club, just as the sun was setting one perfect evening late in September, 192-, his meagre labours finished for the day. He gazed idly around him over one of the finest stretches of golfing country in the world. Duncaster is a remote hamlet on the Norfolk coast and, being twelve miles from a railway station, would have remained delicately secluded if some roaming enthusiast in the late '90s had not felt his heart seized by so fair, so promising, so Royal and Ancient a prospect, and rallied his golfing acquaintance to found the Duncaster Golf Club, with a small and select membership, and small and select it had remained. Almost deserted for most of the year, it was thickly sprinkled in August, and there was always a pleasant gathering of old friends at the Spring and Autumn meetings. Mr. Baxter, the popular and efficient secretary, was a portly little person, kindly, considerate, but not very happy. He let his eye roam placidly just over the superb sand-dune country bordering the North Sea, where gleaming alley-ways of perfect turf burrowed their way through the golden ramparts above them, sweet isolated pathways ending in the World's Finest Greens—so the members considered—where little red flags gleamed, waving gently in a dying evening breeze; then his eyes wandered inland and became for a moment sharply intent as they reached the 17th green, the new 17th placed on a plateau in the big wood, the long shadows cast by the sleepy sun peeping through the trees, playing across it.

Mr. Baxter was in a slightly depressed and introspective mood. Golf secretaries, he decided, were born and not made, and born under no felicitous star. There was he, a student and a philosopher by taste and temperament, condemned to oversee for a slender remuneration the tiny activities of a blasted Golf Club. He had drifted into this blind alley as he had always drifted; it was all due, he supposed, to the fact that one of his glands functioned inadequately. Yes, golf secretaries were only explicable on some such derogatory hypothesis. This 17th green, for example, because it was the only alteration made since the opening of the links, what a "Yes and No," what a discordant clamour of debate, what a fuss about almost nothing! Of course it was an improvement; by hacking a fairway through the wood and making the green on that ideal little plateau a bad 270-yarder had been changed into a very fine two-shotter—the best, though not the most pleasing hole, for the dunes made the real charm of the course. And yet—the student and philosopher rebelled.

He strolled across to the pro.'s shop, whose tenant was standing in the doorway smoking a pipe, and gazing reflectively in front of him.

"Evening, Dakers," said Mr. Baxter, "I thought I saw someone on the 17th a little while ago. Is anyone still out?"

The Pro. took his pipe out of his mouth. His face did not command a wide range of expression, but for a moment a look of a certain sharpness and subtlety flitted across it.

"No, sir, everyone's in. Mr. and Mrs. Stannard finished a quarter of an hour ago; they were the last."

"That's funny," said Mr. Baxter, "I could have sworn I saw someone."

The Pro. paused a moment, as if carefully choosing his reply. "I think, sir, it's the shadows. I've fancied the same thing."

"Well, what do you think of it?" asked the Secretary.

"I'm sure it's a very fine hole, sir, but it's too good for me. I've played it seven times now, and done five fives and two sixes. It's funny, too, because it's just my length—a drive and push iron with the ground as hard as this, yet I haven't found the green with my second shot once. The ball seems to leave the club all right, and then—well, it's something I've never known happen before."

"I hope it's going to be a success, for it's been enough bother and expense," said Mr. Baxter.

The Pro. did not answer for a moment. He put his pipe back in his mouth and looked away over to the subject of discussion. At length he asked, "Did they ever discover what the contractor's men died of, sir?"

"Not for certain," replied the secretary, "blood-poisoning of some kind—a very unfortunate affair."

"The other chaps thought it had something to do with those skulls and bones they dug up. They got talking to the villagers, who put the wind up them a bit, I'm thinking."

"How was that?" asked Mr. Baxter.

"It's some sort of talk about the wood, it seems," replied Dakers.

Mr. Baxter was interested. "I should like to hear more about this," he said, "but I have no time now. I'll see you to-morrow."

The next day, the Saturday before the opening of the Autumn meeting, Mr. Baxter played an afternoon round with Colonel Senlis. It was for both of them their first introduction to the new 17th. The Colonel had taken up the game after he retired, and he served it with an even more fanatical devotion than he had served his King. He was a jolly old maniac with a handicap of 16 and a style of his own. Mr. Baxter might have been a very fine player; he had balance, rhythm, and a beautiful pair of hands, but his heart had never been in it, and he was content to be a perfectly reliable 2.

No incident of any moment occurred during the first 16 holes. The Colonel collected much fine sand in various portions of his attire; Mr. Baxter played sound but listless golf. When they reached the seventeenth tee the wind, which had been wandering vaguely and gustily round the compass, suddenly settled down to blow half a gale from due east, and the seventeenth became a tiger indeed. Mr. Baxter, after a couple of nice blows dead into the wind, lay some twenty yards short of the wood, which was beginning to shout wildly in the gale. The Colonel was in the rough on the right, an alliterative position he usually occupied. He played his fourth—one of the few properly struck golf shots of his existence—dead on the pin. The secretary took his number three iron, and knew from the moment the ball left the club that he didn't want it back. It was ruled on the flag.

As the Colonel came up, a look of swelling pride on his rubicund visage, he remarked, "Did you see mine, Baxter? Never say again I can't play a spoon shot! You hit yours, too, didn't you?"

"Yes," answered the secretary, smiling. "I'm inside you by a yard or two, I fancy."

"I don't," said the Colonel. "You'll be playing the odd, stroke gone, all right."

They walked together along the avenue of lurching Scotch firs and larches, and climbed the bank of the plateau.

"My God!" cried the Colonel. "We're neither of us on! Where the Hades are they?"

An exasperating search followed, which ended when the Colonel found his Dunlop No. 1 dozing behind a tree, and Mr. Baxter detected his No. 2 in a rabbit hole. The Colonel made robust use of an expletive much favoured by the gallant men he had once had the honour of commanding. Mr. Baxter quietly picked up his errant globe and walked off to the last tee.

"Damn it, Baxter!" cried the Colonel, "that hole meant to fight me, I felt it all the time."

The secretary had played many holes with the Colonel on many different courses, but had never noticed any of them displaying any Locarno spirit towards or desire to fraternise with him, but all the same he had voiced his own thoughts. It *had* been a ludicrous incident, but its humour did not appeal to him particularly. Both those shots should have been by the pin. Just what the Pro. had said. It was very curious. "I'm going to hate that hole," he thought.

"There's a damned funny mark on my ball," grumbled the Colonel. "I suppose it hit a tree, though I could swear it didn't. Looks more like a burn. Why, there's the same thing on yours!"

Mr. Baxter examined them. They were funny symmetrical little marks, and they were remarkably like burns. "The wind must have caught them and blown them into the trees," he said, unconvincingly. "It's rather a gloomy spot in there, and it's hard to follow the flight exactly."

After tea the secretary went round to see Dakers.

"Well," he said, "I've tried the new hole."

"I saw you out, sir," said the Pro., smiling. "Did you get your four?"

"I almost deserved it," said Mr. Baxter. "My third was played like a golfer, and lined on the pin. I found it in a rabbit hole underneath the left bank."

"That's what I told you, sir. It's that sort of hole. I shall be interested to see how the members like it next week. In this wind it's certainly *some* hole."

"You mentioned last night something about talk in the village," insinuated Mr. Baxter. "What kind of talk?"

"Well, sir, there's been quite a clack, still is, for that matter; they're a funny, old-fashioned lot, with funny ideas. Do you know, sir, they won't go into that wood after dusk!"

"Why on earth not?"

"They don't seem to think it's healthy somehow; they call it 'Blood Wood,' some old superstition or other. I think some of them were a bit ashamed of feeling that way till the contractor's men died; but that started them off again."

"It's a pretty vague sort of yarn," said the secretary musingly. "Do they go into detail at all?"

"No, sir, it's a village tradition of very old standing, I should say. They are scared of the wood. Old Jim the Cobbler's father was found dead, apparently murdered, in it, and there are other tales of the old times like that."

Sunday was a busy day for Mr. Baxter. The Dormy House filled up steadily, and by the evening the highly satisfactory total of forty-four, mostly hale and slightly too hearty, elderly gentlemen had assembled.

The Autumn meeting opened in a full easterly gale, and it was a battered and weary collection of competitors who arrived back at the club house.

Mr. Baxter, greeting them as they came in, found them on one subject unanimously eloquent. They one and all cherished loathing mingled with respect for the new seventeenth. The secretary examined their cards with curiosity. Only one five was recorded, the average was eight. When young Cyril Ward, the only scratch player in the club, came in, the secretary asked him how he had fared. "My ancient friend," he replied, "I accomplished seventeen holes in seventy-two strokes; good going in this wind; my total is eighty. I give you one guess as to the other hole."

"Oh, the seventeenth, I suppose."

"You've said it. Baxter, there's something funny about it. I hit two perfect shots and then took six more to hole out."

"I'm sure of it," said the Secretary, "but I'm getting most remarkably sick of hearing about it."

After the second round of the thirty-six holes stroke competition Mr. Baxter found himself the centre of one of the fiercest indignation meetings in the history of the golf game. Everyone had something to say. Eventually he was forced to promise that, if at the end of the week they were still of the same opinion, he would have the old seventeenth restored.

"But," said he, "all this chopping and changing will cost us a lot of money."

"More likely save us a bit," grumbled a protestant. "I lost three new balls there to-day. Have you noticed what a stench there was coming from the back of the green?"

Cyril Ward went for a stroll with Mr. Baxter when the debate was over. "I wish the old boys weren't so impatient," he said. "That hole has beaten me badly twice, but I'd like to have many more shots at it. I shall protest strongly if they decide to change back. Look at it now, the green's like a pool of blood!"

("A sinister but apt description," thought Mr. Baxter.)

The sun was setting in a wild and tortured sky, and its fiery dying rays certainly painted the seventeenth a sanguine hue.

"It's funny you should say that," he remarked. "It's called 'Blood Wood' by the locals."

"From what I heard of the expletives used by our worthy fellow foozlers, they certainly agree with them," laughed Ward.

That night Mr. Baxter had a short but disturbing dream. He seemed to hear a deep bell tolling sullenly, and then suddenly a voice cried, "Sacred to the memory of Cyril Ward, who screamed once in Blood Wood," and then came a discordant chorus of vile and bestial laughter, and he awoke feeling depressed and ill at ease.

"This absurd business is getting on my nerves," he thought, "I'm even dreaming about it," and he suddenly felt he wanted to leave Duncaster, and the sooner the better. It was too lonely and idle a life, he decided.

The next day the gale continued, bringing torrents of rain with it, and there was no competition. The course was a melancholy and deserted waste. Mr. Baxter, as he worked in his office, could hear the great breakers booming beyond the Dunes. About six the rain dwindled to a light drizzle, and

Cyril Ward came in to see him, a couple of clubs under his arm. "There's just enough light to let me defeat that blasted hole," he said; "the swine fascinates me!"

Mr. Baxter found himself rather vehemently trying to persuade him otherwise. "I shouldn't; it's still raining, and it will be almost dark in the wood."

"Oh, rot," said Ward, and presently the Secretary saw him tee up and drive off. He watched him until he had almost reached the wood, and then someone called him to settle a point of bridge law. The windows of the smoking room were open, and the gale suddenly increased in fury.

Mr. Baxter had just given his decision when there came a long scream of agony shaking down the wind. He rushed to the door, the other occupants of the room hustling after him.

That terrible cry had come from the wood, and they began running towards it. Suddenly just visible in the gloom, a figure came staggering out from the wood, threw up its arms, and fell. Mr. Baxter dashed towards it as he had not run for twenty years, the others after him.

Cyril Ward was lying on his back, his eyes wide, staring, and horrible—obviously dead.

Amongst those who came up was the local doctor, who knelt down and made a short examination. "Must be heart. I believe he had a weakness there, poor Cyril!" Mr. Baxter helped to carry the body back to the Formy House; his burden was Cyril's left leg, a disgusting dangling thing. The memory of his dream came back to him, and his nerves shook. He tried to find reassurance by telling himself that such premonitions were common enough, however inexplicable.

It was decided at an informal meeting that the links should be closed the next day out of respect for the dead, but that the foursomes should be held on the Thursday. "A very typically British compromise," thought Mr. Baxter.

"Will an inquest be necessary?" he asked the doctor.

"I think not; it's clearly a case of heart."

"Did you notice his eyes?" asked the secretary. The doctor gave him a quick glance. "I did," he replied, "but these attacks are often very painful. But did you notice that appalling stink coming from the wood?"

"Yes," said the secretary shortly.

"Well, I should find out the cause, it can't be healthy."

"I will to-morrow," said Mr. Baxter.

The next day he spent in his office, and never before had a sense of the futility of his occupation so swept over him. This shifting of pieces of india-rubber from one spot to another! Oh, that a man should have to spend his few and gloriously potential days fussing about such banality! Perhaps he was only pitying himself. He went back to his card-marking. He felt utterly weary when he went to bed, and fell immediately asleep. "Boom! Boom! Boom!" there came that terrible tolling. He must wake! He must not hear what was to come. "Sacred to the memory of Sybil Grant, who screamed twice in Blood Wood," and once again came that foul and wicked laughter.

He awoke sweating and unnerved. He got up and mixed himself the strongest whisky and soda of his temperate existence. "Sybil Grant! Sybil Grant!" Thank God, he knew no one of that name! He tried to read, till light came.

He went down to the club house after breakfast, and met the doctor. "Hullo," said the latter, "you're not looking very fit! What's the matter?"

"Oh, just a rotten night," said the secretary. "By the way, I sent the green-keeper to find out about that smell, but he couldn't discover any cause for it; and, as a matter of fact, says he couldn't smell anything."

"Well, he's a lucky man," said the doctor. "It was the most loathsome reek I've encountered, and I've met a few!"

After the foursomes had started, everyone desperately light-hearted and pathetically determined to allow no echo of the horror of a few hours before to disturb the atmosphere of laboured cheerfulness, Mr. Baxter felt he must be alone. He wandered off to the long No Man's Land between the dunes and the sea, a famous haunt of sea birds; the sand showed everywhere the delicate tracings of their soft little feet.

As he reached the darker strata just surrendered by the angry, fading tide, his eye was caught by a patch of scarlet moving down to the sea some distance to his left.—"A girl going to bathe," he thought casually. "She must have warm blood in her to face such a sea on such a day. I hope she knows what she's about. It's none too safe a spot." Presently he saw a man run down to join her, and felt reassured and yet depressed. "To be a dingy old bachelor like myself is the one unanswerable indictment. Ten King's Councillors could not make it seem excusable."

Then his mind turned to the question of the new post he was determined to secure. He would go up to London as soon as the meeting was over and get an exchange if possible.

His work kept him busy all the afternoon, and he did not emerge from his office till dusk was falling. "Best figure in England," he heard the Colonel declaring, as he entered the smoking room. "I believe she's engaged to Bob Renton."

"Who's that?" asked the secretary.

"The Grant girl," said the Colonel, "Sybil Grant."

The secretary felt a tug of horror at his heart.

"Is she coming down here?" he asked sharply.

"She *is* here," replied the Colonel. "If you'd been here ten minutes ago you'd have seen her."

"Well, where is she now?" asked the secretary, seizing his arm. "Where is this girl?" he cried, his voice rising.

"Hullo, young feller, what's all the excitement? I imagine she's about at the seventeenth green; she's staying with the Bartletts at the Old Cottage, and is walking back that way."

At that moment a bell seemed to toll once shatteringly in the Secretary's ears. He put his hands to his head, and without a word started running frantically down the seventeenth fairway. Suddenly there sprang down the wind a terrible cry of terror, followed by a desperate and prolonged scream. Mr. Baxter stopped dead and shuddered. He heard shouts behind him and the patter of others running. He tottered on. Somebody—several people—passed him; as he reeled into the wood he could see the fire-fly gleam of electric torches, and as he neared them he could see they were focused on some object on the ground. It was white, and someone was kneeling over it. When he saw what it was he was suddenly and violently sick. It was flung down the bank, it was naked, its head was lolling hideously. It was sprawling, one knee flung high, its face—but someone covered that face with his coat and told Mr. Baxter to go for the doctor. And that terrible Death stench kept him company.

The inquest was fixed for the following Monday, and Mr. Baxter was told that his testimony would be required.

The little village swarmed with police and reporters. There hadn't been a mystery of such possibilities for many moons, and the whole country was stirred. Murder so foul cried out for vengeance. But there was no arrest, "And there never will be," thought Mr. Baxter as he took his stand in the improvised witness-box in the village school. The Coroner, a corpulent, hirsute and pompous person, soon put to him the question he had anticipated. "I understand that you started to run towards the scene of the tragedy before these screams were heard: is that so?"

"Yes," replied the secretary.

"Why was that?"

And then Mr. Baxter uncontrollably laughed.

"I may be mistaken," said the Coroner, "but this hardly seems a laughing matter."

"I must beg your pardon," said Mr. Baxter, "I laughed against my will, I laughed because I suddenly realised how absurd you would consider my explanation to be."

"That is quite possible," said the Coroner, "but I must ask you to let me hear it."

"I had a premonition, a dream."

"Of what character?"

"Well, I dreamed that Miss Grant would be killed."

"Did you warn her?"

"I had never heard of her except in this dream. I did not know she was here till I was so informed a moment before these screams were heard."

"A curious story," replied the representative of Law and Order, who clearly regarded Mr. Baxter as a person of limited intelligence and dubious veracity.

"Murder by some person or persons unknown," was the verdict, and unknown he, she or they remained.

The nine days ran their course, police and reporters departed, and Mr. Baxter went off to London, where he secured a job at a new course in Surrey. He was to have no successor at Duncaster. Resignations poured in, and it was decided at a final meeting of the committee that the links should be abandoned.

On arriving in London it occurred to Mr. Baxter to call upon a friend of his, a Mr. Markes. He very much wanted an expert confidant, and Mr. Markes, besides being very wealthy, was by some trick of temperament fascinated by all types of psychic phenomena, and had amassed the finest library on such matters in the world.

"Jim," asked the Secretary, "is there any mention of Duncaster in your records?"

"When I read about your troubles there," replied Mr. Markes, "I thought they sounded rather in the tradition, and so I looked up the history of Duncaster and was unexpectedly fortunate; for it is mentioned in a work, which, for the most part, is deservedly forgotten. *The Memoirs of Simon Tylor,* a peculiarly dull dog. I have them here," he continued, walking over to a shelf and taking down a bulky volume.

"In the year 1839 Simon took a walking tour through Norfolk and arrived at Duncaster on September 10th. He liked the look of it, and decided to spend a couple of days there at the inn, 'The Sleeping Sentinel.'"

"It is there still," said Mr. Baxter.

"All this," went on Mr. Markes, "is described at vast and damnable length, but his adventure, which occurred on the second evening of his stay, is much more crisply done. I will read it to you:

"'I spent a pleasing and invigorating morning wandering over the wild expanse of moor and "dunes," as they call the great sand mounds; and afterwards dined, rested and had some talk with my good host of the inn. Late in the afternoon I decided to make further exploration of the neighbourhood, and, noticing a fine wood of tall trees some distance away across the moor, I remarked to my host that I proposed to visit it. Greatly to my surprise he strongly opposed my doing so, but when I asked him for what reason, he returned me evasive replies—"No one wanders there after nightfall," he said, "It has a bad repute."

"'"On account of robbers?" I asked. And though he replied with a short laugh that that was so, I did not believe it was the thought in his mind. To satisfy him, I declared I would but walk towards it, a promise I had better have kept.

"'So I wandered out as the light was fading, and drew near to the wood. Then I put it to myself that such village gossip was in most cases but idle tradition inscribed in the long and sparsely furnished memories of country folk. And this decision prevailing, I entered the wood, following a rough pathway. And then I had reason to doubt my host's word, for instead of it being shunned by the local folk it seemed that the wood did house quite a company. The light being low and the trees growing close, I failed clearly to distinguish my companions, but only, as it were, out of the corner of my eye, I glimpsed them many times. "Lovers," thought I. After I had traversed some two hundred paces I noted some little

way in front of me a low mound with a single fine tree at
its back. I was just fancying that I would go so far and then
return when a movement in the gloom caught my eye, and at
the same instant I perceived a very vile and curious stench.
Something seemed to be reclining on the mound, a beast of
some sort, and slowly gaining its feet. And then I knew the
beginning of fear. This thing seemed to rise and rise till it
towered above the tree, and then it couched its head as for
a spring. I have no wish to see its like again. Seized with a
great loathing and horror, I ran back along the path, and as I
ran it seemed that many were running beside me and closing
in upon me. I felt the Thing was close beside me, but I dared
not turn to look. Just as my breath was leaving me I found
myself at the edge of the wood, and then something seemed
to touch me, and I screamed and swooned.

"'When I regained my senses I found I was prone on the
ground and my host and some others were standing round
me conversing in low tones. They helped me back to the Inn,
no one saying a word. I left early the next morning, that
stench still lingering in my nostrils and the host seeming to
avoid talk with me. All this is the truth as I have set it down.'

"And that's what happened to Simon," said Markes.

"A curious story," said Mr. Baxter.

"Far more curious than uncommon. I could find you a
dozen almost identical experiences. Almost certainly the
work of our friends the Druids, whoever they were! A mound
and an oak—such places are death traps. Not all the time;
the peril is periodic, why, we don't know. But our friend Simon was very lucky to be able to leave 'early next morning,'
though he didn't escape altogether. The rest of his book reads
like a coda to this adventure. Bad dreams, depression and
always that smell in his nose. He died within a year or two.
And now tell me exactly what happened at Duncaster, for I
gather it is still a disturbed area."

So Mr. Baxter told him the curious events connected with
the new seventeenth.

A Peg on Which to Hang—

Before telling Mr. James Partridge's displeasing experience at the Beach Hotel, Littleford, it may be as well to establish that gentleman's credentials by briefly describing him. He is a writer by habit and inclination, though being the fruit of rich but honest parents, he is not in the paralysing position of being compelled to rely on his pen, ink and paper for his means of subsistence. He has made a nice little reputation as an essayist of the lightest sort. He has examined the surface of things, of persons and of life in general with a tolerant, mildly cynical assiduity. Below that surface he very sensibly refrains from looking. It is not in his character. He takes some homely and familiar topic—let us say, a Number IIe Omnibus—as his text, and manages to coax from a ruminating survey of its cargo and its route two thousand bland and gently ironic words of amusement without pedantry, for which he receives 25 guineas from a high-brow weekly.

Though on the whole a modest man, he believes in his heart of hearts that he does this sort of thing better than "Y.Y."—an opinion not widely shared, and least of all by Mr. Robert Lynd.

Being a journalist, you will naturally suspect that he invented this narrative and foisted it on his credulous acquaintance. If so, you will do him a serious injustice, for he has no gift for fiction and, indeed, this is not the type of narrative he would care to pursue if he had. You may take it for granted then that his version of what happened on the night of March 23rd, 1924, at the Royal Hotel, Littleford, is plain, untouched-up fact.

If you would like to know some details of his appearance, he is thin, wiry, but lacking muscle, a mild edition of Sherlock Holmes, facially—a bit dusty and musty and bachelory, a bit donnish and British and formidable—a man's man, but not every man's man. People who like him like him very much—that's all he cares about.

He found himself at the Royal Hotel, Littleford, on March 23rd, 1924, on this account. He has three firm and excellent friends about his own age—which is 47—like himself all keen golfers. Their handicaps range between nine and fourteen—almost certainly the most satisfactory range of all; for those embraced within it are not unduly cast down by the undesired uprising of playful divots, yet they can derive exquisite satisfaction from the production of a Stout Blow, and are sufficiently competent to perpetrate several in the course of a round—humble folk who realise that, if they will never be mistaken for Bobby Jones, it is hardly possible that they will be confused with Harry Tate. Mr. George Dunbar, K.C., masterful, hirsute, with a hypnotic power over juries, Mr. William Cranmer, who knows more about old books than most people, Mr. Alexander Frith, Professor of Moral Philosophy at an Ancient Foundation and a sceptic of sceptics, made up the four who journeyed down to Littleford on this occasion.

It had been their cherished custom for many years to leave their faithful readers, their burglarious clientele, their candidates for firsts in Greats, their cultured bibliophiles to their own disconsolate devices at seasons of the year convenient to them all, and to forgather at certain famous golf courses; and they had chosen that admirable links, Littleford, for their spring pilgrimage in 1924. They intended to stay a week, and had secured their rooms prudently in advance.

They travelled down together in Mr. Partridge's car, and on entering the Royal Hotel were met by a flaccid specimen of the genus Small Hotel-keeper, who was chafing his palms in a deprecating manner.

Mr. Partridge addressed him sternly. "You have four rooms engaged for us in my name, which is Partridge."

"I regret to say, sir, only three," replied the flaccid specimen, "but I have secured an excellent room at a boarding-establishment close at hand," and he frotted his clammy hands again.

If Mr. Partridge had a failing it was a tendency to be choleric at times—and this was one of them. As the organiser of the party it would be his painful duty to sample the boarding-establishment, and, cherishing a peculiar loathing for this type of accommodation, he wasn't having any.

"Look here," he said with truculence, "I have your letter stating you had reserved four rooms, and I must ask you to keep to your word."

Something in Mr. Partridge's demeanour daunted the specimen, and he shuffled off down the passage to his office.

Mr. Cranmer, who is incorrigibly a man of peace, began suggesting he was rather partial to boardinghouses and wouldn't mind a bit, but Mr. Partridge waved him aside and strode menacingly down the passage after the hotel-keeper, who went through the outer office into a small room at the back, which Mr. Partridge saw was already occupied by a female of the Buxom Brighton Barmaid type, with whom the landlord began a colloquy, in a whisper sufficiently audible to allow Mr. Partridge to catch a sentence here and there.

"Well, chance it," murmured the female.

"But supposing—" the flaccid one—obviously a hen-pecked one—started feebly to object.

"*His* look-out," replied the female. "Anyway, you've took a room for him at Mrs. Brown's, it's his look-out."

"I don't like it," said the flaccid one, "honest I don't," and then he shuffled out.

"I find," he said shiftily, "that I *can* manage the fourth room, but I assure you the boarding-establishment is a clean, comfortable house."

"No thanks," said Mr. Partridge. "Show us the four rooms, please."

Leading the way, the specimen unlocked in turn three rooms on the second floor, in which the others were deposited, and then he took Mr. Partridge up to the third and opened a door at the end of a passage.

"This will be yours, sir," he said, his eyes on his fingers, and a moment later Mr. Partridge was alone, and receiving a sharp, vivid yet vague impression of malaise. He had had such impressions just once or twice before—immediate, apparently causeless aversions for certain persons, places, things, rooms—yes, rooms. He experienced again this irritating, irrational distaste when that little worm closed the door of Number 39. It wasn't violently obtrusive, but it was certainly there.

He looked round the room. It was furnished with the conventional Royal Hotel properties—a chest of drawers with a couple of knobs missing, a wardrobe slightly down at one heel, one picture at a rakish angle, depicting Mr. Marcus Stone's reactions to Sacred and Profane Love, a row of pegs with one missing. Mr. Partridge, being an essayist of the lightest sort, was observant of detail, and he noted that a new panel had been inserted beneath one of them. Then there was a loutish wash-stand with a mirror, into which he gazed. Yes, certainly he wanted a holiday—one could almost tell a man's age from his eye-brows, his were growing wispy and errant—and then he stepped back abruptly, for it seemed to him for a moment that the image he saw reflected had changed—as if someone had peeped over his shoulder and—absurd of course! It must be because the room was so dark. He began fussing with the blind, which refused to go right up. Well, curse the thing! He started and looked back quickly over his shoulder—it was only the Boots with his bag. "This is a damnably dark room, Boots," he said testily. "See if you can get the blind up a little."

"Always seems a bit dim," said the Boots, putting down the bag and jerking at the blind cord. "There, sir, that's a little better."

Mr. Partridge changed quickly into his golf attire and went down to lunch. Afterwards they took sides in the traditional four-ball match which inaugurated these reunions. The play was not of a very par standard, and the balls were slyly provocative in concealing themselves, so that it was growing dusk as they entered the little garden of the Hotel. As they came through the gate Willie Cranmer said to Mr. Partridge, "Got a decent room, Jim?"

"No," said the latter. "Dark and poky, but it will do all right. It's that one, I think, next to the chimney, with the small window."

"Well," said Willie, "there's someone in there, I saw him look out for a moment."

Mr. Partridge stared up for a moment. "Probably the Boots," he said, a little shortly.

When he went up to dress for dinner, he found his distaste for Number 39 decidedly intensified. He went to the window and looked out. Yes, it was the one next to the chimney. He could find no trace of any activity by the Boots.

In fact, there was too little activity on the part of everybody in this rotten place—no hot water, for example. He'd let his ancient friend Armitage know what he thought of R.A.C. recommended Hotels! He rang the bell viciously, which presently resulted in a timid knock—a maid with a japanned tin can—who came in with the expression of a heifer facing the pole-axe, hurried across the room, rattled down the can in the basin, and ran out again.

"Do I look as great a menace to rustic virtue as all that?" wondered Mr. Partridge. "I should like to think so, but I don't." And he set himself to a smart piece of changing.

During dinner the conversation took the natural form of a riot of golf-shop—the usual immortality for green-finders, the usual Nirvana for shanks, tops and flubs, but afterwards in the lounge they turned to less momentous topics. For example, Mr. Partridge asked Willie Cranmer if he had secured any notable prizes in the book-market lately.

"Nothing of any great value," he replied, "but one thing which interests me very much. It's a privately printed—very badly printed—account of some troublesome events in an Essex Manor, dated 1754. Its abominable title-page is inscribed as follows:

THE HAUNTINGE OF MY HOUSE
BY
CHAS. SWINTON
A GENTLEMAN OF ESSEX.

"He seems to have inherited the place in 1750, but his joy at such good fortune speedily turned to foreboding and exasperation. He goes into great detail, and certainly Swinton Manor seems to have housed a disturbing company. He must have had his fair share of guts and pertinacity to have stuck it as long as he did. It's the most curious chronicle of its kind I ever read. Eventually he had the house pulled down, having endured enough."

"It's a very curious subject, this business of hauntings," said Mr. Frith judicially. "For one thing it is a nice instance of the scepticism of men, when they want to be sceptical—how often they prefer the greatest credulity! Looked at dispassionately, the evidence for such phenomena is far more catholic and irrefutable than is the evidence for ninety-nine things out of a hundred which are accepted without question. Read that encyclopaedic catalogue of Richet, *Thirty Years of Psychical Research,* if you want to know how full and detailed that evidence is. Yet the average man mocks at the suggestion that even one out of this multiplicity is anything but an invention or an hallucination."

"I think you have suggested the real reason," said George Dunbar. "They pretend to refuse to believe because they'd vastly prefer to disbelieve, and comparatively very few have ever been compelled by personal experience to face such facts. Even then, when the intimidating vision is fading, they are satisfied to mutter something about 'Subjective and Objective'—leave it at that and change the subject."

"If there is one certain thing," said Mr. Partridge, "it is that they can be objective. The identical experience has been shared a thousand times, the same apparition has been viewed by dozens of different people at the same and different times. The evidence for that is beyond argument."

"I believe in such phenomena in a certain sense," said Willie Cranmer, "but I am not prepared to allow them a supernatural—in the more esoteric sense of the word—existence. By some unexplained means, certain places, certain things, become impregnated, kinetic, sensitised. How or why one room, one chair, even one W.C., allows itself to be so impregnated is an utterly inexplicable mystery. One battlefield is 'haunted'; a thousand are as placid as Port Meadow. Usually, I grant you, there is evidence that a potent emanation of some passion has at some time been released and operative in such disturbed areas, though not, I believe, by any means in every case. But the most singular thing to my mind about the supernatural is its caprice, its fortuitousness, its rarity—and indeed its essential lack of purpose. The eloquent and, considering its date, ingenious explanation of Lytton covers but a small percentage of the data and, even if one accepts it in its entirety, a vast legion of instances of hauntings and haunted would be left still as fortuitous, as unrelated, and as inexplicable."

"I knew a house," said George Dunbar, "in which I would not spend a week alone for one thousand guineas. Not merely is it impregnated, it is dripping with horror and beastliness. It is dark and brooding and has—it seems to me—an evil life of its own. Everyone, I know, who has entered it has taken an immediate and increasing loathing for it. It has a shocking record of suicides—eight in thirty years, but I agree with Willie that I never got the impression that there was any mind or will animating those coughs one heard, the steps behind one, the dim, drawn faces one thought one saw at windows; and all the symposium of dread one experienced there I mean that one was left convinced that there was no consciousness working in our space and time—these things seemed to be passing in and out of another dimension— that is vague, but just the impression I got. All these pheno- mena seemed quite purposeless, and therefore should not have been, as they were, frightening—puppets without strings—like the mechanical recording of a gramophone."

"I think that's a better simile than mine," said Cranmer. "Once the record is made by the living it goes on long after the recorder is dead, repeating and repeating until it wears out, and there is evidence that the influence does wear out in certain senses. All such comparisons between affairs on one plane and on another are fallacious, but they help to clear the air of debate."

"But someone has to put the record on," objected Mr. Partridge.

"I suggest it is never taken off," replied Cranmer.

"What a typical ghost discussion it has been," thought Mr. Partridge, "hopelessly inconclusive, tentative, vaguely disturbing, subjective, guesswork."

At a quarter to twelve they decided to go to bed. Mr. Par- tridge and Willie Cranmer went out for a breath of air.

"Did you find you had identified your room all right?" the latter asked.

"Yes," said Mr. Partridge, wondering slightly irritably why the subject seemed to have this mild fascination for his old friend.

The night was fine, with a three-quarter moon. Willie Cranmer stared up at the hard shadows round the chimney for a moment or two, and then said, "Well, let's go to bed. You're sure you're quite comfortable?"

"Oh, quite!" said Mr. Partridge in a clipped, slightly bothered tone, and they went in.

The corner of the corridor in which Number 39 was situated was so dark that Mr. Partridge had to light a match before he could find the keyhole. As he was fumbling with the key he checked himself sharply and listened intently. It seemed to him that a sound, difficult to define, had come from within. He lit another match to make sure this was Number 39. Yes, it was. That little sound must have come from the next room. He went in and turned on the light, which consisted of one blinking and superannuated bulb.

"This is a rotten pub," he thought. "A moribund bulb, blinds not drawn, bed not pulled down! I'll tell that worm what I think of his establishment in the morning!"

He went to hang up his coat on one of those pegs when he suddenly found himself staring uncertainly at them. His subconscious mind had uttered a protest. Then he remembered. "That's rather funny," he thought. "I could have sworn that one of those pegs was missing, and that one of those panels had been renewed." Yet they were all there now, and the panels were identical. He peered at them closely; it was a quite unimportant and yet irritating little puzzle.

The room was stuffy. He went to the window and opened it. He must be getting old and unobservant. He'd never noticed that tree before—what was it?—a yew, and a very fine one. How could he have failed to see it? In how unreal, unearthly a way the moon painted the world sometimes! This view from the window, for example—how uncertain in a sense, unfamiliar, as if it were a reflection from a mind not his own; certain pictures of Cézanne gave one that tingling, groping "let me get back to reality" feeling. Reality! What was it? And what was that? That shifty little noise. Had he heard it or just imagined it? He listened intently. No, there was nothing. An idea for an article! He began to undress, whistling a vague little tune, and pretending to concentrate on pleasant, commonplace things. He pretended to do so because he refused to confess that he had a rather poisonous sensation of being watched and waited for. When he was examining those pegs he had had to exercise considerable self-control so as not to turn round quickly to see who was looking at them too, just over his shoulder. But he had looked round sharply when he thought he'd heard that curious little noise. Well, he shouldn't have done. That way panic lay. Panic! What on earth was there to panic about?

Instead of sinking at once into that ten-fathom-deep slumber to which a flawless conscience and eighteen strenuous holes entitled him, he passed into that exasperating border state where detached and leering images come flocking into one's head, endlessly and inanely telescoping one another, composing indefinable patterns, humiliating puerilities, a state where there is neither the controlled rationality of full consciousness nor the deliciously serio-comic pantomime of the land of dreams. "This region," he decided, "is the nearest approach to an understanding of that buzzing, wavering kaleidoscope called lunacy, which the sane person ever reaches. The mind can neither control, nor quite lose control of, these regurgitations of the memory—for that is what they must be." Yet some of these images did not seem to be derived from the well-stored bins of his remembered experience. For example, he never recalled having entered long rows of figures—wild, whirling figures in a heavy ruled ledger. And that girl's face which kept getting between his eyes and the ruled lines. He did not remember having seen anyone like her before. And there she was, sitting near him in a little enclosed garden, and then back came those figures—into what a raving rigmarole was he plunged! He woke up fully and sharply for a moment, and then—his will surrendering—fell into a deep sleep. Gradually the competing images hardened, and as the confused turmoil of a swiftly rising sea settles into the orderly march of mighty combers, they took unto themselves a sequence.

Rows of figures staring out from a book, and then some-one standing beside him and beckoning him. And then that long room and a table at which two men were sitting with books and papers in front of them, who looked at him search-ingly. It was coming! He sat down on a chair to which one of these men motioned him. Then the other one began pointing at more rows of figures on a paper on the table. It was all over! Then one of the men put down his pencil and looked at him, and that girl's face, placid, smiling, gentle, rose and filled the room. A terrible sense of caged frustration seized him. He walked back to the door and through it, and found himself flinging clothes into a bag, and then he looked up, and there was that lovely childish face looking down so eas-ily at him. A terrible sense of loss—and there he was walk-ing warily and glancing back down a street beside the sea, and there he was on his hands and knees creeping across the floor of a moon-lit room. He reached the window, the moon was pacing rain-bow clouds, but what was that—that shadow flung so silently and so still from the trees? He crawled back to the bed, and his head was in his hands, and they seemed to press and force out that girl's face, radiating love and trust. He staggered up, and a moment later he felt life choking and twisting from him.

Mr. Partridge for good reasons only occasionally and re-luctantly recalls his sensations at the moment when it seemed to him that at one moment he was dangling and gasping, and at the next when he was sitting up in bed watching with horror something which fluttered hideously on the wall, its tortured arms flung out as though from one crucified, its head jerking foully—something which suddenly writhed and crumpled to the floor out of the beam of the moon.

Mr. Partridge shouted and leapt from the bed, overturn-ing as he did so the table by the side. As he reached his feet the door opened, a candle flickered, and there was the manager of the Royal Hotel, in a night-shirt, with terror in his eyes. "I know what's the matter, sir," he mumbled, "it's my fault, I knew it would happen, but my wife thought—"

"Knew what would happen?" cried Mr. Partridge. "Tell me, is there anything on the floor there, is there a tree with a shadow out there? Is there? Is there?" His hands went to his throat.

"No, sir," said the worm, "it's all over, sir. I'm sorry, sir. I shouldn't have allowed it, sir. Come with me, sir."

Mr. Partridge put on his dressing-gown, and after one quick look back followed him down to the floor below.

"This is my room, sir," said the worm, opening a door. "You'll sleep here, sir; I'm sorry, sir."

"What is it? What have I seen?" cried Mr. Partridge, his nerves still dancing, but settling down.

"I don't really know, sir," said the worm. "But something happened in your room twenty-five years ago—long before I came. Some clerk it was, sir. Well, sir, he hanged himself."

"Yes," said Mr. Partridge, shuddering, "I know that."

"It seems, sir, he'd been taking the Bank's money for a good while; he wanted to marry and couldn't afford it, and he slipped away down here, but the police were after him, and followed him. Well, sir, something always happens in your room on the night of it. That's why it's always kept empty."

"Well then," asked Mr. Partridge, "why the devil did you put me into it?"

The worm looked limply and hen-peckedly at him.

"Oh, I know," said Mr. Partridge. "Because your wife hated to see fifteen shillings and sixpence go begging."

"Well, sir, I did take a room at the boarding-establishment."

"Has this happened before?"

"Yes, sir, twelve years ago, sir, the year I took over, and I didn't know about it. A gentleman was in there, and he screamed and woke the whole house. I promise you, it was against my wishes and better judgment that we let you be there, but my wife thought it might have passed off, and we're not usually so full at this time."

"Well," said Mr. Partridge, "before I take some aspirin and attempt to sleep, let me give you a word of advice. Make your wife sleep alone in that room this day next year!"

The worm smiled deprecatingly.

"Your things will be brought down in the morning, sir."

"All right, all right," said Mr. Partridge, "but tell me, is there a peg missing in that wall?"

"Yes, sir, it was the one on which—"

"All right, all right," said Mr. Partridge. "Call me at 8.30."

And, taking ten grains of aspirin, he soon after sank into a dreamless sleep.

At breakfast next morning Mr. Partridge made a brave effort to appear his usual calm, flippant self, but the sharp eye of Willie Cranmer, with whom he was playing a single that morning, was not deceived.

As they walked together to the club-house he remarked, "You had a bad night, Jim, tell me about it."

Mr. Partridge did so.

When he had finished, Cranmer said, "I did not tell you at the time, but that face at the window in the afternoon had not a very reassuring expression, and I saw it again just before we went to bed, but I thought it better to say nothing to you."

"Do you know, Willie, that, now I'm feeling almost all right again, the thing that impresses me is that until I had that experience last night I had never even vaguely conceived what it must be like to be driven to such vulgar lengths as embezzlement by such elementary impulses as love and poverty? Yet that sort of thing has been going on around me ever since I had eyes to see and read, ears to hear, and a mind to understand, though in my vanity I have considered myself rather a knowing fellow where humanity and its motives are concerned. I know now that I knew nothing about anything, above a certain pitch of intensity. I feel humiliated. What is it? How do these things happen?"

"Well," said Cranmer, "as we agreed last night, some of the cleverest minds in the world have been trying to answer those questions for thousands of years. Your experience last night is as inexplicable as it always would have been and, in my opinion, will ever be."

They had reached the first tee. Just below them baby waves frolicked in, chased by a small and scented breeze. Four alert, beady eyes, the property of a pair of black-headed gulls on the beach, regarded them sardonically. Mr. Partridge tried a practice swing, and then his hand went to his throat. He stroked it for a moment as he gazed out to sea.

Willie Cranmer noticed the little gesture, but merely said, "Now let's be serious!" And he teed up. A little later, being an Injudicious Hooker, he disappeared into a bunker on the left, simultaneously Mr. Partridge, a master of cuts, retired into its counterpart on the right. Two little spurts of sand leapt into the air. And then—two more!

An Echo

It was about a quarter past four on September 4th of last year that I knew, as I walked along a ride through Long Bottom Wood, that I was once again to be projected into a Fourth Dimension. I must explain, as well as I can, what I mean.

At irregular intervals I am compelled, though with extreme reluctance, to witness supernatural phenomena. Every haunted place seems longing to reveal its secret to me. There is a ghostly understanding between me and the Restless Ones. The experience I am about to relate was the fifty-sixth of its kind, and experts in this shadowy commerce tell me I am probably the most gifted clairvoyant known to the world.

They yield me this dubious palm for the certainty, precision and vividness of my recorded "successes." For some time I tried to keep my dismal talent secret, but I betrayed it unconsciously far too often.

I regard this peculiarity of mine as a nuisance, often a profoundly disturbing nuisance. From none of my experiences have I gained anything of good, and as far as throwing light on the nature of this or any other world they seem utterly useless. I have called them "supernatural," but they may be nothing of the kind; sometimes I doubt profoundly if they are.

As I say, I have no pride in my performances. I feel myself to be merely a peculiar kind of camera, the lens of which is sensitive to things to which an ordinary camera is insensitive.

The preliminary symptoms are always the same. Suddenly every sound, from the loudest to the softest, seems frozen in dreadful suspense. It is something more active than the mere absence of sound. Simultaneously everything is dimmed—a consistent toning down of every shade. It is as though I am gazing through one of those glasses used by artists when painting outdoors in too dazzling a light, and the world becomes sullen, brassy, livid. I feel that I am both within and without the bounds of reality, as though, as I have suggested, I have strayed into a fourth spatial dimension, a region dim, motionless, soundless. Once, when these first preliminary warnings came to me, I attempted to avoid seeing the vision I knew was coming, but it was in vain; some irresistible force compelled me to go through to the end—and now I never struggle.

The great love of my life is ornithology—to put it less pompously, I adore birds, and have written many articles and a few books about them. And this was the cause of my stay at Balland Manor, for its owner, Ronald Lawton, is an enthusiastic amateur, and had implored me to catalogue the birds on the estate. He and his wife were abroad on this occasion, so I had the house to myself, and very pleasant I found it. I had strolled out for an afternoon examination of the amazing nut-hatch colony in Long Bottom, when, just as I reached the last turn in the ride, there came that silence and that dimming, and I knew that round the corner something was waiting to reveal itself to me. It was there. Some eighty yards ahead of me a man was walking in the same direction as myself. He had a gun under his arm. Suddenly he stopped, looked first to his right and then to his left: as he did so a woman came out a little way from the trees and raised her arm to the level of her shoulder. The man turned to his right again, and then threw up his arms and fell. Then the woman ran out, picked up his gun, held it poised for a moment, dropped it again, and then stepped back to the shelter of the trees. As she did so she paused for a moment and then disappeared. Then the veil came down, rose again, and the birds were singing, the sun shining, and it was over and all trace of it was gone.

I turned at once and went back to the house. These experiences always distress me, and I feel nervous and depressed for some time afterwards. But the period varies; sometimes their memory speedily becomes blurred; sometimes the vividness lingers. It lingered on this occasion. I knew that I had witnessed some tragedy of the past, for these records are infallible, and in spite of my repulsion I felt a certain interest concerning it. I have said that I hate these manifestations; at the same time I must confess I sometimes feel a certain sense of curiosity.

I had never felt this curiosity so strongly on any previous appearance. So I left Balland the next morning, and in the evening went round to call upon a very old friend, Jim Myers, who, besides being an artist of very considerable and growing repute, is a fanatical criminologist. He greatly respects my singular gift.

"Hullo, Robert," said he, "I can see you've had another attack. It's curious, but your personality seems to echo them for days after."

"I believe," I replied, "I have seen the ghost of a murder, and that's why I've come to you."

"Tell me."

When I had finished I could see he was highly excited.

"It sounds marvellously like—where did you see this?"

"At a place called Balland Manor, near—"

But Jim had leapt to his feet. "My God, it is! it's the fifteenth anniversary, too. You mean to say you didn't remember and recognise it at once?"

"Remember what? Recognise what?" I asked.

"You're incredible, Robert. Do you mean to say you've never heard of the Balland Mystery?"

"I don't think so; I take no interest in those things."

"Well, I'm damned! Let me tell you, you've had the amazing experience of seeing solved before your eyes one of the greatest murder puzzles of all time." He went to a shelf and took down a book. "Here it is, a classic of the *Great Trials* series. I've read it a dozen times, and puzzled and wondered. Now, partly for my own amusement—for I love talking murder—and partly to show you what an absolutely marvellous and mysterious person you are, I'll tell you the story.

"Richard Eagles was at Univ, with me. He was a flabby animal of no marked attractions, and lots too much money. He was an orphan, and at twenty-one came into the Barton Estate, amongst a number of other very pleasant things.

"He was by no means a genius where men were concerned, and about women he was a complete ass. He wasn't what we mean by a womaniser exactly, but he had a mania for being seen about with female celebrities of the lighter sort. Most of them spent his money avidly, but he had a streak of caution inherited from his very able father, and, as he was a bore into the bargain, he was forced to change his partner pretty frequently. These ladies pretended to like him at first, but made him realise that "that little more and what worlds away" was only to be obtained via a Registrar's Office; but Richard was not the marrying sort; the streak of caution saved him, and he disappointed them one by one. It used to be quite a joke in the old days, for these so jealously guarded charms were often surprisingly surrendered by their fair owners, and even I remember being present at a capitulation or two. Acquit me of boasting. Like you, Robert, I have reached the age when one is visited neither by pangs of conscience nor gusts of vanity by the remembrance of successful indiscretion; at an age, in other words, when emotions of that *genre* are recollected with tranquility.

"Eventually, probably inevitably, however, he got caught, and one ill-omened evening he was introduced to Miss Patty

Golden at the Regent Night Club, where she was the professional dancer.

"All that could be known about this young person's antecedents and mode of life came out at the trial. Both her mother and father, who had kept a small shop at Luton, were dead. Apparently they had been completely commonplace individuals, but by some Mendelian miracle they had produced between them one of the most fascinating human animals on whom it has been my, or anybody's else's, luck to cast an eye. I tell you frankly that, if she had gone for me, I would have gone to the devil for her myself.

"Her hair was a most shining auburn, her eyes large, violet sirens, her figure delicious—at least by the standards of those times, and they are still mine. But hosts of damsels can display such charms more or less; what they don't possess is the amazing vitality, sparkle and 'devil' which Patty had more than any woman I have ever known.

"That she was a completely immoral little 'gold-digger' was apparent at a glance, but it was not generally realised till the trial that she was utterly vicious, and perhaps something more; but her personal fascination was such that men could not resist her, even though they realised perfectly she was a soulless little tough, out for money and for nothing else.

"When Richard met her she was living with a blackguard called Mason, a man of good family, but born with a seed of evil in him which had flowered freely. He was the leader and brains of a gang who made it their highly lucrative business to complete the education of young gentlemen with money. And brilliantly led as they were, they succeeded in ruining more than one, fleecing dozens, and dodging Scotland Yard. Patty was one of the cleverest and toughest of the bunch, and, as a dancer at a fashionable night club, she occupied an admirable strategic position. Richard was a rich prize. Patty, who had planned the introduction, mobilised all her powers, and he was immediately overwhelmed. They became inseparable. Richard's infatuation made him an abject, drivelling serf, and there is no doubt he bored her to screaming point, and I am certain she resolved to make a quick job of it. But while she could get plenty of small sums and unlimited entertainment out of him, that saving streak of caution stopped him from signing any big cheques, and it was the big cheques she was after. Eventually, there is no doubt, though it was disputed at the trial, she forced him to make a will leaving her £30,000. She claimed in the box that he had done this unknown to her and that she was expecting to marry him.

"By this time Richard's friends—and he had a few decent ones—were warning him very vigorously about the character of the object of his devotion, and one of them at the trial stated that Richard had sworn to him he would never marry her, and would do his best to conquer his infatuation.

"Well, this will was signed on August 25th, and on September 2nd Patty and her 'chaperone,' an elderly shark, also, of course, a member of the gang, and Richard went down to Balland for the week-end. On the Monday afternoon, the 4th, your day, Robert, the two went out, leaving the shark to her 'knitting,' Richard carrying a gun, and walked in the direction of Long Bottom. About half an hour after, a shot or two shots—testimony at the trial differed—were heard, and a little later Patty came running back to the house, apparently in a great state of agitation, saying that Richard had stumbled and as he fell his gun had gone off, and he was lying in the ride dead. According to her story she had been walking behind him, and had not seen very clearly how the tragedy occurred.

"At the inquest she repeated her story, and the local doctor, who obviously and naturally believed her, gave evidence which decided the jury unhesitatingly to bring in a verdict of 'Accidental death.' And that might have been the end of the story but for the fact that Sir Rex Moore, the greatest expert on head wounds in the world, had read the very full description the local doctor had given of the injuries to Richard's head, and considered it his duty to write to Scotland Yard, stating that in his opinion it was impossible for the injuries described to have been caused by a gunshot wound, even if fired at the closest range. About the same time it came to the knowledge of the Yard that the only witness of the tragedy had been someone who was going to benefit to the tune of £30,000 by it, and, moreover, that this person was one to whom their attention had been drawn on more than one occasion. By a coincidence, about the same time they succeeded at last in running Mason to earth for an ingenious fraud, rather luckily discovered. Amongst his papers was found a letter which, combined with the other suspicious circumstances, led to the arrest of Patty for murder. Incidentally the police relied enormously on the evidence of Sir Rex, which he had formulated in great detail.

"Richard's body was exhumed and examined by Sir Rex and the expert medical witnesses for the defence.

"The trial began on November 10th at the Old Bailey, and stirred the interest of the public more than any murder trial of the century. So like you, Robert, not to have heard of it!

"The Attorney General led for the Crown and Sir Leonard Venables, K.C., for the defence. As I don't suppose you have heard of him either, I may say he was the greatest verdict-getter who ever wore a wig. His florid, fruity style exactly suited a jury. His voice was beautifully musical and persuasive, and he used it like an artist. Altogether, he commanded gifts as a pleader which more than one guilty murderer had cause to bless.

"Patty's sojourn in prison had not damaged her looks. She was more beautiful than I had ever seen her, and seemed full of confidence and fight.

"The two strongest cards the prosecution had to play were the evidence of Sir Rex and the letter found in Mason's flat.

"The surgeon was examined and cross-examined at great length. Most of his evidence is meaningless to a layman, but he held unswervingly to his opinion that the injuries to the head could not have been caused by a gunshot, but were certainly the result of a rifle or revolver bullet which had glanced off after striking. He stated that his examination at the autopsy had more than supported his early suspicions. The only admission useful to it which the defence could extract from him was that decomposition had set in strongly by the time the body was exhumed. With regard to the letter, the prosecution merely proved its discovery at Mason's flat and that it was in the handwriting of the accused. It ran as follows:

"Sept. 7th.　　　　　　　　　　　　　　Balland Manor,
　　　　　　　　　　　　　　　　　　　　　　Bucks.

"Dear Tim,
"The agreement all along was for you to get a third and I see no reason to change it. It will be some time before I get anything, and anyway practically the whole risk was mine. I have to stay here till after the inquest. I believe everything will be O.K. But don't ask for more, you won't get it.
　　"'P.'

"The first witness for the defence was a famous hospital surgeon, who was shown to have had wide experience of shooting cases. He had taken part in the examination of the body, and declared that in his opinion the injuries might have been caused by a shotgun in the manner described by the prisoner, but that all possibility of giving a categorical answer was destroyed by the fact that decomposition had proceeded so far.
　　"Briefly and non-technically the whole point lay in whether the injuries were the result of a glancing blow from a charge of shot or a glancing blow from a bullet—in either case fired at point-blank range. All this would remind you, had you read of it, Robert, of that matchless mystery, the Ardlamont Case.

"This witness was examined and cross-examined for a full two hours, and searching questions were volleyed at him. Near the end he was beginning to give ground, but he just held out to the end, and regained some of his confidence in re-examination.

"A curious piece of evidence was then brought forward by the defence. It was that of a local farmer, who stated that about two hours after the tragedy he found one of his sheep dead in the field, and he found on examining it several pellets in its head. It was lying exactly opposite the spot where the body had been found, and it was proved that the trees in between were heavily marked by pellet scars, showing that a charge had been fired from the ride, through the trees, to the sheep. Do you remember, Robert, seeing her pick up his gun?

"Then came the question of the hypothetical revolver. The police were closely examined as to their efforts to find it. They confessed they had searched the whole terrain in the neighbourhood of the tragedy, but had discovered nothing, and there was no evidence to show that Patty ever had a revolver in her possession, either before or after the affair.

"Then Sir Leonard took his courage into both hands, and Patty stepped into the box to give evidence on her own behalf, the first woman to avail herself of that dubious privilege since the passing of the Act.

"She was marvellously composed, and under her counsel's tactful handling gave a consistent and coherent account of her relations with Richard and the events of the fatal day.

"Eventually he came to the letter. Of course the two dangerous sentences were, 'Anyway I took practically all the risk,' and 'I think everything will be O.K.' She explained that by 'risk' she meant the risk of Richard not marrying her after all her trouble. 'Everything will be O.K.' she said, referred to the possibility of the will being disputed.

"Sir Leonard did not question her very closely, preferring to wait for his re-examination.

"Then the Attorney-General rose, and that famous duel began. Patty gave him one of her indomitable looks as he asked her his first question. He went straight to the letter.

"'I take it there was an agreement between you and this man Mason by which you were to share any monies to be obtained from the dead man?'

"'That is so.'

"'How did you expect to obtain these monies?'

"'Do you mean originally?'

"'Yes.'

"'Well, he gave me money at times, but chiefly by my marriage with him.'

"'Did you consider yourself engaged to him?'

"'Informally, yes.'

"'Informally? Do you mean that you knew he didn't want to marry you, but that you were determined to force him to do so?'

"'Certainly not. I believed he fully intended to marry me.'

"'You have heard the evidence of a friend of his implying very strongly the contrary.'

"'Yes, but Richard was rather weak and inclined to agree with the person he was with.'

"'If you were certain he intended to marry, wherein lay the risk to which you refer?'

"(A pause.) 'There was always a risk of the marriage not taking place.'

"'Although you were convinced he intended it?'

"'Yes, but certain things might have prevented it; his death has done so, as a matter of fact.'

"'Did you regard his death as probable?'

"'No, certainly not.'

"'Did your agreement with this man cover any sums obtained in any way?'

"'Yes.'

"'Sums obtained from the will?'

"'Yes, all sums.'

"'But you told us under examination that you did not know you were to benefit by his will?'

"(A pause.) 'I didn't know, but I suspected he might leave me a small amount.'

"'But surely you had no reason to suspect that Mr. Eagles would die for forty or fifty years. Why should anything so problematical have formed part of your agreement with Mason?'

"'The agreement covered all sums. I forget if we actually mentioned anything about a will.'

"'Had you told Mason you suspected he had left you something?'

"'I can't remember, as I say. I don't think so, but it's possible.'

"'You have told us that you did not encourage Mr. Eagles to leave you anything.'

"'I did not.'

"'Nor try to discover the amount?'

"'No, it hardly interested me. I expected to marry him and have money settled on me.'

"'Very well, we will leave that.'

"While the Attorney was looking through his papers Patty passed her handkerchief across her lips and forehead, and then set her teeth.

"'You concluded your letter by saying, "I believe everything will be O.K." Are you sure that doesn't refer to the verdict at the inquest?'

"(Sharply.) 'Yes, perfectly sure.'

"'Then to what did it refer?'

"'I have already said that it referred to the money I should get under the will.'

"'Yet you weren't sure you were to get a penny?'

"'I can't be sure, I thought the lawyer had told me.'

"'You know he has denied that.'

"'Yes, but he may be wrong.'

"'But if he is right, you didn't know you had inherited a penny?'

"'I have told you I strongly suspected he had left me something.'

"'If he had, why was there any doubt about your getting it?'

"'I thought it might be disputed.'

"'On what grounds?'

"'Undue influence, I suppose.'

"'Now I want to be fair to you. Do you seriously suggest that the Jury should believe that "It will be O.K." referred, and referred only, to a legacy the very existence of which was unknown to you?'

"'It is the truth; as I say, I believe the lawyer *had* told me about it.'

"Those are the salient passages," said Myers, "but there was much else. Patty's character disappeared beneath the rain of questions, but her reputation for pluck was never more convincingly justified.

"Her counsel in his re-examination set himself to counteract the very perilous impression left by these answers.

"'Had you heard anything which made you realise there was a serious risk that your marriage would not take place?'

"'I knew that people, enemies of mine, were warning Mr. Eagles about me.'

"'And you were afraid he would act on their advice?'

"'Yes, he had spoken to me about it.'

"'About this legacy—had you good reasons for suspecting its existence?'

"'Yes, Mr. Eagles frequently said he would see that I was provided for if anything happened to him.'

"'When you referred to the risk, can you explain a little more clearly what was in your mind?'

"'Well, I thought it might be disputed on the ground of undue influence—not that I have used any, but, as I have said, I have many enemies.'

"To understand the beauty—to criminologists—of this duel concerning the letter, the whole of Patty's examination and cross-examination should be closely studied. For five long hours Patty's life was hanging by a thread.

"Sir Leonard, in order to neutralise the deadly implications in her letter, had been compelled reluctantly to reveal that she had a very strong motive. If she knew of the legacy she had 30,000 good reasons for shooting Richard; if she was ignorant of it, that terrible word 'risk' could not be explained.

"In my opinion they were the five finest hours the Old Bailey has given us.

"When the Attorney-General got up to make his closing speech everyone felt it was touch and go. He was perfectly fair, but perfectly firm. The evidence he marshalled would have been deadly but for the conflict in the medical evidence and the absence of the revolver. He characterised Patty's answers about the letter as incredible.

"Then Sir Leonard got up and made the speech of his life. He began with one of his most impressive exordia.

"'Gentlemen of the Jury, the prisoner at the Bar is accused of murder. If she is found guilty of that foul crime she will meet in three weeks' time a shameful, felon's death. On my poor efforts depend her defence: on your verdict her liberty or death. Gentlemen, it is an awful responsibility that you and I must share.'

"He made no attempt to disguise the fact that his client was a hardened little scoundrel, but he impressed on the Jury how much more she had to gain, and gain in perfect safety, by marrying Richard than by taking the frightful risk entailed by murdering him. She would not have been the calculating little intriguer which she had shown herself, if she had failed to realise the inevitable suspicion which was bound to fall upon her when the terms of the will became known. People of her type did not commit murders, they steadily fleeced, and so great was the dead man's infatuation she had every reason to believe she could force him to marry her, when she could fleece him to her heart's content.

"So did he dismiss the question of motive.

"He emphasised the sharp and irreconcilable conflict in the medical evidence. Would the Jury ever know a moment's peace if they sent her to the gallows when such doctors could disagree?

"He made much of the absence of the revolver, and—this will interest you, Robert—he asked how could the shot have been fired? The dead man was shot from the front at point blank range. He must have stood stock still and calmly allowed the prisoner to blow his brains out. Was it conceivable?

"The letter of which the prosecution made so much was perfectly capable of bearing the construction the prisoner put upon it. In a peroration of majestic power he demanded that the prisoner be given the benefit of the doubt. 'If she is guilty,' he concluded, 'she will not escape, for there is One Who knows all: Vengeance is His, He will repay!'

"The Judge's summing up was quiet and eminently judicial. On the whole it inclined, and I think rightly to the defence. The police had not made out their case.

"At length the Jury filed out, and Patty was taken out of Court, her eyes blazing with excitement, and two red stains flaming in her cheeks. The Jury were out for three and a-half hours. It was known afterwards that two of them long held out for a verdict of guilty, but in the end gave way, and in a quivering silence the foreman pronounced 'Not guilty,' which would undoubtedly have been 'Not proven' in Scotland.

"And that, Robert, was the end of the 'Balland Mystery'— till you took that afternoon stroll."

"What happened to Patty?" I asked.

"She dodged the vast crowd awaiting her, and disappeared from the knowledge of men till two years later she was found dead from an overdose of cocaine in a Buenos Aires Hotel—she had been 'White-slaving' apparently. She made no attempt to get the £30,000, Richard's next of kin winning the action for undue influence unopposed. Mason died in prison three years after the trial."

"Now tell me again just exactly what you saw."

I did so. When I had finished he said, "There was one little detail you mentioned that time which you didn't mention before: you say she paused for a moment by a tree?"

"Yes, she just hesitated for a moment or two and then disappeared."

"Look here," said Myers, "this fascinates me. Could I come down with you and see the place?"

"Of course you can," I said. "We can go tomorrow if you like."

"We'll go down in the car," said Myers. "I'll pick you up at ten."

We lunched at the house, and then walked down to the scene of my vision. I pointed out to my highly excited companion the exact spot, and he regarded it reverently.

"Was this the tree?" he asked, pointing to a fine cedar.

"Yes," I replied.

"And she paused just here?"

"Yes."

Myers examined the trunk carefully, and then turned to me suddenly. "Look here," he said, and he pointed to a hole of medium size about the level of his waist in the cedar.

"Good Lord!" he said, "I wonder! I wonder! Look here, run up to the house and see if you can find a strong knife, I want to get my arm into that hole."

I eventually waylaid a gardener, who produced a knife, which I took back to Myers. He set to work, and after a few minutes he put down the knife, and with a look of extreme excitement on his face, thrust in his arm to the shoulder. "Empty!" he groaned. "No, by God! it's not!" He drew up his arm. "Robert, you are the most wonderful man in the world. Do you know what I've got in my hand?"

He drew his hand clear of the hole and then opened it, and there was the neatest little Colt revolver. He jerked it open, and there were six cartridges, five unused, one used.

Others Who
Returned

(1929)

"A figure whose right of presence I instantly and passionately questioned."

The Turn of the Screw.

"Treat all supernatural beings with respect, but keep aloof from them—then you may be called wise."

CONFUCIUS.

"I have heard, but not believed, the spirits of the dead may walk again."

. . . .

. . . .

. . . .

(Exit pursued by a bear)

ANTIGONUS.

Old Man's Beard

Mr. Bickley almost precisely satisfies our American friends' definition of a "Regular Feller." That is to say, he makes an article of commerce, and by selling it at seven times its cost of production has prospered greatly. Mr. Bickley has merely supertax worries. He is a good "mixer"—he knows sixty-three persons by their Christian names: he is always ready to talk golf shop, with particular reference to a gross eighty-seven he once shot on a short course burnt to a cinder. He makes almost exactly the same slice off the first tee twice on Saturday and twice on Sunday, and can stow away several rounds of drinks without becoming unduly pugnacious, verbose or pleased with himself. He goes to and from the City in a big car and smokes a big cigar during the process. And so on and so on. But he slightly diverges from type in two respects; he quite frequently reads a book that has neither been written by Mr. Edgar Wallace nor recommended to him for its candid treatment of the Sex Question, and he hasn't got quite the orthodox Regular Feller's life partner. Mrs. Bickley is a bit of an enigma to the other R. F.'s. Sometimes they are reassured that she is just what she ought to be—a "lovely little woman," again in our American friends' idiom—the adjective being a tribute to her character rather than her physical charms—though these are still considerable. But at other times the R. F.'s have an unpalatable impression that she would like to take them by the shoulders and drown them in deep water. And then they are rather afraid of her and very sorry for Mr. Bickley. As a matter of fact her mother was an Hungarian and temperamental, one who found even the Buda-Pesth variety of R. F. so desperately, irredeemably deadly that none such ventured for long into her presence. She had been the Perfect Mistress in her youth, a Perfect Wife to an Englishman of high intelligence in her middle age, and a formidable and indomitable old woman. In her daughter these characteristics were strongly diluted by Anglo-Saxon tolerance and phlegm; though sufficient of the fiery spirit remained to save her from becoming just a British Female Yawn. She was an avid but virtuous flirt in her youth, she is at present a perfect wife for an Englishman of no particular intelligence, and in her old age she will probably be a bit of an autocrat and a nuisance. And there are still to be found traces of that scarifying old mother of hers; sudden sharp explosions caused by boredom; quick, short-lived ardours for good-looking men with brains—though she meets very few—and apparently causeless fits of temper, so uncontrollable and uncompromising that poor Mr. Bickley—that nice little man—has always urgently watched the temperamental development of his daughter and only child, Mariella, for symptoms of that dangerous and irregular Mittel-European strain. And, though they are still further diluted, they are there. She is all right in many respects. She is physically flawless and saved from being merely the ordinary, full-blooded, smooth-skinned, regular-featured *Daily Mirror* bathing belle by a delicate upward slant of her eyelids, and a certain indefinable but captivating chic, by an air of slightly exotic breeding and an absolute incapacity for giggling at little odd erotic moments. Again, though she is as intellectually incurious as a portable wireless set she is as sexually inquisitive as a curate, and in Mr. Bickley's opinion she knew What Every Young Girl Ought To Know much sooner than any young girl ought to know it. At the age of fifteen she had driven the chauffeur—a most high-minded young man—almost out of his mind by the warmth of her feelings towards him, and when they were discovered together by Mrs. Bickley he had spilled indignant protests all over the garage where Mariella had neatly cornered him. After this infatuation faded, she had experienced a succession of hurried, hot passions for a number of hopelessly ineligible youths, so that Mr. Bickley, with a meanness only excused by his desperation, once upbraided her mother for introducing this culpable and devilish strain into the staid and seemly Bickley stock. Whereupon, the Old Lady being in the ascendant, he got about five times as good as he gave and spent a restless night composing a dignified letter to *The Times* on the dangers of mixed marriages.

And then came that most desired return to Bickleyism, for Mariella accepted the hand—the in every way desirable hand—of young Arthur Randall. Six weeks before it hadn't been desirable at all, for then he had been extremely impecunious, and merely—or so at least it appeared—a superlative player of games. Mariella had seen him make eighty-four runs against Larwood, Barratt and Staples when the dust was flying, and beat three men in succession to score the winning try against Wales, and as the applause rose and towered she had made up her mind, and prepared herself for a long and fiercely contested battle with her father. And then Arthur's uncle suddenly slipped his anchor, leaving his nephew £80,000. This timely and unexpected event eased the situation completely, and Mariella was soon flourishing a solitaire diamond ring and the wedding was fixed for the end of October. The beginning of August found them all installed in a well-appointed furnished house at that aristocratic resort, Brinton-on-Sea, which Mr. Bickley had rented for seven weeks.

This confinement within four walls gave Mr. Bickley a not too earnestly desired opportunity of scrutinising the character of his prospective son-in-law, so far as that young gentleman permitted him to do so. Physically he was beyond criticism. Tall, lithe and dark he had exceptional vitality and perfect health. He was a joy to look upon, and the fact that he had stood up to the Notts fast bowlers for two hours, and had picked their short ones off his nose and plunked them up against the square-leg boundary was sufficient evidence of his courage and pugnacity, as was that vicious "handoff" which had turned the Welsh full-back turtle and given him a very sore jaw-bone for a week. It would have been very soothing to have been able to couple these moral qualities and physical attributes with £80,000 and find nothing more to scrutinise. But Mr. Bickley reluctantly and irritably nosed up something else; something enigmatic, elusive, buried so deep, as it were, that Mr. Bickley felt his nose was only long enough to unearth its fringes and vague outline. What was it? Well, it sometimes revealed itself in sudden and most unexpected flashes of brutal, ruthless insight, almost a devilish sort of flourished egoism, most singular in so usually commonplace a master of moving spheres and ovals. Yet was he ever quite commonplace? Wasn't that orthodox exterior possibly a very cunningly adjusted mask? Unpleasant questions which Mr. Bickley reprimanded his mind for asking about his prospective son-in-law. Yet they had some justification. For example, on one occasion they had all been sitting on the beach and he had been reading out from the *Daily Express* an account of the lamentable defalcations of a former business acquaintance, with appropriate comments. And then young Randall had suddenly stared into his face with a most ironical and piercing expression and said, "There, but for a spot of caution and the grace of Old Nick, went Horace Bickley." Which was exceedingly rude, and he hoped, unjustified. It had taken him very much aback, though both Mariella and her mother had seemed amused. And then again, when they had been discussing a peculiarly unpleasant murder of a young woman by a solicitor's clerk, and marvelling how he could have brought himself to commit such an atrocity, young Randall had remarked with frigid detachment, "She

probably bored him, and if by slitting her gullet he prevented her from boring any one else, I consider he did a service
to Society." He said something unexpected and in bad taste
like that quite often. Did he mean such things? He certainly
appeared to. So he couldn't be quite ordinary. Was that a
good or a bad thing? Well, Mariella wasn't quite ordinary
either. All those difficult, adolescent tendencies, now so
pleasantly dormant, that her foreign blood explained but
didn't eliminate, and other little signs here and there showed
she had a slight streak of some kind. Perhaps their prospects
of marital happiness would be increased by the fact that each
was slightly peculiar, and certainly it was most reassuring
that young Randall seemed so utterly devoted to Mariella,
fiercely and fanatically so, and she seemed to have concentrated at last in a sort of smouldering and unvarying way.

Mr. Bickley had waded his way through the evidence to a
fairly favourable summing-up when something else came to
worry him. Mariella didn't seem very flourishing. The family
G. P. had described her as the most flawless physical specimen he had ever examined, and the sun and sea and air of
Brinton should have put the keenest edge on this brilliant
Toledo Blade, and the close presence of her lover should have
made her spirit leap within her. But the actual result was
depressingly different. After the first few days she seemed
limp and lethargic and "snappy" in the mornings. She shook
this off during the day, but began to droop again at sundown
and showed a marked distaste for going to bed; not a distaste
born of overmastering vitality, but something less reassuring,
something less readily explicable. Her mother had noticed it,
of course, and was rather worried, had questioned her gently
and been testily repulsed.

Look at her now, for example, just come in from bathing
on such a glorious day, and young Randall gazing at her with
such undisguised adoration. What more could she want? Yet
she seemed shadowed, brooding over something. She really
almost looked ill and yet, in a purely physical sense, radiantly

healthy—it must be some mental trouble; but what conceivable reason could there be for it? Yes, she was looking in that way worse than he'd ever seen her look, worse even than when he'd kicked that ghastly young dancing partner creature down the steps at home. It then occurred to Mr. Bickley that his old friend, Sir Perseus Farrar, had just arrived at the Royal Hotel, and that he was the greatest authority in Europe on that awful and occult business, the female nervous system. How Mr. Bickley admired a man who had the audacity to make a living out of delving into that monstrous region, that scarifying inferno! He knew it was an unforgivable sin to consult members of the medical profession out of office hours, and especially while on holiday, but Sir Perseus was such an old friend and kindly person and so fond of Mariella that he'd risk it, if she didn't get better. So far from getting better she burst into hysterical tears in the middle of breakfast the very next morning, ran up to her bedroom, locked the door and refused to see any one. So Mr. Bickley trotted round to the Royal. He found Sir Perseus smoking in the lounge, and forthwith burst into a halting recital concerning Mariella, liberally studded with apologies. These Sir Perseus cut short. "My dear Horace," he said, "I was just thinking when you came in how glad I should be to have a little work to do. I'm always like that after a week's idling, and though I am very sorry that that which will rescue me from my sloth is some trouble with my dear and exquisite Mariella, I don't suppose there's much wrong, and if I can set it right, I shall feel doubly grateful to you for allowing me to don my harness for an hour or two. I'll drop in casually after lunch." Which he did, and Mariella came out of her seclusion to greet him. By arrangement Mrs. Bickley and young Randall had gone out before his arrival, and very soon Mr. Bickley found an excuse to absent himself. Sir Perseus was not a famous authority on the female nervous system for nothing, and within a quarter of an hour Mariella was telling him something to which he was listening with an absorbed

and authoritative attention. At the end of half an hour he
began to ask questions, and at the end of an hour he patted her hand and told her there was nothing seriously to
fuss about, but that unless she objected he would like her to
put herself in his hands, by which he meant that she should
tell him at once anything else which happened, and confide
absolutely in him. She agreed thankfully. And then he left
her with a very puzzled and thoughtful expression on his face
and, as arranged, met Mr. Bickley on the front.

They sat down on a seat overlooking the sea, on which
Sir Perseus stared for a time, while Mr. Bickley waited rather
anxiously for him to speak.

"I don't think it's anything at all serious," said Sir Perseus at length, "but very unpleasant for her, poor child. It's
a nightmare she's been having. I asked her if she were accustomed to dream, and she replied with great candour that ever
since she could remember she had dreamed frequently and
vividly of young men."

Mr. Bickley shuffled on his seat, his thoughts winging
back. "I suppose," he said, "that's quite usual, quite natural?
I mean, most young girls dream of young men."

"Oh, quite, quite," replied Sir Perseus; "but I gather that
her dreams have been exceptionally, well—vivid. I was relieved to hear it, for it makes the deep etching of this nightmare less hard to explain. Apparently she experienced it for
the first time ten days ago—on the second evening she was
here. She has had it twice since. It takes this form. As she
relates it, her room appears to be divided into two parts; that
in which she herself is is in darkness, the rest of the room is
highly lighted. In it there is a bed, rather a big bed, and on it
is an old man with a longish, grey beard wearing a nightshirt.
He is apparently writhing in great agony. He is twisting over
and over, his hands to his heart, his head flung back. And
then he suddenly rolls over and drops from the bed to the
floor and is hidden from her. Then the light seems to spread
towards her across the carpet, and she sees between the bed

and where she is placed a coffin on the ground. And it seems to her as though there must be many cracks in this coffin, for long grey hair is streaming through it, some coiled over the lid and some streaming upwards. And presently the lid starts slowly to rise, and then the whole room is in darkness, and she has the impression that something is moving towards her and then bending over her, and she feels something spreading over her face—hair, she thinks; she has a sensation of suffocation, and awakes."

"My God!" cried Mr. Bickley. "That is foul, dreadful! Poor little girl, what a bestial, terrifying experience!"

"Yes," replied Sir Perseus, "it is one of the most disgusting and unnerving dreams of the kind I have ever had described to me. There must be some explanation of it. Recurrent nightmares of this type are invariably the echo—stored in the subconscious—of some sharp experience once upon a time recorded. That sounds obscure, and it is so, but I have known very many such cases. Can you recall anything in Mariella's short existence which, when regurgitated, as it were, might cause this beastly dream; anything to do with a grey-bearded man, for example?"

"Nothing whatever," said Mr. Bickley, emphatically. "I have certainly come across grey-bearded men in the course of business and so on, but I cannot remember that Mariella ever met one." ("But what a lot of men Mariella has taken to," he thought to himself. "It is conceivable there *was* one with a grey beard, but it is excessively improbable.")

"I stress the detail of the beard," continued Sir Perseus, "because it seems to be the *hair* which sharply dominates this dream, and chiefly disturbs Mariella's mind; for example, when she broke down at breakfast it was because, so she told me, she saw some one with a grey beard pass by the window, which shows how sensitive she is to, and preoccupied by, the hair element. And I am convinced that she must have had some shock—long ago quite possibly—connected with a person so adorned, and that this vile dream is a throw-back to this experience. I have told her to sift her memory for something of the kind. I am interested in her case, not only for professional reasons—I am very fond of her—and I feel it is up to me to exorcise this horror. She is too young and too innocent to be made a victim of such devilry. She has agreed to put herself in my hands and consult me at once if there are any developments. I will send her a sleeping-draught, and I suggest she should not sleep alone. She had better have her mother with her in the same room, also a night-light, and try to give her as amusing and *tiring* a day as possible."

"I certainly will," said Mr. Bickley, "and I'm deeply grateful to you for taking up the case—if that isn't too alarming a way of putting it. She shall sleep in our room and I'll move into hers. But, good heavens, if I thought as I got into bed I was doomed to have that dream, I should never dare to close my eyes!"

"Remember this," said Sir Perseus; "if you actually had such a dream it would not seem quite as dreadful as you expected it to be; that is an axiom of human experience. It is not quite as shocking to Mariella as you think it must be. Nevertheless, it is loathsome enough, and therefore we've got to be very gentle and swift-witted with her. Oh, these dreams—how often I've puzzled over them! I've always firmly maintained they were distorted echoes of reality, though I know there is a school which regards them as nothing of the sort, but as reflections from another mode of consciousness, so that they can be prophetic—more than that—definitely another existence as it were, so much so that if the dreaming faculty was fostered to its highest voltage, waking up might be equivalent to slipping into dreamland, and sinking into dreamland really waking up; but that is too hard a saying for my old cranium to digest. But the land of dreams is largely an unexplored terrain, or anyway unsuccessfully mapped and surveyed, and Mariella's case

sharply reminds me of it. And now I must be off, my dear
Horace. Don't worry, we will make her once more as sweetly
light-hearted and fancy-free as she deserves to be."

When Mr. Bickley got back to the house Mariella had
gone to lie down, but her mother and young Randall were
awaiting him. He retailed to them a brief résumé of what Sir
Perseus had told him. Mrs. Bickley had one admirable trait;
in moments of crisis she acted first and talked afterwards,
though most certainly she talked afterwards! So with hardly
a word she bustled off to see about the change of rooms and
the purchase of night-lights. Compared with young Randall's
reception of the news hers seemed almost callous and unfeel-
ing. For he became highly agitated and upset to an extent
that slightly surprised Mr. Bickley, for surely it wasn't as
bad as all that! Young Randall went very white, and cross-
examined him closely and urgently concerning the details of
Mariella's nightmare, and seemed more and more distressed
at every additional detail of it. As if such minutiae made any
great difference, wondered Mr. Bickley. How very much in
love with her he must be! He felt compelled to impress on
him that they must all do as Sir Perseus had decreed and keep
Mariella's spirits up and her mind off her trouble as much as
possible, and so on; but young Randall hardly seemed to be
listening to these excellent platitudes, and if he hadn't been
drinking a good deal when he came down to dinner, Mr.
Bickley was no judge of the earlier stages of intoxication.
Mariella, on the other hand, seemed better, and the doctor's
visit had restored her confidence. And this was justified, for
under the influence of the sleeping-draught she enjoyed ten
hours of dreamless slumber and was very glad to have her
mother by her side and a tiny light shining between them.
The next morning she was in excellent spirits, and once more
keenly appreciative of those glances of masculine admiration
and feminine envy which she always evoked as she slipped
her wrap from her shoulders and stepped slowly down the

beach to the sea. She was—and still is for that matter—five feet nine inches and a half in height, magnificently "marshalled." The peculiar beauty of her figure is due to the fact that while she seems very long from hip to knee, she is one inch longer from knee to foot, and her torso, rippling, taut and beautifully developed, is just exactly proportionately right. When the critical eye of the Brinton visitor turned from her perfection to the many other "very good figures" on the beach, their slight but recognisable flaws seemed brutally intensified. And then those tantalisingly lifted eyelids! Well, young Randall was deemed a damned lucky dog so soon to have all those rare felicities to sample. Yet on that occasion he didn't look as if he sufficiently appreciated the fact. He looked morose and hardly said a word. "A thick night or a tiff" surmised the knowing onlookers.

Sir Perseus looked in during the afternoon and professed himself quite satisfied with the patient. And for forty-eight hours he had every reason to be. But three nights later Mrs. Bickley woke up suddenly and looked across to Mariella. She was lying on her back and moving about with a slight incessant restlessness. "Shall I wake her?" thought her mother. "No, I'll wait a little while, it may be nothing." Presently Mariella's motions became more rapid, pronounced and urgent. And then she sat up in bed and began thrusting with her hands, and then brushing her face as if to free it from something which was spreading over it. This impressed her mother very horribly, and she jumped out of bed and went over to her, spoke her name, and touched her gently. And presently she awoke, her eyes staring, her body trembling. And then she burst into tears. Her mother gave her a sleeping-draught, stroked her hair and comforted her, and took her to her own bed. Soon her sobbing became less violent and, as the drug allied itself with her exhaustion, she fell into a deep sleep. Mrs. Bickley, however, didn't close her eyes again that night. Early next morning she rang up Sir Perseus, who was vaguely reassuring. "Whatever the cause," he said, "it cannot be expected that complete recovery can be immediate." For the present he ordered a sleeping-draught every night.

Mariella seemed listless but fairly cheerful and, after her bathe, almost her usual self. Mr. Bickley was worried, but succeeded in disguising the fact. Young Randall was told nothing about it. And then there was another three days' pause and every one's spirits rose again.

Mariella's temperament demanded a certain amount of solitude. She had found a very secluded spot wherein to rest and read in the afternoons, and she liked to go there alone after tea for a while. It was beside a groin about half a mile from the house. She used to go there in her bathing dress and have a dip just before going back to change for dinner.

On the fourth day after her bad night she strolled down there about five o'clock. Randall and her father were playing golf, and Mrs. Bickley was busy with the laundry. Mariella usually returned about half-past six, but on this occasion a quarter-past seven struck and still she had not appeared.

"We'd better go and fetch her," said Mr. Bickley to young Randall. "She may have gone to sleep." He tried to keep all trace of uneasiness out of his voice, but each knew the other was anxious as they walked at top speed towards that cosy little spot under the shelter of the groin. What they saw when they reached it made young Randall leap recklessly down the fifteen feet from the sea-wall to the beach, while Mr. Bickley ran for the steps. For Mariella lay sprawled down the shingle. Her beach cloak had draped itself over her head so that only her legs were visible. Her book lay where she had flung it, almost at the water's edge. Young Randall pulled back the cloak. Her face was dead white and she was unconscious. He dashed down to the sea, soaked his handkerchief and squeezed the water over Mariella's face, but she showed no sign of recovery. "We must carry her back," said Mr. Bickley. By good fortune a taxi was passing just as they got her to the top of the steps, and three minutes later she was lying on her bed and Mr. Bickley was telephoning to Sir Perseus. He was in, and the taxi was sent to fetch him. Meanwhile Mrs. Bickley and young Randall were busy with restoratives and hot-water bottles.

Mariella was just conscious but quite dazed when Sir Perseus arrived. After a few hurried words with Mr. Bickley he went upstairs and asked to be left alone with his patient. Half an hour later he left her in charge of her mother and came downstairs. He was looking grave as he joined the two men in the study. Though he had something else almost monopolising his mind, the attention of his expert eye was fleetingly seized by the appearance of young Randall, who was looking almost as ill as his young woman, he thought.

"Well," he said, "the bare facts are these. Mariella was resting against the breakwater and reading, when she felt something tickling her neck. She paid no heed for a while, and then the irritation became more insistent. She looked round casually and, according to her account, streamers of grey hair were flowing through the cracks in the woodwork and coiling round her neck. She remembers nothing more." Young Randall poured himself out half a tumbler of neat whisky and drained it.

"What is it? What is it?" cried Mr. Bickley desperately.

"It is, to put it crudely, an hallucination," replied Sir Perseus, "and I will not disguise from you the fact that it is a serious matter. A nightmare is one thing, a violent waking illusion of this kind quite another. I must tell you one thing. She says she occasionally has the impression that some one is whispering in her ear."

"But, good God!" said Mr. Bickley miserably, "that sounds like madness!"

"It sounds like nothing of the sort," replied Sir Perseus sharply; "get any such idea out of your head. Mariella is ill, but she's absolutely sane."

"Of course she's sane," said young Randall violently.

Sir Perseus looked across at him, and once more his expert eye was steeply challenged by that look about him.

"What does she hear whispered?" asked Mr. Bickley.

"She is uncertain about that. She thinks she has heard the words 'September the tenth,' but usually it sounds more like vague chatter. She likened it rather vividly to those soft husky mutterings one often hears between items on the radio. And once or twice she fancies she hears a sort of sniggering chuckle. She believes she heard such a sound first before she felt that tickling sensation. However, I don't think such details have much significance. The point is, she is ill, she has some disturbing, I may say dangerous, symptoms. She must not be left alone; she must have the reinforcement and comfort of you all, and especially of you, Mr. Randall. You are to be her future husband, and she naturally already regards you as the person who will guard and cherish her in the coming time. All this is inevitably a very horrible business for you, but you must do your utmost to conceal the fact in front of her."

"Have you really ever known a case like this?" asked young Randall, leaning forward and regarding Sir Perseus with a haggard gaze. "I mean, I mean, do people have such hallucinations without any real cause for them?"

Sir Perseus paused before replying, "That depends on what you mean by a *'real cause.'* I *have* known similar cases, but only when, as I have told Mr. Bickley, some deep indentation has been made on the patient's mind from severe shock—psychic shock, I mean. I have read, of course, of some alleged phenomena, reported from Eastern lands, which have always seemed to be hopelessly unsubstantiated—witchery, hocus-pocus, mumbo-jumbo. If such phenomena have any basis in fact they can, in my opinion, be satisfactorily explained by the potent influence of auto-suggestion on the primitive mind. It is significant that they seem to lose their force with the donning of trousers. But we are wandering from the point, the subject on hand, and I must go and get something to eat. Mariella," he concluded impressively, "is a healthy-minded Western girl, she isn't a Zulu or a South-Sea islander, and she is in great trouble; I do not wish to minimise the extent of that trouble, but she can and must be cured, and you two, and of course her mother, but you especially, Mr. Randall, can greatly assist the process of recovery by your tact, your love, your intelligent determination."

Mr. Bickley saw him out, and while he was doing so young Randall drank another half-tumbler of neat whisky.

Mariella recovered slowly. The next day she had several attacks of semi-hysteria, and she insisted that everything grey should be taken from her room. And she had a strong but diminishing antipathy for hair, so much so that she asked her mother to wear a shawl over her head. And the latter cut away the ribboned streamers from the electric fan, because she noticed Mariella staring at them in a rather strange way as they fluttered in the draught.

Young Randall spent several hours a day with her and appeared to be attempting—without complete success—to be obeying Sir Perseus's instructions. The latter came every afternoon and was breezily chatty and cheerful, but it was a full week before his patient was well enough to come downstairs, though she had no relapse in the meantime; but Sir Perseus was less reassured by this than he allowed himself to appear. She never referred to her condition or trouble, and seemed indeed rather disinterested in her progress, and yet, so it seemed to Sir Perseus, she was psychically abnormal, subtly so, almost as though she were "entranced"; hynotised, though in a very sly, unobtrusive way. He attributed this vague spiritual eccentricity to shock, and he told himself that she would either make a slow but sure recovery or relapse suddenly and violently and become past his aid. She talked very little and paid the very slightest heed to anything any one else said, and spent most of the day sitting in a chair on the beach and staring out to sea. "Somehow she doesn't seem quite a free agent," thought Sir Perseus. Her mother, who hid a very deep distress with heroic success and had become just the mother of a sick child, had formed the habit of waking up frequently during the night, but only once found anything to report to Sir Perseus, when Mariella had suddenly sat up in bed and said, "Who's that whispering?" and then sank back again and went to sleep, though she muttered at intervals, as if discussing something almost under her breath with some one who was visiting her in her dreams. That happened during the early hours of September 9th. On the next morning there was a remarkable change in her. She came down to breakfast in her bathing costume and seemed her old care-free self. She talked away fluently and flippantly and, one would have judged, kept no remembrance whatsoever of any displeasing experiences. Young Randall, who had been a wretched, withered shadow of himself ever since that evening when he had seen Mariella sprawled down the shingle, and drinking far too much in Mr. Bickley's opinion, responded instantly to his fiancée's changed state, and it was a very thankful and delighted trio which went down with Mariella to the beach about eleven o'clock. It was a blithe day, cloudless and breezy, and the small waves chased in hard on each other's heels.

Mariella and young Randall stretched themselves out and let the searching rays of the sun pour through them, and then, just before twelve o'clock, they got up lazily and dawdled down to the water's edge. The beach was crowded, and Mariella seemed quite content that every one should have a generous opportunity of scrutinising once more her exquisite workmanship and finish.

"I heard a rumour," said one envious damsel to another, "that she's really not quite 'all there'; gets fits about once a week."

"She certainly has got something rather odd about her," said her girl friend. "I expect that's why that Mr. Randall has been looking so worried lately. What a figure he's got and how good-looking! I'd give ten years of my life for a month with him. What a shame he should be tied up to some one who isn't quite sane!"

These charitable and erotic observations had just been exchanged when Mariella began to step delicately into the sea. Young Randall was already swimming about and waiting for her to join him in a cruise to the raft. She forced her way slowly in, rubbing her hands and uttering the conventional light cries evoked by the tart embraces of the North Sea. She paused for a moment as it splashed up over her waist, waved her hands to her parents, and then strode forward again. The water had just reached her neck when she suddenly screamed, flung up her arms and disappeared. In an instant the beach was in an uproar. Those in the sea swam furiously towards the spot where she had last been seen, a dozen sun-bathers dashed in, the boatman struggled at his oars, but young Randall was there first, and he dived for her. To Mr. and Mrs. Bickley, who had dashed down to the sea, it seemed a thousand years till he appeared holding Mariella round her armpits and brought her ashore. A doctor had run up and he got busy with artificial respiration, but Mariella, though she had swallowed more sea-water than was good for her, was in no danger of death from drowning, and though she showed no sign of coming-to she was very soon in a condition to be carried back to the house. A quarter of an hour later Sir Perseus was at her bedside. And then for a moment she recovered consciousness, and after staring fixedly at Sir Perseus for a full ten seconds, she said in a cold, toneless voice: "I put my foot on a face. I could feel it. And then I felt the hair, and it began to come up my legs and pull me down." And then she began to scream and scream and scream, and it took all the strength of Sir Perseus and young Randall to hold her down in bed. Presently her struggles became less violent and Sir Perseus put a hypodermic syringe to her arm.

Five hours later she was on her way to a London Nursing Home in an ambulance which paid no heed to speed limits, her mother and Sir Perseus with her. His last words to her father and young Randall were: "I will save her reason if I can, but you must be prepared for the worst." And then with the light of battle in his eye he leaped into the ambulance. Mr. Bickley and young Randall stayed behind by his orders; they would only be in the way for the present. He would ring up early the next morning and tell them what to do.

Mr. Bickley, who spent the evening in deep and melancholy reverie, hardly noticed the absence of young Randall. He in no way wished for company, and no doubt Randall felt the same way. Could Mariella have had some affair with a Grey Beard? She might have had. Certain horrible conjectures tapped for entrance to his brain. Utterly worn out he lay down on the sofa in the drawing-room, but he could not sleep. At seven o'clock a maid came in and handed him a letter. To his surprise he recognized young Randall's writing on the envelope. He opened it and found it contained two separate enclosures. The first he took up was headed "Letter 2. Letter 1 to be read first." So he unfolded number 1 and read as follows:

"Dear Mr. Bickley,
"When you get this I shall be lying in the gorse patch below the eighth tee, and I shall have even less brains in my head than I was born with. Incidentally it will be the first time I was ever on the left-hand side of that fairway. No doubt that sounds very flippant, but once I had finally made up my mind to shoot myself and knew I should have the guts to do it—four hours ago—I became almost light-hearted, in a way exalted, scrubbed and robed for death. This mood would not have lasted, but it will remain with me at least long enough. The fact is, I poisoned my uncle, which was not nearly so difficult a feat as it sounds, for his doctor was half-witted and I made a careful study of his habits and his medicine chest. He was a vile, disgusting old Sadist and I feel no remorse whatsoever. Killing him seemed as natural a performance as beating down a wasp, and by killing him I did many people

a service, for everyone who served him and was in his employ breathed a sigh of relief when they heard of his death. However, I am no altruist, and I should never have taken the serious risk entailed by experimenting with his sleeping-draught but for one thing. It came to my knowledge that he was about to make a new will, and cutting me right out of it. Consequently I should have to give up Mariella. Now I am not going to dwell on what that knowledge meant to me, for I know you realise how I feel about her. Life without her is unthinkable. Well, why am I going to kill myself? For this reason—my uncle had a rather *long grey beard*. That is why. The moment I heard of Mariella's nightmares I had a dreadful suspicion that my plans had failed. When I heard why she had that seizure on the beach I almost believed it was hopeless. What happened this morning convinced me that the rest was up to me. Now I have no belief in a future life. My uncle was one of the few people I have met who deserved to go to the conventional hell, and I have never met anyone bad enough to merit the conventional heaven. Nevertheless, by some agency Mariella is being attacked, and I have a curious feeling of certainty that those attacks will cease when I am dead. Her sanity, I am convinced, depends on what I am about to do. Now I have worked out what I believe to be a consistent and plausible explanation of this, but I shall not go into it, for I must hurry, and very probably it would sound like lunacy to anyone but me. If, however, I am wrong and I meet Uncle Walter hereafter and find out something, then he'll really know what hell can be! But I'm afraid that is too optimistic a prospect. Now I want you to do something for me. I want you to tear up this letter as soon as you've read it and send the other to the coroner—or whatever the procedure is. I can't bear to think that people might point at Mariella as someone who almost married a murderer, and I don't want her to know I was one. She won't—and I am reconciled to the fact—sorrow for me for long. When she is well again I shall just seem part of a horrible memory, and as she forgets that she will forget me. And I'd rather it was so. Good-bye. I was once so happy with you all.

"A. R."

When he had finished reading it Mr. Bickley tore the letter to small pieces and burnt it in the grate. And then he took up the other and read:

"Dear Mr. Bickley,
"I am about to shoot myself in the gorse below the eighth tee because I have discovered a horrible secret about myself. There is no need to tell you what this is, and I'd rather no one knew it, but it makes it impossible for me to marry your daughter, and life without her is unthinkable, so I am doing this."

"A. R."

Mr. Bickley put this epistle back into its envelope and went to the telephone.

The following April Mariella returned from a long sea voyage perfectly restored to health. The following August she became affianced to a certain Mr. Peter Raines, whose past is as bland and innocent as an infant's posterior, but concerning whose future stupendous prophecies are made. He has just left Oxford, where he was President of the Union, and only the fact that he has been adopted as Conservative candidate for a Midland constituency has prevented him from completing a really "brilliant and daring" novel. As it is, he is about to publish a slim volume of essays entitled, *Constructive Toryism*. Mariella is blissfully happy, and if she dreams at all it is of this formidable young thinker. Except just once when she had a very sharp dream vision of someone dark and lithe, beautifully poised, and flicking Larwood's cannon-balls from his nose to the rails. She has just one idiosyncrasy: she cannot remain in the room with a grey-bearded male person. But the owners of such are fortunately uncommon and, even in Scotland, becoming rarer every day.

Mr. and Mrs. Bickley are very well indeed.

The Last to Leave

Arnott pushed aside the papers on the table in front of him and got up. "Well," he said, "I think that's all the business for to-day, and it's good-bye to Number 5."

"When do they actually begin to murder the dear old place?" asked Walters.

"They start dismantling to-morrow afternoon, I believe. They're in a hurry, as they want to get the mess pretty well cleared up before the end of the holidays. Anyway it's got to be done. If the Borough Surveyor saw the condition of that beam in your room, Bob, he'd condemn the house without a moment's hesitation; for if that worm-eaten old hero did what he has threatened to do for the last six months, and decide he was as tired as he looks, we should probably all be cadavers in the basement inside ten seconds. I hated signing the death-warrant, but it will be a great weight off my mind when we're all safely installed in Russell Street."

"All the stock has been taken round, hasn't it?" asked Moberly.

"Yes," replied Arnott, sitting down again and lighting a cheroot, "and, by the way, *Tambourin* is going very strong. Smiths' had fifty again this morning, Simpkins' another twenty-five, and both *The Times* and Mudie's have repeated."

"Well, it's a good book," said Moberly with a yawn. "The most deliberately naive plot, excellently sardonic characterisation, and charmingly sophisticated dialogue, a young man's pen and an old man's mind, the type of the Best-Seller of the future in my humble and usually inaccurate opinion. To find everything rather ridiculous and yet worth writing about, that paradox which stokes the genuine satirist's mind and keeps its safety-valve screaming."

"And," said Arnott, "no smut for smut's sake and no bunk or James Douglas's. It's very soothing to have one selling like that. One week's sales will pay for the move and then some."

"And to think it's by a *man over* thirty," added Walters. "How rare and refreshing! Thank the Lord we've got him nicely tied up for the next four."

"I hate leaving this room," said Arnott. "I've done so much darned hard work in it, and I have always had a silly feeling that it was the sort of work it respected—making books. Supposing we were in the *brassière* business, for example, how the old aristocrat would have felt his walls degraded, for I bet he's really a hopeless old snob. He'd have collapsed long ago. Whatever authors may say, publishing is a gent's job and, considering what authors are like, the fact that we swindle them so little is a great tribute to our integrity."

"We've a pretty decent bunch on the whole," said Moberly. "Certainly they are the crosses we have to bear, but ours are fairly light, and, provided one always agrees that their last book is their best, and they see their singular countenances in gossip columns at regular intervals, they're not so much trouble as they're worth. As for the old house, I feel like whimpering too, but you, Jack, can't reproach yourself. You've spent your own real money in prolonging its life to the last possible moment, and it ought to be very grateful to you."

"I should like to think so," replied Arnott with a smile. "And now it's half-past five and time for a little farewell ceremony, a little suitable sentimentality." He got up and went to his cupboard, from which he took out a bottle and three glasses. He twisted off the wire, eased out the cork and filled the glasses.

"Now," he said, "let us drink of this quite tolerable Roderer to the memory of Number 5, Equity Court, built in the prosperous reign of King William and Queen Mary, designed by a gentleman to be a home for gentlefolk, a gentleman itself. In a few hours the pick will be laid at its roots, in a few days it will be a vulgar heap of rubble, but it is still a small poem in bricks and mortar. We have looked after it so far as was in our power; it has been a good friend to us. Now we strike our tents. But its memory will remain with us. We have loved it; let us hope it has tolerated us. So here's to the memory of Number 5, Equity Court. . . . My God, what was that?"

He put down his glass and rushed to the bell, and a moment later the manager came into the room, looking nervous.

"What was that row?" asked Arnott sharply.

"You mean that big cracking sound, sir?"

"Yes, of course. It sounded as if someone had dropped a ton weight somewhere in the house. Run up and see if the beam's holding. I'll go downstairs."

The others went with him. All the members of the small staff of John Arnott & Co., Ltd., were out in the passage, looking uncertain.

"I thought it came from your room, sir," said James the clerk, addressing Moberly.

The latter hurried across the corridor. "No," he said after a moment, "everything's O.K. here."

"I thought it came from your room too, sir," added the book-keeper.

"Well, it didn't," answered Moberly, a shade irritably.

Just then the manager joined them. "Beam looks just the same, sir," he said, "and if I may say so, when I've stayed late I've thought I heard noises sometimes."

"Thought!" cried Arnott; "not much thinking about that. Heavens above, I believed it had gone at last! Not a pleasant feeling," he added, wiping his forehead.

"What sort of noises do you think you've heard?" asked Walters.

"Steps and creakings like people moving about."

"How often?"

"Oh, just now and again, sir, Mrs. Rummy, the charwoman, says the same thing."

"Well, those weren't steps or creakings," said Arnott. "Something went then, I'm certain of it, and I thought we were going with it." And he mopped his brow again.

Presently the three partners returned to Arnott's room.

"You two are going off now, I suppose," he said. "I think I'll wait a bit and clear up. I suppose the van comes for the furniture early to-morrow?"

"Yes," replied Walters, "at nine punctually."

"Well, then, I'll clear up everything to-night. There's not much to do, and I don't suppose I'll be late, but I shall feel happier when I've got the Essays' estimates finally worked out."

They said good-night, and then Arnott sat down at his desk, took some papers out of a drawer, opened his estimate book, shook his fountain pen and put himself to work. Half-consciously he heard the staff one by one leaving the house; each time the swing-door, which divided the short outer passage from the rest of the building, groaned lightly, it signalled the homeward exit of another. Presently all was silence save for the light, indeterminate stretchings of the oak panelling. Arnott set himself seriously to the problem of how to lower the production cost of the new series of non-copyright essays, the first four titles of which his firm proposed to publish during the next spring. They must be nice little books, in appearance superior to any rival series, but every fraction of a farthing counted and he must get a penny off the cost if it could possibly be managed. He had just turned to the binding estimate when he thought he heard the swing-door creak again.

He was so absorbed in his figures that for a moment he disregarded this insignificant little sound, but then the echo of it as it were tapped on the back door of his consciousness, and he was saying to himself, "Now, who can that be? The charwoman? No, she comes in the morning." Did it matter? Well, perhaps he'd better go down and see. He went to his door, turned on the light in the passage, and went down the two flights of stairs to the ground floor. There didn't seem to be anyone about. He visited the trade department, the packing and waiting rooms; each quiet and lifeless. And then he went up again to his room. But he found it difficult to concentrate; he was unable quite to expel the problem of the swing-door from his mind. Presently he recalled that it was accustomed to move without human agency when a westerly wind surged rudely into the Court. So he looked out of his window. Heavens! how the fog had thickened. He could only just see across to the Estate Agent's office opposite, a mere eight yards away. That swirling dank curtain completely cut off his view of the entrance to Equity Court, and the tiniest breeze would have parted wide that opaque curtain. It couldn't be the wind then. Well, why worry! Very probably he'd imagined the whole thing. ("No, you didn't," insinuated his subconscious.) He must get back to business.

He picked up the book of cloth samples and went through it carefully and critically. He had just decided that a second quality aquamarine would be quite good enough, would mean the saving of a halfpenny per copy, and look bright and attractive, when his head went up and he appeared to be listening intently. If those weren't footsteps from Wells's room above him, what were they? He'd heard him stumping about a thousand times. He went to his door, opened it half-way, and listened. No, there wasn't a sound now. All the same, perhaps he'd better go up. It was just possible there might be someone in the house. How could there be? That swing-door? Probably his imagination. Well, then, those footsteps? Oh, very well, he'd go up, but he'd never finish this job if there were all these interruptions. He ascended the stairs a shade heavily and opened the door of Wells's room. Of course there was nothing there. This was the last time he'd see the old room It looked bare, and as if laid out for burial, old and tired, reconciled to being a part of a heap of rubble a few hours later. What weird, tiny sounds there were! Just then, for example, as if there were people whispering; yes, it sounded like whispering, but a whisper was a sound made by human agency—a house could not whisper—yet for a fleeting second he entertained the possibility that there might be something neither human nor composed of bricks and mortar, which might make a noise that could be likened to a whisper, for lack of a more precise word—a very far-carrying conception which he succeeded in repressing.

He tip-toed back to his room in a stealthy way which his common-sense derided, but the state of his nerves dictated, and once again tried to lash his mind back to those numerals and abstractions, which faded out with such craven obsequiousness at the suggestion of these small, uncertain sounds. How hard it is, he tried not to tell himself, to concentrate when one is expecting—well, not exactly expecting, some new little interruption. And concentration becomes impossible when that diluted kind of expectation is fulfilled, for if those soft tappings were not made by someone coming down the stairs from the floor above—well, what the devil were they? Now they seemed to have paused just outside his door, just outside. Acting on a sudden and, he realised, ill-advised impulse, he picked up a box of matches and flung it at the door, and then was very angry with himself for having done so, for a person only did a thing like that to drive someone or something away—or to reassure oneself that there was nothing to drive away—no one or nothing to startle. And then, insidiously, the echo of the manager's remark came back to his mind, "When I've stayed late, I've thought I heard sounds sometimes," "and unlike me," thought Arnott, "had the guts to disregard them. But I wonder if he heard steps coming down the stairs and halting outside his room. Well, have I? Why should I call them steps? Instead of just vague, indeterminate—a vague, indeterminate what?"

He got up again to distract his thoughts from their fuddled peregrinations and went to have a last look at his mantelpiece, a masterpiece of its period, about which those who had expert knowledge of such things were enthusiastic. What would be its latter end? It belonged to the ground landlord and he'd probably sell it to a Yank; and it would end up in Park Avenue; and why not? He liked Yanks, admired their taste, and in certain moods preferred them to his own ruddy countrymen. That chap who'd been sketching Number 5 for the *Sunday Budget* had passed his hand up and down the embossed detail of the mantelpiece and told him he got a sharp, sensuous delight from such a contact. Very possible and plausible. Let him see if he got any such sensation. Yes, he did. It was exquisitely smooth, silky—in a way feminine—and warm, yes, most curiously warm. And then he remembered how that person had been surprised to find that sort of cowled head screened in the foliage, and had said he'd never seen a more or less conventional floral design of this period housing any such sly intruder, a joke on the part of the carver, he had considered it. He'd feel that too. And then he swung his hand back sharply. Good God! It seemed red-hot. Yet he'd turned his electric stove off an hour since. Well, his imagination was running away with him. He'd better chuck work and be off. It was natural enough to be a little fallaciously percipient on his last night in the old house.

Good heavens! There was another of those frightful rending sounds, and then he felt something drop lightly on his head and he looked up. Yes, that was plaster falling, and that rent in the ceiling had suddenly stretched two inches. The house was on its last legs, dying slowly—perhaps not so slowly—considering that plaster and that extending crack above him. And then there was a sharp metallic tap and his door wavered uncertainly for a moment, and then swung on its hinges with a decisive, and final, and muted crash. That last settling down of the house must have wrenched the latch out of true. And then in came the fog, questingly and waveringly like a lady curtseying into a Throne-Room. And in with it came that whispering, so that Arnott had a horrible impression that he was no longer alone in his room. He *must, must, must* fight his way down. Could he? Dared he? He must! Never mind his hat and coat. To be outside—that was everything. But supposing he ran down and fumbled with the latch of the front door! Fumbled and fumbled, and those steps kept coming down those last two flights! Would he be able to open it in time and dash outside? To be outside—that was everything!

He had just poised himself to run when there came a dreadful, ripping rending. And then there was a second's pause, and then he felt himself flung forward and down the plaster poured on to him. The window crashed outward, his light bulb swung wildly and shattered, and he was hurled through a splintered wall, his arms flung out beseechingly. And as he dropped through space a fleeting thought came to him—"That was how they said it would go." And then he was prone on his back and a welter of bricks, desks, chairs and tiles splashed wildly down beside him.

His escape was always afterwards described as "a miracle," for he was absolutely untouched. The débris rained down beside him, but not one particle touched a hair of his head. For a moment he lost consciousness and then for a few seconds came to himself. He saw the dust rising up to meet and mingle curiously with the fog, and it seemed to him that out from the piled ruin two little cowled figures stepped delicately; and that one of these figures hesitated for a moment, and then turned back and came and looked down on him, and the impression he received was that he was regarded very benignly and gently and sweetly, and, as it were, said "good-bye" to by something which gazed for a long, deep moment into his eyes and then slipped down the court and disappeared.

The Cairn

"I'd like to go with you," said Welland, "but I think I had better nurse this heel if I'm to get through the rest of the trip."

"Yes, certainly," agreed Seebright, "you'd be a fool to attempt it. But I like the look of those silvery slopes above the wood. Ever since I was a kid I've loved high hills and virgin snow. I don't imagine it will take me more than four hours or so up and down. All the same it might be as well to get one of the locals to go with me—it's easy to miss the shortest way even on such a simple climb as old Brudon looks to be."

"Well, ring for our worthy host and see if he can arrange it."

Seebright pulled the bell-knob, and a moment later the landlord appeared, a tubby, rubicund Midlander, genial, of andante intelligence and consequently at perfect peace with the world.

"Oh, Mr. Reddle," said Seebright, "I'm going to climb Brudon to-morrow. Mr. Welland has a bad heel and I want a companion; would someone from the village go with me?"

"I don't believe they would, sir," replied the landlord.

"What on earth do you mean? Don't they like the look of me?"

Mr. Reddle shifted about on his feet. "It isn't that, sir, but the chaps about here won't climb Brudon when snow's lying."

"Why the devil not?"

"Well, sir, it's just that way. They won't go beyond the wood on any account, and most of 'em don't like setting foot on the hill when snow's lying."

"But why? I can't imagine a simpler or easier climb. Is it because it's too much like work?"

"No, 'tain't that. I'm not a native of these parts, so I don't hear everything as a local chap would; but they've got some reason why they won't go above Dim Wood in the snow."

"Is that big spinney, half-way up, Dim Wood?" asked Welland.

"Yes, sir. The fact is they think there's something that wanders on the slopes above it when snow's there."

"And hides behind the cairn and pounces on the unsuspecting climber?" suggested Seebright, laughing.

"Yes," replied Mr. Reddle, looking startled, "that's just what they does think."

"Well, I'm damned!" said Seebright. "Do they think they've seen it?"

"They're pretty close about it, sir. The chaps get sullen like and changes the subject if it's mentioned, but it seems as though they think they've seen some marks. I gather it's a very old story, a sort of village secret."

"A very typical piece of folk-funk," said Weiland. "A few probably perfectly explainable marks in the snow, and, of course, the devil or some other undesirable is abroad. Away goes the snow, away go the marks and away goes the devil."

"Well, landlord," said Seebright, "you're above that sort of thing. Come with me to-morrow and help to lay what must be rather an inconvenient bogey."

"I don't believe I will, sir," said Mr. Reddle.

"What!" cried Seebright, "you don't mean to say you believe this tripe?"

"I don't say I does, but I believe in being on the safe side in such things. I'd do the same if I was you, sir."

"Be damned to that! I'll climb Brudon if it snows ink!"

"As you please, sir, but in any case you wouldn't want a guide, the way is as easy to find as hard to miss. I'll show you, if you'll look through the telescope. You takes the third turn to the right in the village—Dim Lane—that takes you up to that big clump of oaks; then you follows the hedge till you comes to a gate, and then you goes straight up to the wood. There is a path through that and then it's all plain sailing to the cairn. And now I must go and see about your dinners, sir.

Pat Seebright and Leonard Welland differed in temperament as much as they differed in their command of this world's goods. Yet to have laid down his life for the other would have been considered a privilege by either of them. If the summons had come, neither of them would have hesitated for a moment. They had been the fastest, firmest friends for twenty years. Pat made an easy £10,000 a year in his father's stockbroker's firm. Leonard secured from the National Income a precarious £250 as an usher in a small school. Yet the overwhelming disparity between their income-tax returns had never in the slightest degree tarnished their friendship, and Pat had never lent Leonard a penny. All he had done was to persuade him to allow him occasionally to do a little marginal speculation on his behalf with a rather mythical £50. These occasional flutters came off in a most magical manner, and every year a most welcome little increment was paid into Leonard's bank. Intellectually, Pat was a child in comparison with Leonard, but in the practical affairs of life he was absolutely his master. Each envied and complemented the other. Pat was of an enterprising and inquiring type of mind, and Leonard stimulated and vitalised strata of his brain which would otherwise have perished of malnutrition.

Neither was ever quite happy when separated from the other, though an innate sense of the supreme obscenity of sentimentality would ever have prevented them from acknowledging the fact. Their affection for each other so far surpassed the love of woman that had they been forced to face the conventionally considered ultimate test of friendship by falling in love with the same one, they would have left her to celibacy or a third person with absolute contentment, in the certain knowledge that such a competition would have been essentially discordant and disgusting. Each secretly dreaded the possible marriage of the other, though in the case of poor Leonard, who had to think twice about purchasing packets of cigarettes, and who met about three fresh females per annum, such a contingency was highly improbable. (As things turned out there was no need for either of them to worry.) They always spent their holidays together, and on this occasion were passing the Christmas vacation in tramping the Lake District. Their time was almost up, for in three days' time they were due to drive back to London in Pat's impressive car. Perhaps it was this which seemed to cast a shadow over their dinner together that night. Both felt it and confessed to it. Pat applied his usually infallible antidote to irrational gloom by ordering a bottle of Mr. Reddle's champagne and two large glasses of his mediocre port. However, this medicine was not quite as successful as it should have been—the shadow remained.

"That's a curious yarn about Brudon and the snow," said Welland. "In other circumstances it would be easier to explain. This alleged bogey might be, let us say, the personified terror of avalanches, but I don't suppose an avalanche has sprayed down Brudon since the end of the Ice Age, and even the traditional memory of the good folk of Borthwaite cannot be as long as that. Still, even on Brudon a blizzard might not be too pleasant; are you sure you're wise to go alone?"

"Oh, perfectly," replied Seebright; "anyway I shan't start if the weather breaks. How's the glass, Mr. Reddle?"

"Steady enough, sir. From the looks of the sky I'd say 'twill be fine but dullish to-morrow."

They went to bed early and Welland was asleep at once, but his rest was disturbed by the recurrence of a very idiotic little dream. It seemed to him that it was moonlight and that he was gazing through the telescope at the cairn, which was throwing a hard shadow on to the snow. And then this shadow began to move, and as it moved it changed its shape and became more like a crouching beast of some kind than any such shadow had a right to be. And were those flaming points red eyes? And each time, before he could make up his mind on this—for some reason or other—rather urgent question, he awoke. "Now I will not dream that again," he said to himself, but a moment later he was once more scrutinising with a growing anxiety and distaste this erratic and enigmatic shade. After this had happened five or six times he sat up in bed. Self-flatterers, he said to himself, would attribute this bother to nerves; honest men to alcohol. What should he do about it? Well, it occurred to him that if he crept very quietly downstairs and swung the telescope on to the cairn and proved to his full consciousness that nothing of the sort was abroad, then his subconscious—or whatever it was—would be convinced that no such wearisome phenomenon, such change of shape, was occurring at the crest of Brudon.

The moon was filtering vague rays through light clouds. So much of his dream *was* true. Well, here was the telescope and there was Brudon. He put his eye to the lens and swung the glass to the cairn. And then he put it down and rubbed his eyes, and then he took it up again, stared through it intently for a full twenty seconds and put it down again. And then he returned rather slowly and thoughtfully to bed.

"Of course I must be slightly tight," he said to himself. "That's why I can't sleep, that's why I see things through telescopes. No more double ports for me. All the same—" And for a moment he felt a powerful inclination to go down again and take up the telescope and make quite sure that— He looked at his watch—five o'clock—and he did not feel sleepy. He decided to read till it was time to get up; something which would mobilise his powers of concentration, *Essays on Truth and Reality,* for example. Once he found himself dozing off and there was just the vague, spectral outline of a cairn and a shadow beginning most exasperatingly to reappear. He pulled himself back to consciousness, and taking each sentence slowly etched it on his brain.

As Mr. Reddle had prophesied, the morning was fine but overcast, and the glass remaining high, Seebright announced his intention of starting at 12.30. He would reach the wood about 2.00 and the summit about 3.30—just as dark was beginning to fall. There would be enough light to see him down to the wood and he would be back at the inn before 5.00.

"And you can follow my progress, Leonard, through the telescope," he said, "and mutter prayers for my safety. Now, Mr. Reddle, are you sure you won't come with me?"

"No, thank 'ee, sir, and if you'd take my advice you'd change your mind. Why not have a try for some of them ducks on the marsh?"

"I'm going to climb the Haunted Hill," said Seebright with the utmost emphasis. "I am determined to convince the superstitious natives of these parts that climbing this measly hill with two inches of snow on it is not precisely the perilous ordeal they profess to consider it. I shall—if he appears—tweak the nose of the local bogey, and I am off to do this now."

"Very well, sir," replied the landlord, "and I wish you luck."

Seebright set forth punctually at 12.30 and Welland watched his strong, stocky figure striding away down the village street. As he reached the third turning on the right he turned and waved.

Welland lunched at 1.0, and afterwards sat down by the telescope, and attempted once again to concentrate upon the profound yet racy speculations of Dr. Bradley, but again without much success. His body seemed to protest against its immobility. It joined in a conspiracy with his nervous system to compel fidgets and fussiness and a sort of tingling unease, so that he repeatedly pulled out his watch and yawned and lit cigarettes and shifted his position, and these tendencies developed and became more insistent—they almost took charge of him—and the effort to resist them was exhausting in a small way.

Presently he gave up the attempt to read and took up the telescope. He searched very carefully the slopes between the wood and the cairn. If those weren't footmarks in the snow what were they? Very possibly the locals were in the habit of pulling Mr. Reddle's—"the foreigner's"—leg. Certainly someone had travelled those slopes. Those marks were extraordinarily distinct. Would that be due to their size? He looked at his watch again—five minutes to two. Pat should be appearing at any moment now. Looking through a small telescope like this was a damned tiring business. Ah, there he was! As he came out from the wood Welland saw him pause— he is looking at those footprints—or whatever they are—he thought. Seebright remained peering down for half a minute or so and then began climbing steadily again. Welland found he could just follow him with the naked eye, so he put down the telescope. Mr. Reddle came in just then. "How's he getting on?" he asked.

"He should be at the top in twenty minutes or so."

The landlord seemed not quite at his ease. "Getting a bit misty near the cairn, isn't it, sir?"

"Yes," replied Welland, "the clouds are coming down; looks like a change in the weather, I fancy."

"Well, sir, I shall be in the kitchen for a bit yet. Would you mind letting me know when Mr. Seebright gets back to the wood again."

"All right," replied Welland, looking at him a shade sharply.

"It's just a fancy of mine, sir," said Mr. Reddle, "if it's no bother," and he went out again.

Welland watched the little dark speck climbing steadily towards the cairn till it was but a hundred yards or so from it and then once again put the telescope to his eye. A few minutes later he saw Seebright reach the cairn, slap it with his hand and then turn and face towards the inn and wave his right arm above his head. And then he began rapidly to descend. Welland had started instinctively to wave back and then had smiled at his stupidity. He was just about to put the glass down again when he suddenly became tense and intent. He put the telescope down sharply and rubbed both lenses with his handkerchief, and then he put it to his eye again. For a moment he remained taut and rigid, and then he began to tremble, and then he dropped the telescope to the floor, and then he rushed from the room, out through the front door and down the village street. As it happened there was only one person who saw him pass, old Mrs. Elm, who was beating a rug outside her cottage door. When she saw a hatless figure dash hobbling past, and that queer look on his face too, her mouth fell open and the rug dropped from her hands. A moment later she saw this figure turn up the lane and disappear, and then for several minutes she remained staring open-mouthed.

Now Mrs. Elm's brain never exceeded largo in its tempo, and seldom reached it. At the same time she had a sense for the unusual. She went back to her kitchen and wrestled with the problem of what to do. So presently she put a shawl around her head and trotted up to the Hare and Form, where she found Mr. Reddle squeezing the digestive apparatus from a chicken.

"Mr. Reddle," she began, and fiddled with her shawl.

"Yes, what is it?" asked the landlord, pausing in the midst of his culinary business.

"Well," said Mrs. Elm. "I sees one of those young chaps who's putting up here, and I sees him running by in his slippers and without his hat and he turned up Dim Lane. I thought I ought to tell you."

Mr. Reddle stared at her for a moment; then he rushed past Mrs. Elm and into the guest parlour, stood stock still for a moment gazing round the room, then noticed the end of the telescope sticking out from beneath the table. He picked it up, stared for a moment through it at the dusk-rimmed crest of Brudon, and then rushed through the front door and down the village street. By a lucky chance he met the local representative of Law and Order, Constable Lamb. Mr. Reddle clutched his arm. "I think there's maybe something wrong on Brudon," he said, "maybe something's happened to those young chaps staying with me."

Mr. Lamb stared at him sharply, but something in Mr. Reddle's face, and a rather disturbing memory which had often recurred to lubricate the somewhat sluggish machinery of his imagination, prevented him from asking some rather natural questions. All he said was, "We'd better see if the doctor's in."

They ran together down the street to where a brass plate announced that "R. Ford, M.D., Physician and Surgeon," had there his habitat. He was in and he *did* ask a few questions, but his natural scepticism was also diluted with a certain memory, and presently he picked up his bag, his hat and coat and an electric torch and started off with the other two. Soon they were climbing in panting silence through the dusk, the doctor's torch faintly revealing the way. They had just reached the last turn on the path through Dim Wood when the doctor stumbled over something. . . .

"Just describe to us, constable, exactly how you found the deceased," said the coroner.

"Well," said Mr. Lamb, "Mr. Seebright was lying on his back, his arms thrown out like, and Mr. Welland was about six yards away. He was lying on his face—more crouching than lying—but his face was in the snow. They'd both fallen hard."

"Did you examine the snow for tracks of a third person?"

"Yes, sir."

"Did you find anything?"

"No, sir."

"You saw tracks of Mr. Seebright going up and coming down to the wood, but nothing else?"

"Nothing else, sir."

Dr. Ford was the next witness.

"Dr. Ford," said the coroner, "I take it you have performed an autopsy on the deceased."

"I have."

"Would you tell the Court what you learned from so doing?"

"Both were strong, healthy young men, organically flawless. They had sustained extensive superficial injuries, bruises and so forth, and Mr. Welland had a broken arm. These injuries were consistent with the fact that they had been thrown down with great violence."

"Were these injuries sufficient to cause death?"

"No, emphatically not."

"Then can you suggest why these two young men died?"

"Frankly, I cannot. It is conceivable that some very violent shock, sudden terror for example, may have resulted in heart failure in each case. When I say conceivable I mean just possible, but I am at a loss for a convincing explanation of their deaths. I have known no parallel case."

"Is Mr. Reddle still here?" asked the coroner.

Mr. Reddle was, and returned to the box.

"Mr. Reddle, as I understand it, Mr. Welland had decided not to accompany Mr. Seebright on this climb?"

"Yes, sir, he'd hurt his heel."

"Then the fact that he suddenly made up his mind to go to meet his friend was a complete surprise to you."

"Yes, 'twas, sir."

"Can you account for it?"

"No, but I think he'd been watching Mr. Seebright through the telescope."

"Well, what's that got to do with it?"

Mr. Reddle was silent for a moment, searching for words.

"I should say nothing, sir, like as not. I only mentioned it, sir."

The coroner drummed on the table but there was otherwise no sound. From outside there came the light crack of a whip and the slow rumble of wheels.

"Well," said the coroner at length, "this seems to me an extremely unsatisfactory affair. All I can do is to express my profound sympathy with the parents of these poor young men"—and here he bowed to four persons in deep mourning—"and to express my hope that further light will be eventually shed on this highly mysterious and tragic affair, but I see no object in adjourning the inquest." The verdict was open.

Mr. Reddle followed P. C. Lamb out of the Court and suggested to him that he should come up to the Hare and Form and have some refreshment. The constable had no objection whatsoever. When they were seated in the parlour and furnished with some glossy old pewter, Mr. Reddle said, "You didn't tell the whole truth and nothing but it at the inquest did you, Mr. Lamb?"

The constable put down his mug and looked suspiciously at the landlord. "How's that?" he said. "What makes you for to say that?"

"Because I was watching you through the glass when you climbed Brudon the morning after we found those poor young chaps."

The constable shifted, uneasily in his chair.

"If I tell you what I see'd, will it go no further, will you keep your tongue quiet about it?" he said at length.

"I'll do that," replied Mr. Reddle.

"Well," said Mr. Lamb, "a year or two afore you came, there was a London chap found dead in the wood and that time I did tell all I'd see'd. And the Chief Constable sent for me to Rendle and asked me a lot of questions. And at the end of it he said, with a laugh, 'They brew strong ale in Borthwaite, don't they?'"

"What did you say to make him laugh?"

"I said I'd seen marks in the snow coming along behind the marks made by the London chap."

"What sort of marks?"

"I don't believe I'll be after saying what those marks was like. I don't somehow feel like doing it—not out loud that is, but I'll say this: it seemed to me that whatever made those marks some of the time made four and not two of 'em."

"Sort of crouched down like a time or two?"

"Maybe that," replied the constable.

"About those tracks," said the landlord, "you could make out the ones Mr. Seebright made up and down."

"Yes, I could."

"Would you say he noticed anything? I mean anything that might have to do with them other marks?"

"Well," said Mr. Lamb, "he went up steadily enough, but after he'd come down a couple of hundred yards I judge he'd stopped and looked round; well, you could tell that plain enough, and then he'd started to run."

"Started to run, did he!" exclaimed Mr. Reddle.

"That was easy to read too; his stride got longer and he came down harder, and he kept up the running till he got to the top edge of the wood—where we found him. And just as he got there I take it this Mr. Welland met him, and Mr. Seebright stopped and the two of them faced up to whatever—well—to whatever there was to face up to."

"That's what they would have done," said Mr. Reddle emphatically. "I guess that's the rights of it. They'd face up to it together."

And then there was a long silence in the Hare and Form.

"Snow's off Brudon now, I take it?" asked the constable at length.

"Yes," said Mr. Reddle, "I looked through glass at it round about dinner-time and even that last big patch round cairn is melted."

Present at the End

When Mr. Benchley noticed the rabbit he was for the moment out of sight of the other guns. The rabbit crouched and stared at him for a second or two, and then started to run past him across the ride. Mr. Benchley swung his gun ahead of it and fired. The rabbit somersaulted and then lay kicking. Mr. Benchley went up to it. Some of its fur, cut by the pellets, was shaken on to the pine needles as it kicked. One shot had struck its left eye, which was broken and bleeding. When it saw Mr. Benchley looming hugely over it, it ceased to struggle for a moment, and with its uninjured eye it stared at the other animal who had done this to it. And then it kicked out convulsively once more, trembled throughout its length, and was dead. Mr. Benchley picked it up by the hind legs and walked on. Before he rejoined the other guns at the edge of the wood he had three other opportunities of making the fur fly, but he did not take them. He could hear the other guns taking theirs to right and left of him. It was a very quiet and coldly radiant October morning. As Mr. Benchley strode along, the rabbit swung as it dangled from his hand, and he saw there was a thin trickle of blood pouring down the white patch below its left eye and dripping to the ground. This somewhat distracted his attention from the beauty of the day. As he came out from the wood, an under-keeper took the rabbit from him and flung it down on a rapidly growing pile of its fellows, many of which had rosy cheeks also. One by one the other guns arrived, refilled their pipes and sat down to rest. After a short consultation between Mr. Benchley's host and his head-keeper it was decided to send the beaters round by the road and into the big field of roots facing them, for the purpose of driving the animal inhabitants of that field towards the guns. Those that were edible would be bombarded, and in certain cases the non-edible—stoats, poaching-cats, owls and so on. The guns spread themselves out, lightly concealed by the hedge bordering the wood. The beaters trudged off and Mr. Benchley lit a cigarette. After ten minutes or so he could see the beaters in the distance forming into line and beginning to move forward. Soon he could hear the tapping of their sticks, and almost immediately a big covey rose and flew hard and low towards the wood. As they neared it they rose to clear it. "Bang-bang. Bang-bang-bang. Bang-bang-bang!"

Mr. Benchley got a beautiful right and left and he could hear the birds' bodies crash into the trees behind him. The root field was well stocked and he was kept very busy for the next quarter of an hour. And he was so occupied with events overhead that he had no time to attend to two hares, which dazed by the din ahead of them, hesitated for a moment at the edge of the roots, and then with their ears back dashed wildly past him. When it was all over and the beaters were mopping their brows, the attention of Mr. Benchley was attracted by a fluttering sound just behind him. This he discovered was being made by a hen partridge with a broken wing and leg, which was attempting unsuccessfully to adjust itself to its altered circumstances. When Mr. Benchley went up to it, it paid little attention to the person who had necessitated this adjustment, but continued to flutter and roll itself over on to its side, and, when this hurt, roll back again. Mr. Benchley picked it up and struck its head twice against his right boot. Not hard enough, obviously, for it continued to writhe in his hand.

"Not often you have to do that, Mr. Benchley," said a voice. He looked up and there was his host's rather pretty flapper daughter. He smiled back at her rather uncertainly, and again struck the bird's head against his toe. It became inert in his hand. The girl took it from him, and he wiped the blood from his boot with a handful of grass. It was then time for lunch, which was eaten in a barn near by. A rough count proved that the morning's work had been reasonably successful. The number of hares seen and shot surprised his host. "Too damned many of 'em," he declared. Mr. Benchley agreed with him, but remarked very emphatically that he derived little amusement from killing them.

"No more do I," agreed someone. "Too much target. All right for anyone who can shoot, but the bad shots are always back-ending them, and even if they're stopped, they scream, and I don't like that sound a little bit." And he patted his retriever's rump affectionately.

"All the same," said the host, "there are too many of 'em. So shoot all you can."

Presently they moved off to Pearson's spinney, one of the finest pheasant shoots in the country. Mr. Benchley spent the next half-hour dexterously picking those gloriously high birds out of the sky, and hearing the pleasant plump with which they met the ground. His mind was disconnectedly busy with a certain problem, but he continued to load and fire with the virtuosity born of forty years' practice and training. The flapper, who had heard many tales of his prowess, watched him with bright-eyed enthusiasm, and she never forgot having seen him kill fifty-eight pheasants stone dead with his first seventy cartridges. Mr. Benchley was only vaguely aware of her presence, and it was a sudden sight of her dark blue jumper which made him a shade late on a hare which dashed out straight in front of him and then swung left for cover. It began to drag its hind legs and scream. It managed to pull itself into the heart of a thick thorn bush, and, though Mr. Benchley could hear it well enough, he could not at first catch sight of it. Presently, however, he saw it move and gave it the left barrel. It died at once and he left it there. He jerked out the empty cases, but did not reload. It was near the end of the drive, and when the beaters came up he went to his host and told him he had gun-headache and wouldn't shoot any more.

"All right," said his host; "give your gun to someone to carry back, and if you want tea or a drink, Jenkins will get it for you. There are some aspirins in my medicine chest if you want them. We'll knock off in about another hour."

Mr. Benchley was rather silent during dinner, and pleading a violent headache, went early to bed. He left for London the next morning.

A month later the organising secretary of a certain society for protecting the interests of animals was going through his letters. Eventually he opened one, the contents of which seemed to cause him surprise. He got up and went to the next room, which was occupied by the publicity manager.

"Dick," he said, "I've got a note here from a bloke named Benchley. I seem to have heard of him. Who is he?"

"A famous Mass Murderer," replied the person addressed. "He's put an end to nearly everything which flies, swims and runs, and in most cases in vast quantities. He once killed a thousand grouse in a day—or a million—some charming record or other—one of the five best shots in England, in every sense of the word a Bloody Man, I imagine. What the devil does he want with us?"

The publicity manager was a person of intolerant views and intemperate utterance.

"He says he would like to see someone connected with this outfit," replied the secretary. "Let's look him up in *Who's Who.*" He fetched that encyclopaedia of mediocrity and read out:

"Benchley, Robert Aloysius. Born in 1870. Eldest son of (We'll skip that). Educated at Eton and New College, Oxford.

He took a first in Greats, by Jove! Founded firm of R. A. Benchley & Co., Limited. Recreations: shooting, fishing, golf. Address: 43 Brook Crescent, W.1. —Well, he's less verbose and full of himself than most of them."

"Does he mention how many grouse he once killed in a day?" asked the manager. "Recreations: mangling birds, beasts, fishes and golf balls. Imagine confessing to it! What he wants to bother with us for I cannot conceive, said the Duchess. But go and see him."

The secretary thereupon rang up 43 Brook Crescent, and was told that Mr. Benchley would be glad to see him at half-past three that afternoon.

Precisely at that hour the secretary was shown into a large, quietly furnished, sedately appointed room, and Mr. Benchley got up to greet him.

"It's very good of you to come," he said.

The secretary found himself not quite at his ease. For one thing he was somewhat taken aback by Mr. Benchley's appearance. He had expected to find a hearty, rubicund, confident Mass Murderer; instead he saw before him a pale, soft-voiced neurasthenic. Well, perhaps not so bad as that, but he looked ill and strained about the eyes, and he had some nervous tricks—staring so hard at his boot—and then that occasional and discomforting sudden throwing up of his hands towards his head, a very noticeable and obviously involuntary trick, though he half controlled it.

"I imagine," said Mr. Benchley, "that you are very curious as to my reasons for asking you to come to-day. You probably know me, if you know me at all, as the incarnation of a kind of cruelty; that is badly phrased, but you know what I mean, a Blood-Sportsman, to adapt an epithet of Shaw's. So I have been, but the past tense is appropriate, for I do not intend to merit that epithet ever again."

As he said this his hands once again jumped towards his head, were controlled and brought down again. He wiped his forehead with his handkerchief.

"Officially at least, we do not attack or concern ourselves with fishing, shooting or hunting," replied the secretary guardedly. "Many of our members shoot, fish and hunt."

"I know that," said Mr. Benchley, staring fixedly at the toe of his shoe. "All the same I have fired my last shot and caught my last fish. I fired my last shot exactly a month ago. Do you have many cases of so sudden a conversion?"

"I've known quite a few," answered the secretary. "In fact in a little way I am such a case myself; I shot when I was young and enjoyed it."

"Have you ever in a sense enjoyed anything more?"

"In a limited sense, no."

"Then why did you give it up?"

"Well," said the secretary, "I found that the memory of the movements and sounds made by the animals I had wounded remained with me. I used to dream of them. But besides that, I suppose I grew up *sensitively* as it were." He would have expanded this remark slightly if it had not been for the fact that Mr. Benchley threw his hands up again, which distracted him.

"I believe," said Mr. Benchley, "that the sensitiveness to which you refer is an unchallengeable symptom of intellectual, and to some extent, moral superiority. Highly sensitive people are ahead of their time. A general quickening of sensitiveness in a race is equivalent to a general refinement of its civilisation. One day, it may be, to kill an animal for amusement will be considered an act of flagrant indecency, as serious an offence as wearing a white tie with a dinner jacket. As a matter of fact my conversion was not quite as abrupt as it seems. My father shot all his life, and I killed my first rabbit when I was twelve. It seemed a perfectly natural thing to do. But I can recall certain more or less short-lived premonitions that it wouldn't always seem so natural. Every now and again I felt disgusted and uncertain, and these occasions became more and more frequent until that day a month ago. On that day I had certain experiences, experiences I had had before, but they suddenly seemed vile and harrowing, unendurable, intolerable. As a result of them I had a mild form of nervous breakdown. I have been in the doctor's hands for the last month—I am better now, but not entirely cured, I'm afraid. It sounds an absurd question, but can you see any mark, any stain of any kind on the toe of my right shoe?" He pushed it forward.

The secretary made rather a business of deciding this point, for he was not feeling too comfortable. "None whatever," he replied with great emphasis, after a close scrutiny.

"I thought not," replied Mr. Benchley; "it is simply that I have been a little worried about my eyesight since that trouble a month ago. I quite realise," he continued, "that it would probably split your society from top to bottom if it attempted to tackle the shooting-hunting problem, and the money I am going to give it will be given unconditionally. At the same time I should prefer that some of it at least was expended in furthering the following causes. I will put all this in writing, of course.

"Firstly: To put pressure on the Government to bring in a Bill making it compulsory for all drivers of horse vehicles to pass an examination in horsemastership before they are allowed to drive.

"Secondly: I should like a certain percentage of this money to be devoted to the discovery of a humane trap for rabbits.

"Thirdly: To inquire temperately and impartially into the vivisection question.

"Fourthly: To put pressure on the Government, by arousing public opinion, concerning the export overseas of old horses. Any money within reason you want for rest-homes for such horses will be forthcoming.

"That will do for a start, and now I will give you a cheque." He went to his bureau and fetched it.

When the secretary saw the figures his eyes grew wide and he began to utter fervent expressions of gratitude, to which Mr. Benchley put, almost rudely, an immediate stop.

When the secretary was out in the street again, he set off whistling and swinging his cane. "That old bird gave me the 'willies' for some reason or other," he said to himself. "There's something slightly 'dunno-what' about him. Who cares! It's his money we want! He seems extremely tame. I can imagine him allowing a really fierce snipe to bite his ear. Who cares! It's his money we want!"

After he had left, Mr. Benchley opened and shut his right hand many times, and he did this to convince himself that he no longer had the sensation that he was gripping something warm and feathered which writhed slightly whenever his nails met his palm.

A few days later his drawing-room was transformed into a highly efficient office, with a secretary and three plain but serviceable typists, all of whom were kept exceedingly busy. After they had been at it for three weeks the first-fruits of their labours were seen in the shape of a column long letter to *The Times* signed by their employer. In this he had the cool nerve to suggest that, as a result of many years' desultory, and a few weeks' concentrated examination of the subject, he had come to the conclusion that the utilitarian arguments for hunting and shooting were completely fallacious. He himself had shot all his life, though he had now given up doing so, but he realised he had shot simply and solely because he had found killing animals amusing; obeying a potent, savage impulse. Many people, he believed, salved their consciences when they inflicted gross pain on animals by reflecting that, "some one had got to do it." In his opinion *no one* had got to do it. And an elaborately documented argument followed.

This bombshell started one of the most heated and co-pious controversies in the history of Press debate, for this discordant chatter spread from *The Times* and rippled out over the length and breadth of the British Isles, and wherever two or three were gathered together, the introduction of this tinder topic made for fiery dissension. Mr. Benchley's former friends shook compassionate fists in protest. "The poor old dotard! Incipient senile decay! Nervous breakdown! Blood pressure! Piffling sentimentality! Hopeless bunk!" Such were the exclamatory refutations with which they repudiated such sloppy heresy. Yet he did not lack adherents, and the skirmish swirled into a battle, and the battle surged into a campaign. Mr. Benchley's post-bag was worthy of a filmstar's, though he had few requests for signed photographs; but every communication which deserved one received a courteous, if usually and necessarily a controversial reply. He had always had the capacity to write concisely; now controlled passion lent him a style, so that his short contributions to sympathetic weekly papers were well worthy of their polished company. These little papers usually took the form of impressionist sketches of incidents he had witnessed during his sporting career; vignettes of animals' terror and pain, very often. Sometimes they were dispassionate little studies of the psychology of those responsible for that terror and pain. One and all made a curious impression of authenticity, and many of great horror and distress.

Throughout all this time Mr. Benchley kept himself entirely aloof from his fellow-men. His former friends had no more wish to meet him than he had to meet them. And he was in no mood to make new friends. He worked ten hours a day, making up for much lost time. He left his business to his partner. The secretary dined with him once a week to report progress and plan schemes for the future. He became gradually acclimatised to his host's eccentricities, for which he made St. Vitus responsible. Mr. Benchley still continued at intervals most fixedly and urgently to regard certain apparently blank spots on the wall or the table-cloth, and once in a while he flung his hands up to his head, but he no longer seemed so unnecessarily preoccupied with the toe of his shoe. St. Vitus had yielded a point. He had observed correctly, the explanation being that Mr. Benchley no longer was compelled to accept the fact that he could see a small splashed globe of blood on the toe of his shoe. This visual relief coincided with the patenting of an efficient humane rabbit trap and the initiation of a campaign to make its use compulsory. The bitter controversy started by Mr. Benchley's letters gradually died down, as he had realised it would, but it left, nevertheless, certain permanent results, revealed, not so much by a perceptible but probably temporary decrease in the number of those who hunted and shot, as in a general intensification of that uncertainty and unease which had always troubled humane persons at the thought of at what expense they took their pleasure, a slight moving of the waters of sensitive perception. He was ahead of his time, but his teaching was not merely ridiculed. It was frantically assailed by some, its sincerity was grudgingly conceded by others, it was fervently welcomed as a potent aperient for the bowels of compassion by those who had long laboured in the same cause against apparently hopeless odds.

It was on the day that *The Times* announced it could no longer extend the hospitality of its columns to the debate that Mr. Benchley found himself most blessedly free from another ocular bother. That swollen, red blob which always reminded him so horribly of the pulped eye of a rabbit no longer imprinted itself on flat surfaces, and remained there, as it were staring aloofly at him. This, he had hoped *subjective* appearance, had been both frequent and regular, but like shellfire its effect on his mind increased rather than diminished with repetition.

The day after he was freed from this eccentricity, all the windows on the ground-floor of his house were broken by persons unknown, and some abusive phrases were painted on his front door, a gesture charitably attributed to medical students. This was quite probable, for the society's inquiry into the pros and cons of vivisection had brought some uncomfortable facts to the light, and it was generally known that Mr. Benchley had been at the back of this inquest. He heard the succession of crashes just as he was reading a report from the secretary stating that, since the date when he had first

interested himself in its affairs, the subscriptions and dona-
tions received by the society had increased four hundred per
cent., that a grant of £10,000 had been made to the affiliated
society in Spain, and that the long over-due fight against the
torture of the Indian Water Buffalo was about to be begun
with adequate financial support. Mr. Benchley felt that those
crashes rather appropriately signalled these announcements.
A little later the society announced that a certain person,
who desired to remain anonymous, had subscribed £5,000
to it to form the nucleus of a special Benchley Fund to be
devoted to the further education of the public in regard to
Blood Sports.

The fund reached £20,000 in a week. On the last day of
that week, Mr. Benchley ceased to fling his hands up towards
his ears at regular intervals, for he no longer felt that agonised
scream suddenly shake on their drums. Nevertheless, he went to
bed that night feeling utterly exhausted and ill. The next morning he couldn't get up, and when the doctor came he diagnosed
pulmonary pneumonia and engaged day and night nurses.

Up to the crisis, Mr. Benchley fought for his life, for he
had much still to do, but he had undermined his powers of
resistance by insensate overwork, and presently he knew he
could fight no more. After that he relapsed into gradually
lengthening periods of unconsciousness. When he realised he
was dying he sent for the secretary, to whom he gave certain
instructions regarding the use of the fortune he was leaving
to the society. The secretary had come to regard Mr. Benchley as a very great man, and when he had shaken hands with
him, and said good-bye and left him, there were tears in his
eyes as he swung his cane jauntily.

The doctor came about four o'clock and made his examination. He took the nurse out from the sickroom with him,
and shrugging his shoulders said, "There is nothing more to
be done. He may last one hour or twelve."

"I'm wanted for another case to-morrow," said the nurse.
"Will it be safe for me to accept it?"

"Oh, yes, he can't possibly last through the night. He re-
fuses to have any more oxygen. I can't help respecting him,
though I know he financed that damn-fool inquiry."

During his periods of unconsciousness Mr. Benchley had
dreams. In one of them he seemed to be watching a small excited boy who was staring across a surging field of corn over
which a windhover was poised against the gale. And suddenly
it lifted and soared over the bordering trees, a dark speck
against the green, and disappeared. This dream recurred
three times. And then he awoke full of a great weakness and
a certain sense of peace. The nurse had gone out to pack
her bag. The fire was alive but dying, just one still pregnant
coal was thrusting forth lazy, lolling flames which slightly
darkened the shadows. Mr. Benchley was just about to surrender again to that overmastering weariness when it seemed
to him that something leapt lightly on to the bed beside him,
something which turned and faced him. And at first one of
its eyes was clear, and the other bleeding and broken. With
an effort he turned his head towards it, and then he saw that
both its eyes were bright and whole again. And it nestled to
his side. And after a little while something else fluttered up
on to the blanket, something which for a moment trailed a
wing and writhed, and then settled itself down beside him,
trimly and stealthily. The flames died down, but there was
just enough light left to enable Mr. Benchley to catch the
outline of something big and brown which dragged its hind
legs towards him. Mr. Benchley tried with all his might to
get his hands to his ears, and he shut his eyes. But the silence was unbroken and he opened them again, and that big,
brown shadow moved easily towards him and tucked itself
down beside his arm. And then the fire shook itself slightly
and the room was dark. And Mr. Benchley, feeling three
little pressures against him, rallied his failing strength, and
just succeeded in moving his right hand over and down, and
it closed over two long, soft ears, which twitched gently, as if
with pleasure. And a moment later Mr. Benchley fell asleep.

"Look Up There!"

Why did he always stare up? And why did he so worry Mr. Packard by doing it? The latter had come to Brioni to read and to rest, and to take the bare minimum of notice of his fellowmen. Doctor's orders! And here he was preoccupied, almost obsessed, by the garish idiosyncrasy of this tiny, hen-eyed fellow. He was not a taking specimen of humanity, for his forehead was high and receding, his nose beaked fantastically and the skin stretched so tightly across it that it seemed as if it might be ripped apart at any moment. Then, he had a long, thin-lipped mouth always slightly open, and a pointed beard which, like his hair, was fussy and unkempt. He was for ever in the company of a stalwart yokel—a south-country enlisted Guardsman to the life; a slow-moving, massive, red-faced plebeian who seemed a master of the desirable art of aphasia, for no word ever seemed to pass his lips. But, good heavens! how he ploughed and furrowed the menu!

Mr. Packard was a very important Civil servant, and, contrary to the opinion of the vulgar, Civil servants sometimes overwork. The notion that they arrive at their offices just in time for lunch, and return again to them just in time to sign a few letters and catch a train home, is a fantasy derived from newspapers, and therefore from newspaper proprietors—idle fellows as a rule, for all they have to do is to propagate ideas and employ other people to carry them out. Anyone can have ideas; it is the carrying them out which means work.

Mr. Packard had ideas, usually very judicious and admirable
ideas, and he also had to carry them out, which meant work—
eventually overwork, a threatened nervous breakdown, peremptory advice from a specialist, and three months' leave.
He had been recommended Brioni in June because it was
between seasons for that green and placid isle, and there was
plenty of sun, gentle breezes blown over a purple sea, very
purple, very warm, very salt; a golf course, with seven short
holes, and a reasonable tariff. Perched primly in the Adriatic,
it offered every possible advantage, every chance of speedy
convalescence to an overworked bachelor fifty-two years of
age, with nothing whatsoever organically wrong with him.
So Mr. Packard had found it till his eye had been caught by
this curious couple: one who never spoke, but stolidly filled
his belly, the other who was no more communicative, and
for ever stared upwards at an angle of thirty-five degrees, for
such Mr. Packard, after an exasperating calculation, estimat-
ed it to be. On the first occasion he had noticed him, Mr.
Packard had instinctively stared up also, wondering what object of interest was to be found on the bare, brimstone-tinted
wall of the dining-room at an angle of thirty-five degrees
about. But there was nothing. Yet this midget had continued
to gaze up, even while eating his fish and emptying his glass.
And his companion, that burly proletarian, appeared entirely
unconcerned. Again Mr. Packard's eyes tilted in sympathy,
only to encounter a bare brimstone wall. It then occurred
to him that this angular obsession must be of long standing,
for its victim most expertly neutralised what must have been
a heavy handicap to accurate feeding by an impressive dexterity in the manipulation of knives and forks and spoons,
though his appetite seemed as slender as his physical frame.

So stern and uncompromising had been the specialist's
fiat, that Mr. Packard had been genuinely alarmed about his
nerves; so much so that he almost entertained the possibility
that this upward-peering absurdity was a figment of his dis-
ordered imagination—a very unlovely thought—but he had

dismissed it with a very comforting reassurance when he saw that others among the sparse company then visiting Brioni were also puzzled by this singular prepossession of the hen-eyed fellow.

What an incongruous couple they were! And why didn't the lusty rustic turn his eyes up too—or do something about it? Well, let him take a leaf out of his book, and pay no regard to what was none of his business, and certainly no part of his cure.

If the fellow wanted to stare up, let him. So, by making a considerable effort, Mr. Packard looked away. All the same, he was charged with a tantalising and hard-to-exorcise curiosity about this couple, their circumstances, the connection between them—all this—but, above all, why the devil the tiny one stared up. Knowing such wonderings could only delay the healing of the lesion in his nervous system, he made quite elaborate plans for avoiding the pair. He changed the times of his meals, and if he saw them in a room he went to another, and if he observed them coming towards him he turned on his heel. By these means he freed his mind of them to some extent, but a sneaking, insidious inquisitiveness endured. However, the sun and air and peace of Brioni rapidly restored him, and once again he slept an unbroken eight hours; he found himself with such an appetite as he had not known for twenty years, and the idea that there was someone standing just behind him all the time—a very irritating symptom, this—most absolutely and blessedly ceased. So, reassuringly soon, his inner eye began to turn longingly to a snug though austere office in Whitehall, with neatly raised pyramids of "jackets" and official documents of undeniable secrecy and import. And to that leisurely stroll up to the club at one o'clock so punctually, and that carefully chosen little lunch, and perhaps a game of chess with Lenton, some gossip, and a leisurely stroll back to the Home Office, where there would be decisions to make, questions in the House to consider, a feeling of slight but pleasing importance, and all that regulated system and ordered regime which suited him temperamentally so perfectly.

A holiday in August seemed a justifiable weakness to him, but to idle about in dreamy, flushing, dark-green islands in June was abnormal—a process which should not be prolonged for an unnecessary second. He would stick it out for a week or two longer, and count the days till the hour of his release should strike—release from indolence, strolling about, and from an inclination to uneasy, vague surmisings concerning an ill-assorted couple, one of whom for ever raised his eyes in a sort of viewless intensity, and the other who never spoke but was for ever at his side.

On the evening before his departure, about six o'clock, Mr. Packard strolled along the path through the holm oaks towards the bathing place and sat down on a seat overlooking the shadowed and darkening straits of the Istrian shore. Shadowed and darkening because a slowly marshalling army of clouds was rising above the Dolomites and frowning down over Trieste. The sun, resisting and not yet overpowered, hurled red and gold shafts up through the advancing host. The spectacle had a certain sombre sublimity, and its leisurely shifting pattern pleasantly absorbed Mr. Packard's attention, so much that when a rather high-pitched and deliberate voice remarked, "Some persons have found in such spectacles evidence of the existence of a God," he started abruptly and half rose from his seat. He must have been half-asleep, for he found sitting on the same seat beside him that enigmatic pair, the little one next to him and the yokel—on his other side—smoking a pipe and staring out to sea. Mr. Packard was irritated and taken by surprise, but his natural good manners and subconscious curiosity prevented him from uttering the tart and "snubby" retort which half rose to his lips. Instead, he said dryly, "The particular deity concerned is most certainly Jupiter Pluvius. I imagine that Trieste will get the benefit of that storm soon and it will be our turn in an hour or so."

"From your tone," suggested the little man, "I judge you are of a sceptical turn of mind."

("And what the devil has it got to do with you if I am?") thought Mr. Packard. "If you mean," he said, "that I do not see why all that is beautiful should be put to the credit of what you call God, that is so. For in whom do you lodge the responsibility for the somewhat less palatable spectacles provided by bull-fights and battle-fields? Unless you are a dualist."

"Very possibly I am," said the little man, staring up at the fading sun, now drowning in a majestically pacing cloud ocean.

"Well," said Mr. Packard, "it will be the devil's turn soon enough. Storms in this region are no joke."

"I think I have reason to believe in the devil," continued the little man, taking off his rusty panama and placing it on the ground beside him. As he said this the yokel looked at him sharply, then knocked out his pipe on his boot and began filling it again from an aluminium box.

"Oh, indeed," replied Mr. Packard, his curiosity rising. "I have myself deduced him logically, but I take it you have had a closer view of him."

"Yes," answered the little man, his eyes on the rim of the advancing storm, "I think I can say that. Would you like to hear about it?"

"Certainly," said Mr. Packard.

"I'm glad of that, because it is a relief to me to tell it now and again. Does Gauntry Hall convey anything to you?"

"Gauntry Hall," repeated Mr. Packard uncertainly. "The name seems vaguely familiar."

"It was a famous show place burnt down in 1904. I was there that night."

"Oh, I remember now," said Mr. Packard. "Middle Tudor, near Leicester, famous chiefly for its Long Gallery; and wasn't there some legend about it?"

"Yes," replied the little man; "and the fact that you can recall so much is a great tribute to your memory."

"Oh, I was rather keen on that period once upon a time when I was less busy."

"I went up to Oxford the same term as Jack Gauntry, and to the same college—Oriel," continued the little man, his eyes narrowed and shifting and busy with the sky. "In those days I was keenly interested in the occult: I believe it to have been somewhat of a pose—a dangerous pose. I knew there was some queer story about Gauntry Hall, and made up my mind I would get Jack to tell me about it; not a very creditable ambition, but I was young and foolish, and I have been punished enough. We became great friends, and one evening I had my chance. He came up to my rooms rather late one night, in November, 1896, after dining out. He was a little drunk, and still thirsty. I filled him up, and finally brought the subject round to Gauntry Hall.

"'Funny you should mention it,' he said; 'my people did the annual trek to London to-day.'

"'How do you mean—"annual trek"?' I asked.

"He did not answer for a moment, and I could see he was torn between two impulses—one to cleanse his bosom of this family obsession, the other to keep his mouth dutifully shut. So I gave him another whisky-and-soda. He drank it in a gulp and then became muzzy and garrulous. I could see he would find relief in being unrestrainedly indiscreet. I'm not boring you?"

"Not in the least," Mr. Packard reassured him.

"'Well,' suddenly Jack blurted out, 'No one's allowed to be in the house New Year's Eve.'

"'Why not?'

"'Oh, because the Bogey Man gets busy then. As a matter of fact, no one is supposed to have spent New Year's Eve at Gauntry for three hundred years. So as not to make it too conspicuous, we always clear out during the last week in November. Perhaps it's all bosh—I sometimes wonder. Any way, I shouldn't be telling you this, but I'm slightly tight, and shall tell you some more.'

"I was feeling rather ashamed of myself, and it was on the tip of my tongue to shut him up. But I didn't.

"'No one's allowed there on New Year's Eve, but early next morning old Carrow, the butler—the Carrows have been in our service for years and years—comes to the house and opens all the windows one after the other and shuts them again—the hell of a job. All but one, the one in the middle of the first floor of the south wing. And out of this one he has to hang a white silk banner which is in the Long Gallery and wave it three times very slowly, and then—shall I tell you what he has to do then?'

"'No,' I said, for I knew I was hearing what I should not and that I should be bitterly repentant if I let him go on. 'Shut up, and I'll forget what you've told me.'

"This seemed to sober him up. 'Yes, I hope you will,' he replied, and got up and left the room. We never referred to the subject again.

"I spent half the summer vac. at Gauntry Hall for the four years I was 'up.' It was an exquisite house, gloriously placed, and the grounds were perfection. But you remember it, so I need not describe it. Sir John and Lady Gauntry were sweet survivals from an easier age—a type which began to disappear with the introduction of modern plumbing from America. They were rather slow and faded, their manners were a heritage, their benign suzerainty over the local serfs and villeins a sharp reminder that there was something in consonance with society in the Feudal System. Well, they are dust by now. I grew to love the old place. Its atmosphere seemed so placid, untroubled, unshakable in those long, lovely summer days that I could hardly believe it was ever visited by a curious winter spell; that it ever could cease to drowse and become most malignantly awake. The subject was never alluded to within its walls, but I remember I used to find my eyes wandering up to that window in the middle of the south wing. Yes, I used to find myself looking up—that was all. At least, I think that was all, though one evening when I was taking a stroll after dinner I happened to glance up at this window, and for a second it seemed as if something white fluttered from it and disappeared. But it may have been a projection from my own mind.

"And then came the Boer War, and Jack went out with his Yeomanry and was killed on the Modder. The shock drove the old couple into complete seclusion, and they died within a few days of each other early in 1903. Meanwhile, I had completely lost touch with Gauntry Hall. And then one day I met Teller, the agent, in the street and he lunched with me. He told me the estate had been leased to people called Relf, *nouveaux riches*. Young Relf was the son of a millionaire multiple-shop owner in the North, and he had married some little vulgarian. Teller utterly despised these town-bred parvenus and considered their occupation of Gauntry defiling and almost intolerable.

"'But they may not be there much longer,' he said, 'for the damn fools are going to spend New Year's Eve in the house.'

"'What!' I cried.

"'Oh, yes,' he replied; 'they are greatly looking forward to it. I felt it my duty to warn them, but I might have saved myself the trouble, for when I had said my piece, that little barmaid, Mrs. Relf, who looks like a painted Pekinese, clapped her hands on her knees and declared she simply adored ghosts—didn't believe in them a bit, would have a house-party for the occasion, and wish a very Happy New Year to whoever or whatever came. I reminded her she was preparing to break a rule which had lasted for three hundred years. "Quite time it *was* broken," said she. So I shrugged my shoulders and gave it up. I wish them luck!'

"'All the same,' I said, 'it's one of the most interesting pieces of news I've heard for a long time.

"'Well, if you think that, why don't you make one of the party?' asked Teller, laughing.

"'How could I? I don't know them.'

"'Oh, that doesn't matter. They're very partial to peers.'

"I was about to say 'No' most emphatically when I was seized by a most violent temptation. Here were these fools prepared to put this most ancient and vague and famous mystery to the test. It was a unique opportunity. Dangerous? Yes, probably, but the old house had always seemed friendly to me. Here was I, a professed student of the occult, presented with a glorious opportunity for investigation. If I failed to take it I should never forgive myself nor have any respect for myself. I imagine you can sympathise with my feelings to some extent."

"Oh, yes," replied Mr. Packard; "no doubt I should have done as I infer you did."

"Yes, I accepted."

As the little man said this Mr. Packard noticed the yokel glance across at him, and as their eyes met it seemed as though the fellow wished to convey a message of some sort. A warning, was it?

"Yes," continued the little man. "I accepted. Teller fixed up the invitation for me, and I reached Leicester Station about 5.30 on New Year's Eve twenty-three years ago. The moment I got into the trap and we began to drive eastward through rows of dingy villas, I began to feel a nervous irritation which steadily increased as we drove towards Gauntry. It was a foul night, blowing very hard, and sleeting, and every yard we travelled made me wish the more I hadn't come. I could feel the influence of Gauntry reaching out and attempting to repel me. I'd have gone straight back to the station but for one thing. Supposing I funked it and nothing happened. That story might get round, which wouldn't have been pleasant. All the same, when we reached the house, it took all my resolution to cross its threshold. The old place had always seemed so friendly and welcoming before; now it was sullen, and utterly hostile. I felt as if I were a traitor, as if I had been caught by my best friend in the act of forging his name. I was so seized by dread and nervously unstrung that I hardly noticed the rest of the party. I remember there

were ten of us, five women and five men, and that they all
appeared to be young, noisy and vulgar-—so noisy that I was
convinced they had had a good many of the primitive cocktails which they were drinking as I arrived, and presently I
knew they were almost as full of dread and as unstrung as
myself. The house seemed throbbing with a sinister rhythm.
It seemed as if it had summoned the great wind which leaped
at it in gigantic gusts. By coming there that day I had in-
curred its malignant enmity, and with cold austerity it was
bidding me begone. I had my old room in the east wing, but
when I went up to dress, it was as though an almost materi-
alised force was disputing my entry. I had to breast my way
through it as through a hostile tide. I found they had decided
to dine in the Great Hall instead of the dining-room—why,
I don't know. Round ran a balcony from which a door led
through the famous Long Gallery. When we sat down I knew
them all to be suffering from an acute spiritual malaise, and
that what they had drunk, far from lulling their sensitiveness
to the power which menaced them, had but weakened their
resistance to it. How soon will the storm break?"

"In ten minutes or so," replied Mr. Packard. "I am surprised it has not broken before now. It is reserving all its
venom for us."

"Then I may have just time to finish. I do not remember
whether I spoke a word throughout that meal, but I do know
that I was under such a strain that I had to grip my chair
to stop myself running from the room. The women were on
the verge of hysteria, the men drank feverishly and, as time
went on, a dreadful vague, inane babble came from all of
them. The woman on my right—she had a high, thin voice—
suddenly gulped down a full glass of champagne some of
which swilled over her chin and neck and shouted: 'Well,
when does it begin?' and then went off into peals of hysterical laughter. We did not move from the table, and from
half-past ten onwards, Relf kept getting up to ring the bell,
but no servant appeared. 'Where are those bloody slaves?' he

cried each time, and staggered back to the table and filled his glass again. From half-past eleven I was no longer master of myself. The room was thick with smoke which wreathed itself into fantastic patterns. The pressure grew unendurable, and suddenly my resistance broke, and I ran from the great hall up to my room and lay cowering on my bed. I could still hear the crazy, chaotic babble from those I had left, and then a great bell crashed out. *One-two-three*—and each mighty stroke followed so hard on its predecessor that the vile jangle almost seemed an undivided sound. It was as if a murderer was hammering in my brain. Suddenly it ceased, and I heard no sound from below, and then came one high, piercing scream from a woman: 'Look up there!' and then every light in the house went out.

"Well, when that happened I groped round the room for my electric torch. At last I found it, and I think if I had not found it just then I should have suffered even more than I have suffered. I staggered downstairs and into the Great Hall, and flashed the lamp on the table. They were all sitting rigidly, their eyes looking up and focused on the door into the Long Gallery. I peered into their faces one by one. Their eyes were wide, yet drawn in, as though asquint; their heads were strained back on their shoulders; their mouths were open, and foam was on their lips. And then I flashed my torch up towards the door into the Long Gallery, and there—and there—"

The cloud army had advanced so far that it was looming down on them. Two striding horns of vapour preceded it. As the little man cried "and there—and there—" a blinding flash leapt from one to the other, so that these enflamed and curled tentacles drove down at them, or so it seemed most terrifyingly to Mr. Packard, and the rending crash of thunder which followed hard upon it hurled its echoes round the world. And then, with inchoate fury, the storm drove forward to the attack. And then the little man leapt to his feet and flung his arms above his head and screamed out as

though in agony: "Look up there! Look up there!" Mr. Packard moved towards him, but in a second the yokel had him
by the shoulders. "Leave him to me," he shouted against the
thunder, "I know what to do." And he began to propel the
little man before him. Mr. Packard, oblivious of the rain,
stared after them. With a horrid regularity the little man
flung up his arms and screamed: "Look up there!" and presently they turned a corner and disappeared, and the screams
grew fainter. For a moment Mr. Packard stared upwards too,
and then, as another flash speared down to the sea, he came
to himself, and turning up the collar of his coat, started to
run through the blinding rain back to the hotel.

"Written in Our Flesh"

Mr. Timothy Frone put down his pencil. It was true, he supposed, that one could write poetry, he knew it was true that one could write prose, *de profundis,* but only a human type-writer could pen newspaper paragraphs about inane and despicable minutiae when his heart was in his boots. He couldn't, anyway, though his next meal—his very life—depended upon it. But was he so anxious to live? Three weeks ago he had been, when he had first seen his novel on sale at Mr. Denny's shop in the Strand, and then a little later at the bookstall at Waterloo. He had bought three copies—all he could afford—to encourage the others—the price of a paragraph. That first excitement and tempered elation over, he had waited desperately for news. He had longed to ring up his publishers to learn how it was going. But he had waited three weeks and then gone round to see them, and had sat trembling in the waiting-room till his summons had come. The Senior Partner received him with resigned and practised amiability. "Not very good news, I'm afraid, Mr. Frone," he said, holding out his cigarette case.

And Mr. Frone had said, "Oh, I'm sorry to hear that," and he had fixed his eyes on a pile of manuscripts on Mr. Dickinson's table which seemed to be wavering slightly like an earthquake-shaken pagoda.

"Can't get the reviews," continued Mr. Dickinson. "As you know I have always believed in your novel, but it is impossible for a book, however distinguished, to make its way unless the reviewers help it. We have advertised it, of course, but a book by an unknown writer cannot be helped much by advertising unless we can append to the bare announcement of its publication some extracts from a favourable review by a well-known critic."

"No, I realise that," said Mr. Frone; "isn't it selling at all?"

"We subscribed two hundred and twenty copies—to such depths has the novel business sunk! We have had small repeats here and there, but I'm afraid the total is not yet three hundred."

"Then it's what you would call a hopeless dud, I suppose?" said Mr. Frone.

Mr. Dickinson looked down at his fingers which were tapping his desk.

"Oh, it's too soon to pronounce quite such a depressing verdict as that, and, as I have said, I know it to be good work. It just wants a push and then it would start to sell. For example, if Reginald Stall were to mention it favourably in one of his Wireless talks I am certain we should sell at least five thousand copies."

"Oh, really," said Mr. Frone, "is he so influential as all that?"

"Most certainly he is. He can make or break, but he can only break by keeping silence, for even a slating from him is very much better than nothing. Yet there is no man whose opinion I less respect. All the same, you can't manage anything in that direction, I suppose?"

"I'm very much afraid not. I have a friend on the *Banner* who knows him, but he told me that Mr. Stall never notices any book if he is asked to do so."

"Unless the suppliant has a handle to his or her name," rejoined the publisher dryly.

"Well, then, I suppose there is nothing I can do," said Mr. Frone.

"Only by mobilising any journalistic influence you may possess. I have been in this game too long to retain any illusions. I'd rather be a Charles Garvice with good Press backing than a Joseph Conrad without any. The best may come to the top, but the upward pressure from the right friends in the right newspaper offices is the easiest way for it to do so. Perhaps that is too cynical, but the publication of fiction is not calculated to foster credulous optimism. However, we must hope for the best."

"Poor little devil," thought Mr. Dickinson when Mr. Frone had gone; "he always reminds me of a small bird with a broken wing."

It was the impression left by this interview which had frustrated Mr. Frone's attempts to make much headway with "A Day in the Life of Queen Souriya," although the editor of the *Echo* had been quite enthusiastic, and for three chatty paragraphs on the subject had offered to pay £1 17s. 6d. = one week's rent and seven meals. But Mr. Frone lacked the heart to improvise.

The room in which he lived and worked and slept was the epitome of utter and shameless shabbiness. Had it been on the top floor it would have been quite unarguably a garret. He looked round it, and a sense of final disgust and defeat and nauseating repulsion surged through him; such as greatly oppresses those with the instincts of gentlemen— however simple their tastes—when squalor is their inevitable portion and somehow they feel they have not quite deserved it. And then there was a rap on the door and Mr. Waller thrust his vital, bustling person into the room.

"I've got news for you Tim," he exclaimed, "very, very good news. Stall is going to review your book from 2LO to-night."

Mr. Frone's heart gave a hard thump, missed three beats, so that he leaned forward quickly to get his breath, and then began working spasmodically and uncertainly, and he had to cough sharply to disguise the fact that this rather urgent inconvenience was troubling him.

"Well, that *is* good news," he said; "are you sure?" (How desperately he wanted to be sure.)

"Yes, quite. He was in the office to-day and asked me to tell him about you, as he was very impressed with the book. I filled him up with the right stuff I can assure you. I asked his typist afterwards, and she said you were down for tonight for certain."

"It certainly will make a difference," said Mr. Prone. "I've been feeling rather depressed about it. It hasn't begun to sell yet, and I was afraid it was destined to be a hopeless failure."

"Well, you needn't worry any more; you're a made man. Every library will be clamouring for copies to-morrow morning, and your publishers' Trade Department will look as if it had been hit by a hurricane."

"I'd like to hear what he has to say," said Mr. Frone.

"Then come along to my rooms to-night. My wireless set is primitive, but it usually functions."

"That's awfully good of you. What time shall I come?"

"The rag-time pundit clears his throat precisely at 9.25. Come along at nine and we'll have a drink to to-morrow's Best Seller," said Mr. Waller, and he dashed away on one of his many occasions.

When he had gone Mr. Frone put his hand to his left side. Good heavens! how his heart was going, it seemed to leap, die and then struggle and stutter. That was what the doctor had meant by saying he must avoid sudden strains and shocks, but he couldn't have meant such wonderful shocks as this; no one could die from hearing such news as that. He must go out, he couldn't sit still. He walked to St. James's Park and leaned over the bridge. Small beady-eyed ducks looked expectantly up at him, and then dived, necks strained forward, gleaning stray scraps of fodder from the lake's bottom. Trim, cruising gulls cocked their heads and screamed nervously at him; a gusty breeze raised tiny waves, and a pair of mallards planed down, raised a spray flurry and shook their tails.

Mr. Frone's heart regained its rhythm, his tingling nervousness subsided, and he sat down on a bench overlooking the water. What a blessed relief to be able to think about his book again. Ever since he had felt in his bones it was a failure he had been unable to recall it to his mind without almost physical nausea. The years he had spent upon it! In a sense he had given his life to it, conceived it, borne it, lived with it and known that it was good. He would probably never write another. He knew that he was not a natural novelist, he was too autobiographical, his imaginative power and impulse were sluggish and feeble, and writing a book was a great and agonising ordeal for a person of his intellectual type. If only all the careless people who read a novel a day could realise the sheer, maddening, torturing difficulty of finding words with which to say just what one wanted to say and just as one wanted to say it! One had a sense of death when one wrote "finis." A stage of life was past, a child had been born, a purpose fulfilled, and simultaneously came nostalgia, exhaustion, a sense of nearing death. Perhaps that was only true of novels as autobiographical as his, wherein one's consciousness attempted the miracle of explaining itself to itself. What had it really done? Seen itself in a glass darkly—caught a glimpse, a fleeting glimpse, of reality—certainly it had obeyed an urgent instruction, whatever its origin, whatever its justification. Possibly it was just trying to draw a pig with one's eye shut. Anyhow, when one had done it, one longed, for some obscure reason, to have an audience, even for something so personal and subjective and so self-compelled. That was rather a mystery. The author always wishes for company, always longs to get that warming, quickening certainty that someone is saying to himself as he reads, "I understand. We're in the same boat, even if we're just sinking together." How brutal then, how remorselessly brutal, to know that all had been for nothing, that the audience was amusing itself elsewhere, that one had written an absolute and unsaleable dud. That was how he had felt, but he needn't feel it any longer. By this time to-morrow, if what his publishers said was true, and it surely must be, the audience would be eagerly assembling and some of them would be beginning to say, "I understand," and that life-long loneliness of his would be passing away, that spiritual loneliness. And he'd have money enough for two rooms, no more vile degrading hack prostitution, perhaps enough even to travel—not that he'd ever learn properly how to spend money, for you couldn't teach poor old dogs new expensive tricks. Yes, now he could think of his book with a most bless-ed feeling of happiness and hope and confidence. After all it wasn't so bad. Here and there he had contrived just the effect he had aimed at. It was not too well-constructed per-haps, but well enough; and certain episodes had leaped to life, and he was certain that here and there he had done just precisely what he had tried to do. What had recommended it to this so miracle-working an oracle as Mr. Stall? He must have hundreds of novels to choose from, so that the very few he selected to review must have seized his attention in some sharp and dominating way. Was there anything in *Written in Our Flesh* to attract so eclectic and godlike an authori-ty? Heaven knew he was modest enough; life had given him precious little reason to be otherwise. All the same it might have a certain sincerity, perhaps a precision of attack, an absence of pose. It might carry a conviction that it had all happened and that most of it had hurt. Even a hardened reviewer, if he were as acute and accomplished a critic as Mr. Stall, would take from a book like that what the author had meant to have had taken. Waller had called him "a Rag-time Pundit," but he was not remarkable for reverence towards his colleagues. Anyhow, he'd know the answers to these tentative questions in a few hours. How marvellous, how unbelievable it sounded! These people passing by him in endless, strolling nonchalance might have his name on their lips by to-morrow.

"Have you read *Written in Our Flesh* by a fellow called Frone? Reginald Stall recommended it most highly. I tried to get a copy at Hatchards' to-day but they were sold out, not a copy left." What childish nonsense, and yet how irresistibly exciting! And it hadn't happened yet! But it would. He felt a sudden insistent desire to go back to his room and take his book, from which for the last three weeks he had deliberately averted his eyes, as it lay gathering dust on the top shelf of his tiny bookcase, take it up and open it—as Mr. Stall must have done—and begin to read through it from the beginning and pause, as Mr. Stall must have done, at certain felicities of phrasing, evidences of insight, and those unmistakable shadings of expression, which reveal the born writer. All of which was rather absurd, as he almost knew the book by heart, but to the author a praised passage is always worth re-reading—though there could be for him no such pleasant surprises, such quiet little shocks of appreciation, as must have come to Mr. Stall and persuaded him to select the book containing them from the towering tumulus of fiction at his august disposal, for the subject of part of one of his most potent and oracular disquisitions. Rather absurd, of course, but Mr. Frone felt compelled to do so. He walked hurriedly back to Number 5 Manton Street, smacked the dust from its paper jacket, and settled himself to peruse *Written in Our Flesh*.

There were even fewer women in the book than there had been in its author's life, but there had been one of some significance in each, and in each case she had disappeared rather early from the proceedings.

He turned over the pages, but instead of reading the passages of which he felt fairly satisfied, he would examine again one or two of those which were concerned with his heroine, though that was a somewhat grandiose term with which to describe the fleeting wraith whose breath had barely clouded the mirror of the first third of the book, and whose influence so thinly affected the other two-thirds.

For she had broken off their engagement with him and married someone else when he was twenty-four. Well, then, let him read again that passage where the heroine breaks off her engagement with the hero—God save the mark—aged twenty-four and married someone else.

"Harry, dear, I love you in a way and I don't love this other man, but I'm one of those women who can and must deliberately and in a way contentedly crush their sense of decency, the better but weaker side of them, to powder, if they are compelled to choose between a failure and a success. You aren't and never could be a success. I know it, I know it—as I mean success! If you like I am a frigid, calculating, though, oh, so respectable, prostitute! I am selling myself, but I know I am right to do so, for it is what my nature tells me I must do. I have stated the case to myself fairly. I have set my love for you against the clothes, the luxuries, the ease, the sense of security, the never having to think about money. I was never meant to have to think about money. If you were a different kind of man I'd be your mistress after I was married. I'm that sort of woman, for I love you, I love you, but you are not that kind of man. Harry darling, I can't bear darned socks, darned sheets, darned cheapness any more. I may be selling myself, but think what I shall be able to buy with the price! God bless you!"

Well, what would Mr. Stall think of that? Not much probably. For it was unlikely that he would recognise it as a verbatim report. But it was. That passage occurred at the end of Chapter VI, and then from then on *Written in Our Flesh* was quite lacking in feminine interest or complication.

Mr. Frone then decided to read over some other passages which were more likely to have tickled the highly critical palate of Mr. Stall. He did so, and then began to feel very sleepy. He looked at his watch—5.30. Time to rest a while before going to dinner. But before settling himself down, he took up a foolscap sheet headed, "A Day in the Life of Queen Souriya," and tore it into very small pieces and threw the scraps into the waste-paper basket. And then he lay back in his one easy-chair and closed his eyes. As he grew drowsy a curious picture began to form itself in some back area of his brain. He seemed to be watching an enormous beast, half animal, half reptile, which was stretched back as far as he could view it down a street and cramming the pavement with its bulk. This beast was on the move and passing its length through the door of a building. And above the door was inscribed the motto, "Book Club." The beast was furnished with tentacles and fins, as he could see by glancing through a window, it was seizing with its tentacles books at random and pulling them down from shelves and thrusting them under its fins. And this beast seemed to be so fluid of composition that it was flowing both in and out of the door of this building, and that portion entering seemed to merge in and pass through that portion coming out, and the effect reminded him of an attempted impression of a fourth dimensional figure in a work he had read devoted to the recondite subject. This beast had one other peculiarity—it owned no head. "That," he said to himself, just before he dropped off to sleep, "is the aspect of the reading public which obsesses the Unread, but I cannot imagine why it should have come to me, for after to-day I shall no longer be included in that category."

He woke again just before seven and went out to dine. That was as a rule rather a lavish word to apply to the process of keeping body and soul together for the next ten hours at a cost not exceeding one shilling and ninepence, but it should be justified on this occasion. Before his father lost his last penny and retired to a better world from his bedroom in a nursing home, he had been an admirable judge of good food and the right things to drink with it, and Mr. Frone had had his palate educated during his boyhood and had never quite forgotten how to read a menu, though extracting the utmost nourishment from an expenditure of two shillings (tip threepence) had not improved his taste.

He would go to the Café Royal and spend thirty shillings of the six pounds in his possession on something worth eating for once, and something worth drinking for once, to celebrate the marvellous good fortune which had come to him that day.

He chose nothing very epicurean, just bortsch, a sole, lamb cutlets, half a bottle of Meursault and a glass of good brandy. This programme was carried out, and at the end of it he felt almost gorged, and entirely exhilarated, but as the time approached for him to go to Waller's flat he began to be very, very nervous. He got there punctually at nine. Mr. Waller made him very welcome and poured him out a glass of port. Mr. Waller was very fond of Mr. Frone and till that day had been desperately sorry for him. Consequently he was feeling nervous too. But he efficiently disguised the fact and talked away about Fleet Street "shop" till the clock showed it was 9.25, and then he turned the button of his wireless set to "on." It was the tail-end of a ballad concert, and the grimly familiar strains of a venerable inanity by Tosti slushed through the loudspeaker, then mercifully ceased, and the announcer declared that the stage was set for one of Mr. Reginald Stall's famous talks on "Books of the Day," and Mr. Frone's heart performed those funny—sometimes slightly frightening—tricks again.

Mr. Reginald Stall had ceased to think and formed himself into a company at the age of fifty-two. He had done everything in turns and nothing quite badly and nothing really well, for he was fundamentally superficial. He had once had four plays running simultaneously in London theatres, which fact had formed the text for more than one sermon on the decadence of the British Drama. He knew to a hair's breadth how much sentimentality the public would stand. Though not entirely lacking in literary taste, save where his own work was concerned, he had raised himself by kowtowing, delicately disguised as criticising, to the status of an Oracle, and was paid large sums for not being too darned highbrow, for deeply respecting the half-baked susceptibles of the half-educated. References to the Deity dripped from his pen. Enough of him! On this occasion he announced his intention of dealing in the short time at his disposal with what he might call the Autobiographical Novel, illustrating his thesis by certain specimens of that genre of fiction which he had recently perused. (This piece of information was highly reassuring to Mr. Frone.) Mr. Stall then proceeded to deliver himself of some rotund introductory platitudes. The Autobiographical Novel, in his opinion, was perhaps the most poignant of all, written as it often was in the very heart's blood of its author. It was a *cri de cœur,* a cry from the heart, in many cases, something almost sacred, in the truest sense a Human Document, and it behoved the critic to deal tenderly—very tenderly—with such documents, when it was at once his duty and his pleasure to say a few words about them to such an exceptionally intelligent section of the community as that which through ear-phones and loud-speakers was doing him the honour of listening to his litle talk that night. (There he paused and took a deep pull at a double Johnnie Walker and "Polly.")

The first novel of this type to which he proposed to draw their attention this evening was, *And Then There Were Two,* by Lois Dunt, who, he understood, was a young woman. He would repeat that: *"And Then There Were Two,"* by Lois Dunt.

To Mr. Frone's stretched and aching consciousness this work seemed to be chiefly of obstetric interest, and apparently the description of heroine's extremely protracted, painful, but eventually successful attempts to increase the population was a magnificent piece of nervous prose, and the situation lost nothing of its poignancy from the fact that the masculine responsibility for the event might have been laid equally justly at the door of any one of a platoon of possibles. So "noteworthy" and "arresting" Mr. Stall found this "gripping" presentment of so original and "striking" a theme that it was 9.35 before he had said his last word upon it. Halftime!

By now there was just the trace of tension in Mr. Waller's sitting-room. He himself was smoking rather quickly. Mr. Frone was deliberately keeping his eyes away from him. Then Mr. Stall metaphorically picked up another volume, equally in his opinion a "human document," though in every case he would remind listeners it was only his intuition that told him these works were autobiographical, a necessary warning he wished most emphatically to emphasise; he ought to have done so earlier in his "little talk."

But by this time Mr. Frone could not endure to listen, but could only realise that this torrent of portifical journalese was most sharply connected with the movements of the hands of a clock which terribly soon reached 9.40. And then Mr. Stall—his time he found "running short"—drew attention to another *cri de cœur* entitled "Badinage," but Mr. Frone was finding it harder and harder to concentrate upon these observations. For one thing his heart was not making it easy to do so. At one moment it seemed that he had no pulse and that he was already dying, and then "Thump," "Thud," a horrid broken rhythm the menace of which made it so very difficult to listen. For Mr. Stall's time was almost up. And—and—and then to the dimming consciousness of Mr. Frone came a vast beast with tentacles and fins, and up went those tentacles to shelves and pulled down books, and then, as though from a vast distance, he heard Mr. Stall's voice remarking, "There was another work of this type to which I had intended to introduce you to-night, but I see I have already exceeded my time." And then Mr. Frone sent a curious, twisted glance over to Mr. Waller, which Mr. Waller could not meet—a smile of sorts. And then Mr. Frone tottered to his feet, swayed for a moment, and crashed down. As he fell his head struck the wireless set and brought it with him to the floor, and this in falling jerked at the cord connecting it with the loudspeaker, which swayed a moment and then toppled over and dropped on to Mr. Frone's head, hatting him most fantastically. The effect of this must have

been displeasing, for Mr. Waller, even before he attempted to succour Mr. Frone, clenched his fist and crashed the
loud-speaker into a corner of the room, where it crumpled
sharply.

Blind Man's Buff

"Well, thank heavens that yokel seemed to know the place," said Mr. Cort to himself. "'First to the right, second to the left, black gates.' I hope the oaf in Wendover who sent me six miles out of my way will freeze to death. It's not often like this in England—cold as the penny in a dead man's eye." He'd barely reach the place before dusk. He let the car out over the rasping, frozen roads. "'First to the right'"—must be this—second to the left, must be this—and there were the black gates. He got out, swung them open, and drove cautiously up a narrow, twisting drive, his headlights peering suspiciously round the bends. Those hedges wanted clipping, he thought, and this lane would have to be remetalled—full of holes. Nasty drive up on a bad night; would cost some money, though.

The car began to climb steeply and swing to the right, and presently the high hedges ended abruptly, and Mr. Cort pulled up in front of Lorn Manor. He got out of the car, rubbed his hands, stamped his feet, and looked about him.

Lorn Manor was embedded half-way up a Chiltern spur and, as the agent had observed, "commanded extensive vistas." The place looked its age, Mr. Cort decided, or rather ages, for the double Georgian brick chimneys warred with the Queen Anne left front. He could just make out the date, 1703, at the base of the nearest chimney. All that wing must have been added later. "Big place, marvellous bargain at seven thousand, can't understand it. How those windows with their little curved eyebrows seem to frown down on one!" And then he turned and examined the "vistas." The trees were tinted exquisitely to an uncertain glory as the great red sinking sun flashed its rays on their crystal mantle. The vale of Aylesbury was drowsing beneath a slowly deepening shroud of mist. Above it the hills, their crests rounded and shaded by silver and rose coppices, seemed to have set in them great smoky eyes of flame where the last rays burned in them.

"It is like some dream world," thought Mr. Cort. "It is curious how, wherever the sun strikes, it seems to make an eye, and each one fixed on me; those hills, even those windows. But, judging from that mist, I shall have a slow journey home; I'd better have a quick look inside, though I have already taken a prejudice against the place—I hardly know why. Too lonely and isolated, perhaps." And then the eyes blinked and closed, and it was dark. He took a key from his pocket and went up three steps and thrust it into the keyhole of the massive oak door. The next moment he looked forward into absolute blackness, and the door swung to and closed behind him. This, of course, must be the "palatial panelled hall" which the agent described. He must strike a match and find the light-switch. He fumbled in his pockets without success, and then he went through them again. He thought for a moment, "I must have left them on the seat in the car," he decided; "I'll go and fetch them. The door must be just behind me here."

He turned and groped his way back, and then drew himself up sharply, for it had seemed that something had slipped past him, and then he put out his hands—to touch the back of a chair, brocaded, he judged. He moved to the left of it and walked into a wall, changed his direction, went back past the chair, and found the wall again. He went back to the chair, sat down, and went through his pockets again, more thoroughly and carefully this time. Well, there was nothing to get fussed about; he was bound to find the door sooner or later. Now, let him think. When he came in he had gone straight forward, three yards perhaps; but he couldn't have gone straight back, because he'd stumbled into this chair. The door must be a little to the left or the right of it. He'd try each in turn. He turned to the left first, and found himself going down a little narrow passage; he could feel its sides when he stretched out his hands. Well, then, he'd try the right. He did so, and walked into a wall. He groped his way along it, and again it seemed as if something slipped past him. "I wonder if there's a bat in here?" he asked himself, and then found himself back at the chair.

How Rachel would laugh if she could see him how. Surely he had a stray match somewhere. He took off his overcoat and ran his hands round the seam of every pocket, and then he did the same to the coat and waistcoat of his suit. And then he put them on again. Well, he'd try again. He'd follow the wall along. He did so, and found himself in a little narrow passage. Suddenly he shot out his right hand, for he had the impression that something had brushed his face very lightly. "I'm beginning to get a little bored with that bat, and with this blasted room generally," he said to himself. "I could imagine a more nervous person than myself getting a little fussed and panicky; but that's the one thing not to do." Ah, here was that chair again. "Now, I'll try the wall the other side." Well, that seemed to go on for ever, so he retraced his steps till he found the chair, and sat down again. He whistled a little snatch resignedly. What an echo! The little tune had been flung back at him so fiercely, almost menacingly. Menacingly: that was just the feeble, panicky word a nervous person would use. Well, he'd go to the left again this time.

As he got up, a quick spurt of cold air fanned his face. "Is anyone there?" he said. He had purposely not raised his voice—there was no need to shout. Of course, no one answered. Who could there have been to answer since the caretaker was away? Now let him think it out. When he came

in he must have gone straight forward and then swerved
slightly on the way back, therefore—no, he was getting confused. At that moment he heard the whistle of a train, and
felt reassured. The line from Wendover to Aylesbury ran
half-left from the front door, so it should be about there—he
pointed with his finger, got up, groped his way forward, and
found himself in a little narrow passage. Well, he must turn
back and go to the right this time. He did so, and something
seemed to slip just past him, and then he scratched his finger
slightly on the brocade of the chair. "Talk about a maze," he
thought to himself; "it's nothing to this." And then he said
to himself, under his breath: "Curse this vile, godforsaken
place!" A silly, panicky thing to do he realised—almost as
bad as shouting aloud. Well, it was obviously no use trying
to find the door, he *couldn't* find it—*couldn't*. He'd sit in the
chair till the light came. He sat down.

How very silent it was; his hands began searching in his
pockets once more. Except for that sort of whispering sound
over on the left somewhere—except for that, it was absolutely silent—except for that. What could it be? The caretaker
was away. He turned his head slightly and listened intently.
It was almost as if there were several people whispering together. One got curious sounds in old houses. How absurd
it was! The chair couldn't be more than three or four yards
from the door. There was no doubt about that. It must be
slightly to one side or the other. He'd try the left once more.
He got up, and something lightly brushed his face. "Is anyone there?" he said, and this time he knew he had shouted.
"Who touched me? Who's whispering? Where's the door?"
What a nervous fool he was to shout like that; yet someone outside might have heard him. He went groping forward
again, and touched a wall. He followed along it, touching it
with his finger-tips, and there was an opening.

The door, the door, it must be! And he found himself
going down a little narrow passage. He turned and ran back.
And then he remembered! He had put a match-booklet in his

note-case! What a fool to have forgotten it, and made such an exhibition of himself. Yes, there it was; but his hands were trembling, and the booklet slipped through his fingers. He fell to his knees, and began searching about on the floor. "It must be just here, it can't be far"—and then something icy-cold and damp was pressed against his forehead. He flung himself forward to seize it, but there was nothing there. And then he leapt to his feet, and with tears streaming down his face, cried: "Who is there? Save me! Save me!" And then he began to run round and round, his arms outstretched. At last he stumbled against something, the chair—and something touched him as it slipped past. And then he ran screaming round the room; and suddenly his screams slashed back at him, for he was in a little narrow passage.

"Now, Mr. Runt," said the coroner, "you say you heard screaming coming from the direction of the Manor. Why didn't you go to find out what was the matter?"

"None of us chaps goes to Manor after sundown," said Mr. Runt.

"Oh, I know there's some absurd superstition about the house; but you haven't answered the question. There were screams, obviously coming from someone who wanted help. Why didn't you go to see what was the matter, instead of running away?"

"None of us chaps goes to Manor after sundown," said Mr. Runt.

"Don't fence with the question. Let me remind you that the doctor said Mr. Cort must have had a seizure of some kind, but that had help been quickly forthcoming, his life might have been saved. Do you mean to tell me that, even if you had known this, you would still have acted in so cowardly a way?"

Mr. Runt fixed his eyes on the ground and fingered his cap.

"None of us chaps goes to Manor after sundown," he repeated.

A Coincidence at Hunton

"And how are all the placid and pleasant denizens of East Bucks?" asked Brent. "Not all quite as placid as they seem, so far as I remember."

"Extremely flourishing," replied Lumley. "We have increased the population here and there, and watched with coy excitement some mild and invariably unconsummated infidelities. It was a hot summer, and some of us felt a little experimental. But all is peace again—a little patched up here and there. But our moral standards are high and we make the way of the waverer very hard."

"Does that apply to your local lady-killer?" asked Brent.

"It applies to me, certainly."

"I said 'lady,'" replied Brent. "I mean a fellow who somehow curiously appealed to me, whose tennis attracted me much more than his painting. One on whom even your imperturbably chaste wives found it hard to resist smiling, and upon whom all those 'Sappery' White Men, their husbands, were inclined to frown."

"I take it you mean Bob Harriday."

"Yes, that's the fellow."

"Well, he's dead."

"Dead! How did he die?"

"He was drowned in Hunton Reservoir in November. He went through a hole in the ice."

"And I daresay some of you rather unattractive married men were not overwhelmed with grief. When I last stayed with you in June—just before I sailed—he looked like being hooked by a very plain but affluent maiden whose figure almost made one forget her face."

"You mean Brenda Vandelaar," said Lumley. "Yes, he did get engaged to her."

"Poor devil, was she very knocked up?"

"She hadn't a chance to be, she was drowned in Hunton too."

"What!" cried Brent. "At the same time?"

"No, in September, while bathing."

"Good Lord," said Brent. "These are curious goings-on for the sober and responsible county of Bucks. But seriously that seems rather an extraordinary coincidence."

Lumley looked out from the club window to Pall Mall, where taxis were honking and jostling through the streaming March night.

"Well," he said at length, "I suppose I shall have to tell you the story, though I swear it shall be for the last time. I'm utterly sick of it."

"Why have you been appointed the Kai-Lung of these events?" asked Brent.

"Because I was more or less in at the death, and not so far from sharing the fate of the principals. Also I knew Bob rather better than any of them, I suppose."

"Well, you've got to say your piece again, and if the tale pleases me I will drop some yen into your bowl."

"Oh, all right," said Lumley resignedly. "Now you only saw these people at a few week-ends, so I shall have to tell you more about them. About Bob and Brenda I mean.

"Now Harriday was a very curious and complex person. This was no doubt partly due to the fact that his father had been a fearless and pugnacious free-thinker and his mother a morbidly credulous Anglo-Catholic. Why they ever married was and remained a complete mystery. But this hopelessly

incompatible union had appropriate issue. Bob was a painter
of great promise. I'm no judge of such things, but those who
are assured me of it. But what I *could* realise was that he was
conversationally a genius. We are not exactly a high-brow
colony in East Bucks, but we listened to Bob, though his
talk was informed, highly sophisticated and obviously the
fruit of a very nimble intelligence which had trained itself
by deep and catholic study to the highest degree of precision and subtlety, though curiously enough he never wrote,
or tried to, I believe. Not that he ever preached or paraded
his knowledge, he simply released a spring in his brain and
a beautifully ordered torrent of paradox, aphorism and profound verbal ingenuity poured forth. Not often though. He
was completely silent as a rule. He spent most of his time
quite alone. He came out of his solitude more in the summer,
for he loved tennis and played it, as you know, almost brilliantly. And then there was his Sex Appeal, as I believe it's
called. Sometimes it's also called 'It,' I gather. Well, whatever it's called Bob had it. I once asked Lillian how she felt
about him. She replied, that if he hadn't been somewhat of
a misogynist she would strongly advise me not to leave them
alone together on a hot June night. When I asked what weird
power he possessed through which he could lure into wanton
imaginings the staidest of matrons, she declared she knew
no more than I did. She didn't like him so particularly, but
that something in his personality aroused dreams of primitive ecstasy in every woman of temperament. It wasn't only
his looks and it wasn't his intelligence, it was an amalgam,
and a woman could no more explain his effect on her if
she were temperamental than she could explain the effect
of Beethoven on her if she were musical. That those of her
friends who were sensitive to such influences unanimously
agreed with her that he could be, if he chose, the Pied Piper
of East Bucks, and so on.

"Now you have suggested that we, the jealous husbands
and fathers of Great Wissenden and district, frowned upon

him. Not really, I think. We should desperately have feared
the music of his pipe if he'd ever shown signs of tuning up,
but he never did, and the feminine adulation he encountered
did not give him swelled head, in fact it usually seemed to
embarrass and bore him. He never played up to his attraction
for women, one reason being possibly that he was as poor as
a church mouse, and it galled him and soured him somewhat.
He could just afford that tiny Top Cottage, but not to entertain or really be himself. He occasionally unburdened himself
to me, and I know he felt cribbed, cabined and confined and
ashamed of his poverty. And that was where Brenda Vandelaar came in with her ten thousand a year. If ever I saw a
woman make up her mind to buy a man it was Brenda. Her
will was as strong as her admirable body, her intentions as
plain as her face. She employed the methods of modern War.
Eschewing any strategical subtlety she flung her 200,000
golden mercenaries into the assault. She revealed to Harriday in a dozen ways how he might ease his lot and increase
his felicity by means of her cheque-book. Bob, like most artists who are poor, was weak, that is to say, he most bitterly
failed to see why we, who bought shares and sold soap and
audited account books, should have nice comfortable houses
and motor-cars, and the wherewithal to travel and enjoy
ourselves, while he was condemned to indecorous penury,
though his brain was worth all of ours put together. So in the
end he succumbed and was engaged by Brenda. This was in
the first week of August. Now I watched him carefully about
this time. I watched him as he received somewhat cryptic
congratulations. I watched him in the company of his bride-
to-be, and I knew for certain he regretted his surrender as
soon as he had made it, but he was actually terrorised by
her ardour and potential violence. I could see that he hoped
against hope that he might suddenly find the courage to
escape, and was employing the usual temporising insincer-
ities of the cornered weakling, the trapped gentleman, and
I'm sure that he was always desperately strung between two

opinions. Remember, he was a highly trained judge of what was beautiful. Certainly her money would enable him to travel and see all that was lovely in the world, and all he longed to see. And then her body was aesthetically satisfying, but her face was not merely plain—what we consider plain an artist often finds challenging and stimulating—it was lifeless, badly moulded, and, I can imagine, actually repulsive to anyone acutely sensitive to visual impressions. Anyhow there it was, and it always seemed to me that he was experiencing a sense of disgrace and degradation, that he was writhing in those triumphant coils, so that for the first time he allowed his gaze desperately to wander over the many stereotyped 'pretties' of East Bucks, 'Escape-me-never' hissing in his ears. Psychologically Brenda had the debits of her assets. A strong will, an indomitable determination, is seldom found allied with intellectual suppleness and finesse, and once she had, as it were, put her money down and obtained a binding option on the man she meant to marry, she showed it only too plainly. Her attitude became blandly and confidently proprietorial and possessive. She even had the supreme impertinence to criticise his work, with what must have been a maddening combination of confidence and philistinism. She displayed him and flaunted him before the highly exasperated locals, as if to say, 'Look here, you maidens and matrons, I have secured that for which most of you in your heart of hearts lusted. Remember this, a pretty face is subject to the law of diminishing returns, as each year traces a line and etches in a crow's-foot, whereas £200,000 properly invested increases and multiplies. I may be as plain as a petrol pump, but I've bought the most attractive man within a thirty-mile radius. I've bought him and I'll keep him!' She was not exactly beloved.

"It was not long before Harriday began to feel the strain. He lost his resilience, his face became drawn, and its expression inadequately concealed the molten irritation of his mind."

"He could have broken it off, I suppose?" said Brent. "He hadn't compromised her in any way, had he?"

"Well, concerning that there were rumours. The night he got engaged he did not leave her house till five o'clock. Certainly that was merely servants' gossip, but there's no reason to doubt it. Anyhow if he'd had the guts to break it off, he'd have had the guts to prevent it happening, I imagine."

"Wasn't she the older of the two?" asked Brent.

"Yes, thirty-one to his twenty-six."

"Was she in love with him?"

"Yes, in a sense. She was very passionate by nature but vigorously repressed, and she released all her pent-up emotion on Bob, though it might have been any attractive man, I think. After a bit I kept out of their way, for Bob's wretched attempts to play the lover and pretend he wasn't miserable and utterly ashamed of himself were horrible to watch and got on my nerves. The wedding was fixed for the middle of October. On September 26th I went up to London as usual, and as there was a very heavy American mail I missed my usual train and didn't get home till 8.30. Lillian met me on the doorstep, obviously heavy with tidings. Brenda had been drowned that afternoon in Hunton Reservoir. She and Harriday had gone down there to bathe about four o'clock. Half an hour later he had dashed up to the officers' mess at the Aerodrome and told them that Brenda had suddenly thrown up her arms and disappeared, not to appear again. They were now dragging the lake.

"There seemed to be nothing I could do for the moment, and I was tired and hungry, so I waited till after dinner and then rang up the Top Cottage, and found that Bob had just got in. He said he would like to see me, so I went round. He was pacing up and down his little studio, and he had been drinking. He immediately began to pour forth a rather incoherent account of what had happened, returning over and over again to the fact that he had had no chance of saving Brenda. When she sank they had been at least a hundred

yards apart. He seemed temporarily unbalanced, and I attributed this to those very frequent, if very natural, visits
to the tantalus. At the same time I thought I detected an
intense sense of relief competing with the horror, and not
quite concealed. This made my conventional condolences
sound ridiculous. I advised him to get away after the inquest.
But there was no inquest, for in spite of the most exhaustive
scouring of the lake's bottom, the body was not recovered.
Harriday did go away for a few days, and when he came back
he shut himself up and refused all invitations and was said
to be drinking hard."

"Was there much local gossip?" asked Brent. "I imagine
that such an affair provided a welcome change from baby
talk at tennis parties."

"Some of the women, shall we say 'conjectured,' rather
indiscreetly," replied Lumley, "but we did our best to shut
them up. It was the fact that the body was not found which
lent a certain air of mystery to the business. I couldn't
understand it myself. The dragging might easily fail, but why
didn't it reappear of its own accord? As you can imagine,
Hunton ceased to be a very popular bathing place, for there
was always the chance of finding an old friend at one's side.
Well, as it didn't reappear there were veiled hints and insinuations that it wasn't there at all—never had been and
Harriday's drinking and hiding away, as it were, reinforced
these sinister whispers. For his own sake I made up my mind
to tackle him on the subject, and I went round early one
Sunday morning. He was still in bed when I arrived, so I
went into his studio. It was a glorious early autumn morning, radiant yet deliciously fresh, but the atmosphere of the
studio was almost nauseatingly foetid and stale, though the
window was open. It smelt rank and mildewy, like rotting
weeds, I remember thinking. Presently Bob came down. He
was looking sluttish and ill, another 'morning after' very
obviously. As delicately as I could I stated my case. I told
him that everyone was anxious to help him, and hurt and

perplexed at his refusal to meet us half-way. That his behaviour was causing just a little comment—and then I was
suddenly completely knocked out of my stride. We were
sitting at a table, and I happened to glance down at the
floor, and there, just behind Harriday, were the imprints of
two little feet, and it seemed to me that the rankness of the
atmosphere was intensified. And then these prints seemed
to dry and fade. I pulled myself together and went on with
my piece, but somehow without conviction, and I suddenly
took a distinct dislike to the Top Cottage. Bob was looking
very uneasy and would have visited the decanter if I hadn't
been there, I felt certain. However, he promised to make an
effort. He was very anxious to know what I meant by 'comment.' Did I mean that people thought that he hadn't done
all he could to save Brenda? As he mentioned her name he
turned his head sharply and stared out into the garden for a
moment.

"I replied that nothing like that was being hinted because
there wasn't a particle of evidence to support it, it was simply that his conduct seemed funny. He looked at me search-
ingly to see if I was lying. I was, of course, and probably
showed it.

"'I know you've had a ghastly experience,' I said, 'but
shutting yourself up and brooding on it is the worst possible
method to adopt to recover from such a shock. It is all over.
Brenda is at peace, you have nothing with which to reproach
yourself. Take up your life again.'

"He promised to try, and I left him. There was a mirror
near the door and I could catch his reflection. He dropped
his head into his hands with a gesture of utter dejection.
From then on I found my mind constantly reverting to those
footprints in an urgent search for a rational explanation of
them. As their memory grew dim I eventually decided I had
imagined them. But did I?

"After that he did make an effort, and we all did what
we could to help him, but it never looked like being

successful, for he showed no sign of recovering. He was usually half-tight, and his tennis on the few occasions he played was melancholy evidence of his physical deterioration, though curiously enough he was selling his pictures—and very curious and uncomfortable pictures they were.

"One evening late in November Lillian said to me, 'You know that old hag, Mrs. Colley, who cleans up the Top Cottage; well, she is saying in the village there's something funny about it.'

"I asked her how she knew and what she meant by 'funny.' It was the usual story. The hag had told Mrs. Lent's maid, who had told our tweeny, who'd told the housemaid, who'd told Lillian. Plenty of opportunity for embroidery and expansion of the yarn, I judged.

"As for the 'something funny,' the hag declared she found marks on the stairs up to Bob's bedroom, which looked as if they'd been made by a woman's wet feet. (That made me sit up.)

"'Anything else?' I asked uneasily.

"'Yes, she thinks she's seen Brenda's dog in the garden several times.'

"'What, Stinko!'

"'Well, that's what she says.'

"Now, Harry, Brenda's hound Stinko had been an unmistakable mongrel, but a sweet and most faithful gentleman, who had pined away and died when he found that his mistress was never coming back. And that was why I felt more or less sincere when I informed my good lady that I didn't entirely believe Mrs. Colley, knowing her remarkable capacity for absorbing Bass and Guinness in equal proportions, a beverage which probably made one dog very closely to resemble another.

"'Yes, I thought you'd say something unconvincing like that,' said Lillian, 'but you must remember that Stinko used to spend much of his time hunting rats in the barn behind her cottage, and she knew him very well indeed.'

"'Then do you believe it?' I said.

"'I don't know whether I do or not,' replied Lillian. 'I think I do believe that Mrs. Colley believes she sees Stinko, but whether she really sees him or not is a much more difficult question to answer.'

"'It certainly is,' I said, and feeling ruffled and restless I went out for a stroll after dinner, and I found myself going towards the Top Cottage rather unwillingly and yet from some vague but urgent compulsion. When I reached the gate I saw there was a light in the studio, but the blinds were drawn. I walked up the little path and peeped through a crack in one of the blinds. I saw that Bob had his back to me, and for a moment I was extremely puzzled as to what he was doing. Though he was standing still his whole body seemed in motion. It was as though he was rehearsing a part in front of a mirror. I remember that was the first impression which I gained. Had there been anyone else in the room I should have said he was protesting or arguing violently with that person, but there was no other one—at least no one perceptible to me. And then I could just detect that he was speaking in a steady and seemingly most urgent murmur. All this affected me unpleasantly and I turned and walked back home. It wasn't funk exactly, just a sense of certainty that I was utterly out of place, unwanted, impotent, intruding on something that was none of my business. But when that impression began to fade I began to feel somewhat ashamed of myself, and took a day off from the office and went to the Top Cottage the next morning. I may say I preferred it now by daylight. Bob was painting when I arrived, painting a woman's foot, I noted, a whisky-and-soda by his side. He seemed very nervous and preoccupied. After a few commonplaces he looked at me searchingly and said, 'Look here, there's something I want to show you.' He went to a drawer and pulled out a sheet of paper which he handed to me. It was a beautifully drawn plan of Hunton Reservoir, and on it were letters and a key to them below. For example:

"'A on the chart was shown by the key to be, '*Where Brenda disappeared.*'

"'B,' '*Where I was at the time.*'

"'C,' '*The Boat House!*'

"'D,' '*Where Stinko was sitting.*'

"And he'd drawn several portraits of Stinko in the left margin. On the right he had drawn what looked like rough sketches for his painting of the woman's foot.

"I was somewhat taken aback by this document and said rather fatuously, 'But what does it matter where the dog was?'

"He continued to stare at me with a very curious expression on his face.

"'Well,' he said, 'he must have been able to see what happened; that's important.'

"'He's going mad,' I thought. However, I felt I must make one more effort to pull him round.

"'Look here,' I said, 'everyone knows you did all you could. What's the good of keeping the whole thing alive in your mind and letting it prey on you? Come and stay with us for a time. Why not?'

"'And bring my companions with me?' he replied. 'It's very good of you, but I couldn't do that.'

"'I don't know what you mean, but go away for God's sake,' I cried, 'and never come near the place again!'

"He got up and walked over to his easel and appeared to be examining the painting upon it. 'I can draw that woman's foot rather well, can't I?' he said. 'Of course, as you have guessed, it's done from life.'

"'Look here,' I said, going up to him and taking him by the shoulders; 'tell me, Bob, is it quite hopeless?'

"'Of course it is, my dear Jack,' he replied, staring into my face, 'perfectly bloody hopeless.'

"And I felt it was so, and left him.

"The next morning I received a package from him. It contained a note and a closed envelope. The note ran:

"'My dear Jack,

"'Open the enclosed when I'm dead, and then you'll understand. You have done everything you could.

   "'Bob.'

"A week later came the big frost. It froze night and day for a week, so that for the first time in ten years Hunton was safe for skating. It became so on Saturday afternoon, and a bunch of us arranged to go down there after dinner. The night was sparklingly clear. There was no moon, but the ice shone with a dim starlit glow. There were four car-loads of us altogether. We parked the cars by a little inlet sentinelled by bulrushes.

"After I had got my skating boots on and was daggering down towards the lake I saw a figure a man's—with his back towards me. To my considerable astonishment I saw it was Harriday. 'Hallo, Bob,' I said.

"He turned his head and looked at me intently yet aloofly for a moment and then began to walk out over the ice.

"'Well, if that's how he feels, poor devil, I won't butt in,' I thought to myself. I waited till the others were ready, and then we all began gingerly attempting to recover our skating balance.

"Mine came speedily, and as I hadn't quite liked the look of Bob I went off by myself to find him. I may say Hunton is a good two miles long. Presently the laughter and shouting of the others grew faint, and replacing them came the steady and rhythmic barking of a dog. I could find no trace of Bob and presently skated back to the others. 'You haven't seen anything of Bob, I suppose?' I asked.

"'Bob—is he down here?' asked someone.

"Nobody had seen him, and after we had played about for half an hour or so we decided we'd had enough. I was last off the ice and, just as I was scrambling up the bank, there came a sharp strangled cry from down the lake. 'That may be Bob,' I cried, and I turned and raced in the direction from whence I judged the sound had come. Out of practice though I was,

I got a creditable 'move on.' Suddenly I had a sense of most imminent danger and something dark raced towards me. I flung myself to one side and crashed full length on the ice. I was badly shaken and dazed, but I managed to stagger to my feet, and then I saw that the black patch was a hole in the ice about six feet square and Bob's cap was lying beside it.

"Soon the rest of the men came up. Willy Rankin was the first to arrive.

"'Are you hurt, Jack?' he cried. 'I heard you take the hell of a toss,' and then he stopped short and stared at the hole and Bob's cap. 'My God,' he said, 'who made that?' I can still see the look of utter astonishment on his face.

"'It is rather a puzzle,' I replied, and then for the second time in my life I did a perfectly orthodox faint, but woke up soon after to find my face full of Willy's best brandy, and presently Lillian took charge and drove me back home to iodine, arnica, bandages, sleep and a certain dream."

"What sort of dream?" asked Brent.

"The sort of dream one hopes to forget some day. The others, I learnt next morning, had roused the Aerodrome people, but there was really nothing to be done till the frost broke, which it began to do at noon. The thaw was as violent as the freeze-up and accompanied by sheets of rain, so that by Tuesday morning the men from the camp were at work with drags. I was with a couple of them in the big punt, and we had only been working about half an hour when suddenly the grapnel caught and we began to pull. And then suddenly I saw the back of Bob's head flickering in the water just below me, and that it was forced back between his shoulders and that there was something white around his neck. And then I saw that something white was a circle formed by two small arms picked clean. As we began to tow them ashore I heard the steady persistent barking of a dog."

"My God," cried Brent. "That's the hell of a dirty yarn. Got him round the neck had she? I hate that! Well, what about the hole? Who made it? How was it explained?"

"It wasn't," replied Lumley.

"Well, what about that letter he sent you? He was dead. Did you open it?"

"Yes, I did."

"What was in it?"

"Just a chart, in every respect but one identical with the one he showed me at the cottage. It varied in just this respect.

'A,' *'Where Brenda disappeared,'* and

'B,' *'Where I was,'*

instead of being a hundred yards apart, were 'monographed,' as it were, superimposed."

"Thank you," said Brent, "buy me a *long, strong drink.*"

Nurse's Tale

"Thanks awfully, Nurse; it's just what I wanted. But now that I'm ten you've got to tell me about that kid Layton. You promised you would."

"I don't believe I ever promised."

"Yes, you did, you old fiend."

"You mustn't use such expressions, Master Gilbert, they're rude! You're too old for your age, that's what you are! And you read too many of those ghost books. That James, he gives me the creeps!"

"Oh, I love them, Nurse; especially, 'Oh, whistle and I'll come to you!'"

"That one about the bedclothes getting up and walking about, just when they'd made the bed, too? I can't see why people want to think of such things."

"Well, I'm ten and you promised."

"And I hope you'll behave like ten; it's time you did. I daresay the other Marlborough boys will take you down a peg or two, when you get there."

"I shan't funk them. And shut up, Nurse, and shoot the works!"

"Wherever did you learn that vulgar saying?"

"At the movies. Oh, go on!"

"And give you dreams and get into trouble with your mamma. You're such a pest! Well, I'll tell you, but don't blame me if you can't sleep. Anyhow, I know I shan't have any peace till I *do* tell you. Now, sit still and don't shuffle about.

"It's about twenty-five years since I first went to Layton Hall. Lady Layton died the night I arrived, poor dear, and the funeral and the christening took place within a few days of each other. His Lordship was terribly sad. He was a fine gentleman, every inch a lord. He was very tall, and handsome and quiet, and at first he didn't seem to take to the baby—Jocelyn they named him—but then afterwards he could hardly keep his thoughts off him. At first I wondered why he seemed so watchful and anxious, but one day the head gardener told me there was a sort of mystery about the family. The story was that a long while ago—hundreds of years—they burnt a witch, at least I think she was a witch—some bad lot, anyway—"

"But, Nurse, you don't believe in witches, do you?"

"I don't believe either way, but where I was brought up plenty did. But, as I say, they burnt one of them, and her small boy too. And it seems he was near his sixth birthday, and this witch put a curse on the family—that was the talk, anyway—saying that no Layton's eldest son would live to be six. And they never had done after that. So the place was always going to different parts of the family. And that was why his Lordship was so anxious about Master Jocelyn. He was a beautiful baby, and very good—too good, I used to think. For he hardly ever cried, not even when he was cutting his teeth, and healthy babies ought to cry. You used to cry till I could have choked you, you young limb, but then you were never good. Now, don't pinch or I won't tell you any more. Not that he was sickly, but he seemed to be thinking his own thoughts all the while. But the first time I found something really funny about him was when he was about nine months old. At Layton there is a long drive from the road to the Hall, twisting and hilly, and about half-way up there was a dip in it—a sort of valley. It was a lovely quiet spot, cut off from everything, with fields on either side. It always used to give me the creeps a bit; I mean I wouldn't have walked along there alone after dark if I could have helped it."

"I wouldn't have minded. I bet I'd have gone!"

"Oh, you're very brave and full of swank in the morning with people about. But you weren't so brave in the cloisters at Norwich!"

"Well, something began to tap on the other side of the big door just as I reached it; and I thought it was beginning to open. And there wasn't anyone in the Cathedral. Anyway, I was partly pretending."

"Did you put chalk on your face? That was white enough. Now, don't keep on interrupting. Well, as I said, it was just about Master Jocelyn's ninth month that I found he was queer about that bit of drive. As we got near it he'd waken and sit up in his pram and keep his eyes fixed on the field on the left side—coming down, that is. And he wouldn't lie down until we began to go up the hill on the other side, however much I tried to make him. And then the pucker left his little forehead and he'd lie back and go to sleep again. As he got older he seemed to get more and more interested in that bit of the drive, and when he learned to walk he always insisted on getting out and going into the field, and almost the first thing he ever said after he'd learned to talk was, 'Pitty tees,' when he was out on the grass."

"But I thought you said it was just a field?"

"So it was. There was a tree or two, but they was on the other side of the drive."

"Then—"

"Now, Master Gilbert, don't keep on stopping me in the middle. I'm just telling you what happened. And what happened was that Master Jocelyn always behaved as if there was trees. It used to worry me—it wasn't natural—and I tried to get him past that dip, but he wouldn't let me, and then I tried keeping him in the garden, but he wouldn't let me do that either, but cried and made a fuss till I took him down the drive again. And it wasn't so much that he seemed happy in the field as anxious to be there. And there was he in a wood all the time and me in a field. It seemed to me I ought to mention it to his Lordship. So I did, and for a moment he looked away from me, as if he was upset and not sure what to say. And then he said, 'Have you tried to keep him away from there?' And I said I had, but that it wasn't any use. And he said, 'Well, then—' and he paused for a bit, 'Well, then, let him play there, but don't let him wander off by himself.' I was sorry I'd told him in a way, but I thought I ought to."

"What was the field like? Were there stumps of trees there? Had it been a wood?"

"No, it was just an ordinary grass field."

"Did you see any birds or animals in it?"

"No; why do you ask that?"

"I don't know exactly."

"Well, it's a fact I never saw bird or beast in that field except a dead rabbit once. The gardener picked it up and had a look at it, but he couldn't find anything wrong with it, so he said it must have died of old age, and he threw it away. Master Jocelyn was always drawing pictures of a wood, and he was clever at it and made it look real. But he always drew the same one with a big tree in the middle. But he couldn't seem to draw the big tree properly, but always made a red and black smudge around it. And it was a funny thing how he always made straight for the place where that big tree would have been if there had been a wood, and then he'd look up. And he used to pick his way along as if he was dodging trees, and following some sort of pathway. He talked very little and always seemed to be thinking his own thoughts. He grew up into the most lovely little boy. He learnt his lessons all right, but not as if he cared so much about them, though he was very quick and sharp about some things."

"When he was in the field, could he see you?"

"What questions you ask! Well, I can't be sure; he never looked at me or said a word. He just wandered about, and I got out of the way of speaking to him, though I always kept an eye on him."

"Did it put the wind up you?"

"There you are with your vulgar talk! I always felt a bit uneasy, but I got used to it and didn't bother as a rule. But sometimes when I got drowsy and day-dreaming I'd think for a second or two I was in a wood and hearing a sort of rustle of leaves, and get a feeling that someone was watching me; but then I'd come to myself and know I'd been imagining things. We lived a very quiet life, with just a break of six weeks every summer when we went to Bognor—the doctor said the air there was good for Master Jocelyn. He seemed to like the sea-side though I couldn't get him to make friends with other children. But he liked his bathe and sitting on the beach and watching the water. And he loved the boats."

"You don't see any decent liners at Bognor, only dull old tramps. Deal's the place."

"Oh, well, he wasn't so particular, nor such a Johnny Know-All as you. But I believe he was nearly always thinking of the wood. He used to try and draw it on the sand with a shell.

"Things went on much the same till just after his fifth birthday, and then I felt more bothered about him, for I got the idea that he was seeing someone in the field."

"Why did you think that, Nurse?"

"Now, wasn't I just going to tell you, impatient? Well, mostly from the way he stared and looked about him. He seemed to be following something around—watching it. And as he didn't look up or down I took it that it was something or someone about his own size. I asked him what it was, though I never liked to put questions about the field. He didn't answer, but looked away from me. I felt it was a sort of secret of his and that I was left out of it. His Lordship asked me now and again how I found him, and I had to say he was a queer little chap, though as good as gold. I still love him, the sweet angel!"

"Better than me?"

"Well, you're not so bad, Master Gilbert, when you try to behave, which isn't often. Now, stop rubbing your toes together, those shoes have got to last you.

"I could see the master knew what I meant when I said, 'queer.' He looked as if there was nothing to be done. He used to spend an hour or two a day with Master Jocelyn, but I don't believe they was quite easy together. The little boy was fond of him and liked sitting on his knee or lying back against his shoulder, but it was always the same story, he thought his own thoughts, and neither his father nor me came into them much of the time. And I think his Lordship knew that and felt badly about it; and I used to get the idea that he'd given up hope, though he'd hardly confess it to himself. Layton seemed to make him worried and he used to spend a lot of time in London. He looked ill and tired and restless. But when Master Jocelyn's sixth birthday came near he stayed in the house, and, of course, I knew why. I kept the little boy near me night and day—it made me dream and sleep badly, for I had a feeling that the trouble was coming."

"What sort of trouble?"

"Well, haven't I told you about the curse and what always happened?"

"Yes, but—"

"Now, then, you're interrupting again. I just felt that I'd got to see that Master Jocelyn had someone on his side and fighting for him and that it wouldn't be my fault if the curse worked again. As the birthday drew near, his Lordship was like a cat on hot bricks, and I could have screamed sometimes, my nerves were so on edge. His birthday was on March 21st. During the week before we'd been in the field every day and I'd watched him like a knife. March 20th was a very wild and windy day and Master Jocelyn seemed restless and broody, but all the same, when we went out in the afternoon I felt the worst was over, for what could happen between then and midnight? It was very dark for that time of year. Now, I don't know how to explain it, but as soon as we'd gone into the field everything seemed strange, as if it *was* a wood, and I thought I heard the trees fighting with the wind, and for a bit I forgot Master Jocelyn, and I think I sat down and felt silly—as if I was someone else. And then suddenly I heard a shout and came to myself, and I couldn't see Master Jocelyn. So I started to run, and I remember twisting and dodging as if I was running through a wood, and I turned a corner, and there was Master Jocelyn lying on his face, just about where that big tree would have been. When I reached him it was just a field again and he stretched out on the grass. He was in a faint. I ran with him in my arms back to the house. As I got near, his Lordship came dashing out to meet me, and he took him from me without a word. I was so out of breath that I had to lie down on the lawn, and I thought my heart would burst. As soon as I could manage it, I got to the house. His Lordship was giving Master Jocelyn brandy in his study and the footman was rushing off on his bicycle for the doctor. And then his Lordship carried Master Jocelyn up to my bedroom, where he slept. He was dead white and his eyes was shut, but he couldn't keep still. He kept twisting and throwing out his arms, and then he began to mutter—on and on and on—and presently he'd scream. When the doctor came he asked me what had happened, and I told him, but he never looked at the master. And then he pulled up Master Jocelyn's sleeves, and I could see his little arms was burnt past the elbow. And the doctor said nothing, but got me to fetch bandages and vaseline, and we did all we could for the little boy. But nothing we did was any good. He kept twisting and shifting and throwing out his arms and always gave that scream. The doctor said he wasn't really in pain, for he was quite unconscious. Just before twelve o'clock he cried out, 'Mummie!' very loud three times—and died.

"I can still remember how the wind was roaring, and how when he cried out the wind seemed to catch his cry and carry it far, far away.

"They buried him three days later. The master kept himself shut up in his room all the time. The family had a vault in Layton Church, and the coffin was taken to it in a farm cart. The wind had gone by then and it was a queer, dark, close afternoon, not a bit like any March day I've ever seen. I remember I walked behind the cart with the master, though otherwise I've always been a bit hazy about that day. We had to go down the drive, for the church was just off the main road. Well, just as we reached the middle that field something seemed to flash down from the sky and there was a great flame before my eyes. And I seemed to see Master Jocelyn jump down from the cart and start to run along the path through the wood. And I went after him. And it was a wood this time, and very dark. But ahead I could see a big red glare and, as I got near, flames above it. And they came from the same spot by the big tree. And all the time I could see Master Jocelyn running ahead of me. And then I turned a corner, and there was a great pile of flaming wood and I could hear it roaring. And I seemed to be running through a big crowd of people who made way for me. And Master Jocelyn ran straight into the fire and disappeared. Then, just as I reached the blaze I heard him scream and I saw his little arms flung above the flames. And I tried to reach up to him, but the flames came out at me—and the next thing I knew was waking up at the Klerkley Cottage Hospital and finding my arms all bandaged up and most of the hair burnt off my head. I didn't understand what had happened for a day or two because they wouldn't let me talk. But when I was better they told me I'd been struck by lightning and knocked down silly for three days, and that was really how I got the burns."

"But what happened to Lord Layton if he was walking beside you?"

"Now, don't you worry about that, because I'm not going to tell you. And I suppose you'll have dreams and I'll get the blame. But you pester so and you're always reading those horrid ghost books."

"But tell me, Nurse, why—"

"I shan't tell you another word. You get on with that drawing of the house while I wake Miss Dolly and take her some Bengers. And don't kick your toes together. Those shoes have got to last."

The Dune

Mr. Parsley was in no sense of the word a gentleman. Certainly not by birth, for his father had been a Turf Accountant in a small cop-conscious way of business, though his mother had been superior intellectually, though inferior morally, to her station in life. She had possessed looks, a temperament, too much "sauce"—in the opinion of her neighbours—a red head and a tendency to sour and pregnant utterance. Born under a different dispensation, she might have played a dominating part in affairs, delicately adjusted her existence to the demands of a posse of exigent lovers—been all women to all men who attracted her socially or emotionally. But all she actually did was to hand down to her only son a hard head, a purely pragmatic philosophy and an indomitable self-reliance. She lived and died fighting.

Mr. Parsley was no gentleman by education, for he had sneered his precocious way through a Board School. Sartorially, he was beneath contempt, for he could often be seen strolling on Wimbledon Common arrayed in a bowler hat, a frock coat and brown boots. He wasn't even a Nature's Gentleman, for he drove notoriously hard bargains, spoke disrespectfully of religious bodies, voted Labour, and had attached to his golf-bag a tripodic excrescence which enabled that bag to stand up by itself, so enabling him to dispense with a caddy. He voted Labour for the characteristically realistic reason that he considered the workers should be protected in their unequal combat with employers like him-self, an opinion those employees enthusiastically endorsed

He developed a sound flair for money-making, and after several tentative and insufficiently remunerative essays, he was persuaded by a brilliant young chemist to manufacture and market a most sweet-smelling and emollient substance for removing Superfluous Hair. This far-sighted youth had been one of the first to realise that there *was* such a thing as Superfluous Hair; that hair *could* be superfluous; that such hair obstinately refused to regard itself as superfluous (if there—why not everywhere?), and that it had to be ruthlessly extirpated, in the opinion of females who found the bounty of Nature embarrassing.

From the painless and decorous destruction of millions of bushels of this hirsute paradox, Mr. Parsley arrived at great affluence and a model factory.

He was a very contented, very common and very compe-tent little fellow; as hard as a brick, as nippy as the devil, who believed implicitly in Number One, and in precious little else.

He employed a number of girls in his factory, but that was as far as he had ever gone to living a bisexual life. Girls were cheap, if inclined to giggle and look up at him with a certain nonfactorial freedom when he made his periodic tours of inspection of his highly efficient and compact domain. They were allowed two free tubes of the emollient per month—a piece of payment in kind which they seemed to appreciate highly. Otherwise, women were to Mr. Parsley merely pay-envelope recipients, who occasionally so far for-got the claims of commerce as to get married.

This rather elaborate and expository analysis of Mr. Pars-ley's origins and state of life is necessary to explain why his curious experience at Porthlech made such a profound im-pression upon him. Porthlech is in North Wales, and he had gone there for his summer holiday because he took his holi-day, as he did most other things, alone, and he had heard it had a very good golf links, and that it was easy to pick up matches there. It didn't turn out to be quite so easy, for when his potential opponents saw the tripodic attachment and discovered his handicap was eighteen, they were inclined to remember important engagements and slink away, but those who accepted his challenge, had invariably to pay up at the end of the round, for Mr. Parsley was without exception the best eighteen handicap golfer in the world. He worked as hard to win his five bob as he did to make his fifteen thousand a year, and it gave him just as much pleasure to acquire.

There was another reason for his choice of a Welsh resort. He had been told that when you were in Wales you didn't do as the Welsh did, but you were done as the Welsh decided to do you. Being pretty good at that sort of thing himself, he accepted the implied challenge. So far, in a fortnight, he had only lost one round to the locals, and that was when he discovered an Australian shilling amongst his small change and failed on five different occasions to pass it on to the village tradesmen. He often took it out of his pocket and examined it closely. It had a mild fascination for him, for he was fully determined to get rid of it somehow before he left the Principality. This became a slight obsession which each rebuff intensified. How should he inveigle someone into giving him twelve British pennies' worth of some article of commerce for it? "The dam' Tories," he thought, "always spouting Imperialism. Why don't they make Aussie bobs legal tender?" Yet on the afternoon of his last day in Porthlech it was still in his possession. His hands were sore, and he decided to take a walk instead of playing a second round. Porthlech is famous for its great rampart of dunes between the links and the sea, and he decided to explore them. He found it a very tiring promenade, and about five o'clock sat down to rest on one of the highest summits of the range. He took off his hat, mopped his brow, and stared out over the sea. The weather was breaking, a dark army of clouds was mobilising to the south-west, the wind was freshening and the sea rising.

There was a feeling of menace in the air. He leaned back
and dozed off. Presently he was roused by something flicking past his left leg. He opened his eyes, glanced round and
saw that his hat, caught by the rising wind, had been blown
into a patch of bent grass just behind him. As he twisted
round to secure it, his eye was caught by something which
had not been present when he dozed off. It was a figure, a
man, seated on the twin peak to his, fifty yards away to the
left across a deep sand valley. This person had his elbows on
his knees and his head was buried in his hands. He was quite
motionless.

Mr. Parsley was vaguely irritated by this intrusion and a
little suspicious. Why had this individual selected to plant
himself on that adjacent knoll when he had the whole long
and utterly deserted range of dunes to choose from? It seemed
calculated and deliberate. All the same, this intruder seemed
completely uninterested in him, though that might be a ruse.
Mr. Parsley yawned, put his squash hat beneath his chin, lay
back and—well, he never quite decided what he did do then.
He might have dozed and dreamed, but there *were* other possibilities. In any case, this is what he remembered to have
experienced.

His idea of the sea—which he had never crossed—had
been derived from the advertisements of shipping compa-
nies. To him it was an element blue and bland across which
a golden pathway ran up to the horizon, and, he supposed,
down the other side. And along this gleaming ribbon great
ships strolled with leisurely decision. From their funnels dark
feathers undulated away down the breeze, slowly diminishing
till they were lost in the distance. A churned and milky stir
rose from their propellers and flecked the gold with foam.
And at the end of the pathway were many exotic and strange
harbours where dark boys dived down at the ship's side down
and down, the outline of their bronze bodies becoming oily,
shimmering and shattered. And presently they shot up again
to the surface, breathed deeply, showed white teeth in a

smiling black face, and held up the coin they had stripped from the sand, an Australian shilling quite possibly, if Mr. Parsley had been on the deck. The Seven Seas had seemed to him merely supports for huge, expensive steamers, puffing away to hardly realisable strangeness; bulky, and in no way menacing or formidable fluid highways. A concept as romantic as it was inaccurate, but a considerable tribute to the efficiency of steamship advertisements.

But during his dream, reverie, or whatever it was, the water over which he seemed to be gazing suggested very different ideas. It suggested animosity; it seemed frigidly hostile, yet in a way tempting; something which inevitably carried one away and swallowed one up, however fiercely one strove against it. Something which clutched and killed—and yet invited. For what a quick and merciful sleep it granted to those who entrusted themselves to its austere touch! Why not accept that invitation? Why not run down, plunge in, forget, and leave his shell to dawdle up and down its tides? "What the devil is the matter with me?" wondered Mr. Parsley. "It is as if someone was saying all this for me, and yet these thoughts seem to be mine, though I know they cannot be. I'll stop it. I'll think about something else, the usual things I think about." He grasped for the Australian shilling, vaguely feeling he wanted a material ally in this struggle for his personality. But there was no money in his pocket. Was the stranger still there? No, he wasn't, but then neither was the high dune on which he had been sitting! And then he looked to the *right* and there was a figure lying outstretched on a little summit. He felt dazed and dizzy, as though something passed sharply across his brain, taking with it *his* thoughts and dragging others in.

Supposing he did respond to that sea-beckoning, accept its aid in escaping from intolerable pain. She *had* meant it. She *did* almost hate him. (All this part of Mr. Parsley's reverie was dominated by the mental picture of a woman, a stranger to him and yet someone he knew terribly well.) He

could remember just how she looked when she said, "You
bore me, do you hear? You always have and always will bore
me. I can't say fairer than that!" How that look she'd given
him had seemed to break him. He hadn't any money; that was
it. (Mr. Parsley momentarily rallied to repudiate this libel.
He *had* money, he had £200,000 and an Australian shilling.
But which he? Who was he?) She was, he knew, an utterly
soulless, mercenary little harpy. It was partly the humiliation
of loving so desperately someone so despicable which tortured him. If she were a woman of intelligence and character
he could have borne it far better. "I can assure you I'm not
worthy of a good man's love." She'd meant that to be funny,
but it was God's truth. He wasn't good and didn't want to be,
but he was a cut above that lovely, indecent obsession. What
was it? What was this despicable craving for a tow-headed,
scarlet-lipped, contemptible, shallow little pickpocket? An
animal without a single animal virtue and every animal vice.
And yet—he'd sacrifice anything, anyone, to see her for five
minutes. Supposing he found a telegram when he got back
to the hotel saying, "I'll see you tomorrow"? He'd drive back
through the night insanely happy. But he never would get
such a message. Never, never, never again! Now couldn't he
realise what she was and save himself! She was a pink-and-
white envelope over a system of bones and muscles and fat; a
collection of functions brutally mechanical. Whether such a
functioning hide ever housed a soul was disputable; to suggest
that hers did was a dirty joke. And her brain was such that it
merely intensified the essential beastliness of her body. That
was what she was, and it meant absolutely nothing to him.
Just futile verbiage. Perhaps he was so rotten himself that it
was her very vileness he adored. For let him face the fact—he
couldn't live without her. And he would probably never see
her again. He *couldn't* go back to the hotel and fling himself
down on his bed and go all over that hopeless ground again.
Over and over and over again. "You ought to eat more, sir;
won't you have an egg with your tea?" . . .

Suddenly Mr. Parsley was himself again. He rubbed his eyes and looked about him. "Hullo, that chap was running down the sand. What for?" Without quite knowing why, Mr. Parsley started to run down after him. Good God! He'd gone into the sea with all his clothes on! When Mr. Parsley reached the water's edge he hesitated, for he couldn't swim and he was wearing a new pair of grey flannel trousers. Also, it was rough. And then he saw a pair of arms flung up for a moment above the surge, so he began to wade gingerly in. It was bitterly cold, and a wave bursting against his navel soused him from head to foot. So he staggered back to dry land. "That chap must be drowned by now, and getting wet like that is bad for a man of my age," he thought, "I'd better run for help, run fast to keep my circulation going." He trotted back, setting his course by the peak on which he had been sitting.

On the way he retrieved his hat and the Australian shilling, which he found lying beside it. "Good Lord! Running through this deep sand takes it out of me. Got my heart to think about. No one could say I ought to have done more, could they?" After all, he couldn't swim; he was most convincingly and heroically soaked, and he could say he'd gone right in and been nearly drowned. Thank God! there were the golf links and level ground. The links were deserted, and he met no one till he encountered a group of local larrikins at the bottom of the steep hill which ran past the castle to the hotel. He shouted to them as he ran by: "There's a man in the sea. Go for help. He went in straight past the twelfth green." They stared at him and then burst out laughing. "They don't understand English," he thought, "but what stupid oafs they are. I'd like to have the sacking of them."

When he reached the hotel he found the landlord weeding his flower-beds. "Mr. Gribble," he panted, "a chap ran down into the sea. I went in after him and nearly got drowned."

"Is that so, sir?" said the landlord, startled, and then his expression swiftly changed. "I'd forgotten the date," he muttered to himself. "It's all right, sir," he said, "you go right up and have a hot bath. I'll send a hot whisky up to your room."

Mr. Parsley stared at him in amazement. "But—" he began again.

The landlord interrupted him. "It's all right, sir, you take my word for it. I'll tell you about it when you've changed."

Mr. Parsley began to shiver, and in a hopelessly confused state of mind allowed himself to be ushered upstairs. Three-quarters of an hour later he was sipping shudderingly that vilest of all concoctions composed of whisky, hot water, lemon and sugar, when the landlord came up to his room.

"The fact is, sir," said his host, "a chap *was* drowned there, but that was ten years ago, before I came here. A young fellow staying here went into the sea. As a matter of fact, there is no proof that he did—he just disappeared, and his body was never recovered. But a couple of years after a visitor saw much the same thing as I take it you saw, which seemed to show that he had drowned himself."

"Why?" asked Mr. Parsley.

"Well, sir, it certainly is a funny sort of evidence. A caddie saw the same thing a year or two after, and he got a wetting too. And that's just all about it. It seems to happen only if there's just one person about, for a crowd of fellows used to go down on the right day—to-day that is—sir, and stand on the beach, but they never saw anything."

"You mean I saw a ghost?" asked Mr. Parsley.

"I suppose that's about it."

"But I don't believe in them!"

"Well, sir, if you still believe you saw a real person, go back there and look at the place, where you think you saw him sitting. If you sit on sand you leave marks, you make a hole or two and muck the sand about. See if there's anything like that on the top of that dune."

"I certainly shan't do that," said Mr. Parsley; "I've no wish to see the place again. Tell me; as I came through the village a group of young louts laughed at me when I said someone was in the sea. Did they understand what I was saying?"

"Oh, yes," replied the landlord. "I'm English, like you, sir, though I like the Welsh all right. I've no complaints. But that's their idea of a joke. They wouldn't go alone to that dune on September 10th in the evening for any amount of money, but it makes 'em laugh to think of you getting a wetting for nothing."

"I'd make 'em laugh if I got 'em in my works, replied Mr. Parsley, venomously.

"They're a funny lot," said the landlord; "they believe there's a lot of small men living in the mountains, sort of dwarfs, who chase you and do you in if you're alone."

"I'd give 'em dwarfs!" said Mr. Parsley, "I'd chase 'em!"

"You don't think you've caught a chill?" asked the landlord.

"No, I'm O.K. Did they find out why this chap went into the sea?"

"No, sir, not so far as I know, but it's usually money or a woman."

"Not enough money or too much woman?"

"Or a bit of both," replied the landlord.

Mr. Parsley found it difficult to get to sleep that night. He was just dropping off when all that he had experienced during that reverie on the dune seemed to loom up like a great wave and burst over his memory, and all within a few seconds he understood that agony, and all about that woman, and why men felt like that, and he realised what death was like and why it was sometimes desired.

But the vividness of these impressions faded quickly away and he never felt them so vividly again, except very occasionally in dreams.

The next morning he went back to London, leaving the chambermaid the richer by an Australian shilling.

He returned to work the next day and made a searching inspection of the factory. All was well. The great vats,

simmering and formidable, seemed to hiss forth defiance to
every shade of superfluity; black, auburn, "ripe corn"; a reassuring sight for Iris Storm and her *soignée* and "well-dressed"
sisters. For the first time Mr. Parsley followed up, as it were,
the career, the latter end, the *raison d'être* of his "unique"
eliminator, and he got a curious little vague thrill from
this imaginative mental pursuit. The tow-haired, the scarlet-lipped, squeezing little tubes, and then delicately erasing
with tiny towels, and then going forth to conquer and torture men! Men—*he* was a man! Let them try conquering him!

As he passed through the filling-room he scrutinised each
neat-handed Phyllis with a less detached eye. He regarded
their faces and they stealthily regarded his. Suddenly, this
new, less detached eye of his was caught by a young woman
in the third row by the door. *She* was tow-haired and scarlet-
lipped, and when her eyes met his she looked back at him.
And in that look was surmise, expectation and, as he vaguely
felt, danger. He went back to his office and told the forewom-
an to send the young woman to him. Presently she came in
and gave him that look again. And, suddenly, a wave seemed
to strike his navel and drench him from head to foot. . . . He
took out his note-case and presented her with two months'
wages—and the sack.

Unrehearsed

Mr. Richard Cantelope is one of those happily situated persons who make glad the heart of golf club secretaries, for he is nearly always available for mid-week team matches, and he is just good enough to bring up the rear of hot sides creditably, and not too formidable for a gambol with the "rabbits." Furthermore, he is of a sociable habit, commanding a wide repertoire of seemly anecdote, and packed tightly with entertaining reminiscences of the many persons of note and notoriety with whose friendship he has been honoured. In a word, he can keep the ball rolling admirably both on and off the course and is a most desired acquisition. He is fifty-three years of age, just now retired from a fine old business, a bachelor, and a connoisseur of good food, good wine and good mezzotints. His character is firm but kindly, his outlook on life mildly disillusioned, his health excellent.

On a beautiful morning in June 1927 he was driving himself down to Moor Park to represent that club against the Stage Golfing Society, and musing on an effervescence from a young poet, not remarkable for self-effacement. This fellow had delivered himself of the opinion that actors nowadays were so busy trying to be gentlemen and golfers that they had no time to learn their job. But for the life of him Mr. Cantelope failed to fathom why this criticism did not equally apply to any member of any profession—even to poets. If it were possible to be a well-mannered poet and a good putter, why was it impossible to be a well-mannered mummer and a master of the mashie? A hasty and fatuous utterance this of Mr. S—, Mr. Cantelope decided.

During the ensuing three hours he was strongly entrenched in this opinion through being heavily defeated by a most delightful gentleman and admirable actor whom we will call Mr. Stanley Willoughby. In spite of being outdriven and outputted by him, Mr. Cantelope enjoyed his round thoroughly, for his opponent showed himself to possess a nimble wit, a sunny disposition and a pleasantly cynical outlook on that particular scene of the human tragedy or farce in which it had been his fate to appear. The attraction seemed to be mutual, for Mr. Willoughby appeared delighted to accept Mr. Cantelope's invitation to dine with him that evening at his club. So, after being chiefly instrumental in gaining a point for his side in the foursomes, Mr. Cantelope drove the actor back to London and they met again later on at the Bachelors' Club. For a time Mr. Willoughby greatly entertained his host with his memories (and there is something peculiarly entrancing in being taken behind the scenes unless one is professionally compelled to spend much time there). Mr. Willoughby's gently caustic revelations of the foibles and frailties of his famous colleagues were delightfully instructive to his host, and then, some vague reference to the occult having been made, Mr. Cantelope observed that he was somewhat attracted by such phenomena. "I've never seen a ghost or even thought I'd seen a ghost," said Willoughby, "though I was once mixed up in something which seemed to require more explanation than it got, but I'm insufficiently mediaeval to imagine that what appears inexplicable is necessarily supernatural. However, it may interest you to hear about it, but," he added, laughing, "you must promise not to say you heard it from me."

"Of course you must tell it me," replied Mr. Cantelope, "but may I ask why you feel it necessary to extract such a vow?"

"For what you will consider a ludicrous reason; because members of my profession are the most superstition-ridden creatures in the world. I despise them for it and yet I share their miserable weakness; and were it not for the fact that, as a result of inheriting a modest competency, I have just retired, I should never have even considered referring to the affair."

"I'm sorry to hear we shall see you no more," replied Mr. Cantelope. "Believe me when I say that it means a considerable loss to the stage."

"Thanks very much, but I fancy it will survive. As a matter of fact I am becoming slightly antique for the parts in which I have been usually cast. I can see grey wigs before me, and I find it more and more of a strain to learn my lines. The machine-made and machine-gun dialogue of to-day is far harder to learn than the more leisurely and legato brand to which I have been accustomed. Anyway, I was referring to our professional superstitiousness. It is all-pervasive and the taboos are typically irrational—whistling in dressing-rooms, quoting *Macbeth,* repeating the last or 'tag' line of a play before the first night. No one knows where the interdict will fall next, and it was probably mere caprice that it became an unwritten law that no one who was in the cast of *The Eleventh Hour* should ever refer to it again lest some dire doom should be inflicted on the transgressor."

"Absit omen," said Mr. Cantelope with a smile.

"You mean I may repent my indiscretion in telling this tale to you. No, I take it that the curse only falls on the guilty party in his professional capacity. Well, I have made my last bow and am consequently immune. Anyway, I will risk it. Do you remember an actor-manager named Duncan Littlemore?"

"Very vaguely I do," replied Mr. Cantelope, "but he's little more than—oh, acquit me of the vilest pun—it was absolutely unintentional—he is just a name to me. As I recall him he produced and acted in pieces which did not greatly appeal to me."

"And that is all you remember about him?"

"Yes, I believe that is all."

"Very well then, I shall have to describe him you briefly. Well, he was a highly competent actor, though his methods were florid, stagy and over-emphatic, but he possessed an absolute sense of what his public expected from him. He was extremely good-looking, again in a curled rather vulgar way, and his dressing-room was usually thronged by persons of position, particularly ladies; and there is not the slightest doubt that many a well-known dame entrusted her reputation to his discretion, with justification, for as a snob and a sensualist he greatly appreciated these decorative surrenders, and was sensible enough to know that if he wanted to add to their number he must keep a tight rein on his scurrilous tongue, for he was a vile fellow, vain to a degree, uncultured, the epitome of selfishness, crooked and corrupt. I know of no other profession in which such a loathsome animal could have secured a large and effusive following. There were many tales related of his bumptious insolence. For example, when *A Flight of Birds* was first produced, Eleanor Dundas and Jimmy Block played the leads, and Eleanor as the better-known artist of the two had the Star's dressing-room. When Jimmy surrendered the part Littlemore succeeded him; and without saying a word to Eleanor he rushed down to the theatre and had all her gear shifted to another room, installing himself in hers. That was typical of his caddish little soul. Once he became a manager he never picked a play in which there was a decent part for anyone else; he got rid of anyone who seemed to be making a competitive hit, and no one was ever allowed on the stage when he was taking a 'call.' He was a bully and a 'sweater,' but as his plays usually ran for months, he got the casts he wanted and his own way in everything. And then one day Arthur Wells sent him in a play."

"A drink?" asked Mr. Cantelope.

"No, thanks. Lately I have had some of those symptoms of that Change of Life known as 'blood pressure' in men.

Arthur had had one big success with *Tweedledee,* but he could never 'click' again, and he was in very low water when he submitted, *What Does it Matter?* to Littlemore. He was a huge Irishman, violent-tempered, but generous and greatly loved. His disappointments found a conventional outlet in brandy. About this time, however, he had married and reformed courageously. Littlemore kept the play for five months. But had it been lying idly on his desk? Oh no! He kept an unscrupulous hack called Richards, one of whose functions it was to pinch ideas from plays sent in to his boss and fake up a new play round those ideas. Usually, he chose pieces by obscure individuals who could do nothing but protest and, I suppose, Littlemore considered that Wells had sunk sufficiently low to make it safe to rob him. Apparently *What Does it Matter?* was a fairly good play with a very strong central situation and a really good third act. I never read it myself, but I heard that was so. Anyway, six months after returning it Littlemore announced with a mighty flourish of Press trumpets that he would shortly produce a new play by Samuel Richards. I was engaged for a tiny speaking part, the first time I had ever been paid for opening my mouth on the stage, being eighteen at the time.

"After rehearsals began, Leonard Wilkins, who was also in the cast, happened to meet Wells, and in conversation with him outlined the plot of *The Eleventh Hour.* Wells realised at once that it had been 'lifted' straight from his play, and, beside himself with fury, rushed round to Littlemore. Though they actually came to blows, Wells got no change from the actor, merely insolence and abuse, whereupon Wells took legal opinion, having obtained a copy of the script of *The Eleventh Hour* from Wilkins. This opinion stated that while there were remarkable resemblances or parallels between the two plays they were very general and plagiarism would be difficult to establish. If Wells cared to employ expensive counsel he would have a sporting chance, but no more. The theft—if it was such—had been most carefully and cunningly

perpetrated and would require able and expert pleading to
prove. This was enough for Wells, who had no resources for
employing expensive counsel. So he sat down and wrote the
following letter to Littlemore:

"'You are a blackguard and a thief. You have stolen my
play, as you have stolen dozens of others, you *foul bloody
swine.*'

"He sent copies of this epistle to every member of the cast
and a good many other people. And then he forced his way
into Littlemore's dressing-room at the Thespian and blew
his brains out in front of him. He had always been a great
admirer of Chinese customs.

"This shook Littlemore somewhat, for the inquest might
be unpleasant. So he sent Wells's widow fifty pounds, which
she returned. Sure enough the coroner did want some explanations, for he had been sent anonymously a copy of
Wells's letter. However, Littlemore employed a K.C., who
very delicately suggested that Wells had been suffering from
delusions due to his appreciation of neat brandy. A typically
mean insinuation. But as there was quite a posse of coffins in
the mortuary and the jury were disturbed at being compelled
to get so much close-up evidence of human fragility and
anxious to be through with it, the inquiry was not pursued,
and Littlemore was able to breathe freely once more, and he
returned to rehearsals in the highest of spirits.

"I may say things were made more or less all right for
Mrs. Wells. Our profession is generous to a fault whatever
else it may be, though possibly a realistic psychologist might
suggest that such generosity is to some extent a case of cast-
ing one's bread on the waters, for the many hours come when
all mummers must 'rest.'

"Littlemore personally produced his own plays for the
very good reason that no one with any self-respect would
have done it for him; producing being to him a process by
which his own part became fatter and everyone else's proportionately skimmed, so much so that I began nervously to

conjecture whether I should be able to retain all my eight lines, for he listened hungrily when I was repeating them. As a producer he was a bully with a quick, foul temper and a dirty tongue, and I realised more and more each day what a matchless egoist he was, and as a timid beginner I was absolutely terrified by him, and yet he fascinated me in a way, he was so complete and perfect a tyrant. *The Eleventh Hour* was a dud play, if ever I saw one, simply and solely constructed to permit Littlemore to occupy the centre of the stage for two hours and a quarter out of two hours and a half.

"The theme of *What Does it Matter?* had been that of a man deliberately sacrificing his reputation to save his friend's. So, of course, was that of *The Eleventh Hour;* but Richards had changed the setting from London to the Wild and Woolly West, then a much more romantic region than it is to-day when all the most sex-appealing and expert Cowboys have gravitated to Hollywood or formed Rodeo troupes. Littlemore in the decorative raiment of a Plainsman nobly chose to sacrifice his existence to save that of the brother of his inamorata. Near the end of the third act his neck was encircled by a rope, a sheriff in attendance. However, the brother, overcome by the spectacle, broke down and confessed to a rather amateurish spot of horse theft at *The Eleventh Hour,* and all was well. I have to tell you these dull facts to explain what happened.

"Littlemore had another trait typical of the tenth-rate theatrical mind; he loved a ludicrous degree of realism in his 'props.' With the slightest justification he would bring in real horses, real Red Indians, real gold-fish and that sort of thing, so the gallows in the act was a most serviceable engine, and during rehearsals many longing eyes were directed to it when Littlemore's neck was in the rope. Wilkins— the sheriff—told me it was as much as he could do to keep his feet from kicking the chair from under him.

"Considering everything rehearsals were carried through successfully, booking we heard was very good indeed, and when the first night came we all were confident that the Thespian would be full for many months and that we should not be worrying our agents for a very long time—to the actor a most blessed and soothing sensation.

"I do not think anything out of the way or untoward occurred during the earlier part of that evening. I should not have noticed it if there had been, for the prospect of having to utter for the first time on any stage eight whole lines of melodramatic prose before a first-night audience was so utterly monopolising my faculties that everything else in the world seemed but the vague antics of phantoms. Time after time those cursed eight maliciously eluded my memory, and all the experienced reassurance of Wilkins that they would be duly forthcoming at the critical moment failed to comfort me. But I do remember that for two acts Little-more gave the performance of his life. He was word perfect and full of most convincing fire, so much so that he made that tuppence-coloured drivel almost seem like a decent play. The audience gave him a tremendous 'hand,' and we petty ones were greatly cheered by the success of the Colossus, for it meant economic ease for us for many months. I did not appear in the later portions of the second act, and I went down to see the stage doorkeeper about five minutes before the curtain. I wanted to leave a message with him so far as I remember. I found him in a state of indignation and irritation. 'Blasted sauce, that's what I call it,' he was remarking to one of the orchestra. I asked him what was the matter. 'Well,' he replied, 'about five minutes ago a chap came in without so much as a "by your leave" and shoves past me. I shouted after him, but he takes no notice, so I runs up the stairs after him and sees him go into the Guvnor's dressing-room. I couldn't go in after him, for the Guvnor would fire me in one act if I went into his room.'

"'What was he like?' I asked.

"'A great big chap, very quick and quiet.'

"'Probably only a reporter,' I said.

"'Well, what'll the Guvnor say to me when he finds this bloke in his dressing-room?' asked the janitor in an aggrieved and melancholy tone.

"I had a pretty shrewd idea of the answer to that question, but I wasn't in a position to help, and after leaving my message went back to my room just as a roar of applause announced the fall of the curtain.

"Wilkins came in shortly after, and we were chatting casually as we changed our attire when Mr. Littlemore's dresser burst in with consternation on his face.

"'Will you come up to the chief's room, sir?' he said to Wilkins. 'When I went in I found him in a faint and I can't bring him round.'

"We both dashed off, Wilkins having picked up a flask of brandy from the dressing-table. Littlemore was lying on the floor, his face dead-white, his eyes closed. Wilkins forced some brandy down his throat and I poured cold water over his face. But for some time without result. We sent the dresser off to tell the stage-manager what had happened and to keep the curtain down. We were just beginning to despair of bringing Littlemore round and about to fetch a doctor from the audience when he opened his eyes. Their expression was blank and unseeing for a moment or two, and then a look of extreme terror came into them. We helped him to his feet, but he took absolutely no notice of us, keeping his eyes focused on a spot behind us. Luckily he hadn't to make a change for the last act, so we cleaned him up and gave him another strong tot of brandy. By this time we could hear demonstrations of impatience coming from the audience. And then Littlemore did a very curious thing; he crooked and extended his right arm as though linking it with another's, and he was staring straight in front of him, and, as though being supported and led, went down to the stage. We feared the absolute worst, but to our relief and amazement Littlemore seemed perfectly capable of carrying through. The fire had gone out of him and his acting became strangely mechanical, but he made no call on the prompter and his actions were sufficiently natural. The only time there was the slightest contretemps was when Wilkins as the sheriff was adjusting the rope round his neck, for he attempted rather feebly to resist him, but even that must have seemed all right from the front. But all through that act his eyes were staring into vacancy. For the last ten minutes I wasn't wanted on the stage and went back to my dressing-room. Eventually I could tell by the applause the curtain was down, and then by its renewal and increased volume that Littlemore was taking his call. And then all the lights in the house went suddenly out. For a moment I could hear a confused murmur from the audience, and then a curious cry, half shout, half scream—and then a moment later the lights came on again. And I heard a chorus of cries of consternation, alarm and horror. I rushed out and down the passage, to the steps leading to the stage. At the bottom of them was a scene of the utmost confusion, the members of the company and the staff being in a state of the most intense excitement, and then there was a cry of 'Make way,' and four men carrying a body passed through the throng and came towards me. I drew back against the wall to let them pass. I have seen many dead men since in France and Flanders, but none has filled me with such horror as that thing in Cowboy kit, with its head dangling from its broken neck.

"I believe there was only one person who had even the vaguest idea of what happened between the time the lights went out and when they came on again; and that by chance was a friend of mine named Hawkins, who had always been known for his extremely keen sight. He was sitting in the front row of the stalls when the lights went out. He told me he could just catch a faint view of the stage, and it seemed to him that something or somebody seized Littlemore and drew him back by the neck, so that he seemed to lose his balance and totter on his heels. It was just then that he screamed. Then Hawkins lost sight of him. After perhaps ten seconds he heard a crash, and the lights came on just as the falling curtain was half-way down. And just before it shut out the stage from his view he saw Littlemore writhing on the ground with the scaffold lying crashed down beside him. There was some sort of confirmation of this from the assistant stage-manager who was in charge of the curtain, for he swore that just after the theatre became in darkness he was conscious that someone went past him and out on to the stage. There was one other funny little incident. They had just carried Littlemore's body into his dressing-room when an ambulance dashed up, and the man in charge of it said they had been rung up shortly before and informed that Mr. Littlemore urgently required their services at the theatre."

"What!" said Mr. Cantelope, "could he have done that himself?"

"Not possibly," replied Willoughby, "for he had been on the stage for the last half-hour, and, of course, no one in the theatre was responsible, for why on earth should they have done such a thing."

"What was the verdict at the inquest?"

"Well, Littlemore died from a broken neck, but the doctor was unable to suggest how it had been sustained. Possibly the gallows fell on him as they collapsed, but all he would state definitely was that Littlemore's neck was broken. Verdict—Accidental Death. As I say, I believe Hawkins was the only person who could throw the slightest light on what happened, if you call that light."

"What happened to the play?" asked Mr. Cantelope.

"It had just that one performance, for there was no one to take Littlemore's place, and anyway the public seemed to have acquired a temporary distaste for the Thespian theatre. Personally, after three months' rest I was engaged to play the part of a footman in *Featherbeds,* and had no less than twenty lines of unrecognisable Cockney. After that I never looked back."

"I imagine you've looked back on the first and only night of *The Eleventh Hour,*" said Mr. Cantelope.

"No more than I could help," replied Willoughby, "for when I do I always see four men carrying something past me clad in Cowboy's kit."

A Jolly Surprise for Henri

When a fortnight before she became a widow, Marianna sat down at her "escritoire" (as her pronunciation of French mellowed many familiar articles were Gallicised), she presented a seductive spectacle. She owned what may be somewhat controversially termed the Ideal Female Figure, to which, after many strayings down Schoolboy and other perverted paths, lovely ladies must always, if possible, return. Just thirty-two years of age, just seventy inches high, just under ten stone, she was beautifully firm, strong, rounded, a lovely rippling rhythm of curves. She had made heroic efforts so to defeat the purposes of Providence as to make herself resemble an anaemic and dissolute Etonian, but "redoocing" had made her feel rotten and look worse, so she gave it up, and thereby gained her reward, for it was partly her appearance of plenty in an era of banting which drew all men unto her. She was a little uncertain about her legs, for they seemed rather larger than most women's, but, as she said unexpectedly, "They may be bloody, but they're at least unbowed," and indeed those powerful pillars were perfectly fit columns to support the admirable edifice above them. Certainly Marianna represented good manners in architecture. She looked at herself intensely in the little mirror on the "escritoire." She saw reflected there a blonde of blondes, eyes unexpectedly dark, a nice little nose, a skin which always seemed slightly tanned, giving her a look of radiant wellbeing. She opened her mouth and examined a dentist's nightmare, a flawless set, and then she put down the glass. Though she had seen all this many times before she still enjoyed the reassuring vision. That the ensemble included no indication of any particular intelligence would not have worried her even if she had detected the omission.

She took up the receiver and demanded a number in Mayfair, and her expression became calculating and concentrated. Students of Human Behaviour would have been prepared to wager their shirts that she was about to enter into conversation with a man in whom she was much interested, and it was so.

When Oliver Painter—ten days before he became a wraith—was proceeding in an impressive automobile towards the City, his face showed no sign of any presentiment of his approaching exit. He seemed quite at his ease as he scanned his papers in a knowing manner. He was a big dominating animal, but in no way gross. The reason for his great Stock Exchange renown was revealed by the look of mingled shrewdness and courage which usually occupied his face. It occupied it now as he absorbed the contents of those miracles of dreariness, the organs of finance, but suddenly he put them down on the seat beside him and an expression of fatuous bliss replaced it. Students of Human Behaviour would have had no hesitation in staking the rest of their attire that his mind had suddenly become occupied by "a dear little woman." Some punters!

The two personalities thus briefly described had first met eleven years before in the city of New York, whither Oliver had gone ostensibly on business and Marianna ostensibly on pleasure—but *he* meant to enjoy himself and *she* to put in some spells in the Crow's Nest.

Oliver was then forty-one, already very rich and in the mood for settling down. Marianna was the daughter of the leading dentist of Tickville, a prosperous and rapidly expanding New Hampshire burg, and in some important respects, perhaps, the dullest hole on the inhabited globe—

at least so Marianna thought. Mr. Sheldrake did more poking about in affluent cavities, more gold and porcelain mining than any of his competitors, for his technique was modern, he was extremely handsome and the Life and Soul of a Party. His wife had also been a Grade A looker in her day, and Marianna's face and form were the natural fruits of so pulchritudinous an alliance. She also was in the mood for settling down, or rather settling up. With her looks all things were possible. She found the youth of Tickville intolerable, and so she flirted with them cruelly. Because they boosted Tickville she despised them, and it amused her to torture them. Had Thamar crossed the Atlantic, lived for a number of years in Tickville and drunk nothing but iced water she could only have been distinguished from Marianna by the fact that she was a brunette.

This morbid and complex attitude towards the other sex supplied the only unexpected trait in her character.

So when she came to stay with a school friend in the metropolis she was through with her home town and out for blood. By the time she had known Oliver for half an hour she had begun seriously to consider him. Oliver equally quickly was equally *touché*. She was physically a marvel, he had never imagined such perfection. He found her slight American accent attractive and she had vitality and vivacity, though he was shrewd enough to know that her smooth and glossy brow would never be marred by lines indicating intellectual contemplation, and that her charming little head was as nearly empty as he could have wished, for this eligible *beau* realised vaguely but decisively that while a combination of great beauty and large brains would admirably grace his bed and decorate his hearth, it would be unlikely to do either for very long, for he knew himself to be just a "nice plain business man." He decided after a fortnight's earnest consideration to pop the question.

Marianna coyly did not jump at the proposal, but she never really seriously considered refusing it. Oliver was not so very far from being the incarnation of her girlish dreams—except that he was forty-one. He was rich, he lived in London, he was English, he was not bad-looking, robust and impressive physically, apparently generous, a bit old though; yet Tickville was no place to linger longer in. Having had propositions put up her by all the unmarried and not a few of the married males of that city, she felt confident that she was fully equipped to hold her own in arenas of far fiercer feminine competition. She was just reaching her best, a face and form such as hers should stir even London, and anyway they were being shamefully wasted in Small Town Celibacy. So they were married at St. George's three months later. For a year Marianna was chiefly occupied in getting her bearings, picking her friends with great care, and in giving the rooms in her house in Berkeley Square the appearance of lavishly furnished and decorated stage sets, though, like most American women, she had naturally good taste in such matters. After that the arrival of Oliver Junior took up most of her time. But when the heir was howling masterfully and a strong posse of domestics had been engaged to look after him, Marianna started to set about things. Two years of matrimony had not changed her opinion of Oliver Senior very greatly. Still he was rich, English, *certainly* generous and *now* he had a house in Berkeley Square. He didn't seem quite as good-looking, but she had few regrets. He had revealed rather a thrilling new trait—he was consumed, "literally consumed," said Marianna, by jealousy. She recognised that he had some cause for it. Nine men out of ten made love to her at sight with varying degrees of ardour. She encouraged all the more socially eligible with a rather stereotyped and highly deceptive response. She knew all the tricks of the trade, but there was no real business done. Oliver, apparently a feeble judge of female frigidity, made scenes of great sound and fury over these tightly leashed affairs. Marianna quailed inwardly, but retaliated and defended herself with spirit, and was cunning enough to put a good deal of stock-broking in

Oliver's way. Whenever the pursuer's chase became too hot she pretended to surrender to her lord and master's will, but while the affair was in an early, safe and interesting condition she defied him with perfect success. Consequently it was not a placid *ménage*, but Marianna didn't hanker after placidity if it was to be bought at such a drearily high price. Surely the Terror of Tickville had a right to a run in London. At the same time she had no intention of giving Oliver any real excuse for taking any unpleasant action. He might rage, but there was nothing definite of which he could accuse her. No man was worth the risk of losing an established position as "One of London's most wealthy and beautiful young hostesses" and that sort of thing. Oliver's scenes were rather a bore, but they had their reassuring side, implying as they did fanatical devotion to herself and acting as they did as allies of her conscience. However, as time went on it seemed to Marianna that he was calming down. The tornadoes became less frequent and less sustained, almost they seemed the result of habit rather than conviction.

Why did Marianna dally? She was perfectly happy, constitutionally frigid, and she knew dalliance might be dangerous. Partly from that malevolent and morbid delight in torturing men. It gave her a queer and complex thrill to see them "aching" for her. Never having experienced such an urge herself she found it most amusing to watch it in others, and men behaved in interestingly different ways when properly adjusted to the rack.

But even without this sadistic stimulus she would have dallied, for she considered that her position demanded it. A member of the *Haute Monde*—an expression she had mastered perfectly—should, she believed, reveal some apparent moral levity. Her conversation should be knowing, dashing, occasionally brilliantly shocking. Those saucy anecdotes which commercial travellers are alleged to compose in their leisured moments, and which they certainly exchange in office hours, should form a staple conversational ingredient. Well-bred cynicism, careless opulence, a complete lack of anatomical reticence, sartorial and verbal, and a most catholic and indiscreet intimacy with all that was happening in the realm of aristocratic-cum-theatrical depravity—these, Marianna considered, were necessary constituents of the part she had to play. A "quick study," she made progress rapidly, and when she realised the highest point within her capacity she was a creditably convincing replica of the real thing. But from an examination of the conduct of her friends she saw that something in the way of a lover or two was indicated. Lovers were evidence of admiration and they lent that spice of danger which post-war matrimony demanded. The engagement book of a lady of fashion should include regular entries in code, the planning necessitate some *sub rosa* arrangement with her friends, and she should reciprocate by assisting in the easing of their delicate indiscretions. (So she thought.)

Most of Marianna's friends were British equivalents of herself. Wealthy and aspiring they worked along the same lines and cultivated the same idiom of conduct, but having the sense of it rather more in their blood more nearly approached the original. However, Marianna was much the richest of them and she forced the tip of her pinnacle level with theirs by the fulcrum of a mighty bank balance. One and all devoted their lives to getting to know just the right people. It was hard and sometimes terribly boring work.

Marianna was very charitable. Blue Crosses, Ivory Crosses, Green Crosses, Red and Purple Crosses were all lavishly supported by her, and she even made an attempt to institute a Lemon Cross, the aim of which would have been to provide soup kitchen facilities for the authors of historical dramas in verse, but it was decided at a meeting of the Provisional Executive Committee that such works were so intrinsically unreadable and unactable that it would be kinder negatively to direct the energies of their authors to more marketable expressions of inspiration. But it wasn't all energy wasted, for Marianna got to know her first Duchess thereby.

Along this worthy highway Marianna marched to social repute. The Really Right People regarded her with amusement and some irony, but they rather liked her, and her hospitality was overwhelming. By observing the Really Rights with great concentration and watching her step very carefully, Marianna improved her technique and secured a coveted place in contemporary Gossip Columns.

To her selection of lovers she gave considerable thought. She eventually decided on a "Stand By and Casuals" system. The former to be ardent enough to merit the description, but sufficiently unappetising to make the rejection of his advances—beyond a certain point—no great strain on a robust conscience. But she realized that something more dashing and decorative was also required, and for Casuals she cultivated the middle ranks of diplomacy—Latin diplomacy for choice—for attachés and people of that sort were often attractive and of noble birth, and their response to exceptional charms and the very best food and drink was invariably enthusiastic. These she could exhibit, enslave and exchange for others. It was the Casuals who roused the ire of Oliver.

With the good luck of the pertinacious she carried out this monstrous programme with perfect success. She found an almost ideal Stand-By in a rubicund individual fifty-four years of age, reasonably connected with the peerage, a widower with £10,000 a year. This personage fell an immediate victim to Marianna in the most photographed bathing suit at Deauville. He pursued her in a "never say die" spirit for five years.

Marianna made elaborate assignations with him, exhibited for his benefit all the wiles she realised were appropriate but secretly despised, and finally drove him to an even larger consumption of alcohol than his appearance suggested. He hoped against hope heroically year after year, and then one day they "parted brass rags" dramatically. It was in Marianna's pet private room at the Restaurant Verdi, when she was looking more than usually rakish and tempting. Fortified by oysters and a Porterhouse steak, he advanced once more to the charge. Repulsed as ever he topped his brow, and then poured out a glass of Perrier water and dropped therein two little pellets which friskily dissolved.

"What's that, Snookums?" asked Marianna.

"A farewell oblation," replied Snookums. "And the only sensible draught for a man who *is* a man and has his meals privately with *you,* a bromide and soda. Farewell!"

And so they parted, and for a time Marianna had to depend on Casuals, but though they usually managed to disguise their exasperation and control their disappointment she had one experience which rather alarmed her. A dashing young Italian gave her a very testing afternoon, once again in a private room at the Verdi. As soon as the waiter had brought in the coffee, this hot and ebullient exile came straight to the net. To Marianna's request that he should try to behave like a gentleman he paid no attention at all. To her indignant assertions that she would never have cultivated his acquaintance if she had known what sort of a chap he was he returned blasting and reprehensible replies. In the indecorous and dubious struggle which followed Marianna learned that lunching dangerously has its trying moments, but that her conscience assisted by a hock bottle was equal to them. She left the restaurant with her raiment less intact than her virtue. The thwarted Latin went back to his flat, put on a black shirt and spent the evening cursing his mistress for being a brunette.

Marianna then decided to get a new Stand-By. Stand-By Number Two was of a very different type to his predecessor. He was a novelist of some repute, considerable talent and inconsiderable sales. Happily he possessed means of his own. He was forty-six, a bachelor, tall, thin, rather grizzled, kind, gentle, but for his job rather too limited in interests. Till he met Marianna he had lived a life of cultured conventionality. A novel a year, a few short stories, a month at Cap Martin, some fishing in Scotland, many male acquaintances, a few

faithful female friends. These last he regarded so platoni-
cally that he could only with difficulty distinguish in his
mind one from the other. He dined with them regularly,
spare, terribly *au courant* spinsters, of uncertain age, argu-
able charms and unplumbed possibilities—unplumbed at any
rate so far as he was concerned. He regarded himself modest-
ly as an A1 risk against any serious feminine entanglement,
a man of the world, a man of honour, a man of recognised
intellectual consequence and then he met Marianna! He met
her after a lecture he delivered at the American Women's
Club on "The Technique of Modern Fiction." She came coo-
ing up to him at the end of it, looking dazzling and uttering
five and ten cent appreciation, lion-hunter's guff. A moment
later he found himself accepting an invitation to luncheon
next Thursday, and as he did so he felt the first faint stirring
of that degrading obsession which was destined to harry him
into premature senility. He was—had he known it—already
a C3 risk.

Between then and the lunch date he canvassed his acquaintances regarding his hostess. Something urgent and
disingenuous in his demeanour caused them to regard him
with pity and consternation—an epitaphal pity, a post-mor-
tem consternation. One, a discarded Casual, informed him
with vivacity. He told the novelist that if he liked consuming
vast quantities of iced water in the hope that it would eventually be transformed into Veuve Clicquot he ought to have
been born in Cana of Galilee; if it amused him to lunch in
private rooms with the Curate's Aunt masquerading as Circe,
let him carry on; if it occurred to him as fun to experience all the extra expenditure entailed by furtive sin without
any of its darling compensations, let him step right in; and
finally, after warning him that in his opinion Oliver Junior
had been produced parthenogenetically, he promised to lend
him *La femme et le pantin.* So that when the fatal Thursday
came, Mr. Rupert Shanklin (author of *Sextet, An Anglo-Saxon Chronicle,* etc.) had been sufficiently warned and should

have shown himself of sterner stuff. As it was he never even
squared up but capitulated with shameful celerity, and never
even bargained to retain his sword. His sensations were
entirely new to him, and he realised to his horror that he
was capable of knowing the same erotic agonies as the heroes
of Best Sellers. Up to a point his reactions to close contact
with Marianna were identical with those felt by all her more
intelligent victims. He knew her for an ass in ten minutes,
but that face, that body, that devastating vitality, the glowing animal excitement she aroused! Deplorable! When he got
back to his flat, booked to lunch with her three days later
at "A little place I'm crazy about," he cursed himself in his
despair, for he knew at last the overwhelming power of a
gentlewoman's frame—even a damn-fool gentlewoman's,
over a gentleman's—even a cultured, fastidious, middle-
aged gentleman's mind and peace of mind—a discovery which
had he made it earlier would have had a very beneficial effect
on his sales.

So it began and so it went on for two years and a half.
How its sham furtiveness shook and yet exhilarated him.
How he winced at being addressed as "Snuffkins," and how
he cherished the appellation. How his better self protested
against his employment of the endearment "Sweetheart," and
with what fiendish and gloating bliss his worser nature tri-
umphed. Had he experienced these trials some years later
he might have compared himself to one of those infatuate
hounds who pursue a piece of mechanism inadequately disguised as a hare round stadiums, their cynical quarry disap-
pearing at the moment of triumph, leaving the panting competitors sniffing dejectedly at its burrow. Marianna was his
"Tin Pussy," and whenever an ironic hand "slipped him" he
had to gallop on in vain pursuit. Yet he knew he would have
no peaceful hour till he—till he—let him confess to it—*possessed* her. Oh, how well he knew that this was a shamelessly
degrading goal for a man of culture and refinement in his
forty-seventh year to set before himself; this coarse physical

union with a being intellectually on a level with a half-awakened bird. He used to lie in bed in the morning miserably rehearsing her failings, her kittenish blather, her half-witted Don't-you-thinks, her snobbery, her frigid flirtatiousness, her! her!! her!!! But it was the apparent hopelessness of success rather than his degrading ambition which afflicted him. And with what unblushing fervour he would rush to the telephone at its first siren tinkle. Whole sides of his character hitherto entirely unsuspected revealed themselves; sides far better buried ten fathoms deep, but which had leaped leering from their graves and refused to be re-interred. He felt himself sinking for the third time.

It was having a shocking effect on his writing. He knew that because the sales of his last two books had jumped remarkably.

"Mr. Shanklin seems to have become more human, less aloofly ascetic in his outlook on humanity, most surprisingly here and there a little raffish," said the *Times Literary Supplement.*

"A little raffish!" he groaned aloud as he sneaked off to the Restaurant Verdi. On one such occasion the taximan looked round half-way down Piccadilly thinking he had heard his fare denouncing him. But it was simply that Mr. Shanklin, overwhelmed by his finer self, had exclaimed, "'What have I done to deserve this!" his tortured soul momentarily a prey to *cliché.*

Marianna, for her part, dimly realised that Stand-By Number Two was a cut above any of her other Chambre privée Chums. She had felt that from the moment he had stood up, nervously clearing his throat and rustling a page of notes, to deliver his lecture, and though not one word of the scholarly pronouncement which followed had been intelligible to her, she was vaguely stirred by his personality and carefully regulated voice and forthwith marked him down. And she had found it sharply intriguing to tame so distinguished a literary personality. She became prouder of this conquest than of

any of its predecessors, for he alone of them, she felt, realised she had a very good mind, and whenever he published a
new book she left a number of copies lying about the house
in unmissable places, and she alluded to it with as much coy
pride as if she had written it herself.

"I suppose you're in it?" asked Mrs. Ludlow, an enigmatic
widow of great physical allurement and one of her best
friends.

"Peut-être, chérie," replied Marianna slyly.

The passing of Oliver, like that of his illustrious name-
sake, was accompanied by a mighty tempest, in fact this
formidable blow was indirectly responsible for it, because
his car crashed into a fallen tree between Walton Heath and
Banstead Downs late one afternoon when he was returning
from a game of golf.

Marianna registered an almost unnatural calm or phlegm
when the dire tidings were broken to her, but, like a diffident
dramatist whose opinion of the merits of his play soars with
each curtain demanded, so was she instructed in the true
pathos of her position by the shower of letters of condolence
she received. And finally, when the terms of the will were
conveyed to her, and she learnt she had inherited everything
by that formidable document, she knelt down and thanked
whatever gods were appropriate to such an occasion that she
had been so privileged as to be the relict of so right-minded
and financially perspicacious a Briton.

Gradually out of the mist of her tears emerged a version
of Oliver most flattering to his memory. How he must have
adored her! How unconditionally he had provided for her!
At that reflection Marianna's eyes became less humid and
narrowed a little. A widow—a lovely young widow—black
suited her—with £40,000 a year; how men—those moulded,
imploring, boring—when they came too close—creatures,
peers, tennis champions and *tutti quanti*—she would learn
some more Italian—would hound her and how she'd hound

them back. Memories of Tickville came thronging—a Moment of Moments! Her eyes were bright and dry.

Mr. Shanklin's reactions to the tragedy were more simple and spontaneous. Fate had most fistily and unexpectedly forced him to face the question: "Did he want to marry Marianna?" How he despised her and how he longed for her! He made a melancholy attempt to break up that longing into its component parts, but the result was not flattering to him. It was, he decided miserably, a mingling of crude physical desire, its voltage raised by perpetual frustration, and a delayed burst of procreative instinct rather more creditable. His natural fictional gifts, his flair for the delicate analysis of character, particularly his own, convinced him that once these mingled low and less low desires were satisfied he would regard life with Marianna as a Life Sentence—temporarily at any rate. Ah, there was the rub or snag! for might not this degrading and urgent animalism recur with fiercer force! The image of Marianna drenched his harassed eyes. Poignant memories of her darling scent pervaded his twitching nostrils, and all he could think of was how soon would she be, as it were, out of quarantine and free to flay him once again. He must ring up and find out.

Marianna had been thinking of him quite often. His letter of sympathy had been far the most aptly phrased of all she had received. She had been strongly tempted to show it to her friends, but of course it was too sacred. It would have settled Mr. Shanklin's doubts if he had known that he had been the gauge by which Marianna had tested the question of remarriage. She liked him better than any man in the world, he was the only man she could imagine living intimately with, but she felt no inclination to make the experiment. No more marrying for love, she decided. She had the money, she'd get the title—nothing less than a Marchioness if possible.

When Mr. Shanklin rang up to find out how soon they could lunch together, she reminded him in a rather shocked voice that it was only three weeks since the funeral and it must be a long time before she resumed her old life even in a subdued sort; that he must dismiss the Restaurant Verdi and that kind of thing from his mind for a very, very long time.

That same evening Marianna was sitting in the writing-room with the door open when she thought she saw someone pass into what had been Oliver's study across the passage. Putting down the Elinor Glyn novel which had been "arresting" her, she advanced to investigate, and what she saw made even her robust limbs tremble. For it was Oliver! and he was bending over his cigar cabinet of beautifully blended woods in the act of selecting a Corona. After a moment he turned round, the costly weed between his lips, and walked towards her. He gave her the slightest, most casual glance as he passed her, then went into the hall, chose a felt hat from the stand and passed through the front door.

Marianna went to the dining-room and poured out a full tumbler of the first alcoholic beverage she could find—it was crème de menthe—and took a steadying gulp. "A ghost!" She didn't believe in such things! Oliver's ghost! A Cigar-smoking, Felt-hat wearing Ghost! Why hadn't he taken any notice of her? Where had he gone? She couldn't stay in the house another minute!

Where should she go? A thin but insistent whisper tinkled, "Mildred." (Mildred was Mrs. Ludlow.) She'd see if she was in. She'd ring up. Yes, she was and would be glad to see her. Oh dear, what a terrible shock it had been!

In ten minutes she was sitting beside Mildred in the sumptuous flat which everyone rather wondered how she could afford. "I'm so glad you came, dear Marianna," she said. "I expect you're feeling terribly lonely all by yourself in that great house. However, I don't suppose that poor Oliver's bed will be empty for ever."

"Naturally I'm not thinking of such things yet," replied Marianna. "And I shall never find anyone as generous, faithful and good as Oliver."

"Of course not, dear," agreed Mildred.

It was at that moment that the most magical of all lanterns, that which projects images of the Departed on to the screen of consciousness, projected Oliver's on to Marianna's. There he was walking coolly in without his hat but puffing vigorously at the Corona—Corona—Corona. An emotion stronger than fear seized Marianna. What was he doing in Mildred's flat? That lady remarked, "How intent you look, darling; what's the matter?"

"Nothing," replied Marianna sharply. "I was just thinking of something I wanted to ask you. But first of all tell me what you've been doing lately." To the ensuing monologue she paid no attention whatever, she gave it all to Oliver. He had gone up to and sat down at the writing-desk. Whereupon he proceeded to take a spectral cheque-book from his spectral pocket and write in it with a spectral Waterman. He then got up again, went out and, as the drawing-room door was open, she could see him cross the passage and enter Mildred's bedroom. Marianna ruffled like a douched parrot, then recovered herself and pretended to listen to Mildred's account of the recent follies and frailties of her best friends, a topic which always composed the larger half of her conversation. Five minutes passed and then Oliver reappeared. He was wearing some robustly toned pyjamas and a pair of furry bedroom slippers. He came over to where they were sitting, then stooping down kissed the back of Mildred's neck, letting the cheque flutter down to her lap. And then the unknown operator of that most magical of all lanterns switched off its beam.

Marianna got up, her eyes blazing, her fists clenched, her body quivering.

"Mildred," she said shrilly, "the question I wanted to ask you is, '*How well did you know Oliver?*'"

Mildred was the best liar in London, but she couldn't face those dreadful eyes. Her mouth opened, but a faint rustle between a gasp and sigh was all that emerged. Then her eyes dropped; at the same time the nearest approach to a blush which had visited her face since she had reached the age of puberty lightly coloured it. But it was only after Marianna had slapped it with both hands with all her might that it took on a really warm tint.

Ten minutes later Marianna took up the receiver in her boudoir, and asked for a number in Mayfair. "Is that you, Rupert? I've changed my mind. I'll lunch with you at the Verdi tomorrow at one. Book number eight. Good-night, dear."

And then she went upstairs and gave all her mourning to her maid, save for five pairs of Ebony Satin Pyjamas which certainly appeared quite as appropriate an epilogue to Wedding Tables as to Funeral Bak'd Meats, and three gowns which certainly were more indicative of the genius of M. Paquin than of the pangs of bereavement.

Then she made a tour of the house, collecting the many photographs of Oliver and the one or two of Mildred it contained. Then she returned to her boudoir and flung them one by one into the fire. Her face was impassive, but she clenched and unclenched her left hand. When the holocaust was accomplished she stared into the flames, her upper lip twitching. Then she went to bed.

Henri, the Head Waiter of the Restaurant Verdi, had a far lower opinion of Marianna than she suspected. This was the sort of establishment where tipping was naturally lavish. Ten per cent, was considered a Doric-Semitic recompense for favours received. But the gentlemen, the divers and apparently flush gentlemen who had entertained Marianna in number eight seemed scandalously unaware of this fact. On one occasion a Spanish Grandee had contributed a five-franc note, several other apparently super-tax Latins had proffered sums varying from one and ninepence to half-a-crown. The Honourable James Renton had invariably been unworthy of his line, while even Mr. Shanklin, who looked a nice, generous novelist, stuck to the lamentable ten per cent.

Henri wished heartily that Marianna would choose another rendezvous. It was, therefore, with a gesture of no enthusiasm that he booked number eight for Mr. Shanklin the morning after these mysterious events. At a quarter-past four when the bell rang, a signal for the bill, he placed it on the table without any presentiment of sudden wealth. He noticed that Madam looked flushed and defiant and that her host seemed to have just conceived a remarkably telling plot. And then the latter slipped something within the folded reckoning and passed with Madam from the room. Henri took up the paper, and then his eyes began to bulge, for inside it was that charming token a ten-pound note (and the amount of the bill was £3 11*s.* 6½*d.*!).

The Red Hand

The postman's knock sounded just as the famous writer of ghost stories was drinking his coffee after dinner. There was only one letter for him, and he recognised by the writing on the envelope that it came from his literary agent. It was a handwriting he had learnt to love, for it was also to be found on the fat cheques which came in such envelopes. He opened it and found it did contain a cheque—not quite so fat as usual—and a letter. The first he put in his notecase and then turned to the letter.

"Dear Mr. Rhode,
"I enclose a cheque for your American royalties which I hope you will find satisfactory. Now I have not forgotten that you gave me strict instructions not to approach you ever again with offers for psychic stories on account of doctor's orders, but I have summoned up my courage to disobey you because of the very flattering proposal just made to me by the International people. They want a 4000-word story from you for their Christmas numbers—the *International Magazine* in America and *Brett's* over here, of course. They will pay you £400 for first serial rights, and I thought this such a lavish offer that I felt it my duty to pass it on to you. I hope you will forgive me. They want copy by August 1st, if you accept.
    "Yours sincerely,
    "A. B. Tryon."

"Blast the fellow!" thought Mr. Rhode, "tempting me like that. Certainly it's a good price; quite half what they pay Michael Arlen. I feel like writing a tale called 'Those Alarming Green Rats,' I'm so flattered. But that isn't quite my *métier*. What is it? To fool the myriad, mindless mob and cause their bugle eyeballs to pop from their sockets with the dear old 'Lighted Turnip' bunk. I've done it exactly a hundred times; sixty good, thirty moderate, and ten duds, and they liked the duds best! Who said you couldn't fool all of the people all of the time? That was just a typical piece of greasy politician's slobber. Once they really believed they couldn't they'd go into the Advertising business, or some less cynical profession."

But here he was at the age of sixty-four, still in the ghost-story business, with thirty-six years of it behind him, his tongue so very stiff from burrowing a hole in his cheek. How had it happened? Well, no doubt heredity had something to do with it, for his father had been a Nonconformist parson and his mother the daughter of a nerve specialist—a nasty ancestry, enough to get him dismissed with a caution for any crime tried before a realist judge. But it couldn't all be blamed on his begetters, there must have been a stout dollop of original sin looking for a congenial home when he was brought into the world. For how otherwise could it have happened that he, utterly, unregenerately sceptical, a gross "impercipient," if a more controversially tart epithet were preferred, had written a hundred extremely popular ghost stories, which had netted £40,000? Yet he hadn't the slightest belief in this chain-clanking tripe. Not that he wrote that sort of story, and he knew many of his to be highly disturbing, intensely visualised tales, technically admirable, for he knew his business, and to do himself justice was a decent craftsman who never left a tale till he had tightened and trimmed and polished it to as near perfection as he could bring it.

Yet the deeper question remained unanswered. What fantastic kink had made him the best-known ghost story writer in the world? Certainly he knew authors of such tales were seldom over-credulous, usually were temperamentally disinclined to revue the regurgitations of mediums, weave fantasies with ectoplasm, or join Conan Doyle in a romp with under-vitamined pantomime fairies. Yet none of them shared his unswerving, contemptuous disbelief in the possible existence of the spirits he called up.

Lowell, for example, who had written some decent ones, had told him that while he never expected to see anything of the kind, he would not be greatly surprised if he did so. Agnew, whose reputation was far higher than it deserved to be, had solemnly stated that in a waking dream one morning he had seen the whole universe, like a transparent globe the size of an orange, poised on his hand, and that it had seemed when he peered into it as infinite as when he stared up at the stars, and that he had felt for a moment, with a sense of ecstasy, that he was on the verge of understanding the truth of all things, on the threshold of the final secret. Well, he hadn't put it quite as crudely as that, but what piffling mysticism, what puerile egoism! No wonder he wrote such rot. The universe was as hopelessly inexplicable as the state of mind of those who thought otherwise.

Well, should he write number 101? Four hundred quid was not to be despised. He could buy those oils of Regnier with which Jenkins of the Pall Mall Gallery was always tempting him. And £2000 a year didn't go so far nowadays. All right, he'd do it. But never again, he swore it. He'd better look over his notes for those stories he'd conceived but never brought to birth.

He went to a drawer and pulled out a battered note-book, over the leaves of which he ran his eye. Eventually he paused at a heading—"The Red Hand," and read out to himself: "Suggested title—'The Red Hand.' Central idea—employee

kills head of firm who has discovered his tampering with
the till. Sob relief—employee owns wife and a large family,
destined for workhouse if swindle discovered. Method of
crime—employee sent for by boss after office shuts. Employee, let us call him 'Tonks,' knows why he is summoned and is
desperate. (The fact that he is sent for must not be known to
anyone else.) He comes to boss's office and is shown evidence
of swindle. Asked about it. (Employee better be old member
of firm and trusted.) He loses all self-control, picks up poker
and puts boss to sleep. As boss slips out of chair to floor he
overturns with left hand red ink-pot, which empties contents
over same hand of boss. Tonks tiptoes quietly from room.
Looks back once and sees a red hand sticking out from side
of desk. Tonks makes successful 'get-away.' End of Part I."

"Part II. Mystery unsolved. (Work this up.) Trouble for
Tonks begins few days later. He is in bus. Just handing penny to conductor, when Red Hand materialises and as it were
conducts Tonks's hand to conductor. (This must be subtly
phrased.) Tonks feels this must be a projection from his own
hand, due to its intense preoccupation with the crime. Image
of hand has been etched on mind and therefore appears.
Reassures himself. Not for long. Finds same Red Hand taking letters from him as he signs them and giving them to
typist. Begins to be always at his service—helps him insert
latch-key in front door at home, etc. (Bored for the moment,
will finish to-morrow.)"

"Red Hand becomes ubiquitous. Almost as ubiquitous as
Bolshie red hand to Duke of Northumberland. Sees its im-
print wherever he goes. (Make a point of this.) Eventually,
however, settles in Tonks's home. (Perhaps make it cause nervous breakdown in Tonks, so keeping him at home.) Anyway,
eventually touches forehead of one young Tonks and that
young Tonks dies; kills them all one by one (so increasing
Tonks's Income Tax). Eventually touches Mrs. Tonks's forehead and she goes west. Tonks now on verge of madness and

taken to mental home. He wakes up in middle of night and finds hand stroking his forehead. Screams out a confession and Tonks's family extinct."

"Note:—This synopsis very rough and undeveloped. Full of difficulties and needs most careful working out. No need for elaborate characterisation. All simple types. Actual appearances of Red Hand must be neatly contrasted and most convincingly described."

Mr. Rhode put down the document. "Rough and undeveloped! I should say it was! But the idea isn't bad. I'll put my mind to it."

One had a curious sensation when reading over an old synopsis, almost as if one were stealing the idea, plagiarising from someone else. That *was* so in a sense, for he and the other fellow in a sense *were* different people. He had written it ten years ago. It was all very well for that other fellow to say there was no need for elaborate characterisation, but Tonks had got to be made a convincing murderer and the best type of family man at the same time. And he must have been a tough nut to have stuck it as long as he did. That was good, he was beginning to see him objectively.

First of all he must visualise that hand. He put his hands over his ears and stared down at the blotting-paper, and then after a moment he started back. Well, that had been a very successful attempt. It had actually seemed to be there. Red as hell-fire, and the little finger longer than the ring finger. That was just the bizarre detail he wanted. Rather reassuring to find he could still visualise as well as ever—if not better. So well, that the stain of the hand, the visual echo as it were, seemed still to linger on the blotting-paper.

He must make the boss an unpleasant fellow, rather a sneering bully, a grinder of wage slaves' silly faces. Everyone would cheerfully murder someone—I'd murder "Jix"—and most people would have a sneaking sympathy for Tonks, but it wouldn't do for them to have too much or his persecution would seem intolerable. That was just where it wasn't simple. And he'd only got 4000 words! Well, his capacity for compression had always been pretty good.

He might make Tonks rather a "Red"—Magazine readers hated "Reds" worse than murderers—there were more of 'em. Yes, then he'd break straight into the story with Tonks entering Boss's office; latter with malignant sarcasm tells Tonks he's been found out and informs him that his subversive activities directed against the innocent rentiers have long been known to him. Well, as he has so much sympathy with work-dodgers and dole-snatchers, he could join their ranks. Then Tonks picks up poker ("and so would I and so would any Tonks). Just before that I should make the Boss boast that he always gets his own back (with a bit of someone else's sticking to it), and bang his hand on the table." Then Tonks should notice for the first time that his fingers were eccentric. (Stigma of exploiter, thinks Tonks plinthly.)

Tonks should be a small, beady-eyed chap, big head, tiny body, under-nourished in youth. A measly sort of "Mr. Polly," extremely proud of his family because he believes they "take after him."

Mrs. Tonks should be competent, rather hefty, a natural mistruster of all "isms" and "asms," who, when her temper fails, reads out *Daily Mail* "leaders" on Russia to Tonks after supper. ("I mustn't get too interested in or waste words on her.) I'll keep her conventional type. Tonks's brats are only 'heard off.' But how shall they die?—A Red Hand at night—convulsions all right?" Better make it A Strange Malady—combination of croup and colic.—Well, they all fade out from the same stuff, so I've only got to slay one to slay the quiver-full. Let it be A Strange Malady.

"I think a little morbid psychology can be connected with the first appearance of that hand when Tonks is opening his front door. He should always feel less remorse when he gets home; when he sees his wife and family he should feel it had been ethically expedient that one boss should have died for the little people. All the more unlovely when he finds the hand becoming a member of the family." One other point; though he tries to pretend to himself it is simply an illusion, he doesn't waste—for he knows in his heart of hearts it *would* be waste—any money on nerve specialists. He was already beginning to get the series of pictures sharply "seen" and fitted into their proper sequence. The horror that was Tonks's was coming to be his too. That meant he'd make a story of it. It wouldn't be one of his best. It was rather a conventional idea—rather too much in the tradition. His best plots had always derived from some highly fantastic yet plausible psychic paradox, which it was the peculiar property of his mind to procreate. What a vicious tendency to alliteration lay in wait for him and always had done! Yet somehow as the rhyme often authoritatively dictated the sense, so alliteration sometimes heightened the pressure of an aphorism or any brand of dogmatic, squeezed generalisation.

Irritating though it was, this weakness usually meant he was in a mood to write. How he hated to begin, for once he began he had to finish; and the labour and irritation that was before him! He knew it! The strain was greater in his case because he was a house divided against itself, that aloof contempt for what he wrote about elbowing that infatuate delight in how he wrote it.

If only he'd once seen a ghost, or even successfully pretended to himself that he had, that rupture might be healed. He was too old for that now. Well, it was eleven o'clock and he must settle down to chronicle the dismal history of Sebastian Tonks. He took up a pen, and at once his face took on an expression of extreme concentration. Pictures were coming to him, he was seizing them and transforming them into words. The clock ticked softly, his pen scratched lightly. . . . As it struck four he laid his pen down and read through what he had written, making slight alterations here and there, and

then he leaned back in his chair and shook his hand from the
wrist, for it was numb and yet aching. A smile of sardonic
satisfaction replaced his look of concentration.

"Cheap at four hundred quid," he said to himself. "Just
the stuff to give the mugs," and yet it had given him in
spots that curious, puerile, chill flicker between his shoul-
der-blades. When he got that he knew he'd "clicked." He
would think of little else for a week and then re-write it. He
had a conscience. In his dirty little way he was an artist. But
never would he write another.

Hullo, there was that infernal pain in his heart again.
His own fault for disobeying that specialist, that damned
angina. It took some guts to face even the possibility of such
pain. Must it come? He was already beginning to sweat and
lose his head a little. By God, that was a wicked twinge!
Was there anything in the world so awful? He'd smoked too
much, worked too long at a stretch. What a fool! God! that
one seemed to rend and slash him, and how it brought with
it the fear of death! He must wait for a pause and get his
tabloids. He rallied himself, and putting his hands over his
heart stared down once more at the blotting-pad. That Red
Hand was there again! It just showed how he'd been concentrating! It would fade away, of course. Now the pain was
better. He turned his head towards the little table on which
were a tantalus and a syphon and that blessed little tube, and
started to get up. But the Red Hand swung round with his
eyes and settled itself on the little table, the sharpest illusion
he'd ever known! And then it seemed to Mr. Rhode that the
fingers moved—clenched a little. He thrust his head forward
and stared at it, and then the pain came lashing back. He
staggered to his feet, and as he did so the hand seemed to
slide forward and close over the little phial. And then Mr.
Rhode flung himself forward in his agony and tried to tear
away that hand, and the room went black and he pitched
forward, recovered himself for a moment and then swung
on his heel and toppled over to the floor. And as he fell his

forehead caught the edge of the little table, and, as his head jerked back, the little phial slid from the table to the floor by his side.

And presently the clock striking the half-hour broke the silence.

Surprise Item

The Haunted House Club was founded in 1923 by a group of persons who decided it was high time that the venerable controversy concerning the genuine or concocted, the subjective or objective reality (a loose term, as they knew, but sufficiently precise) of those phenomena, loosely comprised within the elastic definition "psychic," was decided. Quite possibly, this group agreed, no categorical decision could be made. At the same time—and with all due respect to the S.P.R.—it would inevitably be of value that a swift and pertinacious inquiry should be always made into the credentials of alleged haunted places. Therefore, when such alleged manifestations were published or came to their knowledge, it was decided that some member of the group should be ordered to the scene to examine the circumstances and report upon them. Then, if the investigator so recommended, the group should make a pilgrimage to the scene, institute such further inquiries as were feasible, and subsequently debate the case at the quarterly reunion.

The following is the report of Mr. Charles Baber into the Pevesham Wireless Case of April 14th, 1926—the sixth of the series:

In accordance with the instructions of the H.H.C., I journeyed down to Pevesham on June 15th. Pevesham is a medium-sized market town with 10,000 inhabitants. I called first on the local retailer of wireless sets and accessories. He informed me, rather diffidently and without enthusiasm, that there had been an unexplained case of "interruption" on April 14th. When more closely questioned, he stated that he himself had not been listening in on that evening, but he understood the trouble had only occurred over a four-mile radius from the Pevesham Town Hall. I should state that this area is served by the Daventry Station. He grudgingly owned that since the date of the "interruption" the demand for his stock and his services had appreciably diminished.

I then called on the editor of the local newspaper, who agreed to put a paragraph in his next issue stating that I was making this inquiry, and should be grateful for any assistance or information in furthering it. In response to this, I received a number of replies, the most important of which came from the local doctor, Mr. Stokes. Apparently, his son, aged sixteen, was in the habit of practising his shorthand by taking down the wireless talks, and he had an important record of what had occurred on April 14th.

I immediately went round to the doctor's house, and his son gave me a long-hand copy of what he had taken down between 9.15 and 9.40 on April 14th. Having absorbed the contents of this, I visited others who had replied to me, and found that they all agreed that something very closely resembling young Stokes's version had come through their ear-phones and loud-speakers on that occasion.

Young Stokes told me that the interruption had come in the middle of a talk on "Prospects for the Settler in Tasmania." It was broken into after about five minutes. He couldn't swear he had taken down every word of this interruption, as he was startled and perplexed, but he was convinced he had got most of it. The voice of the interrupter he judged to be that of an elderly person, "half-educated," he described it, "with the local twang." This person appeared to be in a condition of extreme agitation, though, of course, it might have been feigned. But he didn't think it was. He also said that many listeners in the neighbourhood had written strong protests to the B.B.C. about this most unpleasant and unnerving practical joke, as they supposed it to be. They had all received replies stating that the B.B.C. was quite at a loss to account for the interruption, but that the fullest inquiries would be made. Here is the long-hand transcription of young Stokes's notes:

"Why is he here? They buried him deep. I'd sooner see him outright than just know he's there. He's been there since supper-time Thursday. He keeps between me and the door and I can't get past him. He stands there always, always facing me. I looked up just then and there he was. I'd sooner see him than just know he was there. I haven't had food or drink since tea-time Thursday, and that's days ago, three maybe. But there's food in the kitchen and a pitcher of water beside the tap in the scullery. Could I slip past him? Shove him aside? I might if his eyes weren't always on me. All on account of that little slut. As if I was the first—twenty-first more likely! What's he want with me? They buried him deep. I saw them lower him down and heard the dirt tap on his box. There's nothing there! I'll look up! Yes, he's there!

"Why couldn't I slip past him? All I've got to do is to walk straight forward and past him, through him, and eat and drink in the kitchen. Easy, isn't it! I'm getting weak; I should have done it in the beginning. I'll think about the window again. It's high but I might manage it. I'll keep my head down and put him off his guard, then run for it—that's what he did before, he's too quick for me. Didn't I drown you, you bastard? Didn't they bury you deep? Didn't they cover you up? That hot little piece! Always hanging round. She got what was coming to her. I wasn't the first, she told me that. Nor second, nor third. If he got that sort, it's his business if she gets into trouble. And then threatening me, asking me what I was going to do about it! Well, I showed him what I was going to do about it—and he swallowed some water. Water! By God, I want water! He's got to let me past. Why is he here? They buried him deep. I'll see what he does if I get up and go towards him. I've tried that too many times. I know what he does. He always goes round with my eyes. All right, stare at me, you bastard! I drowned you, didn't I? You're down deep, aren't you? I'm getting weak. Water! Water!

"I didn't mean to shout out like that, for I've got to keep a head on me and get past him. Now, I'll think out a way of doing it. Suppose I make a move quickly towards the window, then he'll come over and get between it and me. Then if I dodge back and run for it, he'll be behind me. I might have done it on Thursday likely, but I'm weak and slow now. Now, you dead devil, I'm going for the window! And don't you watch me like that. Do you know what I'm planning? If I could see you plainer, I'd know. Yet you go round with my eyes. Supposing I stare one way and then make a dash the other. No, I've tried that. You're always there! I'll make it right for her if you'll let me past. You're dead! I saw the bubbles come up. I saw you buried deep. . . . Suppose I pretend not to be up to anything and then make a dash for it! Or shall I make a show of going for the window? Then he'll come across and I might slip past him and get behind him—"

Young Stokes said that after this there was a moment's pause and then a muffled crash—and directly after the Wireless Symphony Orchestra came through with the selection from *Tosca*.

Now, I did not disguise from myself that this interruption might have been a hoax perpetrated by someone with a perverted sense of humour and a powerful "sending" set. But the phrasing of this monologue did not seem to me such as a hoaxer would employ. I therefore paid another visit to the local newspaper office and went through its files from the 14th of April till the end of the month.

My attention was caught by a paragraph in the issue of April 17th which stated that a farmer named Amos Willans had been found dead in his parlour the day before. He had

been found lying on the floor and had apparently been dead
for about three days. So I asked the editor if I could have a
few words with the reporter who had "covered" the inquest.
He is a lanky, inky, ambitious and thwarted young Scotsman,
longing, of course, to get to Fleet Street, and with precious
little chance of getting there. His name is Donald Paton.
These "small rag" reporters have a disheartening existence,
their hopes crushed and their style murdered by having to
describe "cold collations," the minutiae of a stagnant local
society, and the small, flat beer of a minor country town.
Therefore, as Mr. Paton showed himself intelligent, and
proved of good service to the Club, I should be pleased if his
name could be mentioned in the report of the case we issue
to the Press. This report invariably has a wide publicity and
it may be the means of translating Donald Paton to that
dubious paradise east of Temple Bar of which he dreams.

This is the gist of what he told me:

Old Willans—he was about sixty-four—had been a "character," and a very unpopular one. He had possessed a miser-
ly temperament and an ungovernable temper. He had lived
entirely alone, cooking for himself and only allowing a local
charwoman to come in once a week to clean the place up. He
had, however, sufficiently regained his vital forces to make
himself somewhat of a problem to the better-looking young
women of the neighbourhood. He was said to have had a
certain "way" with him which had occasionally prevented
his solicitations from receiving the rebuffs they merited. He
seems to have been an original, if highly unpleasant, old
person, capable of arousing heightened emotions towards
himself—hate, fear, curiosity and a kind of grudging passion
in the unwise and wantonly inclined local females.

Paton had obviously studied him with insight and understanding, so that he made the old devil stand starkly out
before me as he described him to me. It was known that some
time before his death he had been seen in company with
the daughter of another farmer. She was a notorious young

person, extremely promiscuous in her "love" affairs. She was seen leaving old Willans's farm late one night, and, not long after, suddenly went up to London and no news has been heard of her since.

Her father had been found drowned in the River Axe, two miles from his farm. Since he was given to insobriety this caused little surprise.

To sum up, the facts are so vague and any coherent explanation of them would be so empirical and ill-substantiated that I do not think the Club would be justified in visiting the area. At the same time, a discussion of these events might be of interest.

Hoping that I shall be considered to have carried out my inquiry with zeal, if not with intelligence, I beg to subscribe myself,

Your obedient Investigator,
    Charles Baber
    (Number 5).

A Case of Mistaken Identity

When Dr. Fender retired from an enormous practice in Wimpole Street he built himself a charming specimen of the modern small country-house just south of Poole Harbour, there to watch the changing seasons and the ranging seas, to placate his thin vein of poetry which the grim but absorbing business of earning a living had consistently snubbed, and to write that monograph on Stanzioni, material for which he had been slowly collecting during the last thirty years. Grizzled, humane, cultured, with a brain trained to perfection for its job, he had never taken a fee he didn't consider he had fully earned, and he had relied not at all on a Bedside Manner. He had always been just too busy to think seriously about marrying.

Though he had rigidly retired from practice, he was always at the service of the inhabitants of Comble Churton and neighbourhood if they urgently required his aid. He entertained very little, but always had a small house-party for Christmas, which he refused to allow to break up till January 1st.

On December 31st, 1926, these six persons, besides himself and his servants, were present in Bradlaugh Lodge (the doctor had had to call his house something and he greatly admired that intrepid pioneer). First and most important his sister, Miss Angela Fender, an eccentric spinster with psychic leanings, chronic absent-mindedness and a horrible

tendency to indiscreet utterance. She had been engaged twice
many years before, but in each case the rather conventional
young person had shrunk from her freedom of expression and
thought better of it. So she had been compelled to accept her
celibate destiny, and she did so with a vague resignment.
She was a "Dear Old Thing" in the best sense of the phrase,
devoted to her brother, who regarded her with amused affection.

Then there was a married couple, John and Mabel Kent,
old friends of the doctor. Supers in this drama, they need
no description. Again, there was the person who related to
me some of the events in this narrative of which he was an
eye-witness. I shall not give his name, for he has a loathing
of publicity, with a special reference to his tailor, who might
be encouraged to premature optimism by seeing my friend's
name in print. Let sleeping bills lie!

Lastly, there were the doctor's niece, Mrs. Cannon, and
Rex Lakeford, to whom she had just announced her engagement. After losing both her parents from influenza in 1906
when she was ten years old, she had come to live with the
doctor and had done so till her marriage in 1921 to Robert
Cannon. She had lost him in tragic circumstances six months
before, when he had been caught by the boom and swept
from his yacht, the *Wavelength,* off Bembridge. Dorothea
and Rex Lakeford had been the only other persons on board
at the time. Cannon had been wearing oilskins and sea-boots
and had never reappeared above the surface; the yacht was
out of control for some time, and no attempt at rescue had
been possible. Eventually they had succeeded in bringing her
alongside Seaview Pier.

Both appeared shattered by the tragedy, and the doctor,
who had hurried to Bembridge when he heard of the accident, refused to allow Dorothea to attend the inquest—
Cannon's body had been washed ashore two days after his
death. At the inquest Lakeford, who seemed near a nervous
breakdown, told a rather incoherent story, containing some

confusion and contradictions, but the coroner sympathetically asked him few questions.

The doctor stayed on at a hotel in Bembridge till his niece was fit to be moved to Bradlaugh Lodge. On the evening after the inquest he was sitting in the lounge after dinner, smoking a last pipe before going to bed and reading an evening paper. There was a group of rather noisy young men sitting and drinking at the other end of the room. The doctor attempted to disregard their slightly alcoholic exuberance, but presently his ear was caught by the word "squall." This, very naturally, interested the doctor, so, though pretending otherwise, he listened.

"Damn funny squall, I call it," a rather husky voice was saying; "I must have been within half a mile of 'em and I got nothing more than a decent sailing breeze. The visibility was pretty ruddy, I grant you, but that was a damn local squall."

"Oh, dry up, you blasted ass!" said another. "Think what you like but keep your fool mouth shut!"

"I was not suggesting anything," replied the husky voice in an aggrieved tone. "I merely said it was a damn funny squall. Squalls are damn funny things, some funnier than others. This was a very funny one. And I didn't like the look of the feller, and he's been the subject of gossip—silly thing to be the subject of gossip. Now, how does one square a triangle? Try a squall, a damn funny, damn local squall!"

"Take him home, Bill," replied the other. "He thinks he's damn funny."

The doctor glanced up quickly and saw several pairs of eyes regarding him nervously. And then he heard some whispering and the group presently departed, noisily but in haste.

The doctor had only just succeeded in holding himself in. "That foul young slanderer," he thought. "What is it that makes humanity so devilish that it loves to insinuate vilely when anything like this happens?" He lay awake for many hours. "Silly thing to be the subject of gossip." That sentence kept recurring to him. What had he meant? Were there many people on the island repeating just that same sort of beastly thing? What was the gossip? Probably just the usual dirty-hearted side-long hinting which even the most inno-cent companionship of the kind gives rise to. He thought of his niece and her great sorrow, and his blood-pressure rose and kept sleep from him.

Three days later Mrs. Cannon was well enough to make the journey to Bradlaugh Lodge, and from then on her con-valescence was gratifyingly rapid. So much so that within a month she had taken a flat in London and therein established herself. After that he received an occasional letter from her which told him little of her doings, but at the beginning of November he got news indeed. She was secretly engaged to Rex Lakeford. It seemed rather soon to announce it, she said, but she would do so before the New Year.

In the meantime, the doctor had almost forgotten that young man's existence; he had, indeed, no inclination to remember it. And now he was engaged to Dorothea. The doctor made no attempt to pretend to himself that he felt the slightest satisfaction at this prospective union. Why? Well, what did he know of Lakeford? Apparently he had met the Cannons casually in London, and being a keen yachtsman had arranged to go to Bembridge with them for a couple of months. He remembered hearing that he sold motor-cars on commission, a profession that the doctor had never rated very highly. As far as his accent was concerned, he appeared to be an educated person. He had the knack of wearing clothes or, perhaps, of not wearing them out. Of course, he was in no position to judge him, for he had only seen him in the shadow of a shocking catastrophe, and unnerved thereby. Very possibly he was all right. All right for Dorothea? Faced by this question, the doctor realised he had never attempted any serious analysis of his niece's character. In a sense she was still to him the impulsive, and in a way formidable, lit-tle girl whom he had taken into his care and provided with governesses and schooling, and to whom he had devoted as much as he could of his scanty leisure. Women to him had always been patients, frightened, in pain, dying; battle-grounds between invading organisms and his therapeutic skill. Never wives, mistresses, temptresses, things which dominated and "made" or ruined men; incalculable forces. Only just a species of animal which came to him when in trouble.

On the screen of his inner eye was projected Dorothea's image; those restless, impatient dark eyes; hair, thick gold; a nose, a shade too "full" and dominating; her lips a shade too thin, her chin a shade too strong. He had loved his brother Tom, but had never really been on easy terms with Ethel, who had also possessed uncompromising lips and chin. A wheedling bully and inclined to unscrupulousness, though a beautiful and, within her range, intelligent woman. Dorothea took after her. And that was really all he knew about her; she reminded him of her mother, a woman he had instinctively disliked; but he didn't dislike Dorothea, though he realized she was almost a complete stranger to him. Otherwise he would not have felt so intensely astonished and disturbed on learning that she was going to marry this Lakeford fellow. Well, it was just something to make the best of, and no business of his. ("A damn funny squall.") That sly insinuation of the young fool at Bembridge recurred to him occasionally, and sometimes with an almost ferocious insistence—its echo pouring through his ears.

During the six days between Christmas and New Year's Eve the doctor's guests had amused themselves in such ways as appealed to them. Mrs. Cannon and Rex Lakeford, as was natural in the circumstances, chiefly amused themselves by segregating themselves from the rest of the company. Not, thought the doctor, that it appeared greatly to agree with them. Dorothea was restless, inclined to sudden nervous tricks, almost sometimes as if she could see something or hear something not perceptible to anyone else. The doctor's expert eye diagnosed nervous strain or insomnia. As for Rex

Lakeford, his appreciation of existence seemed to vary in exact ratio with his distance from alcoholic refreshment. ("None of my business," thought the doctor, uneasily.)

My friend—whose anonymity it is so prudent to maintain—also noticed the rather eccentric manifestations of approaching marital felicity exhibited by those two persons. He, himself, has a stout head and a fearless approach to bottles and tantali, but Lakeford's capacity for "shifting it" filled him with amazement. And Mrs. Cannon's repeated inability to concentrate on what he said to her—and some of his conversation, he assures me, was of a high order—somewhat disconcerted him. But he eventually decided that the union would probably be a happy one, because Lakeford's chat was just the sort of chat which it was better not to concentrate upon.

Dinner on New Year's Eve was a qualified success. Miss Fender qualified it somewhat, for she was in a talkative and disconnected frame of mind, and inclined to be "psychic"— the doctor had mixed quite testing cocktails and she drank a full glass of champagne in almost record time. In fact, the heightening of the tension, caused by the nervous emanations from the engaged couple, had affected all the others and there was a prevailing sense of unease.

Miss Fender, after a number of over-pertinent and somewhat disconcerting observations, suddenly lifted her second glass of champagne, and looking across at Dorothea and Lakeford said:

"Well, I hope you'll be very happy and your married life be quite free from squalls."

And then there was a sudden silence; Dorothea's face became dead-white and her hands shook; Lakeford's eyes widened and his lower jaw dropped, and he stared across the table at the smiling and benevolent face of Miss Fender.

The doctor did his best to repair the damage caused by the dropping of this characteristic "brick"—the tension relaxed, and presently a tolerable imitation of care-free conversation was re-established. After dinner they played a game of cards, Lakeford's inability to distinguish between hearts and diamonds complicating it somewhat.

And presently the doctor looked at his watch, and finding the time 11.55 led his party down to the hall. Dorothea, as the owner of the darkest eyes (and the whitest face), was deputed to let the New Year in. They lined up in the passage from the morning-room to the front door, each with a glass of champagne in the right hand.

It was a wild and streaming night, blowing like the wrath of God, and with a driving deluge from the sou'-west, so the doctor told Dorothea she need not go out but just open the door.

They were ready a few moments before their time, but presently the grandfather clock on the landing began striking solemnly. And when it ceased, Dorothea went forward and opened the door.

And there, on the threshold, was a figure clad in dripping oilskins, its face almost hidden by a sou'-wester. And it started to move forward, and Dorothea screamed and slid along the wall and crumpled to the ground. Rex Lakeford dropped his glass and cried out, "Bob! Bob!" and began flinging out his arms as if to thrust that figure back.

But it was only one of the men from the Coastguard Station come up to ask the doctor if he could give him something for his mate, who was queer with influenza.

Stories from 'Weird Tales'

(1948-1951)

Ghost Hunt

Well, listeners, this is Tony Weldon speaking. Here we are on the third of our series of Ghost Hunts. Let's hope it will be more successful than the other two. All our preparations have been made, and now it is up to the spooks. My colleague tonight is Professor Mignon of Paris. He is the most celebrated investigator of psychic phenomena in the world, and I am very proud to be his collaborator.

We are in a medium size, three-story Georgian house not far from London. We have chosen it for this reason. It has a truly terrible history. Since it was built, there are records of no less than thirty suicides in or from it, and there may well have been more. There have been eight since 1893. Its builder and first occupant was a prosperous city merchant, and a very bad hat, it appears; glutton, wine-bibber and other undesirable things, including a very bad husband. His wife stood his cruelties and infidelities as long as she could and then hanged herself in the powder closet belonging to the biggest bedroom on the second floor, so initiating a terrible sequence.

I used the expression "suicides in and from it," because while some have shot themselves and some hanged themselves, no less than nine have done a very strange thing. They have risen from their beds during the night and flung themselves to death in the river which runs past the bottom of the garden some hundred yards away. The last one was actually seen to do so at dawn on an autumn morning. He was seen running headlong and heard to be shouting as though to companions running by his side. The owner tells me people simply will not live in the house and the agents will no longer keep it on their books. He will not live in it himself, for very good reasons, he declares. He will not tell us what those reasons are; he wishes us to have an absolutely open mind on the subject, as it were. And he declares that if the Professor's verdict is unfavorable, he will pull down the house and rebuild it. One can understand that, for it almost seems to merit the label "Death-Trap."

Well, that is sufficient introduction. I think I have convinced you it certainly merits investigation, but we cannot guarantee to deliver the goods or the ghosts, which have an awkward habit of taking a night off on these occasions.

And now to business. Imagine me seated at a fine satinwood table, not quite in the middle of a big reception room on the ground floor. The rest of the furniture is shrouded in white, protective covers. The walls are light oak panels. The electric light in the house has been switched off; so all the illumination I have is a not very powerful electric lamp. I shall remain here with a mike, while the Professor roams the house in search of what he may find. He will not have a mike as it distracts him, and he has a habit, so he says, of talking to himself while conducting these investigations. He will return to me as soon as he has anything to report. Is that all clear? Well, then, here is the Professor to say a few words to you before he sets forth on his tour of discovery. I may say he speaks English far better than I do. Professor Mignon.

Ladies and gentlemen, this is Professor Mignon. This house is without doubt, how shall I say, impregnated with evil. It affects one profoundly. It is bad, bad, bad! It is soaked in evil and reeking with emanations from its wicked past. It must be pulled down, I assure you. I do not think it affects my friend, Mr. Weldon, in the same way, but he is not psychic, not mediumistic as I am. Now shall we see ghosts, spirits? Ah, that I cannot say! But they are here and they are evil; that is sure. I can feel their presence. There is, maybe, danger. I shall soon know. And now I shall start off with just one electric torch to show me the way. Presently I will come back and tell you what I have seen, or if not seen, felt and perhaps suffered. But remember, we can summon spirits from the vasty deep, but will they come when we call for them? We shall see.

Well, listeners, I'm sure if anyone can, it's the Professor. You must have found those few words far more impressive than anything I said. That was an expert speaking on what he knows. Personally, alone here in this big, silent room, they didn't have a very reassuring effect on me. In fact, he wasn't quite correct when he said this place didn't affect me at all. I don't find it a cheerful spot by any means. You can be sure of that. I may not be psychic, but I've certainly got a sort of feeling it doesn't want us here, resents us, and would like to see the back of us. *Or else!* I felt that way as soon as I entered the front door. One sort of had to wade through the hostility. I'm not kidding or trying to raise your hopes.

It's very quiet here, listeners. I'm having a look around the room. This lamp casts some queer shadows. There is an odd one near the wall by the door, but I realize now it must be a reflection from a big Adams bookcase. I know that's what it is because I peeped under the dust-cover when I first came in. It's a very fine piece. It's queer to think of you all listening to me. I shouldn't really mind if I had some of you for company. The owner of the house told us we should probably hear rats and mice in the wainscoting. Well I can certainly hear those now. Pretty hefty rats from the sound of them. Even you can almost hear them, I should think.

Well, what else is there to tell you about? Nothing very much, except that there's a bat in the room. I think it must be a bat and not a bird. I haven't actually seen it, only its shadow as it flew past the wall just now, and then it fanned

past my face. I don't know much about bats, but I thought they
went to bed in the winter. This one must suffer from insomnia. Ah, there it is again. It actually touched me as it passed.
Now I can hear the Professor moving about in the room above.
I don't suppose you can; have a try. Now listen carefully.

Hello! Did you hear that! He must have knocked over a
chair or something—a heavy chair from the sound of it. I
wonder if he's having any luck. Ah, there's that bat again. It
seems to like me. Each time it just touches my face with its
wing as it passes. They're smelly things, bats. I don't think
they wash themselves often enough. This one smells kind of
rotten. I wonder what the Professor knocked over, because
I can see a small stain forming on the ceiling. Perhaps a
flower bowl or something. Hello! Did you hear that sharp
crack? I think you must have. The oak-paneling stretching, I
suppose, but it was almost ear-splitting in here. Something
ran across my foot, then, a rat perhaps. I've always loathed
rats. Most people do, of course. That stain on the ceiling has
grown quite a lot. I think I'll just go to the door and shout
to the Professor to make sure he's all right. You'll hear me
shout and his answer, I expect.

Professor! Professor!

Well, he didn't answer. I believe he's a little bit deaf. But
he's sure to be all right. I won't try again just yet as I know
he likes being undisturbed on these occasions. I'll sit down
again for a minute or two. I'm afraid this is rather dull for
you, listeners. I'm not finding it so, but then of course—
there, I heard him cough. Did you hear that cough, listeners, a sort of very throaty double cough? It seemed to come
from—I wonder if he's crept down and is having a little fun
with me, because, I tell you, listeners, this place is beginning
to get on my nerves just a wee little bit, just a bit. I wouldn't
live in it for a pension, a very large pension. Get away, you
brute! That bat! Faugh! It stinks.

Now listen carefully.

Can you hear those rats? Having a game of rugger from the sound of them. I wonder if you could hear them. I really shall be quite glad to get out of here. I can quite imagine people doing themselves in in this house. Saying to themselves: after all, it isn't much of a life when you think of it; figure it out, is it? Just work and worry and getting old and seeing your friends die. Let's end it all in the river!

I'm not being very cheerful, am I? It's this darned house. Those other two places we investigated didn't worry me a bit, but this—I wonder what the Professor's doing besides coughing. I can't quite make that cough out because—get away, you brute! That bat'll be the death of me! Death of me! Death of me!

I'm glad I've got you to talk to, listeners, but I wish you could answer back. I'm beginning to dislike the sound of my own voice. After a time, if you've been talking in a room alone, you get fanciful. Have you ever noticed that? You sort of think you can hear someone talking back.

There!

No, of course you couldn't have heard it, because it wasn't there, of course. Just in my head. Just subjective, that's the word. That's the word. Very odd. That was me laughing, of course. I'm saying "Of course" a lot. Of course I am. Well, listeners, I'm afraid this is awfully dull for you. Not for me, though, not for me! No ghosts so far, unless the Professor is having better luck.

There! You must have heard that! What a crack that paneling makes! Well, you must have heard that, listeners, better than nothing. Ha! Ha! Professor! Professor! Phew, what an echo!

Now listeners, I'm going to stop talking for a moment. I don't suppose you'll mind. Let's see if we can hear anything. . . .

Did you hear it? I'm not exactly sure what it was. Not sure. I wonder if you heard it. Not exactly, but the house shook a little and the windows rattled. I don't think we'll do that again. I'll go on talking, I wonder how long one could endure the atmosphere of this place. It certainly is inclined to get one down.

Gosh, that stain has grown. The one on the ceiling. It's actually starting to drip. I mean form bubbles. They'll start dropping soon. Colored bubbles, apparently. I wonder if the Professor is okay? I mean he might have shut himself in a powder-closet or something and the powder closets in this house aren't particularly—well you never know, do you? Now I should have said that shadow had moved. No, I suppose I put the lamp down in a slightly different position. Shadows do make odd patterns, you must have noticed that. This one might be a body lying on its face with its arms stretched out. Cheerful, aren't I! An aunt of mine gassed herself, as a matter of fact. Well, I don't know why I told you that. Not quite in the script.

Professor! Professor!

Where is that darned old fuzzy-whiskers! I shall certainly advise the owner to have this place pulled down. Emphatically. Then where'll you go! I must go upstairs in a minute or two and see what's happened to the Professor. Well, I was telling you about Auntie . . .

D'you know, listeners, I really believe I'd go completely crackers if I stayed here much longer. More or less anyway, and quite soon, quite soon, quite soon. Absolutely stark, staring! It wears you down. That's exactly it, it wears you down. I can quite understand, well, I don't say all that again. I'm afraid this is all awfully dull for you, listeners. I should switch off if I were you.

I should! What's on the other program? I mean it, switch off! There, what did I tell you; that stain's started to drip drops, drip drops, drip drops, drip drops! I'll go and catch one on my hand . . .

Good God!

Professor! Professor! Professor! Now then up them stairs! Now which room would it be? Left or right? Left, right, left, right—left has it. In we go.

Well, gentlemen, good evening! What have you done with the Professor? I know he's dead. See his blood on my hand? What have you done with him? Make way, please, gentlemen. What have you done with him? D'you want me to sing it, Tra-la-la.

Switch off, you fools!

Well, if this isn't too darned funny. Ha! Ha! Ha! Ha! Hear me laughing, listeners.

Switch off, you fools!

That can't be him lying there. He hadn't a *red* beard! Don't crowd round me, gentlemen! Don't crowd me, I tell you! What d'you want me to do? You want me to go to the river, don't you? Ha! Ha! Now? Will you come with me? Come on, then! To the river! To the river!

From the Vasty Deep

"You're sure he knows what say, Abdullah?" said Alistair Brayton to the guide.

"Oh yes, sair."

"It's just a joke, a bit of fun; you understand what I mean?"

"Oh yes, sair, just a plaisanterie; I savvy." The big café-au-lait, pock-marked rascal grinned complaisantly. Brayton had already tipped him well and promised him more, and he wanted some quick money for the purpose of buying a new wife, the daughter of a friend of his, a pretty little creature aged thirteen. His present spouse was twenty-nine and already an old, unappetizing thing, as dehydrated as a dried locust.

"We'll be out in about half an hour," said Brayton.

This conversation had taken place outside the Royal Hotel, Biskra, just within the rim of the Sahara.

Brayton sauntered back into the salle à manger where he found Rex Beaumont finishing his breakfast.

"Have you eaten?" asked Beaumont.

"Yes, some time ago."

"You were up early!"

"Yes, the sun blazes right into my room."

Their tones were cordial and their mutual antipathy nearly perfectly concealed. That intensely reciprocated dislike was of long standing, perhaps sufficiently explained by the fact that they were beyond any argument the two leading actors on the contemporary British stage. In fact Beaumont was probably the best mummer in the world, for he had starred in some very good pictures. Their rivalry was bitterly exacerbated by the ferocious partisanship of their respective cliques. Brayton was thirty-six and Beaumont thirty-nine, and those three cursed years plagued his soul. Forty was *such* a milestone, *mill*stone almost to that cynosure of a myriad female eyes.

He was indeed a very handsome comely fellow, dark, slim, lithe and a beautiful mover on the stage. He possessed "classic" features, an intense, somewhat sinister expression, a powerful and dominating eye, mellifluous voice, and, above all that, he was a most accomplished and versatile craftsman. His Iago, both Richards, Antony, Volpone and Shotover were superb, and he was equally esteemed in modern comedy. But he had found a gray hair six months before; that very morning, in the light of the pitiless desert sun, he had spotted several thriving and minatory colonies, and dyeing was a stark reminder of death.

Brayton was a mighty charmer, too, big, blond, smiling, full of red blood coursing radiantly; equipped with a fine resonant baritone and a marvelous sense of character. He filled a stage and held the eye hypnotically. A superlative Macbeth, Othello, Undershaft, and both Caesars. He almost did the impossible with Falstaff, and, indeed, he never really failed; it was not in his character.

Their rivalry was inept and superfluous, for there was plenty of room for both and they clashed in no way, but there it was, and that is the way of things in that logically lawless profession.

Both were vain men, but Brayton's vanity found expression chiefly in praise of himself, Brayton's in dispraise of others. Beaumont was, however, deemed by his colleagues far the better character of the two, a generous and considerate employer, fair-minded, and with a sense of humor sufficiently developed to disinfect and restrain his little failings; and after all, no great actor is ever *quite* human, everyone agreed.

Brayton was generally rated a false bon-homme, catty, uncertain-tempered, inclined to malice and tight in money matters. His nickname in the profession was "Billy Bennett" after a famous comedian whose self-composed description was "almost a gentleman." This judgment was probably a bit harsh and superficial. He was a medium, in a sense only another word for a great character actor—fundamentally a simple, rather impercipient, unanalytic man, with very little personality of his own, being perpetually "possessed" by the "souls" created by others; and, like most mediums, unscrupulous; amoral rather than bad. He did his stuff very well, and his irresistible smile got his fans vapouring with rapture. Neither was married, both preferring a frequent change of leading lady.

A last very important point, Beaumont was now "Sir Rex," having been knighted a few weeks before in the New Year Honours. Brayton had not yet recovered from that fearful right to the solar plexus.

Their meeting in Biskra was, of course, accidental; Beaumont, on holiday at Algiers, had decided to have a look at the desert before going home. Brayton had been yachting in the Mediterranean, got bored and seasick and flown down from the Riviera.

The night before they had arranged with the local Sand-Diviner to have their fortunes told by him at ten that morning. Both men were extremely superstitious. Most gamblers share this frailty as a badge of their tribe, and anyone who relies for fame and fortune on the fickle and callous mob—chiefly female mob—is a "plunger" indeed.

Brayton now reminded Beaumont of this date.

"Oh yes," he said, "I haven't forgotten. One of these days, perhaps, I shall cure myself of this puerile craving for the reassurance of magicians; they've had a lot of my money and habitually contradict each other."

"Well, come on," laughed Brayton, "and let us see what this professor of the mantic art has to tell us."

Beaumont put on his hat and followed him out of the hotel to where Abdullah was awaiting them. He salaamed in his oily, yet subtly disrespectful way. They had not far to go, the seer's pitch was only a hundred yards down the road at the entrance to the little bazaar. As they proceeded, Abdullah kept up a repeated cry of "Imshi" as he shooed away the septic beggars and precociously lewd small boys.

The Sandman was squatting down behind a porphyry bowl three-quarters filled with soiled sand. He was clad in a burnoose over a tiny, grimy pair of linen pants. He looked half as old as time and his face was the color and texture of a swan's paddle, a dark sallow gray etched with a web of tiny lines and wrinkles. He took no notice of them as they halted beside him, nor to some remark of Abdullah's, but continued apparently aimlessly, to stir the sand with a skinny, arid forefinger. This nonchalance was part of his "act," thought Brayton. Abdullah spoke to him again in Arabic and then asked Beaumont to step forward in front of the bowl. For about half a minute the old man went on scrabbling in the sand more slowly now, less aimlessly and seemingly in a more concentrated way. And then presently he mumbled a short sentence. Abdullah spoke to him interrogatively and he replied again.

He seemed out of temper.

"Well?" said Beaumont.

"It is not very good news, I fear," smiled Abdullah.

"Never mind, let's have it," said Beaumont uneasily and with a forced smile.

"He say gentleman have not one year to go."

"To go! Go where?" asked Beaumont sharply.

"He mean to go on living, I think," replied Abdullah smiling and giving Brayton a quick glance.

Beaumont flushed and gave a clipped, uneasy laugh. "That's nice of him," he said. "Is that all he has to tell me?"

"That is all," replied Abdullah.

"Well, it's your turn," said Beaumont to Brayton. He was obviously much disconcerted. He took off his hat and mopped his forehead.

Brayton moved forward and took his place before the bowl. Again the old man scrabbled in the sand for a while, and then looked up suddenly and for the first time. There was a look of extreme malevolence in his vulture eyes. Then he spoke a very long sentence. Abdullah looked baffled and the two of them had a short tart colloquy. At length Abdullah shrugged his shoulders and said, "It is difficult to savvy what he say. He say you will meet other gentleman at a feast and then by the sea, and then Allah will be very good to you. I dunno what he mean. He say he finish now."

The séance was over. Beaumont immediately excused himself and hurried away. Brayton handed Abdullah a roll of notes. "It was just a joke, of course," he said quickly. "I'll tell the other gentleman it was just a joke before he leaves."

Abdullah smiled, salaamed, gave some of the notes to the Sandman, who took them without a word.

"He is angry," said Abdullah, "he does not like doing such things. He believes he see *true* things in the sand."

"Well, tell him it was only a little joke," muttered Brayton, "and that I'll put it right." He walked away leaving them together.

He had, of course, by bribery and corruption deliberately queered the prophetic pitch, moved by one of those sudden, malicious impulses which had contributed so much to his unpopularity. He had just wanted to give that conceited, over-rated person, Beaumont, a bit of a shock, a jolt. Well, he had done that, all right—quite obviously. Now he had better repair the damage. If he could have met him at once he would probably have done so, but he was not to be found

till lunch-time, and by then Brayton had had time to think
it over. When explained, it would look such a very poor joke,
one requiring rather a lot of difficult explanation. He knew
Beaumont would be furious and certainly spread the story
when he got back to London. That would not do him any
good. "Just typical of the blighter!" would be the general verdict. Whereas, if he kept his mouth shut, Beaumont would
soon forget all about it, of course. No, he felt he just could
not bring himself to confess and humiliate himself to such a
spoilt, vain, over-rated person as "Sir Rex"; everyone knew
how he had worked and wangled for that knighthood! His
sense of guilt intensified his hate, so spreading and thinning
his good impulse till it was impotent. No, he would let it go!

There was a famous Parisian nerve specialist staying in
the hotel, a man of formidable presence, patriarchal beard
and piercing sardonic eye. Beaumont asked him to lunch
at their table, not feeling in the mood for a "head-to-head"
alone with Brayton. He was too full of that sombre oracle
to keep it to himself, and presently told the Frenchman, in
a failed-facetious way, what the Sandman had divined. The
specialist was not deceived and set himself to undo what
might well, he saw, be a serious mischief.

"Do not alarm yourself, Sir Rex," he said with a smile;
"let me assure you the future *does not exist,* and precognition
of all modes is pure fake, as you would put it, and a logical
absurdity."

"Yet such foreseeing has a very long history," remarked
Brayton, and then wished he hadn't. The Frenchman glanced
at him in a cold appraising way. Brayton could not meet his
eye.

"Yes, indeed," he replied, "and so have a myriad other
childish superstitions. I have read your English philosopher,
Dunne, for example. His *Time* is grossly spacial, his *Serial
Selves,* the product of a radical psychological confusion,
and his *evidence, pour rire.* Let me tell you all such stuff—
prophetic dreams, palmistry, crystal-gazing, and this sand

nonsense—is all part of the clever charlatan's stock-in-trade. I say *clever* because some of them are endowed with a peculiar faculty. Let me give an example of what I mean. I am very musical, but what is called absolute pitch, the immediate intuitive recognition of all the relationships of a note, is a profound mystery to me. Now these magicians have an equally strange power, called clairvoyance, which is really nothing but just an immediate, intuitive recognition, not of a *note,* but of a *man* from his face and general deportment. *Deportment* is not quite the word, but you will understand what I mean. By means of it they can make very good guesses as to a man's past, and even his future. In fact I myself have some small gift of this kind. It is a true faculty, but never results in more than a clever guess; there is nothing occult about it whatsover. No, be reassured, Sir Rex, I say with the utmost emphasis the *future does not exist,* and that is the only thing we can know about it. I must say I am surprised at that Sand-Fellow, he is usually more discreet in his humbug."

"He made a highly nebulous divination about me," said Brayton, "and ended up by saying 'And then Allah will be very good to you.' What did he mean by that?"

The Frenchman paused before replying and then said very stiffly, "I do not know, Mr. Brayton, the expression is not familiar to me. Forget all his nonsense, both of you!"

"He's lying, I think," said Brayton to himself. "Anyway Beaumont won't worry any more. That lets me out!"

But he was wrong. Beaumont remained depressed and full of foreboding. Why *hadn't* the Sand-Diviner been more discreet and pronounced the usual smooth things? Because he profoundly believed in the truth of his grim oracle and wished to warn his client. So Beaumont argued. He had always been physically robust enough, but his nervous system was innately fragile, and had been for some time flawed by over-work. He had a heavy programme ahead of him and had been worrying about the maze of detail involved in it during his holiday, which had consequently done him little good. He was in no state to out-face any further strain on his psyche. So Brayton's "joke" had stabbed deep through an impaired organism, and one by nature highly vulnerable to such a thrust.

His first role to tackle was the Inquisitor in *Saint Joan* in which he was as good as any Englishman could hope to be. He started re-studying it, and found to his intense dismay that he could not memorize the great speech at the trial. He "fluffed" time after time and always at the same place. He cancelled the revival because he was hopeless. His doctor recommended six months' complete rest, "But what is the use of that," he drought to himself, "when I have less than eleven months at the best to live!" Still he listlessly took the holiday, a sea voyage round the world.

Unluckily he went alone save for one companion, John Barleycorn. That boon comrade and he became inseparable. "Why not," he told himself, "if I am doomed!" Of course he got no better. In fact he threw himself overboard on the last night before the ship reached Southampton and though they searched for a while, they could not find his body.

When Brayton heard of it he felt very, very badly. Indeed he had been greatly troubled ever since Beaumont had broken down. He kept wanting to tell him it had been a joke, but he just could not. He could not say it to his face and he could not write it. He could go so far as getting writing-paper and shaking his fountain pen, but he could write nothing. He could look down at the paper and see in his mind's eye the letter coming into spectral being line by line, but he could not write it. This had been getting on his nerves. When Beaumont jumped overboard he shut himself up in his room to think. And he had begun to make a confidant of John Barleycorn, too. Of course he had not been responsible for Rex's over-work and break-down, but he knew that some people, if they knew about the "joke," would have called him a murderer and nothing less. It was very lucky no one *did* know—in a way. In another way he would have liked to have got it off his chest. Why had he ever done it? Because Rex's conceit had disgusted him and, yes, because he had got that *knighthood*. Yes, *that* was it. *That* had done it. That's what he wanted to get off his chest and confess loudly and bravely. "It was a lousy trick, a silly, sudden, sodden notion. I was off-balance when I did it and I hadn't the guts to confess to Rex." But he could not face it. It would ruin him, his many enemies would see to that. "I wish to hell I'd never done it, though! It's done me no good and that's a certainty. Actually I miss Rex. I can see now the rivalry between us stimulated me. The bell has tolled for me, too. It was a rotten thing to do."

Whether this belated remorse was due to a sense of sin or a feeling of vague nervous discomfort is doubtful, but he can be given the benefit of it, and, perhaps, after all, the two emotions are pretty much the same.

Certainly it did not, as he had hoped, wear thinner. Rather it steadily intensified, for he was very superstitious, too. He could not get Rex out of his mind, especially as he began dreaming about him and, what was worse, always the same dream. He was standing on a beach gazing out to sea over some rocks. The sea was breaking lightly over the rocks and he was looking for something he knew he did not want to see. He stared hard, watching the lift of each small wave. Presently he saw something white rise on a crest, surge forward and disappear. There it was again, a bit nearer this time, and the next time and the next. And then whatever this was reached the rocks. He wanted to run away but he could not move. Then he saw it climb up on the rocks and come toward him and it was something like a naked man, only there was a difference. For instance where the face should have been, he presently could see was the big ochre shell of a crab, and he could see the claws moving, and that was the worst of all. Just then he always woke up. He had a pretty good idea what that thing was.

It can be imagined that knowing he was going to have this dream, or being almost sure of it, made going to bed a daunting business for Brayton, because it filled him with a great horror, and he was sweating all over and feeling very sick when he woke up. It was not always as clear as has been described, and he had an idea that the more he'd drunk the less clear it was; so he naturally drank a lot just before turning out the light. And after a time he did not turn out the light at all.

Then there was another bother. He was rehearsing *Macbeth*, his best part, now ripe for revival. He had a great natural sympathy for Macbeth with his huge ambition and also his ghostly fears. If the end was the integration of a superior personality and the satisfaction of its potent, clamant rights, then any means were justified; and, again, such a great man was a natural focus round which the Fates—materialized and conflicting tendencies—should gather. He could call spirits from the Vasty Deep and they *would* come when he did call for them. Something like that. Now, however, he saw there was a good deal to be said for Duncan's point of view. Remorse partly and partly, perhaps, that very phrase, "the Vasty Deep" had something to do with it.

The back parts of theatres during the throes of rehearsal of a big play like *Macbeth* are crowded, scurrying places; chaos to the uninitiated, but really that odd, motley section of humanity on the move about its business is a good example of organized division of labor. Brayton was, of course, quite at home in this come-and-go and could perfectly distinguish the wood from the trees, the combined effort from the atoms composing it.

Yet one of these "trees" began to worry him. Whether it was in a group of sceneshifters, or Scottish Noblemen, or the orchestra, or any grouped bodies contributing to the enterprise, an intruder was sometimes to be seen furtively lurking; very furtively, for the moment Brayton got him properly in his gaze, or rather just before he succeeded in doing so, he at once dissolved and disappeared, presently to reappear elsewhere. During one rehearsal he saw him for a second watching from the Royal Box. The curtains of the box were of light ochre silk and Brayton noticed a certain resemblance.

Of course his colleagues noticed something was the matter with Billy Bennett and whispered and wondered, but they had to confess he had never acted better. He was word perfect and never more moving and intense; the tortured Thane and he seemed absolutely one in spirit indomitably defying all the legions of Earth and Hell and Heaven.

For the first night he plugged himself with as much Scotch courage as he dared, and Dulcinea Delavere, the Lady Macbeth, turned up her nose when she accepted his bouquet and hoped for the best. It certainly was the best; he had never given such a terrific performance, in spite of, perhaps partly on account of, the fact that there was someone who had no business to be there, standing for a flash in the shadows behind the weird sisters, and then entering for a second with Duncan's retinue, and just visible out of the corner of his eye as he tried to seize the phantom dagger. But he was very near breaking-point in the banquet scene, for when he and his lady were surveying the assembled guests and the ghost of Banquo should have entered, it was not Banquo who came in, but someone Brayton had seen terribly often coming towards him across the rocks.

"Which of you have done this?" he cried, and pretty well everyone in the audience felt a quick, damp fear break out on them at the way he spoke that mighty line. Dulcinea, who was watching his face as he spoke it, says she knows she will never forget it, but hopes very much she is wrong.

To the audience he seemed entranced and inspired in the true sense of the word, breathing in unearthly air. Indeed at the end of the act the famous critic, Charles Straker, who almost always treats plays and actors as cats treat mice, first lying in wait for them, then playing sadistically with them for a while, and finally driving his claws right home in them, declared loudly in the bar it was the greatest piece of acting he had ever seen and that he'd almost have paid for his seat to witness it. But it wasn't acting, something had snapped in Brayton's brain and he was only vaguely conscious of where he was or what he was doing. However, he carried through to the end, and the expression on his face during the last scene was almost more than the people in the stalls could bear.

When the curtain come down, there was someone waiting for him in the wings. He ran from the stage, floored his dresser with a brutal blow, flung off his motley and dashed from the theatre. He was last seen alive running into Trafalgar Square.

Some mornings later, a prawn fisherman, who was netting the rock pools off Ventnor in the Isle of Wight, came to one of these pools just surrendered by a savage ebbing tide. He peered hard for a moment, and then started to run back to the beach.

The doctor said Brayton had been dead for about three days. The other body, which was resting up against Brayton's, had been dead for very much longer. That body was never certainly identified.

The prawn fisherman said in the pub on the evening of the day he made his discovery: "One thing I'll swear; I'll never eat crab again! Pity, as I liked it more than most things. But not after that!"

Out of the Wrack I Rise

"Chu Chin's in," said the Assistant Stage Manager to the Manager of the Blackton Empire.

"Oh yes. How's he seem?"

"A superb conjurer," said the manager, "but between ourselves a very nasty bit of work."

"You *could* be right!" laughed the assistant stage manager.

"Watch his turn tonight," said the manager. "A pal of mine told me he was slipping."

"I was going to—for another reason. D'you remember what this is?"

"How do'you mean?"

"Anniversary of his wife's death."

"Good Lord! How time skips. He has married again, hasn't he?"

"Yes," said the assistant stage manager, "that assistant of his."

"There was a certain amount of—well—talk, when his wife was drowned, wasn't there?"

"Yes; may have been unfair. It always looks a shade odd when you take your wife out night-bathing and she doesn't come back."

"Her body was never recovered, was it?" asked the manager.

"Well, no, but oddly enough a trawler landed a skeleton, believed to be a woman's, this morning. It had been caught in their nets. It's in the mortuary round the corner now.

There'll be an inquest in a day or two, but I understand it's quite unidentifiable."

"He treated her pretty rough, didn't he?"

"She certainly looked as if he did. And then of course getting married again within a couple of months to a girl half your age and such a bold, designing minx into the bargain! As a matter of fact I didn't think she looked too happy just now."

"I can understand *that!* Is there feeling against him in the town, d'you think? Will they give him the bird?"

"I don't think so. Anyway I'll watch carefully and report to you."

"Okay."

Chu Chin's real name was Jerry Pullin. He had adopted this stage name because he had the Mongol fold to his eyes and a vaguely Oriental cast of countenance. With a mandarin's skull-cap, a black bootlace moustache, and enveloped in a voluminous priest-robe, he looked the part well enough. He was very tall and always paced the stage in majestic Mr. Wu attitudes. He used no patter at all, never opening his mouth from start to finish of his turn. He "distracted attention" by two means. He fixed his queer eyes on the audience, and the female members of it were often slightly hypnotized by this piercing stare. To lull male alertness he relied on his assistant, a big bold-eyed strapping wench. He dressed her in the briefest and tightest of shorts, a low-necked almost transparent blouse, and a Coolie hat. He made her move frequently behind him, as though arranging the things on his worktables, and the men gave her plenty of eye. She also did any talking that was necessary. Jerry was around fifty and cordially detested in the profession, being sly, grasping and utterly unsociable, but he was recognized as a master of his craft, his manual dexterity being unrivalled and his over-all technique superb. He topped the bill everywhere.

The assistant stage manager took his stand in the prompt wing as the curtain rose and Chu Chin and the girl came on the stage. His reception was damp and unenthusiastic, but there were no boos or other manifestations of hostility. The assistant stage manager was himself a competent amateur conjurer, and always watched Chu Chin when he got the chance, to sharpen his skill; just as a golfer or billiards player studies a "Pro," to absorb something of his balance, touch and rhythm, the essence of his mastery. And on this occasion he was particularly concerned to decide whether the manager's suggestion about Chu Chin's decline was true or not. His was, as ever, the last turn of the evening.

He had two work-tables, one on each side of the stage, some chairs for volunteers from the audience, and at the back was a high contraption, a three-sided screen with an orange silk curtain making the fourth side. And always behind him moved the big girl, smiling and showing off her points.

His first trick was about the oldest on the list, just pulling things out of a top-hat, but he made it fresh and amusing. He would place in the hat, say, a miniature baby's feeding bottle and extract a small bottle of whiskey, replace that and produce an imitation red rose. The assistant stage manager knew how it was done, but he never ceased to marvel at the slick virtuosity of Chu Chin's execution. He usually ended by flashing out the flags of all the more respectable nations, but on this occasion he drew out a woman's black bathing-cap.

The assistant stage manager frowned and shrugged his shoulders. What an incredible and monstrous error of taste! But was it that? Jerry stared at it for a second and then flung it down like a hot coal. Then he glared out at the audience as though demanding, "Which of you has done this?" And somehow at that moment the assistant stage manager knew beyond all doubt that Jerry had drowned his wife. From the audience came a short-lived, puzzled murmur. The girl ran forward, picked up the cap and put it on a work-table. The assistant stage manager watched her do this. The brazen smile had left her face, and when she was standing still again, he saw she was trembling violently.

It then became her business to appeal to the audience for four volunteers to come to the stage and cooperate in the next trick. Her voice as she did so, the assistant manager noted, was not quite under control. After some hesitation four persons responded; a girl, two young men, and a tall woman dressed in unrelieved black and heavily veiled. She looked, thought the assistant stage manager, extremely out of place.

Chu Chin took up a pack of cards and the assistant said, "Each of you, please, take three cards and memorize them."

The woman in black took three cards and at once held them up for Chu Chin to see. The assistant stage manager could see them, too. They were the eight of spades, the ace and the nine of spades, in that order. Now, the assistant stage manager, like all conjurers, did a little light-hearted fortune-telling for the amusement of his friends; so he knew that was the most sinister combination of all, spelling a sudden death and very soon. Then the woman in black let them fall from her hand and left the stage, and, apparently, the theatre also. In his subsequent investigations the assistant stage manager had reason to doubt whether she had been in the house at all until the girl called for volunteers. The door-man denied having seen her come in and, still more oddly, ever seeing her go out. Her appearance and disappearance remained a complete mystery, which was never solved.

Jerry took this contretemps fairly well and went on with his trick, but the assistant stage manager could see the audience was getting restive. They vaguely sensed something was going wrong; and there was much shuffling and some murmuring.

The assistant stage manager himself was perplexed in the extreme. Was there a conspiracy on? Had certain persons determined to wreck the turn? If so, it had been most subtly organized, for how had they been able to tamper with Chu Chin's props? He knew the discomforting sense that there was something afoot of which he could not grasp the significance, as though there was being enacted some play within a play, as it were.

Chu Chin finished the card stunt, a very clever and difficult one, satisfactorily, and there was some applause from the audience, which had quieted down. The assistant stage manager, who understood audiences like the back of his hand, and could register their reactions with delicate certainty, realized it was still on edge and embarrassed; about twenty persons even left the house. But if all went well from now on, it would settle down. Any further irritant, or upset, however, might send it right out of control. He'd seen that happen once and it was a daunting memory.

Chu Chin's next offering was his famous Poster Illusion, which he kept a tight secret; the assistant stage manager had no notion how it was done. The conjurer took a large sheet of paper, about the size of a newspaper bill, on which was inscribed in the boldest scarlet lettering the legend, "Today's date is—" Then, in full view of the audience he screwed up the paper into a tight ball, then unscrewed it again, smoothed it out, and what *should* have appeared was "August 21st, 1947," the current date. Instead the "7" was a "6," so that it read "August 21st, 1946," the date of his wife's death.

At once there came a loud murmur, a loud and *angry* murmur from the audience, and the applause was still-born.

"Who is doing these things," thought the assistant stage manager, "and how is he doing them?" And now for the first time he felt fear. Chu Chin had unrolled the paper without glancing at it, but now he hurriedly inspected it. Once more his face was convulsed with rage, and he screwed it up again and hurled it into a wing.

Realizing his act was on the verge of disaster, he omitted some further business and hurried on preparations for his final illusion. For this he employed the screen-contraption. First of all the girl called for a volunteer, and after some delay an elderly man came up. She asked him to pick out any spot near the middle of the stage on which he would like the contraption to be placed, first assuring himself there was no trap-door, by scrutiny and stamping. He did so, and

the contraption was erected over the indicated spot. As the
elderly man turned to leave the stage he slipped and fell
heavily, and was in obvious pain as Chu Chin assisted him
to his feet. "Why don't you keep the stage dry!" he angrily
exclaimed. "Look at that damp patch!" Refusing to be molli-
fied, he hobbled from the theatre.

The audience began whistling and shouting, and a number
began hurrying out. The assistant stage manager later asked
one of them why he had done so and he replied, "It was
simply that I had a feeling something horrible was about
to happen, something I had no wish to witness." There was
consequently much stir and some confusion as Chu Chin
went on with his trick, and the girl in a vibrating falsetto
asked for silence. The illusion consisted, the assistant stage
manager knew, in the girl entering the tent. Then Chu Chin
would lower the silk curtain, raise it again and reveal the
tent empty. He would then enter the tent himself and lower
the curtain, and a little later they would both come onto the
stage from different sides. It was a brilliant mirror invention
entirely undetectable by the audience.
    Now came the moment for the girl to enter the tent, but
this, it appeared, she refused to do. The audience became
very quiet and watchful. The assistant stage manager was
utterly baffled and more than ever conscious of strangeness,
unreality, and growing apprehension. After a moment Chu
Chin, his face a mask of fury, thrust the girl hard through
the curtain. Just at that moment the assistant stage manager
saw something white—could it be a fleshless arm?—flung up
above the screen and down again. There came a high thin
scream of agony and terror and the tent was violently shaken.
    The assistant stage manager turned and shouted an
order for the curtain to be lowered; instead every light in
the house went out. Now the audience started shouting and
screaming and surging towards the exits. For a moment the
assistant stage manager felt inexorably compelled to watch

the stage. He heard the tent crash over, and then he could just discern in that dimmest of glows, three—he could swear it was three—figures struggling violently near where it had stood. Still in wild motion they staggered down towards the footlights, and then the iron safety curtain roared down like the blade of a huge guillotine, and all the lights came on again. Another shriek of terror came from the crowds milling around the jammed doors.

"Play something!" yelled the assistant stage manager to the dazed conductor of the orchestra. He could see runnels of red seeping through below the curtain, and dashed round onto the stage. The bodies of Jerry and the girl were lying in their blood. The heavy safety curtain had crushed their skulls and then hurled them aside. After stage hands had carried them to the dressing-rooms and the ambulances were summoned, the assistant stage manager returned to the stage. In the middle of it lay the eight, ace, and nine of spades, in that order. By the side of one of the work-tables lay the black bathing-cap. He picked it up—it was damp to the touch.

The Third Shadow

"And the other man on the rope, Andrew," I asked, "did you ever encounter him?"

He gave me a quick glance and tapped the ash from his cigarette.

"Well, *is* there such a one?" he asked, smiling.

"I've many times read of him," I replied. "Didn't Smythe actually see him on the Brenva Face and again on that last dread lap of Everest?"

Sir Andrew paused before replying.

No one glancing casually at that eminent and superbly discreet civil servant, Sir Andrew Poursuivant, would have guessed that in his day and prime he had been the second-best amateur mountaineer of all time, with a dozen first ascents to his immortal fame, and many more than a dozen of the closest looks at death vouchsafed to any man. One who had leaped almost from the womb on to his first hill, a gravity defier by right of birth, soon to revolutionise the technique of rock-climbing and later to write two of the very finest books on his exquisite art. Yet there was something about that uncompromising buttress, his chin, the superbly modelled arête, his nose, those unflinching blue tarns, his eyes, and the high, wide cliff of his brow, to persuade the reader of faces that here was a born man of action, endowed with that strange and strangely named faculty, presence of mind, which ever finds in great emergency and peril the stimulus to a will and a cunning to meet and conquer them.

We were seated in my state room in the *Queen Elizabeth* bound for New York, he for some recurrent brawl, I on the interminable quest for dollars. The big tub was pitching hard into a nor-west blizzard and creaking her vast length.

I am but an honorary member of the corps of mountaineers, having no "head" for the game. But I love it dearly by proxy, and as the sage tells us, "He who *thinks on* Himalcha shall have pardon for all sins," and the same is true, I hope, of lesser ranges.

I dined with Sir Andrew perhaps half-a-dozen times a year and usually persuaded him on these felicitous occasions to tell me some great tale of the past. Hence on this felicitous occasion my "fishing" enquiry.

"Yes, so I remember," he presently said, "but are there not nice, plausible explanations for that? The illusions consequent on great height, great strain? You may remember Smythe, who is highly psychic, saw something else from Everest, very strange wings beating the icy air."

"He isn't the only one," I said, "it's a well-documented tradition."

"It is, I agree. Guides, too, have known his presence, and always at moments of great stress and danger, and he has left them when these moments passed. And if they do not pass, the fanciful might suggest he meets them on the Other Side. But who he is no one knows. I grant you, also, I myself have sometimes felt that over, say twelve thousand feet, one moves into a realm where nothing is quite the same, or, perhaps, and more likely, it is just one's mind that changes and becomes more susceptible and exposed to—well, certain *oddities.*"

"But you have never encountered this particular oddity?" I insisted.

"What an importunate bag-man you are!"

"I believe you have, Andrew, and you must tell me of it!"

"That is not quite so," he replied, "but—it will be thirty-five long years ago next June, I did once have a very terrible experience that had associated with it certain subsidiary experiences somewhat recalcitrant to explanation."

"That is a very cautious pronouncement, Andrew!"

"Phrased in the jargon of my trade, Bill."

"And you are going to relate it to me?"

"I suppose so. I've never actually told it to another, and it will give me no pleasure to rouse it from my memory. But perhaps I owe it you."

"Fill your glass, mind that lurch, and proceed."

"I haven't told it before," said Sir Andrew, "partly because it's distasteful to recall, and partly, for the reason that the prudent sea-captain turns his blind eye on a sea serpent and keeps a buttoned lip over the glimpse he caught; no one much appreciates the grin of incredulous derision."

"I promise to keep a straight face," I assured him.

"Yes, I rather think you will. Well, all those years ago, in that remote and golden time, I knew and climbed with a man I will call 'Brown.' He was about my age. He had inherited considerable position and fortune and he was heir, also, to that irresistible and consuming passion for high places, their conquest and company, which, given the least opportunity, will never be denied, and only decrepitude or death can frustrate. Technically, he was a master in all departments, a finished cragsman and just as expert on snow and ice. But there was just occasionally an unmastered streak of recklessness in him which flawed him as a leader, and everyone, including myself, preferred to have him lower down the rope.

"It was, perhaps, due to one of these feckless seizures that, after our fourth season together, he proposed to a wench, who replied promptly in the affirmative. He was a smallish fellow, though immensely lithe, active, strong and tough. She was not far short of six feet and tipped the beam at one hundred and sixty-eight pounds, mostly muscle. With what suicidal folly, my dear Bill, do these infatuate pigmies, like certain miserable male insects, doom themselves with such Boadiceas, and how pitilessly and jocundly do those monsters pounce upon their prey! This particular specimen was terribly, viciously, 'County', immensely handsome, and intolerably authoritarian. Speaking evil of the dead is often the only revenge permitted us and I have no intention of refraining from saying that I have seldom, almost certainly *never* disliked anyone more than Hecate Quorn. Besides being massive and menacing to the nth degree, she was endowed with a reverberating contralto which loaned a fearsomely oraculate air to her insistent spate of edicts. Marry for lust and repent in haste, the oldest, saddest lesson in the world, and one my poor friend had almost instantly to learn. Once she'd gripped him in her red remorseless maw, she bullied him incessantly and appeared to dominate him beyond hope of release. Such an old story I need enlarge upon no more! How many of our old friends have we watched fall prostrate before these daughters of Masrur!

"She demanded that he should at least attempt to teach her to climb, and females of her build are seldom much good at the game, particularly if they are late beginners. She was no exception, and her nerve turned out to be surprisingly more suspect on a steepish slope than her ghastly assurance on the level would have suggested. Poor Brown plugged away at it, because he feared, if she chucked her hand in, he would never see summer snow again. He did his very desperate best. He hired Fritz Mann, the huskiest and best-tempered of all the Chamonix guides, and between them on one searing and memorable occasion they shoved and pulled and hauled and slid her on feet and rump to creditably near the summit of Mt. Blanc. She loathed the ordeal, but she refused to give in, just because she knew poor Brown was longing to join up with a good party, and have some fun. I need say no more, you have sufficient imagination fully to realise the melancholy and humiliating pass of my sad friend. And, of course, it wasn't only in Haute-Savoie and Valais she made his life hell, it was at least purgatory for the rest of the year; his was eternal punishment, one might say. A harsh sentence for a moment's indiscretion!"

"What about those occasional feckless flashes?" I asked; "had she quenched and overlaid those, too?"

"Permit me to tell this story my own way and pour me out another drink. In the second summer after their marriage the Browns had preceded me by a few days to the Montenvert, which, doubtless you recall, is a hotel overlooking the Mer de Glâce, three thousand feet above Chamonix. When I arrived there late one evening I found the place in a turmoil, and Brown apparently almost out of his mind. Hecate had fallen down a crevasse that morning and, as a matter of fact, her body was never recovered. I took him to my room, gave him a stiff drink, and he blurted out his sorry tale. He had taken her out on the Mer de Glâce for a morning's training, he said, determined to take no risks whatsoever. They had wandered a little way up the glacier, perhaps rather further than he'd intended. He'd cut some steps for her to practice on, and so forth. Presently he'd encountered a crevasse, crossed by a snow-bridge, which he'd tested and found perfectly reliable. He'd passed over himself, but, when she followed, she'd gone straight through, the rope had snapped—and that was that. They'd lowered a guide, but the hole went down forever and it was quite hopeless. Hecate must have died instantly; that was the only assuaging thought.

"'Should that rope have gone, Arthur?' I asked. 'Can I see it?'

"He produced it. It was poor stuff, an Austrian make, which had once been very popular but had been found unreliable and the cause of several accidents. There was also old bruising near the break. It wasn't a reassuring bit of stuff. 'I realise' said Brown hurriedly, 'I shouldn't have kept that piece. As you know, I'm a stickler for perfection in a rope. But we were just having a little easy work and, as that rope's light and she always found it so hard to manage one, I took it along. I'd no intention of actually having to trust to it. We were just turning back when it happened. I swear to you that bridge seemed absolutely sound.'

"'She was a good deal heavier than you, Arthur,' I said.

"'I know, but I made every allowance for that.'

"'I quite understand,' I said. 'Well, it's just too bad,' or words to that effect. I was rather at a loss for appropriate expressions. He was obviously acting a part. I didn't blame him, he had to. He had to appear heavy with grief when he was feeling, in a sense, as light as mountain air. He got a shade tight that evening, and his efforts to sustain two such conflicting moods would have amused a more cynical and detached observer than myself. Besides, *I* foresaw the troubles ahead.

"The French held an enquiry, of course, and inevitably exonerated him completely, then I took him home to face the music, which, as I'd expected, was strident and loud enough. How far was it justified? I asked myself. He should, perhaps, not have taken Hecate up so far. Even if that rope hadn't gone, he'd never have been able to pull her up by himself—it would have taken two very strong men to have done that. He could merely have held her there, and she would, I suppose have died of slow strangulation, unless help had quickly come. Yet there is always risk, however prudently you try to play that game: it is the first of its rules and nothing will ever eliminate it. You must take my word for all this, which is rather outside your sphere of judgment. All the same the condition of that rope—and I wasn't the only one to examine it—didn't help things. Still, all that wouldn't have mattered nearly so much if he'd been a happily married man. I needn't dwell on that. Anyway the dirty rumour followed him home and resounded there."

"What was your candid opinion, Andrew?" I said.

"I must ask you," he replied, "to believe a rather hard thing, that I had and have no opinion, candid or otherwise. It *could* have been a pure accident. All could have happened exactly as he said it did. I've no valid reason to suppose otherwise. He may have been a bit careless: I might have been so myself. One takes such practice mornings rather lightly. There *is* risk, as I've said, but it's miniscule compared with the real thing. The expert mountaineer develops an exquisitely nice and certain 'feel' for degrees of danger, it is the condition precedent of his survival,—and adjusts his whole personality to changing degrees. He must take the small ones in his stride. The errors of judgment, if any, that Brown committed were petty and excusable. His reason for taking that rope was sensible enough in a way."

"Yes," I put in, "I can more or less understand all that, but you actually knew him well and you're a shrewd judge of character. You were in a privileged position to decide."

"Was I? A very learned judge once told me he'd find it far easier to decide the guilt or innocence of an absolute stranger than of a close friend; the personal equation confuses the problem and pollutes the understanding. I think he was perfectly right. Anyway I am shrewd enough to know when I am baffled, and I have always felt the balance of probability was peculiarly nicely poised. In a word, I have no opinion."

"Well, I have," I proclaimed. "I think he had a sudden fearful temptation. I don't think it was exactly premeditated, yet always, as it were, at the back of his mind. He realised that bridge would go when she had her weight on it, knew a swift, reckless temptation, and let it rip. I think he'd kept that rotten rope because he'd always felt in a vague half-repressed way, it might, as they say, 'come in handy one day'."

Sir Andrew shrugged his shoulders. "Very subtle, no doubt," he said, "and you may be right. But I know I shall never be able to decide. Perhaps it is that personal equation, for I was always very fond of him, and he saved my life more than once at the greatest peril to his own; and since his marriage, that ordeal of thumb-screw and rack, I had developed profound sympathy for him. Hecate was far better dead. I greeted his release with a saturnine cheer. We will leave that point.

"Well, he had to face a very bad time. Hecate's relatives were many and influential and they pulled no punches, no stabs in the back, rather. No one, of course, actually cried: 'Murder!' in public, but such terms as 'Darned odd!', 'Very happy release!' 'Accidents *must* happen!' and so on, were in lively currency.

"Very few people comprehend the first thing about mountaineering, just sultry, celluloid visions of high-altitude villains slashing ropes, so this sepsis found receptive bloodstreams. I did my best to foster antibodies and rallied my fellow-climbers to the defence. But we were hopelessly outnumbered and out-gunned, and it was lucky for poor Brown he had more than sufficient private means to retire from public life to his estate and his farming, and insulate himself to some extent against the slings and arrows which were so freely and cruelly flying about.

"I spent a week-end with him in April and was shocked at his appearance: even life with Hecate had never reduced him to such a pass. His nerves were forever on the jump, he had those glaring insomniac eyes, he was drinking far more and eating far less than was good for him; he looked a driven, haunted man."

"Haunted?" I asked.

"I know what you mean," said Sir Andrew, "but I don't think I can be more definite. I will say, however, I found the atmosphere of the house unquiet and was very glad to quit it. Anyway, something had to be done.

"'You must start climbing again, Arthur,' I said.

"'Never! My nerve's gone!' he replied.

"'Nonsense!' I said. 'We'll leave on June 3rd for Chamonix. You must conquer all this and at the very place which tests you most starkly. You will be amongst friends. It will be a superb nerve tonic. This tittle-tattle will inevitably die down—it has started to do so already, I fancy. There is nothing to fear, as you'll discover once you're fit again. Come back to your first, your greatest, your only real love!'

"'What will people say?' he muttered uncertainly.

"'What say they, let them say! Actually I think it'll be very good propaganda: no one'd believe a guilty man would return to the scene of such a crime. My dear Arthur, you're a bit young to die, aren't you! If you stay moping here you'll be in the family vault in a couple of years. I'll get the tickets and we'll dine together at the Alpine Club on June the second at eight p.m. precisely.'

"To this he promptly agreed and his fickle spirits rose. So the fourth of June saw us entering the Montenvert, where our reception was cordial enough.

"It took him over a week, far longer than usual, to get back to anything like his old standard, but I'd expected that. On the ninth day I decided it was time for a crucial test of his recovery. It was no use frittering about, he'd got to face the hard thing, something far tougher than the practice grounds.

"After some deliberation I chose the Dent du Géant for the trial run. It was an old friend of ours, and the last time we'd done it, four years before, we'd simply raced to the aluminum Madonna which more or less adorns its summit. The Géant, I will remind you, is a needle, some thirteen thousand feet high, situated towards the southern rim of that great and glorious lake of ice, part French, part Swiss, part Italian, from which rise some of the most renowned peaks in the world, and of those the acknowledged monarchs are the Grandes Jurasses, the Grépon Aiguilles and, of course, the Mont Blanc Massiv itself. It is sacred ground to our fraternity and the very words ring like a silver peal. The Géant culminates in a grotesque colossal 'tooth' of rock, some of which is in a fairly advanced state of decay. These things are relative, of course, it will almost certainly be standing there, somewhat diminished, in five thousand years time. It provides an interesting enough climb, not, in my view, one of the most severe, but sheer and exposed enough. Nowadays, I understand, the livelier sections are so festooned with spikes and cords that it resembles the fruit of the union of a porcupine and a puppet. But I have not revisited it for years and, for very sure, I never shall again.

"Brown agreed with my choice, which he declared himself competent to tackle, so off we went late on a promising morning and made our leisurely way up and across the ice to the hat. He seemed in pretty good shape, and once, when a most towering and displeasing sérac fell almost dead on our line, he kept his head, his footing and his life. Yet somehow I didn't quite like the look of him. He didn't improve as the day wore on and, to tell the truth, I didn't either."

Here Sir Andrew paused, lit a cigarette, and continued more slowly. "You are not familiar with such matters, but I will try and explain the cause of my increasing preoccupation. We were, of course, roped almost all day, and from very early on I began to experience those intimations—it is difficult to find the precise, inevitable word—which were increasingly to disturb and perplex me on that tragic expedition. It is extremely hard to make them plain and plausible to you, who have never been hitched to a manila. When merely pursuing a more or less untrammelled course over ice it is our custom to keep the rope neither trailing nor quite taut, but always—I speak as leader—of course, one is very conscious of the presence and pressure of the man behind. Now—how shall I put it? Well, over and over again it seemed to me as if that rope was behaving oddly, as though the 'pull' I experienced was inconsistent with the distance Brown was keeping behind me, as though something else was exercising pressure nearer to me. Do I make myself at all plain?"

"I think so," I replied. "You mean, as though there was someone tied to that rope between you and Brown."

"Nothing like so definite and distinct as that. Imagine if you were driving a car and you continually got the impression the brakes were coming on and off, though you knew they were not. You would be puzzled and somewhat disconcerted. I'm afraid that analogy isn't very illuminating. It was just that I was conscious of some inexplicable anomaly connected with our roped progress that day. I remember I kept glancing round in search of an explanation. I tried to convince myself it was due to Brown's somewhat inept, sluggish and erratic performance, but I was not altogether successful in this attribution. To make it worse a thick mist came on in the afternoon and this increased our difficulties, delayed us considerably, and intensified my sombre and rather defeatist mood.

"Certain pious, but, in my view, misguided persons, profess to find in the presence, the atmosphere, of these doomed Titans, evidence for a benevolent Providence, and a beneficent cosmic principle. I am not enrolled in their ranks. At best these eminences seem aloof and neutral, at worst, viciously and virulently hostile—I reverse the pathetic fallacy. That is, to a spirited man, half their appeal. Only once in a long while have I been lulled into a sense of their goodwill. And if one must endow them with a Pantheon, I would people it with the fickle and malicious denizens of Olympus and Valhalla, and not the allegedly philanthropic triad of heaven. In no place is the working of a ruthless, blind causality more starkly shewn. And never, for some reason, have I felt that oppressive sense of malignity more acutely than during the last four hours of our climb that day, as we forced our groping way through a nightmare world of ice-pillars, many of them as high and ponderous as the Statue of Liberty, destined each one of them soon to fall with a thunder like the crack of doom. And all the while I was bothered with that rope. Several times, as I glanced round through the murk, I seemed to sense Brown almost at my heels, when he was thirty feet away. Once I actually saw him, as I thought, near enough to touch. It was a displeasing illusion."

"Were you scared?" I asked.

"I was certainly keyed-up and troubled. I am never scared, I think, when actually on the move. It was just that there was a noxious puzzle I couldn't solve. We were in no great danger, just experiencing the endemic risks inherent in all such places. But I was mainly responsible for the safety of us both and my mode of securing that safety was impaired."

"I imagine," I said, "that the rope establishes, as it were, some psychic bond between those it links."

"An unexpectedly percipient remark," replied Sir Andrew. "That is precisely the case. The rope makes the fate of one the fate of all; and each betrays along its strands his spiritual state; his hopes, anxieties, good cheer, or lack of confidence. So I could feel Brown's hesitation and poor craftsmanship, as well as this inexplicable interruption of my proper connection with him.

"When we eventually reached the hut I had in no way elucidated the problem. I didn't like the look of Brown; he was far more tired than he should have been and his nerves were sparking again. He put the best face he could on it, as good mountaineers are trained to do, and declared a night's rest would put him right. I hoped for the best."

"Did you mention your trouble with the rope?"

"I did not," said Sir Andrew shortly. "For one thing, it might have been purely subjective. For another, what was there to say? And the first duty of the mountaineer is to keep his fears to himself, unless they are liable to imperil his comrades. Never lower the 'psychic temperature' if it can possibly be avoided. Yet somehow, I cannot define precisely how, I gained the impression he had noticed something and that this was partly the cause of his malaise.

"The hut was full, but not unpleasantly so, with young Italians for the most part, and we secured good sleeping places. Then we fed and lay down. It was a night of evil memory. Brown went to sleep almost at once, to sleep and to dream, and to tell of his dreams. He was, apparently, well, beyond all doubt, dreaming of Hecate and—how shall I put it?—in contact, in debate with her. And what made it far more trying to the listener, he was mimicking her voice with perfect virtuosity. This was at once horrible and ludicrous, the most pestilential and disintegrating combination of all, in my opinion. He was, it seemed, pleading with her to leave him alone, to spare him, and she was ruthlessly refusing. I say 'it seemed,' because the repulsive surge of words was blurred, and only at times articulate; just sufficient to give, as it were, the sense of the dialogue. But that was more than enough. The sleep-hungry Italians were naturally and vociferously infuriated, and I was compelled to rouse Brown over and over again, but each time he relapsed into that vilely haunted sleep. Once he raised himself on his elbow and thrust out blindly with his arms. And Hecate's minatory contralto spewed from his throat, while the Italians mocked and cursed. It was a bestial pandemonium.

"The Italians left early, loud in their execrations of us. One of them, his black eyes wide with fear and anger, shook his lantern in my face and exclaimed 'Who is this woman!' 'What woman?' I replied. He shrugged his shoulders and said: 'That is for you to say. I do not think I would climb the Géant with him if I were you! Good luck, Signore, *I think you will need it!*' Then they clattered off, and at four o'clock we followed them.

"I know now I should have taken that Italian's advice and got Brown back by the easiest and quickest route to the hotel, but when I tentatively suggested it, he almost hysterically implored me to carry on. 'If I fail this time,' he said, 'I shall never climb again, I know it! I *must* conquer it!' I was very tired, my judgment and resolution were at a disgracefully low ebb, and I half surrendered. I decided we would go up some of the way to a ledge or platform I remembered, at about the twelve thousand foot level, rest, eat, and turn back.

"We had a tiresome climb up the glacier, Brown in very poor form, and that nuisance on the rope beginning again almost at once. We crossed the big crevasse where the glacier meets the lower rocks and began to ascend. There was still some mist, but it thinned as the sun rose. I led and Brown, making very heavy weather, followed. The difference between his performance this time and that other I have mentioned, was gross and terrifying. I remember doubting if he would ever be a climber again and realising I had made a shocking error in going on. I had to nurse him with the greatest care and there was always that harassing behaviour of the rope. Only those with expert knowledge of such work could realise the great and deadly difference it made. I could never be quite sure when I had it properly firm on Brown, and he was climbing like a nervous novice. My own standard of the day was, not surprisingly, none too high. I'd had a damned bad, worried night and my mind was fussed and preoccupied. Usually one climbs half-subconsciously, that is the sign-manual of the expert, a rhythmic selection and seizure of 'holds,' with only now and again a fully controlled operation of will and decision. But now I was at full stretch all the time and ever ready for Brown to slip. Over and over again I was forced to belay the rope to some coign of vantage and coax and ease him up, and there was forever that strong interruption between us. The Géant was beating us hands down all the time and I hadn't felt so outclassed since my first season in the Alps. The light became most sinister and garish, the sun striking through the brume, creating a potent and prismed dazzle. So much so that more than once I fancied I saw Brown's outline duplicated, or rather revealed at different levels. And several times it seemed his head appeared just below me when he was still struggling far down. And then there were our shadows, cast huge on the snow-face across the gulf, vast and distorted by those strange rays.

"That there were *three* such shadows, now stationary, now in motion, was an irresistible illusion. There was mine, there was the lesser one of Brown, and there was another in between us. What was causing it? This fascinating and extraordinary puzzle served somewhat to distract my mind from its heavy and intensifying anxiety. At last, to my vast relief, I glanced up and saw that hospitable little platform not more than sixty feet above me. Once there, the worst would be,

I thought, over, for I could lower Brown down more easily than get him up.

"I shouted down to him. 'We're nearly there!', but he made no reply. I shouted again and listened carefully. And then I could hear him talking, using alternatively *his* voice and Hecate's.

"I cannot describe to you the kind of ghostly fear which then seized me. There was I fifteen hundred feet up on a pretty sheer precipice with someone whose mind had clearly gone, on my rope. And I had to get him, first to the ledge, then try and restore him to a condition in which descent might be possible. I could never leave him there; we must survive or die together. First, I must reach that platform. I set myself to it, and for the time being he continued to climb, clumsily and mechanically, and carrying on that insane dialogue, yet *he kept moving!* But for how much longer would that mechanism continue to function and bring him to his holds? I conquered my fear and rallied again that essential detachment of spirit without which we were both certainly doomed.

"So I set myself with the utmost care to reach that ledge. Between me and it was a stretch of the Géant's rottenest rock, which I suddenly remembered well. It is spiked and roped now, I believe. When that gneiss is bad, it is very, very evil indeed. Mercifully, the mist was not freezing or we should have been dead ere then. How I cursed my insensate folly, the one great criminal blunder of my climbing career! This rush of rage may have saved me, for just when I was struggling up that infamous forty-five feet I got a fearful jerk from the rope. I was right out, attacking a short over-hang, exposed a hundred per cent, and how I sustained that jerk I shall never know. I even drove my teeth into the rock. It was one of those super-human efforts only possible to a powerful, fully-trained man at the peak of his physical perfection when he knows that failure means immediate death. Somehow then he draws out his final erg of strength and resilience.

"At last I reached the ledge, belayed like lightning, gasped for breath and looked down. As I did so, Brown ceased to climb, screamed, and then a torrent of wild, incoherent words spewed from his mouth. I yelled at him encouragement and assurance, but he paid no heed. And, though he was stationary, clawing to his holds, the rope was still under pressure, working and sounding on the belay. No explanation of that has ever been vouchsafed me. For a moment my glance flickered out across the great gulf on to the dazzling slope opposite; and there were my shadow and Brown's, and another which seemed still on the move and reaching down towards him.

"I could see his body trembling in every muscle and I knew he must go at any second. I shouted down wildly again and again, telling him I had him firm and that he could take his time, but again he paid no heed. I couldn't get him up, I must go down to him. There was just one possible way which, a shade technical, I will not describe to you. Nor is there need or point in doing so, for suddenly Brown relinquished all holds and swung out. As my eye followed him, once more it caught those shadows, and now there were but two, Brown's hideously enlarged. For a moment he hung there screaming and thrashing out with his arms, his whole body in violent motion. And then he began to spin most horribly, faster and faster, and almost it seemed, in the visual chaos of that whirl, as though there were two bodies lashed and struggling in each other's arms. Then somehow in his writhings he worked free of the rope and fell two thousand feet to his death on the glacier below, leaving my shadow alone gigantic on the snow.

"That is all, and I want no questions, because I know I should have no answers for them and I am off to bed. As for your original question, I've done my best to answer it. But remember this, perchance such questions can never quite be answered."

Woe Water

WEAR LODGE.

Oct. 3rd: At last! What a huge relief to be away from all that foul publicity, the brutally cynical reporters, the cruel animal stares of the mob, those hard-eyed detectives, hoping to get their hands on me, and all the bestiality I've been through during the last month. This house is, of course, much too big for just Barratt and me, but I was in no mood to be selective and took the first more or less suitable place that offered. One thing, my privacy will not be violated here. We are two miles from the village and the grounds are extensive and well wired-in. I shall be merciless to trespassers.

Only ten anonymous letters this morning—the rush is over! This experience has taught me what sub-human devils people can be, and what a lust consumes them to believe the worst and grind into the mire the unfortunate who is *down*. As if any sane person could possibly believe I wouldn't have done, and didn't do, my very best to save poor Angela? Of course that perverse fool of a Welsh coroner was responsible for much of my tribulation. He should have realized that when I said it was Angela who suggested going bathing that night it was simply a slip of the tongue. (What a strange displeasing cry that is! Bird or beast?) As for that bruise on the head, it could *not* have been acquired *before* death, as that fool of a doctor suggested. Absurd! Impossible! And what conceivable motive had I for ridding myself of her! We

had our differences like any other married couple—no more,
no less. She was a little difficult at times and no doubt, I
was too.

As for her money—I never wanted it; I had enough for
my simple wants, and I didn't care if she didn't leave me a
penny, though I'm quite sure it was untrue she was thinking
of making a new will disinheriting me. Sims, her lawyer,
must have misunderstood her, and his evidence, again, made
a very bad impression. Everything seemed to conspire against
me at that inquest and the "Open" verdict was meant as a
slur on me. Of course it ought to have been "Misadventure"!
I am becoming more and more convinced that some men are
born unlucky, born in the Red, destined inevitably to suffer,
the pack of Fate stacked rigorously against them, always that
Red turning up to consolidate their doom.

I am going to keep a diary for the future. It will be something to do, and help, perhaps, to comfort and clarify my
mind. I shall be very lonely for the rest of my life, I suppose.
Barratt is an excellent servant and a good enough fellow, but
an uneducated man is never really company for an educated
one, and I don't believe he really likes me, even though he
has been with me so long. Angela was his favorite. I am
also going to prepare a statement giving the true version of
these events, so that when it is read after my death it will be
understood how terribly I've been the victim of circumstance,
of shameful suspicion and malignant tongues. (There's that
cry again!) It is strange and awful to realize how a perfectly
innocent man can be slandered and tortured as I have been.
It has made me much more sympathetic and understanding
towards unlucky men, so-called "failures," for I see clearly
how easily they can fall into ghastly traps, as I did, and how
their fate can pursue them to the bitter, hopeless end.

I still dread the postman's knock, but, though I'm sleeping very badly, I think that recurrent nightmare of choking
and struggling, which is so unnerving, is, perhaps, not quite
so vivid. Curiously enough, I have at times a powerful sense

of Angela's presence after dark; so odd because she never entered, or even heard of, this house. It will probably fade after a while. If only the dead could speak! (There is that cry once more! What can it be?)

Oct. 4th: I took this place in such a hurry—almost panic— that I had never properly explored the grounds till today, when I strolled around with old Carlman, the gardener. He is a grizzled and rather unforthcoming rustic, at least he was hardly polite to me, though I provide his bread and butter. Of course he has heard things and I am hardened to that sort of treatment by now. To my astonishment I found there is a pool, a small lake, actually, in the southeast comer of the estate. I suppose the reason I didn't notice it on my one hurried visit is that it is entirely surrounded by a barrier of weeping willows. It is an ellipse in shape, about a hundred yards across the major axis, eighty across the lesser. It is an odd, slate-back hue, due, perhaps, to the over-hang of the willows and the shadows they cast.

The old man surveyed it with some solemnity, and al- most made me laugh for the first time since *it* happened, by informing me its depth was unknown, bottom in the mid- dle never having been reached, a ludicrous yarn which I'll disprove before long. I got the impression he is somewhat nervous of it, and it is undoubtedly sombre and forbidding. He told me it was called "Woe Water" and used to be on common land, but was enclosed—polite term for "stolen"— many years ago, and that the villagers have never forgiven this. "It's always been a place of sin and death," he said, an enigmatic remark, which I found by cross-examination meant a favored venue for suicides—fifteen in his lifetime! This sounds hardly credible, and no doubt he was drawing the long bow. I asked him in a joking way why the sparse inhabitants of Drarley Parva were so addicted to self-slaugh- ter. "There are wicked men here as everywhere," he replied, "and they come to the water to cleanse away their sins." By which I deduced he belongs to the Bible-thumping brigade. "And their scarlet sins color the water," he went on, "so that when there is a body within it, it takes the look of blood, and the body troubles the water while it is lying within it, troubles it for seven days, and on the seventh day the people come to meet and greet the dead man, and his sinful body comes up white as snow and picked clean of its evil flesh."

"How d'you mean 'troubles it'?" I asked as seriously as I could manage.

"It is all astir," he replied, "wind or no wind, and the dead man's wave runs across it."

Just a bit of yokel myth-making, of course. I asked him if there were any fish in it, and he said he didn't think so.

At that very moment there was a huge "rise" out in the middle—a monster carp, I imagine, and I said mockingly, "What about *that!*" But he just muttered and hurried away.

Paid the bill for Angela's funeral today, as they've been pressing me. A hundred and forty pounds; extortionate, of course, but then they know I daren't query anything in my position, and naturally nothing could be too good for her. A peculiarly infamous anonymous letter this morning—fifteen pages! Would you credit that anyone could be so sparking with venomed malignity as to spend what must have been hours composing such a vicious screed? And the writer's no half-wit either. He makes what he is pleased to call "six points which indicate irrefutably your guilt." In the course of time I am going to get down on paper a complete answer to this cowardly, knavish brute, point by point.

I have several times alluded to a strange piercing cry which I hear as I sit writing late at night. It comes from the direction of the pool and is made presumably by some water bird. A heron? I do not know. Apart from fishing, I am very ignorant of country matters, and I mean to study the birds and beasts which visit my domain. There it is again! It is an almost human, despairing note. Rather blood-chilling, rather too reminiscent of—no! I won't even think of such a comparison. That is craven and contemptible, and I must train my mind away from all such frailties. My nerves have enough to carry as it is.

I'll order a small rowboat for the lake and try for that big fish. I've drunk too much whiskey today. I never used to indulge like this, but I think it will help me to sleep. Sense of Angela's presence very strong at the moment.

Oct. 5th: Been in poorish spirits today, bored and lonely. Thinking too, of my poor dead father, who suffered, as I am suffering, and from that odious woman, my mother. Getting tired of my own company, I suppose, but it can't be helped and must be endured. Everyone of my so-called "friends" would cut me dead if he met me in the street. Barratt is no good to me; he is sullen and irresponsive. That cry is becoming rather too *much*—very oppressive. It starts at dusk and recurs at intervals from then on. Curiously enough, I could see no signs of any water fowl when I visited the lake today. Perhaps they just come there to roost. I'll go out there one night with a gun, for I fear that thing responsible, whatever it may be, will have to die. There it is again!

That anonymous slanderer's first point was that Angela was afraid of water and would never have bathed that night unless I'd forced her to. What nonsense! I'm the one who fears water, always have done so since that fortune-teller warned me against it years ago, but I've fought the phobia with some success. It is true, as that chambermaid said, that I wanted Angela to come with me. It was a lovely night, I dislike being alone in the sea, and I thought a bath would be good for her nerves. But that spying maid was lying when she swore she overheard me *threaten* Angela. It was spite; I should have tipped her more at the end of the first week in the hotel.

I wonder if cotton wool in my ears would help to damp and dim the stridency of that cry? I'll try it. I've finished a whole bottle today. I must strive to cut down.

Oct. 6th: Seven anonymous letters this morning. One included my horoscope, says I'll be dead before the end of the year, which "will be good riddance of a bestial wife-murderer." Some nice people in the world. Took another stroll with old Carlman this morning. We visited the pool and I questioned him some more. He says they never drag for the bodies which, he repeated, always surface again on the seventh day and the villagers flock down to see them rise. Well, they won't do that again while I'm here. There'll be no more suicides in my time, the suicidal trespasser will be prosecuted as rigorously as all others. He'll have to select another spot. I asked him about water-fowl.

"None ever come here," he said, "and no bird visits these trees." And, indeed, I confess I haven't seen or heard one in the neighborhood of the pool *by day*.

The second point made by that cowardly swine is that I am a strong swimmer and that Angela was a poor one. Not so poor, really! And that I deliberately took her too far out, and asks, why I didn't stay near her? Why did I swim so far from her? according to my account. "In reality," he writes, "you did stay close to her and struck her over the head with your fist and let her drown." And that I didn't expect the bruise would be discovered because of her thick hair. That shows to what lengths a foul, diseased imagination can go! The fact is I was floating on my back, and Angela swam away from me, not purposely, but pursuing her own way, until she was dangerously far from me. I called her, but got no reply and must have swum in the wrong direction. The tide was on the ebb and we must have been carried out further than I expected. She must have got a cramp, and it was then she cried out so horribly—like that! No *not* like that! Curse that creature whatever it may be! As for the bruise, the body was not recovered for twelve hours, and some flotsam must have struck her during that time. I shan't deal with any more of the vicious brute's insinuations in this diary. I find doing so troubles me and racks my nerves, and these sleepless nights are wearing me down. I keep looking up furtively to see if there's anyone in the room. There comes that devilish cry again; cotton wool does no good. I am going out now to kill that bird. I can stand it no more.

Later. No luck! There was some moonlight, but I could see nothing. Yet the cry came both as I was going out and returning. The pool looked very sinister and forbidding. I can understand, in a way, how it might lure a suicide to his doom. It even exerts a certain perverse attraction over me. It works on that phobia of mine. It is often, too often, in my thoughts. I am half-drunk again, utterly exhausted, and may sleep for once.

Oct. 8th: The rowboat came this morning and was launched on the lake. I rowed out into the middle with a leaded line, but, oddly enough, I couldn't find bottom. There seems to be some sort of current which swings the line. I don't think any pole would be long enough. It doesn't matter, but I'd like to have shown old Carlman, who I spotted peering at me through the trees. What a superstitious old fool he is! In the afternoon I tried some fishing, and again with no luck at all. There was not a breath of wind and the pool lay black, thick, a lake of oil, it seemed. I gave my float a lot of line and at once it received a tremendous tug which almost jerked the rod from my hand and started the reel screaming. Then the line went slack, and on reeling in, found it had been snapped well above the float. This seemed very queer and I tried once more, with the same startling result. It must be, I suppose, that the reeds grip it in some way, but I have known nothing like it in a long piscatorial experience. It does seem to be true about the birds. After landing I carefully searched the trees, but didn't see or start a wing.

Yet what is that cry I hear? There it comes again. I have definitely come to the conclusion that the lake is a very strange place, almost, it seems, with laws of its own. Nothing seems quite normal about it. I shall keep away from it as much as I can. I'm sorry I wasted money on that boat, it was impulsive and heedless.

Oct. 10th: Barratt came to me this morning. I could tell by his face something was wrong. I haven't liked the look of him for some time. He had the impudence to say he could no longer keep silent about that *other* matter. It was too much on his conscience. His conscience! He should acquire a brain first. I swore to him, almost desperately, that it had been a pure accident, that Angela must have somehow switched on the gas as she was undressing. He said truculently that that might be so, but the authorities should be told; that they'd left the verdict "open" to see if any more evidence came out, and this should be made known. The ignorance and insolence of the man! I can see he hates me in his heart. We argued for over an hour, and at last I said, "Why this sudden change of mind? I've paid you well. You promised to keep your mouth shut. Why this new resolve?" At first he wouldn't say, but at last he blurted out, "It's that screaming every night. It's the voice of the Missus. And I feel her about, too, and she wants the truth known." I pretended to laugh heartily at this, and told him it was just a bird at the pool. "I've seen it," I said, "and tried to shoot it!" He appeared unconvinced; so I went on, "Come to the lake tonight and I'll show it to you. Will *that* satisfy you?" "If you show me the thing that makes that cry, sir, I'll think it over," he replied. "Otherwise I'll have to tell what I know."

"Remember," I said, "if you do that wicked, stupid act, I'll sack you without a character and say you tried to blackmail me, and good jobs aren't so easy to come by for men of your age."

"Never mind about that," he replied with effrontery, "you show me the bird which screams like a drowning woman!" And he went on his way. I'm writing this in great agitation. I've burnt my boats. I shall have to fool him now. I daren't let him tell of that incident. It was a pure accident, and if Angela had let me share her room it would never have happened. It would mean reopening the whole thing and I cannot face it. I daren't, especially as the doctor who attended Angela was very "sticky" about it at the time, and his evidence would be dangerous. I can stand no more persecution. I must use my wits tonight.

Later. A terrible thing has happened—Barratt was drowned at the pool! It was a pure accident. We went there together at ten o'clock, as arranged. It was dark except for starlight. As we approached, that cry came, but it was *no nearer.* I was terrified lest Barratt should realize this. As it was, he hesitated. I put my hand on his shoulder and found he was trembling violently. "Don't be a coward!" I whispered, "That is the bird. I'll show it to you. Keep quiet and move stealthily." I led the way till we reached the tree barrier and, moving a branch, peered through. Then I whispered again to Barratt. "Come up beside me and try to follow the direction of my arm." He did so and I said, "There, man, on the shore, can't you see it!" In his eagerness he moved still further forward. The bank was damp, he seemed to slip, and the next moment he was in. There was a splash but no other sound. It was a *pure accident!*

I dashed round to the boat and searched the spot, but could find nothing. And then, heaven be my witness, I saw a wave moving across the face of the water. It swung the boat high and broke on the further shore. And that fearful cry came and its echo screamed in my head. What to do now? It was an accident, but dare I tell the truth after all that has happened? No, I dare not. I must plan otherwise. Luckily Barratt has no relatives alive, no friends, I fancy; no one will enquire after him. I must impersonate him for a week till his body comes up, and then I must dispose of it. I'll weight it heavily and sink it again for ever. Then I'll take the car and drive up to town very late at night, tell the agent I found the place too lonely and unsuitable, and tell him to put it on the market. Then I'll go abroad—the Argentine, which I know well, and have all my funds transferred there. I'll burn Barratt's trunk and all his clothes save one suit and his cap. Luckily he was about my height and not too unlike me in build and appearance. I swear to God it was an accident!

This has shattered my nerves. I thought I *saw* Angela just now, standing by the door in her shroud, her eyes hard on me. Just an illusion. I've been drinking too much, that is it I'm near drunk now. My one longing is to leave this hellish place. There is that cry again! I must stick it out this week, drunk or sober, and then my troubles will be over.

Oct. 11th: All went well. I rose early and dressed in Barratt's suit and cap, which I pulled down over my eyes. I knew him so long I can imitate his walk and even his voice. I took a short stroll in the garden to show myself, and when the milkman came, I waved to him from a distance. There will be the butcher tomorrow and I shall just say, "Nothing this week," through the door.

Then I changed into my own clothes and carefully surveyed the pool just in case. I have prepared some weighted ropes and will bury them near the pool tomorrow. I searched it again in the evening just before dark. It is very strange and inexplicable, but it seems to have changed color. It is now a sinister, sullen carmine in hue, so that it resembles a lake of blood, and it is continually disturbed by a huge ripple which passes across it. I noticed old Carlman kept out of my way. I don't know why, but it was quite obvious. I mistrust this. I shall have a hard struggle to fight myself through this week. Every time I doze off I wake from hideous dreams. I have to drink to keep sane. Thought I saw Barratt in his pantry when I was getting my supper. I keep fancying I see Angela—keep glancing up. The day seems endless.

Oct. 14th: All goes well. My impersonation of Barratt has worked perfectly. Tradespeople not calling again. Old Carlman still avoids me, that is all that worries me, during the *day*, but, O God, the evening and the night! The body should reappear Sunday, but I am keeping the closest watch. I shall spend all day on the lake on Sunday pretending to fish. How fortunate it is so hemmed in; little chance of being overlooked while I'm doing the job. There'll be a risk, of course, but, by God, I'm hardened to those by now! The pool is still that horrid hue and is continually disturbed, ever restless and reeking—yes, it stinks! Wants rain to freshen it I shan't write in the diary again till it is over. The trembling and sweating of my hand makes it almost impossible. Oh, these fearful, endless days! Sometimes I have to force my lips together with my hand lest I start to scream, and if I started, I could never stop. Am as far gone as that! Only four days to wait, only four. Supposing it doesn't reappear! I dare not think of that. That cry again, that death cry. Angela is standing by the door.

Oct. 19th: What can have happened? When I looked out of my bedroom window at dawn this morning, I could see a number of people moving towards the pool and breaking down the wire fence. I hurried out to them and bade them be gone, threatened to prosecute every one of them. They took not the slightest notice of me, completely ignored me, simply looked through me, and continued to pour through the gap. They even shouldered me brutally aside when I tried to dispute their passage. Even old Carlman forced his way past me, his eyes, like theirs, rapt and staring. They are like devotees obsessed and absorbed in some rite and drilled in its enactment. I saw not one speak or smile, and each took up his place on the bank till the pool was entirely surrounded, and then they fixed their eyes on the water. I know why they are there! I cursed and raved at them, but they had not ears for me.

So I came back to the house and am watching from the window. How did they know! How could they have known! It is deadly still and I could hear any sound they make, but they make no sound. What shall I do? Angela and Barratt are here in the room with me. Speak! Speak, you dead and absolve me! So it has come to this. Water! Water! As was prophesied. Shall I get the police? Shall I take the car and fly? What will they do when—I shall swear to them Barratt fell in. I'll defend myself to the last. I did my best to save him. How much longer to wait? Shall I—? Hark! Hark! A great and dreadful shout comes from them! He has risen! I know it! Father! Father!

(On December 16th, 1921, James Greville Leas was hanged for the murder of his servant, George William Barratt, at Reading Jail.)

A Black Solitude

I have no explanation of this story, in fact, one of my reasons for telling it lies in the hope that some reader of it may provide one. I rather dislike being left in such an elucidatory void. I got permission to tell it from Lady Foreland; she is sure the Chief would not have minded. I shall probably tell it very badly, for I am an organizer of writers by profession, not a writer myself. The "Chief" was Lord Foreland, the first and greatest of the newspaper peers; none of his many successors can hold a candle—or should it be a telephone?—to him. I was his personal, private secretary for six years. I got the job directly after the Kaiser War when I was twenty-two. I was a callow, carefree, confident youth in those days, still housing a number of small pieces of shrapnel, but otherwise healthy enough, and very proud of serving such a celebrity.

The events in this narrative occurred at Caston Place, the Chief's most renowned country house. This was a famous specimen of early Tudor manor house, in Surrey, charming rather than beautiful, perhaps; though never have I seen such exquisitely mellow brick. The grounds were unarguably lovely. The great lawn—finest turf in the world—lined by Lebanon cedars, the flower, rock, water and kitchen gardens, all showpieces, and deservedly so, the best private golf course in the Islands, snipe in the water, meadows down by the strolling serpentine Wear. Well, if I were a millionaire, that's the sort of cottage I would choose. The interior, too, after the Chief's purse had mated with "Ladyship's" taste, had been most delicately modernized without a trace of "vulgarized." I was there about thirty week-ends in the year and I grew to love it. It was a great old gentleman, an eternally young old gentleman and it died, like so many other gentlemen of my times, in the wars. And also, like many such gentlemen, it had a secret which died with it.

My little bedroom was almost at the end of the east wing. It had once been, I fancy, the dressing-room of the big bedroom next door to it. To my surprise I found that this big bedroom was never used, even when the most lavish house-parties came for the weekend. It was not kept locked, but no one ever slept there.

One day I went in and inspected it. By any standards I had known up till then it was a *vast* room, and somehow vaguely unprepossessing. It had very dark oak panelling and a great oak bed. Two full length portraits flanked the fireplace.

The owners of Caston had fallen on sufficiently mediocre days not to be able to afford to live in it, though the rent the Chief paid for it must have gone far to reconcile them to such exile. Portraits of their forebears—the majority third-rate daubs to be accurate—liberally littered the walls. The Chief told me there'd always been a "sticky" streak in the family (though the latest generation were tame enough) with a notorious name for cruelty, improvidence and various and versatile depravities. These portraits certainly, for the most part, bore this indictment out. They were a baleful-looking crew, men, women and children, and their decorative value exceptionally meager. But the two in the room, as I will call it from henceforth, struck, it seemed to me, a new and noxious low. They were man and wife, I suppose, and fitting mates. They were both in the middle forties, I should say, period, early Stuart, judging from their garb. The husband had a very nasty pair of close-set beady eyes and his lower lip—a family stigmata this—was fleshy, puffy and pouting, the lip of an insatiable and unscrupulous egoist and sensualist. He carried his head bunched forward and his chin down, as though staring hard at the artist and giving him the toughest piece of his mind. The lady was a blonde, and sufficient in herself to give blondes a bad name. She had the lightest blue eyes I ever saw in a face, almost toneless. They were big, too far apart and as hard staring as her spouse's. Her mouth was just one long, hard, thin line of scarlet. Her expression was ruthless and contemptuous, as though telling the painter he was an incompetent—which was true—and informing him it would be a case of "off with his head" if he didn't hurry up. I remember thinking that if he'd ever seen the color of his fee, he was lucky. When I looked at them I found them staring back at me and I felt I would *not* let them stare me down. I thought how lowering it might be to find those four evil eyes on one when one woke up in the morning, and that it might not be too jocund to turn the light out knowing they were there. (In some frail moods it is difficult to differentiate entirely man and his effigy. And that goes, if you know what I mean, for *dead* men—and women—too.) These twain looked, if I may so put it, as though at any moment they might step down from their frames and beat me up.

Well, here was a small mystery and I made up my mind to solve it. It wasn't as if Caston was over-supplied with bedrooms. Those old houses are smaller than they look, in this sense, that many of their rooms are, to our ideas, ludicrously large, and there are too few of them. I knew Ladyship could have put the room to very good purpose if she'd so chosen. Why didn't she so choose? It was puzzling. I was new to the job, and it was not part of it to ask possibly awkward domestic questions. So I waited my chance and presently it came.

One day, when I was on my own down at Caston making arrangements for a big staff party the Chief was throwing, I took a stroll round the grounds with Chumley, the butler and a great character. The very first time I stayed at Caston, the Chief sent for Chumley and in his presence said to me, "This is my butler, the best butler in England, and a very great rogue. Owing to his defalcations and the house property he has purchased therefrom, he is also a very rich man. No doubt eventually he will go to America, the devil, the spiritual home of the best British butlers. Never, my boy, let me catch you giving him a tip."

"Well, sir," I said, "may he give *me* one sometimes?" The Chief was in a good humor, luckily, and passed this rather saucy remark. In fact, he said it showed I had a promising eye to the main commercial chance. (After the Chief died he *did* go to America, and some years later he sent me his photograph seated at the wheel of a Rolls-Royce, a cigar in his mouth and an Alsatian sitting beside him. An eagle amongst doves!) Well, on this occasion we were strolling about on the lawn and I asked him, glancing up at its windows, why the room was never occupied. "His Lordship's brother, Sir Alfred, had an unpleasant experience there," he replied, "but please do not say I told you."

"What sort of experience?"

"I don't quite know, but he started screaming out one night and went straight back to London first thing in the morning. He never came here again and died very soon after."

"And it has never been used since?"

"Only on one occasion, sir; the editor of the *Evening Sentinel* slept there later on and he looked very *green* at breakfast the next morning. I think he must have said something to his Lordship, for he gave me orders the room wasn't to be used again."

"Was that, Mr. Spenland, the present editor?"

"No, sir, Mr. Cocks, the former editor. He also died soon—within a week, as I remember it."

"Odd, Chumley!"

"Possibly, sir, but keep what I've told you under your hat, if I may use that expression. I made some inquiries in the village and they weren't surprised at all. Until his Lordship took the house the end of that wing was blocked up and never used."

"Why?"

"Hard to say, sir. Not considered lucky, I gathered."

"That's nice for me, sleeping there!"

"Have you been bothered, sir?"

"I don't think so. I get some funny dreams, but that's the food and drink, I expect. Not what I'm used to. But how d'you mean, not lucky?"

"They kept a tight mouth about that, but Morton, the game-keeper, told me there's supposed to be somebody or something still living on in that room."

"*What* a yarn!"

"Yes, sir," agreed Chumley doubtfully. "None of the maids will go in there alone after dark."

"Just because they've heard tales about it!"

"I suppose so, though one of them got a fright some years back. Anyway, don't tell his Lordship I said anything. He's a bit touchy about it; he likes all his possessions to be *perfect*." A very shrewd remark!

"No, all right," I promised, and we resumed discussing the business of the hour.

That night, just before going to bed, I paid a visit to the room. I had been busy with mundane and concrete matters. I had dined well, so it was with a very disdainful and nonchalant air that I climbed the stairs. At once, it is no use denying it, my psychic outlook changed. I suddenly realized that Caston when empty, was a very quiet, brooding place, and that I had never quite liked being alone in it, it was a bit "much" overpowering for a "singleton."

The weather had soured during the evening, clouding over with a falling glass and a fitful rising summer wind. My little enclave at the end of the passage seemed peculiarly aloof and dispiriting. Chumley's enigmatic remarks recurred

to me with some force at that moment and with a heightened significance. I thought of those two dead men, the one
who'd screamed and the other who'd looked "green"—what a
word!—at breakfast. However, you know the feeling. I didn't
want to open that door, and yet I knew if I didn't, I should
have kicked myself for a craven and never—or at least not for
a long time—got it out of my system. My year at the War had
taught me that each time one funks one finds it harder not
to do it next time. All of which may sound much ado about
precious little, but you weren't standing facing that door at
midnight on July 20th, 1923! Well, with a small whistle of
defiance I turned the handle of that door and flipped on the
lights. Anti-climax, of course! Just a huge old room like any
other of its kind. And yet was it quite normal? Well, there
was that commonplace feeling everyone has experienced that
someone had been in there a moment before, that the air
was still warm from that someone's presence; perhaps rather
more than that; perhaps, quite absurd, of course, that one
was being observed by someone unseen. My eyes ran round
the room swiftly and then settled on those criminal types
athwart the fireplace. They had their eyes on me pretty
starkly. "Avaunt!" they seemed to be saying, or whatever was
the contemporary phrase for "Beat it!" I stared back at them.
"Not till I'm ready!" I replied out loud in a would-be jocular
way. There was an odd echo in that room. It seemed to swing
round the walls and come back to hit me in the face. Then I
heard a scraping noise from the chimney, Jack-daws nesting
in it, no doubt second-brood; my voice had disturbed their
slumbers. I moved further into the room. The rustling in the
chimney grew louder. "Well, good night, all!" I said face-
tiously, but there was no echo. I tried again; no echo at all.
That was a puzzle. I shifted my position and said good night
to them once more. This time the echo nearly blew my head
off and something tapped three times on one of the windows. I suddenly felt that uncontrollable atavistic dread of
ambush and glanced sharply round behind my back. "I'm not

afraid of you," I said loudly. "Do your worst!" But somehow
I knew it was time to go. I paced back slowly and deliberately, turned out the light, banged the door and went to bed.

What a history that room must have had, I thought, to
have been blocked off from the world like that for years. And
now the ban was up once more. Strong medicine there of
some sort! What sort? And there was only some thin panelling and plaster between me and it. I kept my ears pricked,
for I was a bit on edge, my subconscious was alert and receptive.

I went to bed and presently to sleep. Sometime in the
night I awoke hearing something, which, my subconscious
told me, I had heard several times before, but now, *consciously*
for the first time; it was a kind of *crack* like the flipping of
giant fingers, twice repeated. A displeasing, staccato, urgent
and peremptory sound, the source of which I quite failed to
trace.

Now the Chief, like most self-made men, especially in his
profession, had some queer "old friends," many of whom had
been associated with him in his days of struggle, but had, for
the most part, been left far behind in the success marathon.
The Chief had not a trace of snobbery about these; so long
as he liked them and they amused him they remained his
friends, rich or poor, successes or duds and, in several cases,
reputable or not. Perhaps the queerest of all these was one,
Apuleius Charlton. This person was generally deemed a very
dubious type and a complete back-number, the last belated
survivor of the Mauve decade, with a withered green carna-
tion in his frayed buttonhole and trailing thin clouds of
obsolete diabolism. Incidentally, he belonged to a cadet
branch of a very "old family." As a sinister monster of depravity I found him sheer Disney and so did the Chief, but
he had unarguably superior brains, a kind of charm, and an
ebullient personality. In fact, *personality* is quite too flaccid
a word; he was *sui generis,* the sole member of his species.
There was a strong tinge of Casanova about him; he shared

his brazen candor, occasional brilliant insight, his refusal to accept the silly laws of God and man as binding upon himself, his essential spiritual loneliness. He was a big hefty creature, an athlete by right of birth, with a huge domed head, large watery eyes and jet-black hair, the fringe of which he tortured into twin spiral locks. Between them was a small, red magical mark, a three-pronged "moon" swastika. He had been everywhere in the world, I think, and his travel tales were legion and sensational and owing something, no doubt, to an ebullient imagination. He was then barred from a number of countries, rather unhumorously, for while his bark was Cerberian, his bite was vastly over-rated. He had, no doubt, acquired certain monies by various modes of false pretenses, but never a sizable hoard; and those he diddled were, I am sure, consummate mugs who just asked to be "taken." He said so himself and I believed him.

He had written copiously on many subjects with an air of complete confidence and authority, and in his youth had been a goodish minor poet of the erotic, adjectival Swinburne school, but somehow he never had any real money. That was his incurable malady. There are a number of such vagrant oddities in the world, lone wolves, or rather, I think, they remind me of great ostracized, solitary birds, forever winging their way fearlessly and hopefully from one barren place to another, wiry, wary, and shunned by the timorous, and "respectable" flock. He had written stuff for the Chief's publications before his name became so odoriferous, climbed with him in several parts of the world, for he was a brilliant and scientific mountaineer, and gone with him on esoteric drinking bouts in the wine countries, for he knew his epicurean tipples and taught the Chief to judge a vintage. Lastly, and immensely most important to himself, he was a magician with a cult or mystery of his very own invention and a small band of very odd initiates indeed. Hence the swastika and much ponderous and Eleusinian jewelry on convenient parts of his person, including a perfectly superb jade ring. I know jade and this piece was incomparably fine. (You will hear of it again.) For this aspect of his ego the Chief, not necessarily rightly, expressed the most caustic contempt, telling him the only reason why he and his rival Merlins and Fingals shrouded their doings in veils of secrecy—and this went for Masons, Buffaloes, Elks, and all other mumbo-jumbo practitioners—was that they had nothing to conceal except the most puerile and humiliating drivel worthy of their Woolworth regalia, and they were ashamed to disclose such infantile lucubrations and primitive piffle. All the same some people were definitely scared of old Apuleius, and no doubt he had a formidable and impressive side. He was sixty odd at this time and very well preserved in spite of his hard boozing, addiction to drugs and sexual fervor, for it was alleged that joy-maidens or Hierodoules were well represented in his mystic entourage. (If I were a Merlin, they would be in mine!)

Of course he never figured in house parties, but the Chief had him down to Caston now and again and, I know, sent him a most welcome cheque at regular intervals.

In November of this same year, the Chief and his Lady went away for a month's holiday to the Riviera, and just before he met old Apuleius in the street looking a bit down at heel and told him he could doss down at Caston while he was away, that I would look after him, and that the cellar was at his disposal, but that this invitation did *not* extend to his coterie, particularly the Hierodoules! Poor Apuleius leaped at this timely and handsome offer and the day after the Chief's departure he appeared at the house bearing his invariable baggage, one small, dejected cardboard suitcase—at least, it looked like cardboard. I was on holiday, too, or rather half-holiday, for I got six to a dozen telegrams a day from the Chief and had made a rash promise to begin the cataloguing of his library. (I may say he had two other secretaries to do the donkey-work.) But I had plenty of spare time to shoot, golf and catch some of the nice little trout in the stream. So there were old Apuleius and I almost alone for a month and all the best at our disposal. He treated me always with some pleasing but quite unnecessary deference, for I was the Czar's little shadow and a lad worth cultivating. Besides he liked me a little and he didn't like anyone very much. I resolved covertly to examine this psychological freak, because I never could decide how much of a charlatan he was and how much he believed in his own bunkum. Such characters are very dark little forests and it's a job to blaze any sort of trail through them.

He arrived, very sensibly, just in time for lunch and did himself extremely well. He was in great spirits and splendid form talking with vast verve and rather above my jejune head. I quite forget what it was all about. He slept for a while after lunch and then began a prolonged prowl around the establishment, which he had never properly inspected before. I went with him, for the unworthy reason that the house was full of small, highly-saleable articles and he had a reputation for sometimes confusing meum with tuum when confronted with such. At length we reached my little enclave and there facing him was the room. "What's that?" he asked, staring hard at the door. "Oh, just a bedroom," I replied. Suddenly he moved forward quickly, opened the door, and drew a quick, dramatic breath. At once he seemed transformed. You have seen the life come to a drowsy cat's eyes when it hears the rustle of a mouse. You may have noted the changed demeanor of some oafish and lugubrious athlete when he spies a football or a bag of golf clubs. Just such a metamorphosis occurred in Apuleius when he opened that door. He became intent, absorbed, *professional.* I felt compensatingly insignificant and meager.

"Nobody sleeps here?" he said.

"No," I replied.

"Not twice, anyway," he said sharply.

"Why?" I asked.

He went up to the criminal types and scrutinized them carefully. And then he pointed out to me some things I had not noticed before, a tiny figure of a hare with a human and very repulsive face at the right-hand side of the gentleman, a crescent moon with something enigmatic peering out between its horns on the same side of the lady. "As I expected," he observed in his most impressive manner, and left it at that.

"Well, what about it?" I asked impatiently.

"That would take rather a long time to explain, my dear Pelham," he replied, "and with all respect, I doubt if you would ever quite understand. Let me just say this. Such places as these are as rare as they are perilous. In a sense this is a *timeless* place. What once happened here didn't change, didn't pass on, it was *crystallized*. What happened herein eternally repeats itself. Here time, as it were, was trapped and can't move on. Man is life and life is change so such places are deadly to man. If man cannot change, he dies. Death is the end of a stage in a certain process of change. Only the dead can live in this room."

"And do they?" I asked, bemused by this rigamarole.

"In a sense, yes."

This effusion didn't commend itself to me. (Besides it was still daylight.) I countered with vivacity. "Well," I said, "you may be right, but the moment anyone begins philosophizing about time I get a bellyache. It is one of the prevailing infirmities of third-rate minds. Personally I believe it to be no more a genuine mystery than say, money, with which it is vulgarly identified. All this pother about both is due to a confusion of thought based on a confusion of terms. The word 'time' is habitually used in about sixteen different senses. If I were asked to define metaphysics, I should describe it as an acrimonious and sterile controversy about the connotation of certain abstract terms. But I'll give you this, the room has a bad name." (There was no getting round that, and he'd instantly spotted it. How?)

"It should not even be *entered* after dark," he said, "save by those who—well—understand it and enter it fore-armed."

"You say something happened here and eternally reacts itself. What?"

"Those two," he replied, pointing to the types, "made an experiment which in a sense succeeded."

"And that was?"

"Once again I am in a difficulty. These dark territories are such new ground to you. You must understand there are no such entities as good and evil, there are merely forces, some beneficent, some injurious, indeed, fatal, to man. He exists precariously poised between these forces. Those two, as it were, allied themselves with the forces noxious to man; what used to be called selling oneself to the devil. These things are beyond you, my dear Pelham, and I should not pursue them. It is one of the oldest mysteries of the world, the idea that if one can become all evil, drink the soma of the fiend, one immortalizes oneself; one becomes impervious to change and so to death. Actually, it is not so. It cannot be done. One cannot defeat death, but one can become what is loosely called an evil spirit, a focus for a concentration of destructive energy, and, in that limited sense, undying."

"Of course, you're right, that's all cuneiform to me," I replied staring up at the ambitious pair. "But what's the result? What happens then?"

"Well, those two made that attempt. I can tell that for certain reasons, and achieved that limited success. They practiced every conceivable wicked and unspeakable thing. This room was their laboratory, their torture-chamber; it reeks of it. When they died, they became chained to this room. It is their *Hell,* if you like so to put it."

"In what state are they?" I asked not knowing whether to laugh or cry. "I mean are they conscious? Do they know, for example, you are discussing them?"

"To begin with 'they' is a misnomer. 'They' are *one;* male and female principles have been fused and the feminine predominates, for it is the more primitive, potent and dangerous. The resultant 'It' is not conscious in our sense of the word, it has no illusion of *will*. It is a state we cannot understand and so cannot describe. It has been absorbed into the very soul of that power which is inimical to man and is endowed with its venom. But it cannot roam; it is anchored to this room. To destroy man is Its delight. In that It finds Its *orgasm*. What occurs in this room is the eternal generation, condensation and release of murderous energy. After dark, for it cannot be released in daylight, this whole room will be soaked in and embued with that energy."

"How does It destroy?"

"It can do so simply by fear and fear can kill. Once in India I passed through a cholera-infected area. The very road was thick with bodies, but more of them had died from sheer fear than the disease. It would kill you by fear, but It could not so kill me. It would have to—well—*overpower* me to destroy me. I am coming here tonight."

"I shouldn't!" I said hastily. "I'm not sure the Chief would permit it. If anything happened to you, he'd be furious."

"It will not. I know the only safeguards against and antidotes to these forces. So leave me now. I will start to prepare my defenses. I will see you at dinner."

So I went off to do some work, completely baffled and somewhat uneasy in mind.

At dinner Apuleius was preoccupied and portentous, and actually drank nothing but water, a sure sign he was taking life seriously. I was preoccupied too. I knew perfectly well the Chief would have shoved down a formidable foot on the whole thing, but I wasn't the Chief, Apuleius had been given the run of the house and I had no authority to control his movements within it. All the same, looking back on it, I think I acted feebly and that I should have exercised a veto however arbitrary, and kept him out of that room that night. All I did was to employ persuasion, and quite ineffectually.

"My dear Pelham," he propounded, "this is a challenge I must accept. I have devoted much of my life to this crusade of safeguarding man from those black forces which, unknown to the blind and impercipient, are forever striving and with ever increasing success to break down his resistance and shatter him. If I fully succeed tonight I shall cleanse that room and make it harmless, white and habitable again. I shall be very thankful if I can do the Chief this service."

"But supposing they are too strong for you?" I protested. "That energy may be more virulent and vicious than you reckon on."

"That is a risk I must take. So far I have always conquered them, and I can rally mighty forces to my aid. In this sign,"—and he touched the swastika on his forehead—"I shall conquer once again. Have no fears."

I must say he looked impressive, exalted, when he said this.

After dinner he again disappeared for a while and I tried to do some more work, but of all jobs cataloguing a library is the most soporific. I dozed off and presently woke to find him standing before me. He had repainted the swastika, which gleamed somberly.

"I am ready," he declared, "and now I will rest for a while. I will enter that room at five minutes to midnight."

"What kind of ordeal do you think awaits you?" I asked. "Or do you mind telling me?"

"The moment I enter that room I shall pronounce certain formulae, what you would loosely call incantations. I shall then, to use a military metaphor, entrench myself within a defensive ring and concentrate my whole spirit on rallying to my side the powers of white, the forces of salvation. They will come to me. Already the black forces will be concentrating upon me, the tension will increase every moment. Sometime the black will strike and the white will lash back, the grapple will be joined. When those dark forces have done their worst and been repelled, white will have been reestablished in that room, the sting of evil, of destruction and of black will have been drawn. I shall be exhausted and soon pass into a coma from which I shall awake refreshed, hale and with added powers. And then we will enjoy our holiday together, my dear Pelham, and drink deep, having cleansed this lovely house of its ancient doom."

"I wish I could be with you in that struggle," I said doubtfully.

"It is unthinkable," he replied forcibly. "It has taken me forty years to learn how to conduct this fearful quarrel. I could not extend that which protects me to you. You would be inevitably destroyed."

"Just killed?" I asked repressing a nervous and blasphemous itch to laugh.

"More than that, though that for certain. You might never be seen again."

Now, I will be frank, it did seem to me that already there was a tension, a sense of malaise in that great room where we were sitting. The wind had risen to half-a-gale and the rain had come with it. The old house seemed like a ship heaving at its moorings. The windows shook, the curtains stirred, the wind went roaring by. And really for the first time I knew old Apuleius to be a strange and formidable fellow and no figure of fun, and that that shining emblem on his brow might have more than a derisory significance. I grew very restless, the current stirring my nerves seemed to have had its voltage raised. I should have liked to have gone out into that storm and walked the tension down. Odd, distorting little pictures formed and vanished in my mind's eye; masks of evil, a flaming body hurtling through the sky, a ring of sultry fire, a dark stream of birds, a bloody sword. I shook myself and fetched a drink. Apuleius was sitting down now, motionless, his chin on his breast, his hands gripping the arms of his chair. And presently the clock chimed three times, it was a quarter to midnight.

"No drink, Apuleius?" I asked, to break the silence.

"No," he replied. "Alcohol relaxes, and I require the utmost stiffening of my spirit. If I had known what was before me I would not have drunk at lunch."

"Then put it off till you've prepared yourself properly!"

"No," he replied, "it must be tonight."

"Look here," I urged, "you realize there will only be a thin wall between us. If you're in any trouble bang on that wall and I'll come fighting."

"Have, no fear," he said, "all will be well."

"Yes, but if it isn't will you bang on that wall?"

"In the last extremity I will, but it will not be necessary. And now the time has come."

We got up together. I took the tantalus of whiskey with me and a syphon. I had no intention of sleeping and I felt like some Scotch courage. The gale was now at its height, screaming wickedly round the house; a fit night for black and white, I thought, as we mounted the lightly creaking stairs. We parted without a word at the door of my room and Apuleius went on. Just before he opened that door he raised himself to his full height, touched the mark on his forehead, turned the handle and strode in. To this day I can see him there in my mind's eye as clearly as I did twenty-three long years ago. Then he disappeared, and I went in and closed my door. I sat down in an armchair, knocked back a big drink and tried to read. But I was half-listening all the time and couldn't concentrate. What was happening on the other side of that thin wall? I cursed the wind which waxed and waxed in venom drowning all small sounds. I could hear their straining timber roar as the great cedars fought the gale. The room seemed charged with a heightening tension. I had felt something like it before in the dynamo room of a great power station, when those smooth spinning cylinders seemed to charge and shake the air with the huge power they so nonchalantly and quietly engendered, a power that in its essence remains a mighty mystery to this day.

I tried to visualize what Apuleius was doing. Sitting inside his magic circle, I supposed, murmuring his protective runes, straining to keep back that which strove to pass the barrier. I concentrated all my will upon it and presently I had the strangest illusion of my life. It was as though I *was* seeing into that room, as though the wall had become almost transparent and I was gazing through its thinning veil. Apuleius was sitting there in the middle of the room surrounded by a faintly illuminated ring. His eyes were staring, his face contorted into an odious rixus, his mouth moving convulsively. On the carpet just outside the ring huge shadows were crouching, other shadows of dubious and daunting shape were leaning down the walls. All seemed to have their heads pointing at him. All the time the lighted ring grew slowly dimmer. Suddenly there came, repeated over and over again, that horrid cracking of giant fingers, the lights in my room flickered, reddened and sparked. And then there was a dazzling flash of lightning and a blast of thunder which went roaring down the gale. I could stand no more and leapt to my feet.

Suddenly I heard Apuleius scream, once quickly, the second a piercing, drawn-out cry of agony. And then came a frenzied beating on the wall. I dashed out into the passage and flung open the door of the room. It was dimly lit, it was quiet, it was empty, the only movement, the slight stirring of the long, dark window curtains. I ran along to his room. Save for the little cardboard suitcase it was empty too. I shouted for him until Chumley came to investigate whether I had really gone crazy, or was merely very tight. He was wearing, I noted, a mink-collared dressing-gown over a pair of the Chief's most scintillating monogrammed silk pajamas.

And on that mildly farcical note I will end the story of that night. For Apuleius was never seen again. Of course, most of the few people who cared in the least whether he was alive or dead believed he'd done a bunk for reasons not

unconnected with the constabulary. He was soon forgotten
for he had long ceased to hit even the tiniest headlines. He
had disappeared before and now he'd done it again. Good
riddance! When the Chief heard my story he flew into a
considerable fury though not with me, for he was a fair man
and agreed it was not my function to control his guest and a
man more than twice my own age. He wanted to believe the
done-a-bunk theory naturally enough, but he realized it was
dead against the weight of evidence. He had the room locked
up and gave orders no one was to enter it without his or
Ladyship's permission in the future.

The years passed and so presently did the Chief, no doubt
to put some ginger into celestial or infernal journalism. I
got a very nice job in his organization for life, I hoped, but
then came the war and I transferred my talents temporarily
to the M.O.I. In 1941 I was for a time bomb-jolly through
being flung out of bed and hard up against a wall when my
Kensington house was next door to a direct hit.

I had still kept in touch with Ladyship, then living very
sensibly in a safe area, and one morning in June, 1944, she
rang me up to say she had just heard Caston had been damaged by a fly-bomb and would I go down and see what had
happened.

Poor sweet old place! The doodle had dived clap in the
middle of the courtyard which had, of course, enclosed the
blast—and that was that. Those Tudor houses were lightly
built of delicate brick and lots of glass, so Caston was no
more. Center block pulverized, right wing still collapsing by
stages when I arrived. My old left wing just a great mountain of debris, brides, beds, furniture, pictures, clothes—an
incredible chaos spangled everywhere with that lovely old
glass. The rescue squads were digging in the center wing for
the bodies of the caretaker and his wife. A bulldozer and
cranes rolled up while I was there. I climbed up the monstrous and pathetic pile feeling sad and full of memories.
On the summit I picked up a piece of canvas and, turning

it over, found I was being regarded by the palest eyes which ever stared from a woman's face above a long, thin, streak of scarlet. I threw it down again, *that* was not the sort of souvenir I relished. As I did so, I saw something glitter from between two broken bricks. I pulled it out and there was a sea-green jade ring on the splintered bone of a fleshless finger. I got the rescue men to dig around there, but we found nothing more.

That ring is on the desk beside me as I write these words. It is lovely beyond all telling. How it happened to be where I found it is, as I have told you, a matter for you to decide.

THE SUPERNATURAL
STORIES OF MONSIGNOR
ROBERT H. BENSON

THE LIGHT INVISIBLE
A MIRROR OF SHALOTT

DANCING SHADOWS

TALES OF THE SUPERNATURAL
BY BERNARD CAPES

BLACK SPIRITS
AND WHITE
RALPH ADAMS CRAM

TALES OF THE
SUPERNATURAL
JAMES PLATT

SHADOWS GOTHIC
AND GROTESQUE

STRANGE
HAUNTS

STORIES BY
F. MARION CRAWFORD &
H. B. MARRIOTT WATSON

Coachwhip Publications

CoachwhipBooks.com

TALES OF FRIGHT
AND FANTASY BY
E. F. BENSON

SECRET
WELLS

THE
SPECULATIVE FICTION
OF
A. C. BENSON

INTRODUCTION BY TIM PRASIL

ARTHUR MACHEN

THE DYSON
CHRONICLES

THE INMOST LIGHT · THE SHINING PYRAMID
THE RED HAND · THE THREE IMPOSTORS

LONELY HAUNTS

Coachwhip Publications

CoachwhipBooks.com

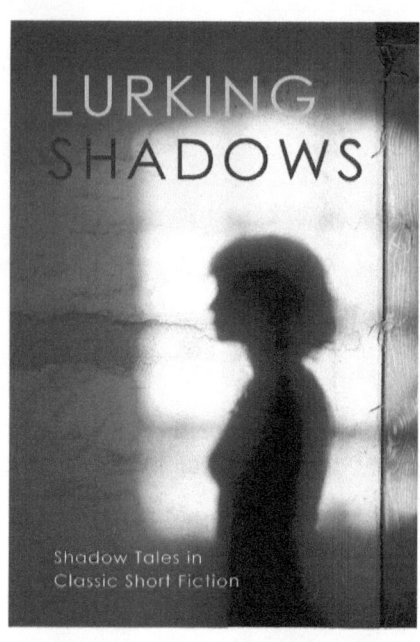

Coachwhip Publications

CoachwhipBooks.com

Coachwhip Publications

CoachwhipBooks.com

Bestiarium
Cryptozoologicum

Mystery Animals and Unknown Species
in Classic Science Fiction and Fantasy

zoologica
fantastica

SAURIA
MONSTRA

Dinosaurs, Pterosaurs, and Other
Fossil Saurians in Classic
Science Fiction and Fantasy

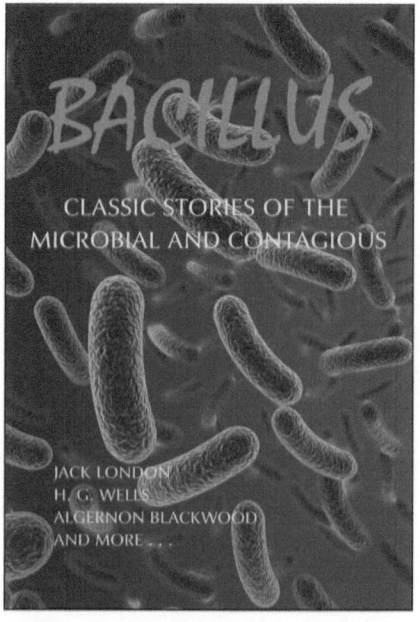

BACILLUS

CLASSIC STORIES OF THE
MICROBIAL AND CONTAGIOUS

JACK LONDON
H. G. WELLS
ALGERNON BLACKWOOD
AND MORE . . .

Coachwhip Publications

CoachwhipBooks.com

Coachwhip Publications

CoachwhipBooks.com

www.ingramcontent.com/pod-product-compliance
Lightning Source LLC
Chambersburg PA
CBHW020924020726
47495CB00002B/339